CRUEL SENTENCE

A NATE SHEPHERD NOVEL

MICHAEL STAGG

Cruel Sentence

A Nate Shepherd Novel

Copyright © 2024 by Michael Stagg

All rights reserved.

All characters in this book are fictitious. Any resemblance to an actual person, living or dead, is purely coincidental.

For more information about Michael Stagg and his other books, go to https://michaelstagg.com/newsletter/

Want to know when the next Nate Shepherd book is coming? Sign up for the Michael Stagg newsletter here or at https://michaelstagg.com/newsletter/

No part of this book may be reproduced in any form or by any electronic or mechanical means, including information storage and retrieval systems, without written permission from the author, except for the use of brief quotations in a book review.

❦ Created with Vellum

PART I - OPEN

1

A rock concert doesn't usually lead to arson and murder. Sure, there's always that guy who caught the Stones in California who'll say that was par for the course back in the day, but he's mostly full of it and another beer will usually shut him up. But when I went to Ford Field to see Lizzy Saint on the Detroit stop of her latest tour, that's what happened—it was my first step on a journey toward arson and murder.

I didn't know that when we left for the concert that night. Northlake, Michigan is so far from Carrefour that the tragic news of the death of a child and a firefighter hadn't really made it down to us, nor had the outrage that burned toward Brock Niesen, the teenager accused of starting the fire who now faced charges of arson and murder.

I've been around grief and loss, but nothing as white hot as what exploded in Northlake that fall. At a time when northern Michigan was normally winding down from the frantic summer season into the more sedate pace of apple orchards and winery tours, this town was frantically focused on making a young man pay the price for the death of a toddler and a hero.

I wasn't aware of any of that as I drove a carload of my family to see Lizzy Saint, just like I wasn't aware of who was leading me straight into the heat.

2

"This can't be right," I said.

"You're Nate Shepherd, aren't you?" said the Ford Field worker.

"I am."

"And these young ladies would be Reed and Taylor Shepherd?"

"I'm Reed," said my oldest niece.

"Taylor." My second oldest niece raised her hand.

The man nodded. "And this young man is?"

"Hunter," said Reed's boyfriend.

The man checked a tablet. "Yes, here it is, Hunter." The man grinned. "You're all in the right place."

"But I thought we just had a backstage pass for after the show?"

The man tapped the badge hanging from the lanyard around my neck. "This symbol here in the corner, or 'the rune' I'm supposed to say, gets you access to Ms. Saint's meet and greet. But those tickets I just scanned on your phone say this suite is yours for the concert."

I looked at the spread of food that ran down one wall and the bar that covered the other. "How many other people are in here?"

"Oh, it's just you and your party, Mr. Shepherd. If you're in the mood for something different though, you have access to all of our restaurants on the club level and if each of you will just put on this red wrist band—here you go, yes right next to the green one—you'll find that all of your concessions have been paid for. Just have the server scan that code there."

I was too busy being bewildered to object as the man slipped the band on my wrist and then handed more to the kids, who slapped them right on.

The man looked at his tablet. "And are there four more adults and one young man joining us?"

"Yeah, I think they just stopped at the concessions there."

The man smiled. "Here are their wristbands. You make sure that's the last thing they buy. My name's Malcolm and if you need anything, just tell me, I'll be checking in."

I shook my head. "I can't imagine we'll need a thing, Malcolm. Thank you."

Malcolm smiled. "You'd be surprised. Have you seen Lizzy Saint before?"

I nodded. "Once."

"Then you know you're in for it. She blew it out last night! Enjoy the show!"

I thanked Malcolm, texted my brothers our suite number, then joined my nieces in checking out the spread.

∼

My brothers, Tom and Mark, their wives, Kate and Izzy, and my nephew Justin joined us a few minutes later. Tom's reaction was predictable—he blinked when he saw the suite, then cursed me out for letting him buy his own beer on the way up. His wife Kate hushed him, oohed and ahhed over the set-up, and went to check out the view of the stage.

"Mom, check out these seats," said Taylor.

Kate went out onto the balcony. "We get all these?"

Taylor nodded.

"Will we be able to hear up here?"

Reed and Taylor looked at each other and laughed. "Don't worry about that."

The kids, I keep saying kids but they were all high schoolers now, went back to crowd watching and guessing the set list while the adults grabbed some food and drinks.

"Did Lizzy set you up like this last time?" asked Tom.

I should back up—a few years ago I'd represented Lizzy Saint's sound engineer, a guy named Hank Braggi, who had been accused of murdering a guy who tried to slip Lizzy some heroin. Hank had actually killed the crap out of the guy, but the jury found that it was justified and Hank was set free. The next time Lizzy had come through town, I'd taken Reed and Taylor, who were big fans, to see her.

I shook my head. "We met her afterward, but we sat out there with the common folk."

"How'd you get this?" asked Kate.

"I reached out to the tour director, and he said he'd talk to her. He sent us the passes to the meet and greet, then a couple of weeks later, I got the email with the concert tickets. I had no idea it was going to be all this."

Mark popped a beer. "And they say crime doesn't pay."

A little later, Malcolm stuck his head in. "Mr. Shepherd? I can take you down to the pre-show meet and greet now."

"Thanks, Malcolm. Let's go trolls," I said to the kids. "Time to meet Lizzy Saint."

Reed, Taylor, and Justin shot over to the door.

"Guess we know how to get them in the car for school," said Kate.

~

MALCOLM LED the five of us—Reed, her boyfriend Hunter, Taylor, Justin, and me—down to the floor. The parents had stayed behind in the suite, both to sample the bar and as a gift to their teenagers, since there's nothing more embarrassing than meeting a rock star with your mom and dad.

As we made our way down a cramped hallway behind the stage, I fully expected to arrive at the back of a long line, but instead, it was just us as we walked right up to an enormous man with short hair, a black diamond earring, and the tattoo of a crow's head stretched across his massive right arm.

Malcolm seemed confused too as he frowned and said, "Sorry, the pass said 6:15."

The big man nodded. "You're right on time, Malcolm. I can take them from here."

Malcolm hesitated, then nodded and left.

"Still at it, Rick?" I said. I'd gotten to know Rick Reynolds, Lizzy Saint's security man, during the Hank Braggi case.

"Living the dream, Nate." He turned and gestured for us to follow him down the hall.

A little ways down, a woman was leaning against a wall, alone. She wore black leathers and a scowl made more fierce by her theatrical eyeliner as she stared at her phone.

"Lizzy?" said Rick.

Lizzy Saint looked up and her scowl vanished. "Counselor!" she said, pushing off the wall with one boot. "Glad you made it! And the nieces! Ready to blow it out again, girls?"

I'm not going to say my nieces squealed, because they're

teenagers and too cool for that, but they squealed, and then were mortified.

Lizzy talked to them for a moment, about how they were doing and how high school was and how this guy Hunter better treat Reed right, then said how glad she was to meet a young heartbreaker like Justin before she said to me, "Thanks for coming to my show."

I'd forgotten how raspy her everyday voice was compared to the one that ranged over four octaves.

"Thanks for seeing us," I said.

"You can't see enough of good people. You have an open invite to the after party, of course."

Reed and Taylor clamored to go.

"I don't think—" I said.

Lizzy Saint smiled. "But your uncle is wise, so I thought of something that might be more fun."

Reed and Taylor's cries of injustice stopped.

"We're shooting part of the video for 'Drop the Hammer Down' right now. You know, one of those where I sing to the empty seats that we're going to mash together with shots of the full stadium."

"Can we watch?" said Reed.

Lizzy nodded. "You can. But I thought you'd rather be in it. You'd be part of the road crew setting up equipment."

Four teenagers looked at me.

I knew what my brothers' instincts would be. But that's part of being an uncle.

"Sounds like fun," I said.

The kids about burst as Lizzy Saint said, "Let's get things going then. We ready, Rick?"

Rick opened a door. "All set, Lizzy."

And off they went.

Twenty minutes and two versions of the song later, they were done. The kids were out of their minds, not only because they got to keep their "Saint Road Crew" t-shirts, but because each member of the crew, including them, did a close-up shot mouthing "Drop the hammer down!" on the chorus. When they were done, Lizzy Saint said goodbye to them and they headed back up to the suite, each talking a mile a minute.

Lizzy Saint waved me over from where I'd been watching.

"They'll never forget that, Lizzy. Thank you."

She smiled, shrugged, then looked away. "Have you seen him?"

"Hank?" I shook my head. "Not since right after the trial. You?"

"I thought so, twice, in the crowd at shows, but I might have imagined it."

"It wouldn't surprise me if he were around."

Lizzy Saint put her full gaze on me. "If you see him, tell him to reach out, would you? He's welcome again. *Runes* sold so many copies, the label will do whatever I say."

"Sure."

"Time, Lizzy," said Rick.

"Right."

I was surprised then when she reached out and hugged me. "I'll never forget what Hank did for me, Counselor," she said. "And what you did for Hank."

I smiled as she let go. "The suite was incredible enough, but the video too? That was over the top."

Lizzy Saint smiled. "Over the top is how we roll. But I can't take credit for the suite. The venue controls those. You'll tell Hank? If you see him?"

"I will."

Then Lizzy Saint left, and I headed back to the suite that neither Lizzy Saint, nor I, had paid for.

∽

WE WERE six songs into the concert when I found out who did. When the woman walked into our suite to claim the tenth seat, I instantly recognized the blood red hair and ice green eyes, and when she spoke, it was with a familiar cool tone, as if it had only been a moment or two since we'd last spoke.

"Hello, Nathan," said Cyn Bardor. "How do you like your seats?"

3

I smiled. "A little cramped, Cyn, but we're making do. Thank you."

Cyn extended her hand, formally as always, and I took it. "Don't thank me, Nathan. They're from my firm."

"Then thanks to the Firm." I raised an eyebrow. Cyn's firm had hired me to act as local counsel in the Hank Braggi murder trial. I'd eventually taken over when the lead attorney died. They'd been very generous then, but I hadn't heard from them since. "It's been three years since the Braggi case."

"It has."

"This is...unexpected."

"What you did wasn't easy. My firm, and our clients, remember it. This seemed like a fitting gesture."

"And?"

"And what, Nathan?"

"Why did you bring me to Detroit?"

Cyn smiled. "Did there have to be a reason?"

"For the suite? No. For you to be here? Yes."

Outside, Lizzy hit the chorus of "Protector." I was sorry to miss it as Cyn shut the glass door to the outer seats and stepped further back into the suite. My family didn't notice.

"I happened to be in town," she said. "I just landed in Detroit." She gestured to a carry-on bag in the corner, one of those aluminum ones that cost more than a mortgage payment.

"Connection or destination?"

"Destination. Well, south of my destination, but this was where my flights ended. I'll drive the rest of the way tomorrow."

"Where to?"

"Northlake."

"What's in Northlake?"

"A case my firm is handling."

Northlake was a small town in the northwest corner of the Lower Peninsula of Michigan. If you're one of those people who use your hand to describe where you live on the mitten, it would be right on Lake Michigan where your ring finger touches the top of your pinky.

Yeah, welcome to my state.

"That's still a long drive. Couldn't you have flown into Traverse City or Petoskey?"

"I could. But then I wouldn't have stopped in Detroit."

"Meeting?"

"Yes."

"Tomorrow?"

Cyn smiled. "Now."

"You want me to work on the case."

"We do."

I looked around. "You do know how to butter a guy up."

"We also know the butter won't matter to you."

"Northlake is literally the other end of the state, Cyn. I don't have any connections up there. I'm sure I can help you find someone better to be local counsel—"

She shook her head. "We want you to be lead counsel, not local."

"What kind of case?"

"Arson, leading to murder."

"Don't you have a whole fleet of lawyers that travel around doing this?"

"We do. I could say it's a scheduling conflict, but that's not it."

"What is it then?"

"You're perfect for this case."

I suspected that one of the main reasons Cyn's firm had picked me for the Braggi case was because of the way my wife had died, of a drug overdose. Cyn had never admitted it then, and definitely wouldn't admit it now, but that didn't mean I didn't know.

I shook my head. "I have no interest in using my personal history to defend a case."

"I wouldn't ask you to."

"You mean you wouldn't ask me to *again*?"

"What are you talking about?"

"You know."

"I don't."

I sighed. "Then what do you mean?"

"Northlake isn't that big a place. The good lawyers are either conflicted out or don't want to touch the case. You're from Michigan, but not from Northlake, and you win murder cases. That's why you're a perfect fit."

"Why don't they want to touch the case?"

"A teenage boy allegedly started a fire that killed a small child and the firefighter trying to rescue him. Feelings are running high."

"Arson and murder, you said?"

Cyn nodded. "Two counts. And he's being tried as an adult."

"They've already determined that?"

Cyn nodded.

"That's usually the subject of hearings and briefing—"

"That's already happened. And part of the reason why our firm is getting involved."

"How far along is this case, Cyn?"

"Trial is in one month."

I shook my head. "Do you folks ever get involved at the *beginning* of a case?"

"Sometimes. Other times, it takes people a while to realize they need us."

I looked out at the concert where some type of pyrotechnics were being fired. "You'll be working on the case, I take it?"

"Yes. We expect that whoever handles the case will have to be in Northlake for the next month."

"That would take some doing with my practice."

Cyn nodded. "Besides your fee, we would expect to pay any related expenses, including any temporary staffing that may be required if Daniel needs assistance handling matters while you are gone."

"Keeping tabs on us?"

"Monitoring resources. We will also pay for whatever staff you feel is required to manage the case in Northlake."

I nodded and thought. "You've caught me kind of cold here, Cyn. Let me think about it?"

Cyn nodded. "Certainly. I'll email you a summary tonight to give you a flavor of the case."

"Fine."

"I need your decision by midnight Saturday."

I started to protest, then realized trial was only a month away. "So you can contact the next lawyer?"

"Whomever is handling this needs to be in Northlake Monday morning."

"Do you still have the same phone number?"

"Yes."

"Then I'll call you tomorrow."

"I've kept you from your concert long enough." Cyn extended her hand. "Thanks for seeing me, Nathan."

"No, thank you. I'll let you know."

She nodded, grabbed the handle of her case, and headed for the door.

"Cyn. Have you seen Hank?"

She stopped, looked. "Why?"

"Lizzy was asking after him tonight."

"I haven't. I think people from my firm have been in touch now and then."

"She wanted to pass along that she wouldn't mind him coming around again."

"I see."

"Could you tell him?"

"I can't Nathan, no, but I'll pass it along. No promises."

"None taken."

"I look forward to hearing from you."

Then Cyn Bardor left, and I went back out to our seats on the landing to catch the second half of the concert.

My mind was elsewhere though, on a paralegal that could arrange for an entire suite at a Lizzy Saint concert to make it more convenient for her to meet with a potential lawyer on her way up north. And on a firm that was willing to pay for it.

Damn them.

4

It was a little after one in the morning when I got home from the concert. That didn't matter to Roxie, who greeted me with a sniff to make sure that I hadn't been out with other dogs. Roxie was a retired service dog, a brindle boxer if you keep track of such things, and, after we took a quick trip outside to do what dogs do, she followed me to the kitchen, waited with sublime patience as I grabbed a beer and my laptop, then curled up on the floor right next to my feet as I sat down at the table.

Cyn's email was right there at the top of my inbox, sent immediately after she'd left me. Knowing her, it had been ready to go.

Her succinct email summarized what she'd told me at the suite: her firm, Friedlander & Skald, was looking to hire me to defend a murder case set for trial in Northlake, Michigan at the end of October, just one month away. They offered a flat fee for my time that was eye-popping and made clear that all expenses —food, lodging, travel—would be paid on top of it. As big as the fee was, they offered an even larger one if I felt my associate should sit second chair and try the case with me. I'd also have free rein to hire whatever other support I thought was necessary—experts, investigators, process servers—with no budget. They just asked that I have Cyn pay those directly.

I'd worked with them before, so I knew that the Firm would be true to their word and that Cyn would be a proficient marvel. The only hitch was that I had to let them know by midnight Saturday. Twenty-three hours from now.

Cyn had also attached a Case Summary. I clicked it open. The defendant, Brock Niesen, was a fifteen-year-old boy who'd been accused of setting fire to the Lakeside Drive-In. The fire had spread to a U-Store facility and from there to a small home that had housed a family with three small children, all under eight years old. The mother and two of the kids had made it to safety.

The youngest, four-year-old Liam had died in the blaze. A firefighter, Eli Tripp, had died trying to get him out.

A local attorney named Luke Mott had represented Brock Niesen through the first part of the case. The Court had held a hearing this past summer on whether Brock should be tried as an adult. Normally, a kid Brock's age would be tried as a juvenile, but Michigan law allowed kids between fourteen and seventeen to be tried as adults in special circumstances.

The judge found that arson and murder were special circumstances. Fifteen-year-old Brock faced the same penalty an adult would face—life imprisonment.

Cyn had more details to share but, as she knew I would understand, she would only do so with the attorney who would be representing Brock.

She added two more files for flavor. The first was a screenshot of the lead story in *The Northlake Ledger*: "Troubled Teen Starts Mission Road Fire that Kills Two." It included a picture of Brock pulled from social media, sneering at a camera, hair drooping over one eye, making a devil sign. Next to it was a

Cruel Sentence

double inset of little Liam's baby picture and Eli Tripp's official firefighter picture.

The second attachment was a local television news story reporting on the joint funeral. The footage included video of two hearses driving down a street between lines of firetrucks, cranes raised, and firefighters standing at attention.

I watched the whole thing, then watched it again.

I stared at the screen, then shut it off. I could see what we were up against. I also wasn't sure I wanted to immerse myself in that for the next month.

But I could also see why Brock Niesen needed someone like me. And Cyn.

I wasn't sure yet which way I fell. I knew that I'd have to check on some things to see if this was even possible for me, but that would have to wait until the morning, so I turned off the computer, and Roxie and I called it a night.

∼

THE CALLS STARTED the next day. Personal first.

I started with my sister-in-law. "Hey, Izzy."

"Nate? The single man up this early after the concert?"

"Impressive, right?"

"I was going to say sad. You should be getting out more. If the boys hadn't woke me up an hour ago, I'd be pissed at you."

"About that. I may be going out of town for a little while."

"It's about time."

"For work."

Izzy sighed. "That doesn't count."

"I have a chance to take a case that would put me in northern Michigan for a month."

"And you're looking for room and board for a certain boxer?"

"I could probably take her with me for part of it, but you know how it gets toward the end."

"Don't take her at all. Roxie is staying with us."

"Are you sure? It would be for a month."

"Not a problem. My boys love that dog more than me."

"It would start tomorrow."

"I wish you showed that kind of initiative with your dating."

"Who says I don't?"

"Literally everyone. Tomorrow is fine."

"Okay. I'm still figuring out if I'm going to do this, but I'll let you know by tonight."

"Don't think twice about it. Roxie stays with us."

The next call was to my mom.

"Nathan, why are you calling so early?"

"Just checking in. How did Dad's appointment go yesterday?" My father had a home improvement encounter with electricity this past summer that had stopped his heart. They'd been able to restart his heart, but his kidneys had lagged behind.

"His kidney function is improving, so that's the good news," she said.

"And the bad?"

"He still needs dialysis, but the doctor was hopeful that the next thirty days might turn things around."

"How'd Dad take it?"

"I think you can imagine his view of being 'hooked up to that contraption' for another month."

"But he's improving?"

"Not as fast as he'd like, but yes."

"How about around the house? Are you two doing okay?"

"We're fine. You all have been a great help while your dad's getting back on his feet. So what's this about?"

"Can't a son be concerned about his parents?"

"Of course. But rarely early on a Saturday morning."

"I might have a case that would take me out of town for a month."

"Might?"

"I'm deciding whether to take it."

"Oh, don't worry about us."

"You're sure?"

"Positive. Where would you be going?"

"Northlake, up by—"

"—Oh, I know exactly where it is! It's beautiful there this time of year! You'll have to go to one of their orchards!"

"I don't know that I'll be sightseeing much."

"That would be a shame. We're fine, son. Your father's on the mend and your brothers are here if something comes up."

"You can still reach me. It's only four hours away."

"Good. And make sure you give me an address so I can send food. You know you never eat during these trials."

"I haven't decided if I'm going yet, but I'll let you know. Thanks, Mom."

I thought about the next call. I was pretty sure I knew what her answer would be, but I was concerned that the question wasn't fair. Still, best to face these things head on, so I called my associate, Emily Lake.

"Hi, Emily."

"We're up early today, Boss. What's up?"

"I'm thinking of taking a murder case."

"Good! We haven't had a trial in forever."

"It's barely been two months, Emily."

"Exactly. Forever ago. It'll be good to get things fired up again."

"There's a hitch. The trial is in a month."

"Now you're talking!"

"Out of town. In Northlake."

"I've been there."

"You have?"

"On our way to Sleeping Bear Dunes. When do we leave?"

"I haven't agreed to take the case yet."

"Why not?"

"I'm making sure we can handle it."

"Why couldn't we?"

"That's what I'm doing, checking for personal and professional conflicts."

"We don't have any trials set for that week, do we?"

"No."

"Did you run a conflict check?"

"Yes. It's clear."

"Then what are we talking about? Let's go!"

"I may need you to cover a few things down here this month like the pretrial in—"

"Oh no you don't. No, no, no. You know Danny can cover any court appearances in other cases here, and I can handle any filings electronically from up there."

"Emily, the trial is at the end of October."

"Right. It's going to be a fun month. What's the name of the client—"

"What else is happening at the end of October?"

Emily cursed, not in general, but at me. Directly. Then she said, "Don't you dare, Boss. Don't you freakin' dare."

"I was concerned that you're going to have so much to do—"

"It'll get done."

"You also have to physically be there you know, for the ceremony."

"Josh?!" Her voice was fainter as she held the phone away.

"Yeah, baby?" came a faint voice.

"You'd never let our marriage get in the way of my career, would you?"

"Never," came the distant reply.

"You can handle anything I can't, right?"

"Always."

"Mind if I'm late for the rehearsal dinner?"

"Do I get your steak?"

"If you ask nicely."

"I'll marry you anytime, anywhere, baby."

Emily's voice came back to me. "No more of your nonsense."

"Northlake is a long way from Columbus."

"That's it, Boss. If we take a murder case, I'm going with you. My wedding will take care of itself."

"I had to check."

"I appreciate that. Now what's the case about?"

I told her about the young man accused of murdering a child and a firefighter, about the terms of the engagement, and about my meeting with Cyn.

"So I would finally get to work with Cyn Bardor?" Emily said.

"You would. Why?"

She chuckled. "Anytime Danny talks about her, he drops something. I have to see why."

"If we take the case, you will."

"Sounds like we'll have our hands full."

"We will, if we take it."

"So are we a go?"

"Just about. I have to check with Danny to make sure."

"Start with the retainer. It'll be a short conversation."

"I'll let you know by tonight."

"I'll start packing."

Some things like the course of rivers, gale force winds, and rolling waves are almost impossible to divert. I didn't tell her to hold off and hung up.

She was right, of course. Daniel Reddy, my former associate and now partner, had no objection to taking the case. He was thrilled at the influx of cash from the retainer and was more than able to manage the office while we were gone.

"Is your dad okay?" was the only real question he asked.

"He is. Not out of the woods yet but getting close."

"Then don't worry about anything here. And tell Cyn I said 'hi.'"

"Thanks, Danny."

"No problem, Partner."

I took a quick look at my calendar to make sure there weren't any lurking time bombs that I needed to handle personally. There weren't. Then I took Roxie for a walk, both because she needed it and to give everything a little time to settle.

When we returned, I'd decided and, if we only had a month, there was no reason to wait until midnight to make the call. I started to email a reply, then picked up the phone instead.

"Hello, Nathan."

"Time to talk, Cyn?"

"Yes."

"I'm in."

"Good."

"I'm going to bring my associate, Emily Lake."

"That's your call, Nathan, but I think it's a good one."

"I have some logistics to work out—"

"Only for your office in Carrefour, Nathan. Everything's taken care of in Northlake."

I chuckled. "My apologies."

"Not necessary. I'll wire the money today."

"That's not necessary."

"It is. We have a lot to do."

"I'm sure. Any more you can tell me now?"

"We can get into the details when you get here."

"You're up there already?"

"Yes."

"How about the big picture?"

There was a pause, then Cyn said, "The big picture is that it appears our client did it."

"Did what exactly?"

"Purposely started the fire at the Lakeside Drive-In, which spread until it killed two people."

"Is there some wiggle room there? Fire in a barrel or a campfire that spread by mistake?"

"It appears that our client attached twenty-five pounds of ammonium nitrate and aluminum powder to the drive-in screen and shot it with a high velocity rifle, causing the mix to explode and start the fire which eventually spread to the victim's house."

We were both silent for a moment.

"Previous counsel did not find any wiggle room," Cyn said.

"I'll see you tomorrow."

5
___

The next morning, I dropped Roxie off with Mark and Izzy, gave a chin of doom to my youngest nephew Joe, and set out for Northlake.

I live in Carrefour, a town that sits on the southern border of Michigan, near Ohio. I've described it now and again, but this case didn't have anything to do with my hometown. I was headed to the northwest end of the Lower Peninsula of Michigan, about four hours away.

The first half of the drive—north on 69 to Marshall to west on 94 to Kalamazoo before turning north on 131 through Grand Rapids—is no different than many drives in the Midwest. Two and three lane highways cut through farmland and woods that are green in the summer and brown topped with white in the winter, punctuated by regular stops for fast food and gas along the way.

It changes once you get north of Grand Rapids, especially on the west side of the state. The towns get farther apart, the hills roll more, and the woods become forests that encroach on the road. Finally, at a point which is debated that might start when you cross Route 10 in Reed City but certainly occurs by the time you hit Cadillac, you are Up North.

That September had been warm so the leaves hadn't turned in Carrefour, but I could see the first signs as I angled northwest from Cadillac for another hour until I arrived in the town of Northlake. Nestled between woods and inland lakes on the east and sand dunes and the vast coast of Lake Michigan on the west, it was a little larger than I expected. It had a walkable downtown of lake-themed tourist shops, which was no surprise, but there was also a commercial district of box stores, a group of government buildings appropriate for the seat for Sable County, and housing developments that indicated a year-round population greater than the typical summer resort town.

I followed Cyn's directions and headed for Bluffside Farms.

∼

CYN WAS WAITING for me outside the condo. Her blood red hair was pulled back, and she was dressed casually in flowing pants and a sweater.

"Couldn't find anything fancier?" I said, pointing at the condo.

"We're going to be here for a month," she said.

"I didn't realize Bluffside Farms was short for Bluffside Farms Golf and Country Club."

She shrugged. "A motel or a lake cottage wouldn't be conducive to work."

"And the gate and security guard will keep out the riffraff?"

"I'm sure the Holiday Inn Express will take you."

"I'll make do with the condo. Where are you?"

"I have the unit on this side. Emily will be in the other."

"Three?"

"A month, Nathan."

I shook my head. "Your firm never skimps."

"That's because Friedlander & Skald is focused on results. Why don't you get settled? I'll order dinner and we can talk about the case."

I took the key from her, and she was down the path before I opened the door.

It was a luxury two-bedroom condo, and if you want all the ooh and ahh description, you're probably better off watching one of those Lakefront Bargain Buy shows than listening to me. There were wood floors and stone countertops and shiny appliances, but I wasn't really interested in where I'd be watching the sunset or sipping my coffee. I put my laptop and file on the kitchen table, dumped my suitcase on the bed, and hung a garment bag of suits in the closet, then fidgeted around for a minute or two before texting Cyn to make sure it was all right to come over. It was and I did.

"Done already?" Cyn said.

I shrugged. "Not much to do."

"The food's on its way. Chinese okay?"

"Fine."

She gestured, and I followed her into a condo which was larger than mine, featuring a large dining room in the middle. Or I should say that it had been a large dining room. Now it was an office with multiple monitors, a deluxe high-speed printer, a...you get the idea. If I didn't see something we needed, I was sure it would be there soon.

"That's the former attorney's file, those are the filings to date, and those are the prosecutor's *Brady* disclosures and investigation materials." Cyn tapped three neat binders in succession. "I'll set up your computer again so that we're on my firm's electronic file system." She held out a hand and I gave her my laptop.

As she opened it, she said, "I know you like to do your own

highlighting, but I've tabbed some things I think you'll want to check."

"Perfect."

"The hearing on whether to try Brock as an adult was interesting. I think it gives you a pretty good road map of how the prosecutor's going to argue the case."

"Who is it?"

"A woman named Astrid Olsen."

"Local?"

"Through and through. She's been the chief prosecutor for ten years. Long-standing ties with law enforcement. And the firefighters."

"Ah."

"Right. She's taking this personally. And she knows what she's doing."

"Okay. Any surprises on her strategy?"

"Not so far. But she's not offering any deals."

"I suppose she wouldn't."

Cyn typed a few more things, then handed the laptop back. "There, you're in. The electronic filing system is in that folder on your desktop."

"Thanks. So it sounds like we're going to have a tough time arguing that the fire was an accident?"

"A good lawyer can argue a great many things."

"But it needs to be based in truth to be effective, so tell me about this twenty-five pounds of...?"

"Ammonium nitrate and aluminum powder."

"Right. What's that about?"

"Are you familiar with SafeBoom targets?"

"No."

"They're targets that explode when you shoot them."

"Oh, right. My brother had some with a different name, I think. You mix it yourself, right?"

Cyn nodded. "SafeBoom ships separate, pre-measured quantities of ammonium nitrate and aluminum powder, which the user then mixes himself in a separate container. When it's shot by a high velocity round, it explodes."

I nodded. "People use them for distance shooting to know when they've hit the target."

"One pound is the maximum recommended quantity. The police say that Brock Niesen used twenty-five."

"To do what, exactly?"

"They say Brock climbed up a support pole of the drive-in movie screen, nestled the SafeBoom into a ledge in the support structure, then went across the street and shot the SafeBoom with his Savage AXIS bolt-action rifle, causing the SafeBoom to explode, blowing a hole in the screen, and starting the fire."

I raised an eyebrow. "He shot at an upward angle?"

Cyn nodded.

"I take it the bullet didn't hit anyone?"

"No, but the prosecutor did include an unlawful discharge of a firearm charge."

I frowned. "I assume Brock didn't mean for the fire to spread, but that doesn't matter. If he intended to set fire to the movie screen, then that's arson, and he can be held liable for murder if the fire kills someone."

Cyn nodded. "Correct."

I tapped the table. "Shooting a massive exploding target that you strapped to a screen seems an awful lot like intent."

"Agreed. You see our problem?"

"I do. Do we know why Brock decided to blow up the movie screen?"

"I have not spoken to our client, but I have a guess."

"Which is?"

"His dad owns it."

I frowned.

"And his dad is no longer married to his mother," Cyn said.

"Ah. How long?"

"Five years."

"Who does he live with?"

"Technically both."

"I see. Any insight into why he'd wreck his dad's theater?"

"Like I said, I haven't spoken with Brock. I do know that his father had put the drive-in up for sale shortly before this happened."

"I imagine this has put a damper on that."

Cyn nodded. "His father still owns it, yes."

"Does the dad have any businesses besides the drive-in?"

"He runs a propane business—delivery for houses, filling and exchange for smaller tanks."

"Hmm. And the mom?"

"She runs the family orchard."

"Apples?"

"Mostly. Some cherries."

"I take it business has been good?"

"Why would you assume that?"

I waved at the luxury condo. "We're here."

Cyn's gaze was cool green ice. "The Niesens' resources are limited."

"Interesting. Friedlander & Skald doesn't exactly seem like a firm of the people."

"My firm has a variety of relationships. Our responsibility isn't to check the Niesens' balance sheet. It's to win an acquittal for Brock."

"So it is. I'll need to get in to see Brock as soon as—"

Cyn clicked a key. "You're scheduled for 8:30 tomorrow morning. The Sable County jail is expecting you."

I blinked, then smiled. "Are you coming?"

"No. I'm going to keep setting up here. We only have twenty-nine days."

I smiled. "I'd say that I should meet Brock's mother, but I have a feeling I already am."

"6:30 a.m. at the Golden Apple Orchard, before she opens and before you meet with Brock. I'll send you directions."

"You've thought of everything."

Cyn shook her head. "No one can think of everything."

The doorbell rang. Cyn answered and returned with boxes of Chinese.

She handed me the Mongolian Beef I'd wanted but hadn't asked for and we ate.

6

I was on my way to the Niesen family orchard by 6:15 the next morning and, no, the sun is not up in Northlake at that hour. If, like my youngest brother, you've already started your shift by that time, then you probably don't think it's worth mentioning, but it seems to me that if the sun hasn't seen fit to start its day, then we should get a gold star for starting ours. I have enough to share.

It took me a little longer than I'd anticipated to find the place —there were no lights outside of town and one street sign was both twisted and hidden by a tree branch, but eventually the sky lightened and my navigation improved, and I arrived at the Golden Apple Orchard.

There was a sign pointing the way to pick your own apples and fun for the whole family, but I really just had to follow orderly rows of trees along a gravel drive back to a cluster of buildings. It's too strong to say that I found the parking lot— what I found was a square area of depressed grass with a line of yellow rope down the middle that seemed to indicate that you could park on either side. I parked my Jeep opposite the only other car in the lot and went to the only building with a light on, a big wooden barn with a covered wood deck in front of a sturdy shop door.

There was a flip sign in the window that said *Closed* but, before I could knock, the door opened.

"Mr. Shepherd?" the woman said.

"Nate. Mrs. Niesen?"

"Dagmar. Come in."

Dagmar Niesen was tall, only an inch or two shorter than me in her work boots. She wore jeans and a padded flannel shirt that was closer to a jacket. Her hair was blond, on the long side, and held in place by a couple of loose twists at the base of her neck. It was hard to tell her age—the blond was paler in places that could have been the product of years or a very particular hair stylist, and she had fine lines at the edge of her eyes and mouth that could have been from time, a fair complexion working in the sun, or, I suppose, your son being accused of murder.

Dagmar Niesen held the door open, then led the way into an open two-story building. A row of concessions lined one side, ending in a cash register, with three long rows of heavy wooden picnic tables stretched across the center of the room. She gestured to the center table on the near end where a couple of carafes of coffee and a plate of donuts awaited.

I took a seat on a bench as she slid me a carafe and a mug. "Sorry to meet this early," she said. "It's our busiest time of the year."

"I bet. How long's the season?"

"October, give or take, depending on the weather. Here." She cut a square piece of pastry out of a tin pan, plated it, and slid it over. The smell of apple and frosting wafted up.

I smiled. "Apple turnover?"

"Made it this morning."

With that kind of invitation, I couldn't very well turn it down so I took a fluffy, light, tart, and sweet bite and decided the sun would rise just a little earlier if this were its reward.

"This is delicious."

Dagmar nodded in assured acceptance. "Old recipe. How are you going to save my son?"

"I don't know yet." I set down my fork, took a sip of coffee to chase the turnover, and met her gaze. "First, I have to learn everything I can. Then, we figure out how to defend him."

That didn't seem to faze her. "What do you need to know?"

I thought. "I know how they say he did it, started the fire. As far as you know, did he?"

"Shoot the SafeBoom target at the drive-in?"

"Yes."

She nodded. "He did."

"How do you know?"

"He told me. Eventually. It wasn't that hard to figure out though."

"Why?"

"His dad, my ex-husband, owns it."

"The drive-in?"

Dagmar nodded.

I took another bite of the turnover. "Brock and his father were having trouble, I take it?"

"They always do."

"What happened?"

Dagmar appeared to think for a moment, then said, "Kevin told us he was moving."

"That's Kevin Niesen?"

"Yes."

"Tell me about it."

Dagmar paused again, then said, "Last winter was hard. Come spring, Kevin said he'd had enough and was moving back to southern Indiana. He had an opportunity to buy another propane business there and was planning to move just as soon as he sold the drive-in and a couple of other things."

I gestured at the barn. "Is this one of those things?"

Dagmar shook her head. "My great-grandma Iduna planted the first trees. The orchard is mine."

"So Kevin moving to Indiana made Brock mad?"

"No. Kevin insisting that Brock come with him did."

I nodded. "What's the custody arrangement?"

"Shared. Since the divorce we made sure we lived in the same school district so Brock could alternate weeks living with us."

"That doesn't seem possible from southern Indiana."

"No. Kevin was willing to let Brock go to school here but expected him to spend summers and holidays in Indiana. Or vice versa."

"I see."

Dagmar shook her head. "My son didn't. He wasn't going to go and told Kevin so."

"And?"

"Kevin insisted that he was. Brock might have come around, or at least softened to it, but my husband can be a—" she said a word I didn't catch.

"A what?"

Dagmar smiled. "Sorry, it's an old word that loosely translates to 'willful butthole.'"

"Ah."

"And so Kevin said he was moving as soon as he sold the theater and Brock would be living with him for the summer."

I nodded. "And next thing you know, the drive-in screen has a hole in it?"

"A big one." Dagmar looked down and those fine lines around her mouth deepened. "And two people are dead."

I thought. "So no question he did it?"

Dagmar shook her head. "None. Nate, my son would never kill anyone."

"That doesn't matter. Did Mr. Mott explain that to you?"

Her blue eyes were intent. "Why don't you?"

"Arson is intentionally setting a structure on fire. If the fire kills someone, it's murder."

"Even if you didn't mean to hurt someone?"

"Even then. All that matters is that you meant to set the fire."

"I don't know that he meant to start a fire."

"Or that you meant to destroy the property."

Dagmar exhaled. "He did mean to do that."

"That's our problem."

Dagmar nodded again. "That's what the first attorney, Mr. Mott said. Does it matter if the death occurs in a different building?"

"No. It's predictable that fires spread. So is harm coming to firefighters."

We refilled our coffees. The turnover smelled delicious, but I left it where it was as Dagmar said, "Do we have any defense at all?"

"That's what I'm working on. The prosecutor still has to prove every single thing in her case beyond a reasonable doubt. My job is to find the weak link in her case and poke a hole in it."

"That doesn't seem like a strong strategy."

"It's a start. Did Brock use his own gun?"

"Yes. A Savage AXIS 270."

"Did he order the SafeBoom?"

"I didn't know that until after."

"But he did?"

"Yes."

"Were you aware he was gone the night of the fire?"

"He told me he was with friends. He came home late that night."

"Where's home?"

She pointed over her shoulder. "Behind these buildings, a quarter of a mile or so up the road."

I thought, then nodded. "That gives me enough to get started. I'll be in town through trial. Here's my contact information. Call me anytime. I can't tell you everything but, since you're Brock's mother and he's a minor, I get a little more leeway."

"Can they really put my son away for his whole life?"

"Yes."

"For an accident?"

I shook my head. "For killing two people who died in a fire that he started."

She held my gaze, then nodded. "I suppose that's why we hired you."

That made me curious. "How did you come to do that, by the way? Hire Friedlander & Skald?"

"They came to me."

That surprised me. "What? What did they say?"

Dagmar cocked her head. "You don't know? Isn't it your firm?"

This didn't seem to be the time to get into the nuances of local counsel arrangements. "I came on later. I wasn't part of that."

Dagmar stared at me, then shrugged. "They said they'd heard about Brock's case and were willing to take it on."

"For free?"

She chuckled. "No. They offered me a price I could manage, and I paid it." Dagmar's brow furrowed. "You really didn't know about all that?"

"No. Why?"

"Because they said you'd handle the case. And that you could save my son."

Now was also not the time to say how bleak the chances of that seemed, so I said, "I'll try."

Two young women walked through the door chatting, then stopped when they saw us.

Dagmar waved them in and told them to start setting up. Then she stood and said, "Sorry, we have to open. We have a field trip coming in this morning."

"No problem. Thanks for the turnover."

Dagmar nodded, picked up the turnover tin and the carafes, and started to leave. Then she turned back to me and said, "I didn't mortgage my orchard to *try* to save my son, Nate."

I didn't answer, but I nodded before she walked away.

A school bus was pulling into the Golden Apple Orchard lot as I left to go meet Brock Niesen.

7

I had to go through town to get to the jail on the other side, so I stopped for coffee at a promising place called Maggie's that had a steaming cup next to the name. I parked in the street two storefronts away, peeked in the glass window to confirm my choice, and went in.

Maggie's had a deli counter along one side and a collection of booths and two top tables on the other. It was more wood than metal, which would have made the place dark if the whole front wall hadn't been a window to the street. The menu behind the glass deli counter promised traditional sandwich options all day with specialty breakfast sandwiches until ten unless you asked nicely. More importantly, I saw big vats of coffee behind the register at the far end.

"Help you, sir?" said a man behind the counter.

"Large coffee, please."

"You can get that at the register. Can I help you, ma'am?" He said to the woman behind me.

I moved down the line to the register where a woman with short black hair sporting a green *Maggie's* t-shirt beamed a smile and said, "You appear to need coffee."

Cruel Sentence 39

I couldn't help but smile back. "Please."

"How many?"

"One, black, please."

"You got it." She whirled back to the coffee, grabbed a cup, and flipped the spigot in a blink. "Seeing the sights today?"

My mind had been on murder and life sentences so I blinked before I said, "No, here on work for a few weeks."

"Oh, for the seawall project? You just missed the rest of your crew." She turned back around and handed me the coffee with another smile. "Like I told them, we're open seven days a week, seven to three. You can order here or if you're in a hurry, say because you're late for work, you can order online, and we'll have it ready for you when you get here."

She rang me up and I paid as she was still speaking. I took a sip of her handiwork, and said, "I'll be sure to do that. And tell Maggie she knows how to make coffee."

She smiled. "You did. See you soon." Maggie smiled at the next woman in line. "Mrs. Watson, did you see the cranberry muffins?"

As I circled back to the door, a man blocked it, and when I say blocked it, I mean he blocked all of the doorway and the sun behind it. He was six and a half feet tall and broad enough that his shoulders filled the entrance. He had a shaved head and a once broken nose and looked as if he'd woken up that morning chewing glass. I'd have guessed he was a bear wrestler or nineteenth-century bareknuckle prize fighter, but he also wore a suit that billowed around his waist and fell just short of his wrists as if it too couldn't get over how big the man was.

The man nodded to me and tried to step to the side, but the doorway wasn't quite big enough. We both stepped back, then both stepped forward, then I stepped back again and said, "Please. I already have mine."

The man nodded and came in. I heard Maggie say, "Your

order's over here, Mason," as I took my turn and walked out the door.

I'd only taken a few steps down the sidewalk when a man strode up to me and said, "Go home."

I stopped. The man looked to be in his thirties, was big and round with a goatee, a ball cap, and, more immediately interesting to me, an open carry pistol at his hip.

"Excuse me?" I said.

He took another step forward. "We don't need your kind up here."

That can mean a lot of things to a lot of different people in a lot of different places and at that particular moment, I had no idea how my new friend meant it toward me.

I gestured. "People who drink coffee? Seems like quite a few of them in there."

"Carpet-bagging lawyers flying in to defend murderers. You need to take your big-city ass back downstate."

Ah.

I pointed at my Jeep. "No propellers on this model."

I made my way around him. He stepped sideways and blocked it.

I exhaled and straightened.

He stepped closer and said, "Mott said he was off the case, that some hot shot was taking over from downstate." Flecks of spit came out with his venom. "But we know what that little shit Niesen did. We know he killed Eli and Liam, and no one is getting him out of it."

Mott complaining would explain how people knew he was off the case. I didn't see how a random passerby would know that I was the one who was taking over, but small towns are small towns. Either way, I'd had about enough.

"Are you going to get out of my way, friend?"

"I'm not your friend."

"No, but that seemed more polite than coital visage." I took a sip of coffee.

He blinked. "That fancy word shit's not going to work up here."

"Neither is the bully shit. Get your hand off your gun and move. Please."

He stared, I stared; you know the deal. But, eventually, he stepped aside. He didn't take his hand off the butt of his pistol, but you take victories where you can.

I got in my car, continued on my way to see Brock, and thought about the new friends I was making in Northlake.

8

Northlake is the seat of Sable County, so it houses the courts and the county government. It's also a tourist town, and the good citizens had found that, while travelers didn't mind strolling past a stately courthouse on the way to their next shop, a stark, institutional jail put a bit of a damper on things so I drove out past the edge of town until a sign told me that I'd found the Sable County Jail, proudly managed by Sable County Sheriff Sean Sizemore.

It was institutional—square, brown, and brick—but I have to say it was nicer than I expected for an out of the way county up north. The gates and razor-wire fence were shiny, the visitor intake involved a high-tech scanner instead of metal detectors and wands, and I saw more monitors and cameras than I'd come to expect. It was brightly lit, clean, with more windows than normal. Another, more subtle, feature took me until I was walking down the hall to the interview room to place.

It didn't stink.

As the guard dropped me off, he said, "We have to bring him over from isolation, so it'll be a minute."

"Isolation? Has there been a problem?"

The guard shook his head. "He's a minor, so it's for his protection."

I nodded, took a seat, and had finished reviewing the Sheriff's report again when Brock Niesen was escorted in.

He was a little taller than average but gangly, as if he'd been stretched and his body hadn't had a chance to catch up yet. He had shaggy hair that was more red than blond and a cluster of acne on one cheek. His orange jumpsuit seemed all arms and legs as he dropped into a chair and put his cuffed hands in his lap.

In other words, he looked every bit a teenager, no different than one of my nephews.

"Can you take off the cuffs?" I said.

"No," said the guard as he left. "Hit the button when you're done." The door snicked shut, followed by the sound of an electronic bolt.

"Who are you?" said Brock Niesen in a voice that was mostly, but not quite, changed.

"Nate Shepherd. I'm your lawyer."

"What happened to Mott?"

"Mr. Mott is withdrawing and I'm taking over."

"Did my mom do that?"

"Yes."

"Figures."

"Why?"

"Because my cheap ass dad wouldn't."

"You don't get along with your dad?"

"What was your first clue?"

"Your mom said he was going to move?"

"He *has* moved."

"When?"

"I don't know." He wiggled his fingers and jingled his cuffs. "I've been in here."

"Were you trying to stop him?"

"From what?"

"Moving?"

Brock shrugged. "Nothing stops him. This is all his fault."

"What is?"

"Me. Here."

"How?"

"If he wasn't such a pussy about winter up here, none of this would have happened."

"Is Indiana that bad?"

Brock shook his head. "You don't get it."

I sat back and crossed my legs. "Probably not. Why did you shoot the screen?"

"Because he was being a dick!"

"Your dad?"

"Were we talking about another one?"

"Tell me about the SafeBoom."

"What about it?"

"Had you used it before?"

Brock nodded. "Last few years."

"How much are you supposed to use?"

"A pound or two."

"How much did you use?"

He shrugged.

"I need to know so I know if the cops are telling the truth."

He looked down. "Twenty pounds, I guess."

"The Sheriff found packaging for twenty-five pounds."

He shrugged.

"Brock."

"Does it matter?"

"Everything matters."

He stared at the table, then said, "Twenty-five."

"Why so much?"

He rubbed his nose. "I wanted to make sure it went through the screen."

"What's the most you'd ever used before?"

"Ten."

"Was this a bigger explosion?"

He grinned. "Lots."

I stared. His grin faded. Eventually, he looked down.

Once he did, I said, "Had you ever seen it cause a fire before?"

He shook his head. "It's not supposed to."

"No? How do you know that?"

"Videos online. There's plenty of guys that blow stuff up and never set fire to anything."

"Did you want to cause a fire?"

"No, I just wanted to blow a hole in the prick's drive-in screen."

"Is that what caught fire?"

"I don't know if it was the screen or the bushes, but it's his fault! What kind of asshole plants bushes at a drive-in?"

"If you meant to blow up the screen, it doesn't matter—"

"—Then it doesn't matter if I meant to start the fire. Jesus, you sound just like Mott! I didn't mean to hurt anyone! No one was even there! The drive-in wasn't supposed to open for another month! How can that make me a murderer?!"

"Because it started a fire and the fire spread."

"I didn't mean to catch anything on fire! It was an accident! It was all an accident! They can't say I'm a murderer for an accident!"

"They can, Brock."

"That's not fair!!"

"Maybe not. But it's true."

Brock's chest was heaving as he gripped the edge of the desk with two cuffed hands. I waited until his breathing slowed and he let go, then I said, "That's why I need your help. Was there anyone with you?"

He shook his head.

"Where did you get the SafeBoom?"

"Big Bob's Online Armory."

"Did you mix it yourself?"

He nodded.

"No friends, no one helped?"

"No."

"When did you order it?"

"Last fall."

"Do you have the email receipt?"

He shrugged. "If it wasn't auto deleted."

I couldn't think of anything else and was about to wrap things up when another thought hit me. "Brock, did you see the fire start?"

Brock shook his head.

"Are you sure?"

"Yeah. I took off as soon as it blew. Why does that matter?"

"It's one thing to accidentally start a fire. It's another to see one going and run away."

He looked at the table. "I didn't see the stupid fire."

"Did you talk to anyone about what happened?"

He shook his head.

"How about your mom?"

"Yeah, I guess her."

"When?"

"That night."

"How about your dad?"

Brock sneered. "No, my mom told my dad. He screwed me!"

I sensed a theme. "Didn't talk to any friends? A girlfriend?"

"No."

"How are you doing?"

Brock looked up. "What?"

"How are you doing? In here."

"Bored. Can you get me my phone?"

"No."

"My Switch?"

"No handheld games either."

"Can you do anything?"

I ignored that. "Have you been in danger at all in here?"

"I'm by myself all day, but I suppose that's better than crapping in front of a roommate."

"I'll see if they allow any computer time for you here. I'll check back in and tell you how the case is going."

I stood and rang the buzzer.

"Tell my mom—" Brock said.

He stopped as the guard opened the door.

"—never mind," he finished.

I nodded. "I will."

The guard led me out.

9

When I'm getting close to trial, I have a tendency to lose track of what's going on around me. You know, I leave the headlights on, forget my wallet, that kind of thing. One time, I was halfway out of the parking lot of a shopping center before I remembered that I'd come with my wife Sarah and had to circle back around and play it off like I'd been getting the car for her. She didn't buy it for a second and took every opportunity to hassle me about it until she died.

This walking around in a comic book thought bubble doesn't usually happen to me until right before the trial, but I was so focused on how I was going to find an angle in this dead-bang loser of a case, and how stupidly evasive teenagers can be, that I didn't even see the women with the signs until I just about ran into them.

In fairness to me, they didn't start shouting until I was right in front of them.

"Justice for Eli! Justice for Liam!"

They were blocking the sidewalk that led to the jail parking lot. A woman with mousy brown hair and plastic red glasses thrust a sign at my face, a sign with a large picture of a firefighter in his dress uniform, a flag behind him.

"Justice for Eli! Justice for Liam!" she shouted again, thrusting the picture at me each time she said a name.

A woman next to her stood a pace or two back. She had the same hair but longer, no glasses, and was a little thinner, but the family resemblance was clear. Her sign was a baby picture of a little boy sitting upright, grinning, holding interlocking teething rings of blue, red, and yellow. She didn't chant, but every time the other woman yelled "Liam," she pushed the baby picture forward.

"Justice for Eli! Justice for Liam!"

I didn't know the ladies, but I knew pain when I saw it. I stepped off the sidewalk and made my way toward my Jeep.

"Justice for Eli! Justice for Liam!"

The women followed me along the sidewalk, parallel to my path.

"Justice for Eli! Justice for Liam!"

The chant was fainter when I closed the car door, but I could still hear it, and I could see them as they took a position at the parking lot exit.

"Justice for Eli! Justice for Liam!"

As I drove away, I waited until I couldn't hear it anymore before I turned on the radio.

∼

I ARRIVED BACK at the condos that served as our makeshift office just before lunch. I saw a new car in the drive of the third condo, and when I knocked on Cyn's door, Emily Lake answered.

"Boss, you gotta see this spread."

Emily Lake was my associate. She was whip-smart and had so much enthusiasm for trial work that she had complained to me, more than once, that there are not enough murderers who need defending.

I smiled. "I didn't think you'd see it until tonight."

She blew a constantly stray strand of hair out of her eyes. "Couldn't sleep. Once I woke up, I couldn't stop thinking about everything I had to do."

I grinned. "With juggling the wedding and all?"

"Josh is the juggler. And if you mention my wedding again, *Boss*, I'm suing. You're my witness, right, Cyn?"

Cyn didn't look up from her keyboard. "Witness to what, Emily?"

"The Boss is harassing me. You heard him."

Cyn put her hands in her lap and looked up. "That's a serious accusation. Did his comments about your wedding make you uncomfortable in any way?"

Emily kept grinning but when Cyn just put that green stare on her, it faded.

Emily turned to me. I held both hands out. "It's not my place to comment on whether I was making you feel uncomfortable. *Ms. Lake.*"

Cyn nodded. "We at Friedlander & Skald take a healthy workplace environment quite seriously."

"Um, right," said Emily. "No, Cyn, I was joking."

"Harassment is no joke, Emily."

"Yes, I mean, no, er, of course not."

"Please don't hesitate to tell me though if you ever don't feel comfortable in the work environment here. We've all been transplanted for the next month and part of my job is to create the optimal conditions for our performance."

"I will, for sure."

"Excellent." Cyn turned to me. "So what did you learn, Nathan?"

I couldn't swear to it, but I'm pretty sure the side of her mouth ticked up as she said it.

"I learned the State has arson cold," I said as Emily and I sat. "Brock blew a hole in the movie screen and he did it on purpose." I told them what I'd learned from Dagmar and Bronson Niesen about the gun, and the SafeBoom, and the explosion.

"Why did he do it?" said Emily.

"To delay the sale of the drive-in so that he wouldn't have to move. And I think generally to piss his dad off."

"So it was his gun, his SafeBoom, and he did it on purpose?" said Cyn. "Where does that leave us?"

"I was thinking about it on the way back. There's no question he meant to blow the hole in the screen. I don't think he meant to start a fire."

"Why do you say that?" said Emily.

"He's shot the stuff before and it's never happened, never started a fire, that is, and he was mad at his dad for having dry bushes. I think I've heard that some of these products advertise that they're fire-safe. Brock was certainly under that impression from some videos he'd watched."

Cyn's fingers flew across the keyboard. "I've already pulled the SafeBoom product specs. I just sent them to you and put them in an electronic research folder."

"Good. Next, I want us to double check the ruling that Brock can be tried as an adult. Emily, take a look at the statutory standard then review the hearing transcript and the Court's ruling."

"I've obtained the transcript and put it in the 'Adult Trial Determination' file," said Cyn.

Emily blinked at Cyn before she said, "On it."

"I'll talk to his former attorney Luke Mott to see if he thinks there was any error, but I'd like your opinion too."

"You have a meeting with him set for tomorrow afternoon," said Cyn.

I nodded. "We have a hearing on…"

"Wednesday," said Cyn.

"Wednesday, to enter our appearance and confirm Luke Mott's withdrawal as Brock's attorney. I'm going to hold off on talking to the prosecutor until then. What was her name again, Cyn?"

"Astrid Olsen."

"You said she's local?"

Cyn nodded. "Born and raised. Family here for at least three generations. University of Wisconsin for undergrad and law school, one year of a federal clerkship in Chicago, then home where she spent one year under the outgoing prosecutor and won an unopposed election."

"Unopposed? At that age?"

"Yes. And each time after."

"So we have to assume that she knows where the bodies are buried and that she's connected to the political machinery here."

Cyn nodded. "That's typical when we arrive to handle a case."

"How has she done?"

"Well. The usual high conviction rate you'd expect in a semi-rural county, but there have been a couple of high-profile convictions too."

"Murder?"

"Two of them were. A well-connected Chicago man who shot a local and a woman who killed her boyfriend when she blew up his boat."

"I suppose that is high profile."

Cyn didn't smile.

"How about arson?" I said.

"No trials. Looks like she's had a few plea deals involving burning down barns and businesses for insurance."

"So not a ton of experience, but she's going to have home field advantage on us."

"We can expect her to be tapped into the community, yes."

"Speaking of which, I encountered the community a couple of times today." I told them about the encounters with Holster Dude and the Sign Ladies.

"I don't know who the man was," said Cyn.

"Slacker."

She ignored me. "But one of the women with the signs was Kim Tripp, Eli Tripp's mother."

"Eli is the firefighter?" Emily said.

Cyn nodded. "She's been demonstrating anytime there's been a hearing or action on the case. She was instrumental in creating public pressure to try Brock as an adult."

"Looks like she's going to do the same for trial."

"One would expect."

I checked the time. "I'd like to go through some witnesses, but do you all want to get some lunch first?"

"Sure," said Emily.

"In a minute," said Cyn.

I raised an eyebrow.

The doorbell rang.

"You didn't," I said.

"I have worked with you before, Nathan," she said as she went to the door.

Emily watched her go. "She couldn't have."

I shrugged.

A moment later, Cyn returned with a bag. "I found a delightful place called Maggie's that specializes in deli sandwiches." She started handing out delicious smelling wrapped packets. "Pastrami for you, Nathan, and I took a guess on tuna for you, Emily."

Emily's mouth was open. She closed it, then said, "Is that a wrap?"

This time, Cyn's mouth definitely ticked. "It is. Did you want something else?"

"No. That's exactly what I want." Emily turned to me. "Why haven't you hired her?"

I gestured to Cyn.

"Nathan can't afford me," Cyn said.

I made a voilà gesture to Emily.

"I suppose not," Emily said.

"Why don't you get started, Emily," I said. "I have something else to discuss with Cyn."

"You got it, Boss." She collected her laptop and sandwich. "I'll be at my palatial estate if you need me."

When the front door clicked shut, I said, "I have questions from my meeting with Dagmar."

Cyn stopped typing, faced me, and folded her hands. "Yes."

"I don't feel right about all this."

"All what?"

"The palatial estate as Emily put it."

"Why?"

"I don't think Dagmar Niesen can afford it."

Cyn didn't blink. "No need to worry about that. Mrs. Niesen isn't being charged for these expenses."

"Who is?"

"My firm pays for certain overhead expenses on every case no matter what we charge."

"How can it do that?"

"It evens out with cases where we charge a premium."

My skepticism must have showed because her green eyes became more intense as she said, "Winning cases is what matters and, once we take a case on, we pay what's necessary to do that whether the client can afford it or not. We've also found that it's necessary to retain good lawyers, which is the most important part of winning."

I thought, then said, "She still had to mortgage the orchard."

Cyn nodded. "I'm not surprised. Land rich, cash poor is part of life for orchard owners. Our fee was significant but reasonable."

When I didn't say anything, Cyn said, "Nathan, I promise you are not running up a tab on her. The people paying for the extra expenses believe it's how a case should be tried. And they can afford to pay."

Cyn could be cagey, but her word was her word, so I was satisfied. "Thank you."

"You're welcome. Is that all?"

"No. She said the firm contacted her."

Cyn nodded. "We did."

"That seems pretty unusual."

"We became aware of her situation, or Brock's I should say, and the partners decided to act on it."

"How did they learn about it?"

"A client told one of the partners about it."

"Who's the client?"

"The partners haven't authorized disclosure of that information."

"Why would your firm take on the case?"

Cyn smiled. "I imagine to see justice prevail. Or as close as we can get."

Her gaze was a cool green wall.

"That's all you're going to say right now, isn't it?"

"Yes. Now did you say you wanted to go over the witness disclosure?"

10

Lawyers have to file lists of every witness they intend to call at trial. I've mentioned before that lawyers tend to name every person they can think of and, when they run out of people, list all sorts of categories of people, which they say is prudent caution and a normal, healthy person would say is runaway paranoia.

This case was no exception. Before we became involved, both sides had filed witness lists that went on for pages.

Emily rejoined us and, together with Cyn, we spent some time getting a handle on the people who were listed and their roles. The professionals weren't too hard to figure out—there were a number of police officers and firefighters, paramedics and hospital personnel named. There were property owners listed: Kevin Niesen who owned the Lakeside Drive-In, Devin Wright who owned the U-Store, and a man named Corey Linden, who owned the house where Noah and Maura Carmody had lived.

"The Carmodys were renting?" I said.

"Yes," said Emily. "The lease was in the documents somewhere."

"Bates page number 1302," said Cyn without looking up.

Emily did a double take and looked at me.

I smiled and said, "These next three names—Benny Bird, Tommy Chase, and Naomi Hoppel. Are they the people who were renting the U-Store units that burned?"

"I believe so," said Cyn as she clicked. "But we don't have a full roster of the renters. I'll add it to the list for your discovery requests, Emily."

"Thanks," Emily said, scribbling.

I paged through the list slowly, then more quickly to the end. I checked one more time to be sure, then said, "You know what else I'm not seeing?"

"What?" said Emily.

"Expert names."

Emily scrolled on her screen, then swore. "Mott listed categories and topics but no particular person. He had to have retained some experts, right?"

"When do we have to disclose them by?"

Cyn clicked. "Friday."

It was my turn to swear. "I think my meeting with Mott just got moved up."

"To when?" said Emily.

"Right now." I turned to Cyn. "I assume Friedlander has a roster of technical experts we could reach out to on short notice?"

"We have a list of people we can contact," said Cyn. "But they're the best so they might not give us the opinion we want."

"One step at a time. I'll go talk to Mott to see if he's done anything. Can you pull together a list of fire experts while I'm gone?"

Cyn nodded and was typing as I left to hunt down Brock Niesen's former attorney, Luke Mott.

It was mid-afternoon so Mott's office seemed like a logical place to start. I called on the way and learned from his assistant that I'd have more success at the Northlake Middle School where an afternoon reading program was underway. I pulled over, plugged in the new address, and made my way to the home of the Northlake Middle School Frost Giants.

The school was already locked down for the afternoon, so I had to wait until a custodian saw me, let me in, and directed me to the office. I checked in, received a visitor's badge even though school was over, and was directed to the library. I found it and joined four parents who were waiting in the hallway.

I peeked through the window and saw a man sitting next to a girl, pointing at a page, speaking. She smiled, nodded, and he stood up. The man was thin with pale hair, a pale complexion, and brown, square glasses. He sat next a boy then, who grabbed a section of pages as if showing how much he'd read. The man smiled, patted the boy's shoulder, and nodded.

"Which one's yours?" said a woman next to me.

"I'm here to see the teacher," I said.

"Oh, Luke does such a good job with this program."

"It sure looks that way."

"I'm so glad he's off that nasty trial so that he can keep working with the kids before standardized testing starts."

"Definitely."

"What did you need to see him about—?"

I was spared the task of deflecting her when Luke Mott dismissed the group and eight kids piled out the door in a rush. The crowd dissipated with the familiar hustle of over-scheduled families until Luke Mott and a girl stepped into the hallway.

"Luke Mott?" I said.

He looked up from the girl and his eyes immediately narrowed with what appeared to be lawyer radar.

He didn't even ask. He just said, "I'm with my daughter right now."

"I'm Nate Shepherd. Can we talk for a moment?"

"No," he said, put a hand on his daughter's shoulder, and started to walk.

"I wouldn't bother you, but it's time sensitive."

He stopped, sighed. "Go ahead, honey. I'll meet you at the car."

"Dad! You said you were done with work today!"

"I'll catch up before you get there."

His daughter walked away. Fast.

Luke Mott turned back to me. "You're not going to make me a liar for a second time today, Shepherd. What's so important that it can't wait until tomorrow?"

"Have you retained any experts?"

He shook his head. "No. Why?"

"Fire causation? Medical?"

Luke Mott looked irritated. "When you talk to Brock—"

"I have."

"Then you know he shot the SafeBoom target that started the fire. There's no question the fire killed the fireman and the Carmody kid." We both glanced over as his daughter disappeared around the corner.

"Did you get any negative reviews?"

"I didn't get *any* reviews, Shepherd. Dagmar Niesen didn't have the money to pay for experts and Brock doesn't either. If you and your fancy-condo, spare-no-expense team want to pay for a review, knock yourselves out."

"Sorry, with the Friday disclosure I needed to know as soon as—"

"I'm late for ice cream, Shepherd. I'll see you tomorrow afternoon. At my *office*."

He walked down the hall and, when he got to the corner, started to jog.

I didn't blame him a bit.

I gave him a head start, then called Cyn.

"Yes, Nathan?"

"No expert reviews. Do you have a fire expert?"

"Three. I'll have their CVs for you when you get back. Pick one and I'll reach out."

"Perfect. I want a certified coroner too. Nothing fancy, just a quick double check of the findings."

"Done. Any other areas?"

"Probably, but I don't know what they are yet. Let's decide by tomorrow night. Email me the CVs so I don't have to bother you."

"My dining room is our office, Nathan. It's no bother for the next month. But I'll send them to you anyway."

"Thanks, Cyn."

The thing was, I couldn't really blame Mott. The case against Brock seemed rock solid, and it's reckless to spend money clients don't have for a bunch of experts who can't help.

Money apparently wasn't a problem now and, even when a case looks grim, you don't know what you don't know until you know it so I hurried back so I could decide on an expert who could guide me through what happened during the Mission Road Fire.

PART II - MEASURE

11

The next morning, I went over to knock on Cyn's condo door and found a note in a clear, concise hand that said: *Come in.*

A second note, written in a familiar scrawl, said: *Beat you.*

I sighed and went in. Emily and Cyn were sitting at the dining room table.

"Was he always the last one to the office during the Braggi trial?" said Emily to Cyn.

"Most of the time," Cyn said.

"I remember beating Christian Dane," I said as I sat.

"True," Cyn said. "But he had died."

Emily cackled.

Cyn ignored it. "Did you decide on a fire expert?"

I nodded. "Bret Halogi seemed like the most qualified."

"She is."

"We only have until Friday. Can she review the case in time?"

"I'll find out." Cyn gathered her phone and left the room.

Emily shook her head as Cyn left. "She's amazing."

"You get used to it."

"She really travels the country trying cases?"

"Far as I can tell."

"She must know so much."

"She does. And we're going to need every bit of it. What can you tell me about the Court's decision to try Brock as an adult?"

Emily scrolled on her computer. "I don't think we have much there, Boss. You know kids between fourteen and seventeen can be tried as adults under special circumstances?"

I nodded. "And arson and murder are special circumstances, right?"

"Top of the list, yes. The juvenile court is also supposed to consider other factors including the use of a firearm, the extent to which the defendant planned the commission of the crime, and the impact on the alleged victims."

"Check, check, check."

"Exactly. I think we're stuck there. What I'm concerned about is evidence that came in on some of the other factors."

"Something besides arson and murder and firearms has you concerned?"

"You wouldn't think so, but yes. The Court also considers the juvenile's police and school records."

"I take it that's a problem?"

"It is. School-wise, he has two fighting suspensions, one excessive absence suspension, and one athletic suspension for alcohol use. Police-wise, he has a juvenile conviction for trespassing and criminal damaging."

"Sounds like we should be able to keep all that out."

"Yeah, about that."

I smiled. "Of course. Hit me."

"The alcohol suspension was for being at a party."

"Happens often enough."

"The party was in a field near, but not on, the Niesens' property."

"And?"

"It was a bonfire."

"High school kids do that, don't they?"

"Yes, but usually with permission from the property owner."

"Okay."

"And they don't usually tear up his field with their cars, scorch a big tract of grass, or burn his bait piles so that the owner has to hunt a different plot."

"Brock can't have been the only one at the bonfire."

"No. But he is the one who lit it."

I sighed. "Did he put it out?"

Emily shook her head. "The rain did that. And there's another thing."

I smiled. "I don't know why there wouldn't be."

"I'm concerned about the juvenile judge's tone in his decision."

"How so?"

"When he said Brock should be tried as an adult, he described the 'alleged acts' as," Emily read her notes, "'heinous and callous actions that have stricken our community and destroyed two families.'"

I nodded. "He did say 'alleged,' I guess."

"The community's pissed, Nate. And small enough that we're going to have trouble getting a neutral jury."

"Do you think we could use some help on that, with investigating potential jurors and taking the local temperature?"

Emily nodded. "I'm going to be chin deep in legal briefing and witnesses—I am going to take some witnesses, right?"

I nodded. "We'll divide and conquer."

"Then we'll need help with investigating jurors, the town, and all of their social media."

"I agree. I'll tell Cyn we want to get Olivia involved."

Cyn returned. "I just spoke to Bret Halogi—she'll review the case. I'll send her our file now."

"Perfect. We need some social media and local research. I'd like to get Olivia Brickson involved."

"Approved. Let me know if she needs to come up here and I'll arrange lodging."

"Not yet, I think, but thanks."

Two phones went off at once. Emily picked up first, rolled her eyes, and said, "Hi, Mom. No, I haven't looked at the florist quote, Josh is..." Her voice faded as she moved to the next room.

My buzzing phone showed a Northlake area code, so I picked up.

"Is this Nate Shepherd?" said a voice before I could speak.

"It is."

"You're in town now?"

"I am. Who's this?"

"Judge Roderick."

I mouthed "the judge," to Cyn. "Good morning, Your Honor."

"If you're going to be mucking around town on a case in front of my court, I want your appearance filed."

"We were going to efile it this morning, Judge."

"Bring it with you."

"Where?" I said before I thought.

"To my courtroom. Be here at 11:00 a.m. I want all this nonsense squared away today."

Before I could say, "Yes, Your Honor," Judge Roderick hung up.

12

A lot of courthouses in Michigan are institutional-looking products of the 1960s and '70s. The Sable County Courthouse was no such thing. It was a four-story edifice of squared limestone and granite topped with an honest-to-God copper-domed, circular tower. You'd expect a courthouse built like that on the outside to be an ancient, drafty relic on the inside, with ill-fitting doors and clanky steam boilers, but the interior of the Sable County Courthouse was sleek and modern, with state-of-the-art security scanners, gleaming floors, and screens outside each room announcing the day's schedule.

Emily and I hurried through security to a swift elevator that zipped us up to the third floor directly in front of a door bearing a brass plate that said, *Judge Lancaster Roderick.*

We went in.

A group of people were already there. They stopped talking as soon as we entered. I resisted the urge to check my fly and moved toward them.

Luke Mott broke off from the group and opened the swing gate.

"Come on up," he said. "The Judge said he'd take the bench when you get here."

"He said 11:00, right?"

Luke Mott nodded. "That means 10:45. He's waiting."

As I joined Luke Mott at one table, a woman wearing a light blue suit with pale blond hair pulled back in a single braid nodded to me and moved to the other one. When we'd taken our places, a man sitting at a desk over on the side of the courtroom rose. And rose and rose and rose until I recognized the tall, bare-knuckle boxer-looking guy I'd seen at Maggie's the day before. The man knocked on the judge's door, cracked it open, and a second later, Judge Roderick appeared.

"You're late, counsel," the judge said as he swept to the bench.

I looked at the time. 10:55. I'd normally let that slide with a new judge, but I saw the court reporter was poised to record us.

"My apologies, Your Honor. I was told 11 a.m."

Judge Roderick nodded and waved us all to be seated. "Like I said. Identify yourselves for the record, all of you."

"Astrid Olsen for the State, Your Honor," said the woman.

"Luke Mott for defendant Brock Niesen, Judge."

"Nate Shepherd for Brock Niesen, Your Honor."

"Emily Lake also for the defendant, Your Honor."

"A regular cavalcade of counsel," Judge Roderick had a thick head of hair so brown it was almost black, swept up and back to the side. He wore brown-framed glasses that bobbed and jerked as he spoke. "Mr. Mott, why don't you tell me how you're trying to screw up my trial."

Luke Mott stood. "Your Honor, I'm seeking to withdraw as counsel and have Mr. Shepherd and Ms. Lake enter their appearance in substitution."

"What possible reason do you have for that?"

"My client wishes to discharge me and retain Mr. Shepherd."

"And you're going to just let him?"

"I really don't have a choice, Your Honor. Mr. Niesen wishes to discharge me."

"That wouldn't be the first stupid decision your client has made. And you, Mr. Shepherd, you're just going to gallivant in here and pop off a murder trial?"

I stood. "Ms. Lake and I are prepared to represent Mr. Niesen, Your Honor."

"My understanding is that you already are."

"Your Honor?"

"You've been banging around town looking at things for a couple of days now, haven't you?"

"Mr. Niesen has engaged us, yes, Your Honor."

"Were you going to get around to telling me about it?"

"Yes, Your Honor."

"Took your sweet time. Ms. Olsen, what's the State's position on this?"

Astrid Olson stood. "The defendant is free to hire anyone he wants, Your Honor, whether that be a trusted local attorney or a foreign firm staffed by downstate lawyers. The State has invested considerable time and resources planning for a trial at month-end, though, Your Honor, and so it is our position that the trial date should remain in place."

"Oh, the trial date's not getting moved, don't you worry about that. I trust a continuance wasn't part of your plan, Mr. Shepherd?"

"No, Your Honor, we'll be prepared to go at month end. And as to Ms. Olsen's comment, we're working with a Minnesota firm, not a foreign one."

"I don't know how you read maps down where you're from, Mr. Shepherd, but this ain't Minnesota. Now how in the name of God's green gravy are you going to be ready to try this murder case in a month?"

"Mr. Mott has done some of the work, Your Honor. We anticipate being ready to go but if something comes up, we'll let you know immediately."

"I'll save you the trouble, Mr. Shepherd. Nothing's going to come up that's going to postpone this trial. Nothing. Understand?"

"I do, Your Honor."

"And you still want the case?"

I shrugged. "My client wants us, Your Honor."

"Your client apparently wants a lot of things. Have you been paid, Mr. Mott?"

"I have, Your Honor."

"Very well. The Court has no reason to save Mr. Niesen from himself in this regard. Absent objection from the State —"

"We have none, Your Honor," said Astrid Olsen.

"—The Court grants the motion for Mr. Mott to withdraw and for Mr. Shepherd and Ms. Lake to enter their appearance on behalf of the defendant, provided, however, that Mr. Shepherd and Ms. Lake comply with Local Rule 3.4(a) prior to any further appearance in Court."

I looked at Judge Roderick. He looked at me, smiling.

I wasn't going to ask. He wasn't going to tell me. So we stood there for about thirty seconds before Luke Mott finally said, "I hereby sponsor Mr. Shepherd and Ms. Lake to join our local bar association, Judge."

Judge Roderick smiled. "Excellent, Mr. Mott. Of course, they do need *two* sponsors."

Astrid Olsen started collecting her things.

"I'll do it, Judge."

The quiet voice came from the desk at the side of the courtroom. The man from Maggie's. "If you don't mind."

"Are you sure, Mason?" said Judge Roderick. "You'll be

vouching for them to our local bar." Though he sounded serious, the Judge was smiling.

"If Luke is comfortable, I'm sure I am, Judge."

"All right then, make sure you take them up to the library right after the session. And payment up front."

The man, Mason, nodded.

"Alright, the motion's granted. Work your discovery disputes out among yourselves. The trial order is confirmed." Judge Roderick stood and left.

As soon as he passed his chambers door, prosecutor Astrid Olsen turned and offered her hand to Emily and then me. "Welcome to Northlake."

"Thanks."

"I hope you're serious about maintaining the date," she said.

"We are, but never say never and all that," I said.

She didn't smile as she shook her head. "Never is exactly what Judge Roderick will say."

As Astrid Olsen turned to leave, I said, "I put my office number on the appearance, but let me give you my cell, just in case—"

"—That won't be necessary," she said and kept packing. "I'll see you at the final pretrial in a couple of weeks."

I've never been a part of a trial where the attorneys weren't calling each other after hours to inform each other of something or work something out. It appeared I might have my first.

"If you have any other disclosures—"

"—You have all of mine." She put her last folder in her file. "I look forward to receiving yours this Friday. Nice to meet you."

Astrid Olsen shook our hands formally one more time, then walked out.

Emily watched her go. "This should be fun."

"Mr. Shepherd, Ms. Lake," Mason said. "I can take you up to the law library if you like."

Mason had ditched the suit coat, so he was wearing a long sleeve white Oxford, which revealed just how big he was. Not necessarily muscular, like Cade Brickson, but just *big*, and standing next to Luke Mott, he looked even bigger.

"Nate, please," I said.

He smiled. "Mason Pierce," he said, and shook my hand.

I've told you dozens of times that I've shaken someone's hand. This was different from any other handshake I've had, ever, in two ways. First, I'm not small, but his hand swallowed mine whole.

Second, the skin of his hands was creased with calluses and hard as horn. It was like shaking a deer antler.

When Emily introduced herself and offered hers, Mason Pierce hesitated, then shook it, looking like he was being careful. Her hand disappeared.

Emily laughed. "I'm not glass, Pierce."

He smiled, but only a little, and put his hand in his pocket. "I can take them up if you like, Mr. Mott."

Luke Mott looked relieved. "Would you, Mason? I'm due in juvenile court in ten minutes."

Mason Pierce turned back to his desk and produced a paper. "I knew the judge would require it, so I've already drafted the sponsorship petition. If you sign there, I'll take them up and finish."

Luke Mott took the paper, signed it. Mason Pierce gave him another one. "And this one for Ms. Lake."

"Right, right." Luke Mott signed the second one. "Thanks, Mason." Luke Mott turned to me. "I've given you everything I have, but call if you have any questions. I have to run. Good luck."

Luke Mott scurried out the door. When he was gone, Mason Pierce said, "Let's go make you members of the Northlake Trial Bar."

13

"Welcome to the Northlake law library and Bar Association," Mason Pierce said, and opened the door to one of the most striking local courthouse libraries I'd ever seen.

The rows of bookshelves with tables in the center was typical; the series of stone arches and columns and church type windows around the outer walls were not. In the center of the room, the ceiling opened to a second level, a circle about twelve feet above us with its entire circumference lined in books, and above that there was another series of smaller windows and stone columns that supported a domed ceiling.

"Is that the tower?" said Emily, pointing up.

Mason Pierce nodded.

I ran one hand along the ridges of a column. "This stonework is incredible."

Mason Pierce smiled slightly. "My family helped build it, way back."

"I wouldn't mind research so much if it were in here," said Emily, still looking up.

Mason Pierce shrugged. "Most people use the computer now."

He led us to a small office tucked away on one side where he introduced us to the secretary of the Northlake Bar Association, a pleasant woman named Nina, who took our applications and our one hundred and fifty dollars, each, and proclaimed us official members of the Northlake Trial Bar.

No, charging us that fee is not really fair; yes, it's protective and colloquial; and while not every jurisdiction requires an entrance fee to play ball, many of them do. It protects the local lawyers, fills the local coffers, and, prevents some downstate yahoo who doesn't know the local rules from swooping in and mucking up big murder trials.

I paid my fee, completing my transformation from downstate yahoo to respected member of the local trial bar.

Right.

When we were done, Mason Pierce said, "Here's my cell. If you need to reach the Court, call me."

"Thanks." We exchanged numbers.

Mason Pierce nodded and made to leave before he turned back and said, "Atti—Ms. Olsen, I mean, wasn't exaggerating. Judge Roderick won't move this case."

I nodded. "I imagine his constituents wouldn't stand for it?"

Mason Pierce appeared to consider, then tapped a stone column. "No. He's just decided when it's going to go."

"Understood. Thanks, Mason."

With a nod to Emily, Mason Pierce left.

"Oh, Mr. Shepherd," said Nina, smiling. "Here's a copy of our local rules, and a link to our bar directory, without you in it yet of course. And you just missed our golf outing, that's in September, but I do hope we see you next year."

I smiled. "I hope our trial doesn't last that long."

"I'm sure it won't but, now that you've been here, I'm sure you'll want to come back. Have you been to the Bluffs yet?"

"Not yet, no."

"Well, that will change your mind. And you too, Ms. Lake."

We thanked Nina and left.

"We going to the Bluffs, Boss?"

"Murder first, Emily."

She grinned. "Good."

∼

It was lunchtime on the way back from court, so we stopped at Maggie's to pick up sandwiches and yes, she remembered our order from the day before. My order stayed the same, Emily changed hers up, and we got a surprise for Cyn, then took it all back to the condos. We told her how the hearing went, about our status as shiny new members of the Northlake Bar, and the fact that Judge Roderick wouldn't allow any continuances of the trial date.

Cyn nodded. "He'd never get re-elected if he did."

"That's what I said. Did the materials go out to the fire expert?"

"As soon as you left."

"Thanks. You said you had pulled the product materials and instructions for the SafeBoom targets?"

"In the efile under 'SafeBoom specs.'"

"I'm going to take a look at that."

"What for?" said Emily.

"I wanna say my brother Mark has used it before. I thought he'd said it was fire-safe, but I may be misremembering. Either way, I'll have to know it for trial. Emily, dig deeper into Brock's school and police record, then start drafting a motion to exclude."

Emily frowned. "Starting a bonfire and destroying property is pretty close to what we have here, Boss."

I nodded. "That's why we have to get it excluded. It's one thing to use that information to decide to try a kid as an adult. It's another thing to let it in as evidence of a pattern to support arson and murder."

"On it."

There's a sense lawyers develop over time, where they get a feeling about whether a case is actually going to go to trial or not. Sometimes a trial date is approaching, and you can just tell that the case isn't ready to go and either the judge or opposing counsel or all of you together just kind of agree that it should be moved to a later date. It's a lot more cooperative than people think.

Then there are other times when you know the case is going to go, when there will be no continuances. It's a disruption to your everyday life, going to trial, so when you can tell it's coming, you clear your schedule, make arrangements for your dog or your kids or your spouse, depending on what your life looks like, then put your head down and plow ahead through all the things that have to be done because you know that relief isn't coming and the last thing you want is to be standing unprepared in front of a jury with the legal equivalent of your pants down.

Emily, Cyn, and I went to work as if there would be no continuances.

14

That afternoon I pulled up the product information for SafeBoom exploding targets. If you've never used them, or don't have a mischievous younger brother who has, SafeBoom ships two dry chemicals to the customer—little black balls of ammonium nitrate and white aluminum powder. The end user then pours a pre-measured bag of black balls and a pre-measured bag of white powder into a clear plastic jar, shakes it until it's all gray and, voilà, you have yourself an exploding target.

One thing that makes SafeBoom so appealing is that it will only explode if it's shot by a high-velocity bullet; so it's pitched as a fairly stable, "safe" product if you store it, handle it, and mix it correctly.

Of course, the company also assumes that you'll use it in the proper amount. It recommends using no more than one pound per target. Brock had used twenty-five.

As I reviewed the specs, I saw that I wasn't misremembering—SafeBoom targets were pitched as having no fire risk when you used them right.

I dove into the history of that claim. Government officials, especially out west, had asked folks not to use exploding targets in the woods or desert because of the risk of forest fires. Met with skepticism from enthusiastic users, the US Forest Service conducted a series of experiments to see if it could make exploding targets ignite common forest materials under certain conditions. The test results were mixed but showed enough of a fire risk that SafeBoom responded by developing what it claimed was an ignition-free target, without of course admitting that their original target could have, under any circumstances, started a fire.

This led me to another paper about a test of the new and improved SafeBoom targets. It had been issued the previous spring by a group of enterprising Michigan DNR officers in conjunction with the Forestry Department of Michigan's finest agricultural university.

I recognized the name of one of the DNR Officers.

Samson Ezekiel Wald.

I looked and yes, his number was still in my phone, so I called.

"Sam Wald," he said.

"Officer Wald, this is Nate Shepherd. I don't know if you remember but we met—"

"—On the Colt Daniels case, the former football player accused of killing his dad with a crossbow arrow in a hunting blind. You cross-examined me."

"About coyotes and dogs, yes. How have you been?"

"I heard you got the kid off the hook."

"I didn't, Officer Wald. The facts did."

Officer Wald was quiet for a moment, and I wasn't sure what his attitude would be. I hadn't gone after him too hard, just gotten out some facts that supported our case about how a coyote would eat a body, but you never know how a witness feels he was treated.

"I liked your evidence on arrow flights," he said finally.

I hadn't asked him anything about arrow flights at trial. "You read the transcript?"

"I was curious about what had happened. The department let me order it for our coyote research."

"Our expert helped me put that arrow-flight thing together."

"He was effective."

Officer Wald sounded mildly positive, so I pushed on. "Speaking of experts, that's why I'm calling. I came across your research paper today."

"Which one?"

I raised my already high estimation of Officer Wald and said, "The one on exploding targets and wildfire risk."

"Which target are you interested in?"

"SafeBoom."

He grunted. "What do you want to know?"

"Is it true that SafeBoom didn't ignite any materials during your testing?"

"For *our* experiment, yes. It doesn't mean it won't under the right conditions."

"Sure. It looked like you tested some dry conditions?"

There was a pause, then, "We used straw, dead grass and leaves, and dead wood."

"How about arborvitae bushes?"

"Dead?"

I thought. "Probably live bushes with some dead needles underneath."

"Hmm. It's harder to ignite live material, but arborvitaes go up easier than most things. Maybe I could include that in our next round."

"You're going to keep testing?"

"Yes. At least one manufacturer has altered their product based on our test findings. Listen, Mr. Shepherd, regardless of our tests, we don't want you shooting these targets out in the woods. The risk of wildfire is just too—"

"—It's not that, Officer Wald. I'm trying to figure out how likely it is that a SafeBoom target started a fire."

"So hire a fire investigator."

"I did. But I saw your paper."

"I'm not interested in going after target companies, Mr. Shepherd. I'm trying to keep people educated about the risk of wildfires. As targets go, SafeBoom is a good product from everything I can see."

"No, no, I'm not going after SafeBoom. I'm trying to figure out if a kid started a fire."

"What's a kid doing with a high-powered rifle?"

"He was fifteen. It was his hunting rifle."

"I take it the fire started on arborvitae bushes?"

"That's what they're telling me."

"When was the last rain?"

"I don't know."

"That's important. Not just the rainfall in the previous twenty-four hours, but the prior thirty days. Moisture levels have an impact on ignition for us. How about temperature and wind?"

"I don't know that either."

"Find out. Just like wildfires, those affect ignition and spread."

"Thanks. I just got involved in the case this week so knowing what I should be looking at helps quite a bit."

"We're not the only one to look at this. The US Forestry department did some experiments with other types of exploding targets too—"

"—I saw that."

"Good. Then you know there was a significant difference in ignition between when it was cold and wet out and when it was warm and dry."

"Do you have any opinion on flammability of dead arborvitae needles?"

"Yeah. They are."

"How about the live bushes?"

"Still extremely flammable. Live and wet are harder to catch than dead and dry, but if they catch, there's so much resin in them that you've got a problem. I'd say if your boy put an exploding target under an arborvitae bush, there's a good chance it could catch. The conditions would push the likelihood of that chance in either direction."

The way he said it made me realize a factor that was common in his tests. "Your tests had the targets on the flammable material, right? Sitting on the leaves and dead grass?"

"Yes."

"What if it was above it?"

"What do you mean?"

"What if the target was above the arborvitae needles and away from the bushes?"

"What, like suspended on a rope?"

"Like attached to a platform."

"Made of what?"

"Some wood, some metal."

"How far above the bushes?"

"About ten feet. I'll have to get an exact measurement."

There was a pause on the other end of the line.

When the silence continued, I said, "Would that make a difference?"

Officer Wald waited a little longer before he said, "I'm not interested in defending someone who started a wildfire, Mr. Shepherd. Even if he is a kid."

"It wasn't a wildfire."

"Not a...then what was it?"

"A fire at a drive-in theater."

"There are arborvitae bushes at the drive-in?"

"Around the border of it. The target was up on the movie screen. The arborvitae were below it."

"Even a six-foot elevation has a significant impact on ignition. Ten feet, or more, would be almost im—would make it very difficult for the ammonium nitrate to ignite the tinder except in precise conditions."

"If you looked at the materials, is that something you could have an opinion on?"

"I might. And you're saying it's not a wildfire case?"

"No. It's worse."

"How can it be worse?"

"It's an arson and murder case. The fire spread to a nearby house and killed a child and a firefighter."

Officer Wald was quiet and this time I let the silence sit.

"Why did your client do it?"

"*If* my client shot a target at the drive-in movie screen, I would guess that it was because his father owns the drive-in and his father might be forcing my client to move away after the theater sells. That's the prosecutor's theory anyway."

"And they're saying the fire was caused by the target and spread to a nearby house?"

"To a U-Store facility and then a nearby house, yes."

A pause. "They've charged him with murder?"

"Yes."

"I'm going to have to think about this."

"We have an expert disclosure deadline Friday. All I would be looking for is an opinion as to whether it is probable that a SafeBoom target ten feet above a row of arborvitae bushes ignited them."

"Probable?"

"I would send you the materials. Then you tell me whether

you think there is a 51% likelihood that the target caught those bushes on fire. Or not. Whatever your opinion ultimately is."

"What's your client's name?"

"Brock Niesen. The case is in Northlake."

"I'll get back to you by tomorrow night," Officer Wald said, and he hung up the phone.

I couldn't tell if I'd been able to convince Officer Wald to come on board. His answers convinced me, though, that I was on the right track. He seemed to think that it would be hard for anyone to say definitively that the SafeBoom target had started the fire.

But, of course, there had been a fire.

That thought made me realize we had another angle to investigate. I went to find Cyn.

15

"Do we know if the drive-in is insured?" I said to Cyn.

She stared at me. "We should." She turned to her screen and typed. A moment later, she said, "We don't."

"Do we have the contact info for Brock's dad?"

She typed. "We do. Just sent it to you."

"Thanks. I'll call him. I think it's time to get ahold of Olivia."

"I agree with both," Cyn said, and went back to work.

I stepped outside. I called Kevin Niesen, Brock's dad, first. Voicemail. I left a message saying who I was and asking if we could talk about his son, then hung up.

Next, I called Olivia.

"So which gym did you pick?" she said.

"Gym?"

"Murphy's looks promising and offers a thirty-day trial."

"We've been a little busy, Liv."

"Shore's Gym seemed more like a hotel rec room but would be better than nothing."

I sighed.

"You're not doing nothing, are you, Shep?"

"I'm definitely not doing nothing. I'm working up a murder case, which is why I called."

"You can't work a murder case more than fourteen, sixteen hours a day, which gives you plenty of time to squeeze in a workout."

"We've had some things come up I could use your help with."

"Otherwise, you'll certainly be squeezing into something."

"Please?"

"Fine. What's up?"

I told her the basics about the trial and the timeframe we were up against.

"Not enough hands?"

"Not nearly."

"How can I help?"

"This place seems like a powder keg with the trial. To start, I need you getting the lay of the land on social media and letting me know where the hotspots are."

"Done. What else?"

"We have new things coming up every day that need investigation. You game?"

"Always. I'll need to work some things out for the Brickhouse with Cade, but it won't be a problem."

"I don't think I need you physically up here yet."

"A lot of my investigation is electronic, but I'll want to put my eyes directly on some things, or people, at some point."

"The travel budget is unlimited. Just give me a heads up and Cyn will have a place for you ready to go."

"That'll work. So besides the social media climate and looking for gyms for you, what else do you have for me?"

"I want to know all about the victims."

"How many are we dealing with?"

"The firefighter, Eli Tripp. His mother, Kim Tripp, has been organizing demonstrations reminding the town of the fire."

"On it."

"The child who was killed, Liam Carmody. His mom, Maura, and his sisters survived."

"Okay."

"Those were the only fatalities, but there are three property owner victims too. Kevin Niesen owned the Lakeside Drive-in. That's Brock's dad."

"Right."

"Devin Wright owned the U-Store facility that was damaged. We're working on a roster of the tenants who were renting storage units that might have been affected."

"Got it."

"And Corey Linden owned the house the Carmodys were renting."

"Have all of them made insurance claims?"

"I don't know. I'm going to start by checking with the prosecutor and sheriff, but I expect I'll need your help on that too."

"Never fear. I'll get started on this today. Oh look, I found something already!"

"Really? What?"

"There's an All-Day Fitness less than a mile from you."

"See ya, Liv."

"Bye."

My thoughts hadn't crystalized until I'd spoken to Officer Wald and Olivia, but it was true—I needed to run down whether any of the property owners benefited from the Mission Road Fire. Insurance money was always a motive for arson. It probably wouldn't be relevant, what with my client blowing things up and all, but I needed to explore every potential avenue for any possible doubt, reasonable or otherwise.

I was about to search our electronic file for references to

insurance when Emily stuck her head in. "Boss. I think you need to see this."

I raised an eyebrow.

She waved for me to follow, walked to the front door, and pointed out the window.

A woman was standing on the sidewalk in front of our condos. She had a sign with the two familiar pictures on it, pictures I'd seen when she'd been outside the jail. There was one thing that was different about her this time though.

This time, Kim Tripp had a bullhorn.

"Justice for Eli! Justice for Liam!" pierced through the door.

"What do you want to do?" said Emily.

"Talk to her. But not without a witness."

I picked up my phone and called a new number.

"Sable County Sheriff's Office."

"Hi, could I speak to Sheriff Sizemore, please?"

"Is this a scheduled call, sir?"

"No, I—"

"I'm sorry, Sheriff Sizemore is in meetings this afternoon. Should I direct this call to 911?"

"No, that's not necessary—"

"Would you like to schedule a call? I have an opening next Tuesday at 3:00 p.m."

"Could you give him a message for me?"

"Certainly."

"Could you tell him that Nate Shepherd, the attorney for Brock Niesen called. Kim Tripp is demonstrating outside some condos in Bluffside Farms, and I'm concerned that some of our neighbors might not take kindly to that."

There was a pause, then, "Mr. Shepherd, could you hold a moment?"

"Certainly."

A minute later, a voice said, "Sheriff Sizemore here. Is this Shepherd?"

"It is, Sheriff. Thanks for taking my call."

"Heard you came on the case the other day. Darlene said Kim Tripp is demonstrating outside your condo?"

"She is."

"Is she on the sidewalk or up in the drive?"

"On the sidewalk."

"I can see how that might be an unpleasant reminder for you, Shepherd, but if she's on the public sidewalk, I can't remove her."

"I understand that would normally be the case, Sheriff, but we're over at Bluffside Farms, in the condos."

"You are? How'd you get in there?"

"A friend. Anyway, the security guard at the gate gave us some pretty particular restrictions for the community, one of which was that the use of the facilities and walkways were for members and invited guests only. Said something about residents getting tired of people walking their dogs on their sidewalks and bringing kids in on Halloween and such. I can't blame them; it really is beautiful in here."

"Uh-huh."

"Anyway, I understand why she's using her bullhorn—"

"—She's using a bullhorn in Bluffside Farms?"

"Yeah. Seems like one of those coast guard versions with the industrial strength amplifier. Like I said, I understand what she's doing, but it seems to me like the other residents here might not."

"I'll be down, Shepherd. Don't go out there, please. I don't want anything to escalate."

"Sure. Thanks, Sheriff."

I hung up. "He's on his way."

Emily grinned. "Look at the Boss getting results."

I shook my head. "Not me. I imagine Bluffside Farms has some important donors living in it."

Ten minutes later, a Sable County Sheriff's vehicle pulled into our drive.

16

Sheriff Sean Sizemore stepped out of the car. He was wearing the brown shirt and khaki pants of the office but didn't put a hat over his slicked back black hair. He took his aviators off as he approached Kim Tripp, tucked them into the top of this shirt, and held both hands out to the side as he spoke.

Kim Tripp stopped shouting momentarily. I opened the door and stepped onto the porch.

She whirled on me, raised the bullhorn, and "Justice for Eli!" rang through the neighborhood again.

"Kim!" said Sheriff Sizemore. "C'mon now!"

She paused, but she didn't lower the bullhorn.

He pointed at me. "Shepherd?"

I nodded.

"Wait inside."

"I'd like to speak with you, Sheriff."

Kim Tripp squeezed the bullhorn trigger. "Justice for Eli! Justice for Liam!"

"In a minute!" Sheriff Sizemore said.

I looked at Kim Tripp's face and decided it wasn't going to stop while she could see me, so I went back inside.

She belted one more refrain, then stopped as the door closed.

I watched as Sheriff Sizemore turned back to her. His tone was low enough that I couldn't hear him through the door, but his mouth moved non-stop as he walked closer to her. He pointed up and down the street, pointed back to the gate, and kept talking.

At one point, Kim Tripp pointed at the sidewalk herself, but Sheriff Sizemore shook his head and spoke some more.

Finally, Kim Tripp stomped and shouted, "You can't let him get away with it, Sean!"

Sheriff Sizemore kept talking and moved closer with his arms out. Kim Tripp held up a hand. He stopped. Then she snapped one last thing at him, turned, and got into the car she'd parked across the street.

Sheriff Sizemore watched her go. Then he took a deep breath, put his sunglasses back on, and came up the walk.

I stepped out onto the porch to meet him.

He stopped on the walk, hitching his thumbs into his gun belt. "This isn't a call I'd normally take," he said. He looked to be in his mid-40s and was trim, as if he didn't spend a lot of time behind his desk.

I nodded. "This struck me as a place that might not appreciate a protest."

"That's true enough."

"I didn't want her to get in trouble with someone else. She's been through enough."

Sheriff Sizemore stuck his sharp jaw out. "It seems to me you wouldn't know a damn thing about that, Shepherd."

"You don't have to be from here to understand loss, Sheriff."

"But you'd have to be to understand hers. What did you want to talk to me about?"

"Insurance."

"What about it?"

"Did any of the owners of the properties that were destroyed in the Mission Road Fire file insurance claims?"

"Why would I know that?"

"I thought it might be part of your arson investigation."

Sheriff Sizemore gave me a black-lensed aviator stare. "I take it you just got into town?"

"A couple of days ago."

"Well when you get around to talking to your client, you'll learn that our arson investigation ended when we figured out your client had blown a hole in his daddy's drive-in screen and set his bushes on fire."

"I've spoken to him."

"So he told you what he did?"

I didn't answer him. Instead, I said, "I didn't see any insurance information in the file I've been given. I just wanted to find out if you'd checked into it before I bother people."

"Bother away, Shepherd."

"So you don't have anything?"

"Only the killer. In my jail."

He turned back down the drive. "This was a one-time thing, sending Kim away."

"I understand public places. And I'm sure the guards at the gate do too."

Sheriff Sean Sizemore didn't wave or nod as he climbed into this patrol car and drove off.

"Always making friends," said Emily as I came back in.

"He didn't check on the insurance."

"He had a point."

"I'll tell Olivia we're starting from scratch."

I'D WORKED the rest of the afternoon and was turning my thoughts toward dinner when my phone buzzed. Brock's father, Kevin Niesen.

"I got your message," he said. "You're the new lawyer representing my son?"

"I am."

"His mom's been handling most of that."

"I understand. I've spoken with her."

"I don't know what she said, but I told that last guy, Mott, that I don't have any extra money for Brock's defense."

"I'm not calling to ask for money, Mr. Niesen."

"Oh." I could practically hear the tinkle of shattered arguments falling away as he paused. "What do you want then?"

I hadn't been sure what Kevin Niesen's attitude would be toward me and given his defensiveness about the money, I decided a softer touch than, "Did you collect insurance on the drive-in?" was required.

"I wondered if you might let me see the drive-in so I can see how it is set up, and you can explain a few things to me."

"I'm really pretty busy, Mr. Shepherd. I don't know if Dagmar told you, but I'm trying to wrap up a business here."

"She did. Brock did too."

"You've seen him?"

"I visited him in jail as soon as I got here, yes."

"How was he?"

"Holding up. For jail. I don't know how he normally is."

"He probably blamed me for all this."

"I can't relate any conversations I had with him, Mr. Niesen."

"You lawyers."

"I'm obliged to protect your son."

"And I'm not?"

"I didn't say that."

"No, no, I suppose I should have just stayed here in these piss-cold winters for the rest of my life so he'd be happy, right?"

"I didn't say that either."

"No, but Brock did, right? Blamed my moving for him being so damn stupid and ruining his life?"

"Mr. Niesen, I'm not involved in any of that. I'm just trying to put together the best defense I can for your son. Part of that is understanding how the fire started and where it spread."

"And I'm supposed to drop everything and go out there?"

"We can do it whenever you want, Mr. Niesen. But I'd like to do it soon."

"Aren't things pretty cut and dried? That's what Mott said."

"Brock's looking at a life sentence, Mr. Niesen. I owe him to check."

"And I do too, I suppose?"

I didn't say anything.

"Fine. You're lucky you caught me. I'm moving soon. Let's get this over with. When can you be there?"

"As soon as you say."

"Twenty minutes."

"I'll see you there."

PART III - MIX

17

I drove to the southwest side of town then a bit beyond until I came to the site of the Mission Road Fire. Coming as I was from the east, I saw the Carmody house first. I slowed to a crawl as I idled by the wreckage of what had been a small, pillbox ranch. The roof and three walls were down, the remaining wall too burned to tell the color. It didn't look like any work had been done to tear down the structure.

I continued to idle, following the path of the flames upstream to the U-Store facility right next door. Demolition had been done there—the line of the street-most units were gone, leaving only a flat concrete slab covered in scorch marks.

From there, I arrived at the street marquee of the Lakeside Drive-In, which declared that it was *Closed for the Season*. A little farther back, four charred poles rose like jagged burned bones out of the ground.

I followed Mission Road past the marquee, using the path the cars would normally take to enter the drive-in itself. There was no barrier at the ticket booth (intact), so I went through and circled around past the concession stand and projection room (also intact), until I was in the parking lot/viewing area. There was one other car toward the front, waiting, so I drove up.

Kevin Niesen was standing there next to his Ford Expedition, arms crossed. He wore a quarter-zip pullover, khakis, and loafers, and had sunglasses pushed back into reddish-blond hair that was apparently where Brock got it from. I parked next to him and got out.

"Thanks for meeting me," I said.

Kevin Niesen gave me a perfunctory handshake, then waved. "Welcome to my son's mess. What do you want to know?"

"Can you show me what you think happened?"

"I've only got about twenty minutes, but it won't take that long. Come up here."

He gestured and we walked toward the screen—or, I should say, where the screen used to be—to the four charred poles.

"This was the screen, obviously," Kevin Niesen said. "It was the original, had stood here since the 1950s. See how it was oriented north, that way?"

I visualized a screen on the poles, nodded.

"For up here, that's perfect. The sun crosses the sky far enough to the south that the north side is always in the shade and the customers don't have to stare into the sunset like they would if the screen faced east. It let me open a full half hour earlier than some other places and increased my concessions revenue by seven percent."

I contemplated a man who thought about his concession revenues while talking to the lawyer defending his son from a double murder charge, then said, "I take it parts of the screen were made of wood?"

Kevin Niesen nodded. "The modern ones, they tend to be metal or concrete, but this one was built back in the day with wooden poles and plywood backing. Old enough that it was grandfathered in from some of the regulations they make you follow today."

"Regulations?"

"Wind ratings and such. Nonsense really. I mean the thing had stood here for seventy some years."

I'd driven through the wreckage of the Glen Arbor and Gaylord tornados on other trips up north, so I had some thoughts about Kevin Niesen's "nonsense" but again didn't think it was relevant. "You cleared out what was left of the screen?"

He nodded. "I left it for a month or so until the police said it was okay to clean it up. The delay totally screwed me."

"How so?"

"By the time I had it cleaned up, there was no way someone would be able to get the place up and running this season." He shook his head. "The little shitbrain got that part right."

"Brock?"

"I couldn't sell it this spring. Hopefully I can line up a buyer now that they will have a full off-season to work on it."

I nodded and walked closer. To the right of where the screen had been was a row of arborvitae bushes between eight and ten feet tall, grown together so that they formed a hedge. The first few were scorched and burned bare, the next browned, then gradually they transitioned to the soft, green, dense, evergreen bush that they normally are.

I pointed at the green ones. "Is that what was under the screen?"

Kevin Niesen nodded. "I had a whole row of them facing the street there. It was a perfect curtain to block headlights from the street and keep people from sneaking in. Here, I'll show you."

He led me so that we were standing between the poles and indicated just to the street side. "The arborvitae were right here, running in a straight line that way, toward the U-Store."

I looked both directions and lined up the existing arbs with where the burned ones used to be. I walked down the line of former bushes. "Are these the stumps?"

Kevin Niesen nodded.

"Were they the same height as those?"

"Yeah. I kept 'em trimmed to about eight feet."

"And they all burned?"

"Every one." He shook his head. "The fire chief said I couldn't have picked a more flammable bush. Apparently, they go up like candles."

I walked down the line, following the path of the flames to the drive-in's boundary with the U-Store, which was marked by a rickety old wooden privacy fence, its wood gray with weathering. A large section was missing, about thirty feet in each direction, replaced with a plastic orange snow fence held upright with long green garden stakes. Following the path, I stood right in the middle.

"So it followed the bushes here then burned the fence?"

Kevin Niesen followed me and pointed. "Yeah, see how the front of the U-Store fenced area is closer to the road than us? Me and Devin had talked about splitting a chain link but, well, it just never worked out."

"Devin Wright, the U-Store owner?"

He nodded.

"Money?"

Kevin Niesen shrugged. "Times were tight. So the fire burns all the way over to here and unfortunately that's exactly where one of Devin's tenants had stored a pile of wood. For cooking or something, I guess."

"Right up against the fence?"

"You'll have to ask him, but I guess so. The Fire Chief told me that the wind blew the fire right into the U-Store and that was all she wrote. Boom, boom, boom, one storage unit after another until..." He trailed off and stared down the empty cement pads where the storage units had been, which left the wreckage of the Carmody house clearly visible.

He cursed, then said, "My son really screwed this up."

"Do you think he meant to?"

"Kill that kid? Of course not, but you can't plead stupidity. That's how Mott explained it to me, anyway. It doesn't matter if Brock meant to kill someone or not, if he meant to start the fire, he's a murderer. Is that right?"

I nodded. "That's the law, yes."

"Well, the little shitbrain got his wish. He won't be moving to southern Indiana anytime soon."

He checked his gold watch. "I have to go. Are we done?"

"Yes, thanks. I'm going to be hiring a fire expert. Do I have your permission to bring her out here to inspect if I need to?"

Kevin Niesen stopped. "How did Dagmar afford that?"

I shrugged.

"Lawyers. Sure, I mean, Brock's a dumbass and he screwed me over, but if it helps him, inspect away. Just text me that you'll be out here."

As we made our way back, I said, "So what's next with this place?

"Not sure yet. It's been for sale since May, since I cleaned it up."

"You don't see many drive-ins anymore."

He nodded. "Or people that know how to run them. Thank God the little shitbrain didn't blow up the concession stand or the projection room. That would have made the place unsellable."

"Was the damage insured?"

He shrugged. "Some. Not enough to rebuild the screen

though. Whoever does that will have their hands full complying with all that wind rating nonsense."

We got back to our cars. I thanked him for coming out and Kevin Niesen nodded, opened the door to his Expedition, and said, "Are things as bad as Mott said?"

"I don't know what Mott said."

"That the cops have a dead-bang case?"

I thought. "They have a very, very good one."

"Is he screwed?"

"We'll know at the end of the month."

He shook his head. "If I'd known everything that had happened, I never would have called."

"Called who?"

"The Sheriff."

I stopped. "You called the Sheriff?"

Kevin Niesen raised his hands. "Dagmar called to tell me what had happened. I thought the little shitbrain had just destroyed my screen, so I wanted to teach him a lesson, you know, scare him some." He shook his head. "But I had no idea he had done all this."

He looked stricken for a moment before his face clouded over again and he said, "The little shitbrain never thinks things through! We went through this with him in school all the time. He gets mad, and he goes off and before you know it, I'm eating a turd sandwich."

I stared at him. "It's certainly a tough break for Brock."

Kevin Niesen shook his head. "It's bad enough I had to carry the note on this place with no revenue coming in. Do you know my propane business is down twelve percent?"

"Oh?"

"That Tripp woman has been convincing people to change propane delivery services! Says my business is funding her son's killer's defense. I mean, I'm one of the victims here!"

"I see."

He swore three more times about his son, then he got in his car and left.

I stared at the jagged poles, looked at the line of destruction of the Mission Road Fire one more time, and decided which victim to see next.

18

It was harder to track down the next person who might have collected insurance from the Mission Road Fire, U-Store owner Devin Wright. Calls to the U-Store number went to voicemail. He had a residence address on one of the inland lakes north of town, but no one was there, which wasn't surprising if it was a summer home or if he was a hunter. Emily even asked Maggie at the deli one day and Maggie had just smiled and said that he would pop up sooner than you wanted or later than you'd like.

It was Olivia who finally tracked him down. She called me that Thursday to fill me in.

"Devin Wright ran a plumbing supply business downstate for years over on the west side near Grand Rapids. He bought a summer place in Northlake fifteen years ago so now he summers there in Northlake, winters downstate in GR, and spends the fall splitting time between those places and a hunting property in the UP."

"So we have no idea where he is right now?"

"That would be the case for a normal investigator."

"Am I about to hear that you are an abnormal investigator?"

"A poor choice of words, Shep. Superior, amazing, unbelievably skilled, and resourceful investigator. All of those are better choices."

"And what did my amazingly abnormal investigator find?"

"Mr. Wright is a Green Bay Packers fan."

"So we're adding Green Bay, Wisconsin to the list of places?"

"That's what a pedestrian, unimaginative lawyer might think, but no. You may be aware that Green Bay Packers fans and Detroit Lions fans don't get along."

"I've come across the phenomenon."

"You may also know that there are plenty of both in northern Michigan."

"A poor by-product of interstate travel, yes."

"So there are Green Bay Packers bars and Detroit Lions bars in northern Michigan so that never the twain shall meet."

"Excellent, so this Sunday I just go to all of the Green Bay Packers bars in northern Michigan to find him."

"That is what a dull lawyer with more time than sense might do, but what an incredibly talented investigator would find out is that Mr. Wright has been gathering bits and pieces of businesses up north ever since he arrived. Part of a hardware store near Empire, a carwash in Frankfort, the U-Store facility on Mission Road. And a fractional share in a bar that shows Packers games right there in Northlake."

"I suppose that narrows things down a little."

"And an even better investigator, one who is worth more than her weight in gold, would learn that the Packers play tonight on Thursday night football and that Mr. Wright always makes a point of watching those games with his brethren at that bar."

"Perfect, Liv. Thanks."

"Do you have any palm fronds?"

"Palm fronds?"

"Now would be the time to wave them."

"I just used my last one."

"A hosanna will suffice."

"You're amazing, Liv. Thanks."

And that was how I found myself wandering into The Beach-Head on a Thursday night.

~

If you've never been to Lake Michigan on the west coast of Michigan, the word "lake" gives you the entirely wrong impression of that massive body of water. To all appearances from the shore, it is the ocean without the salt. It's clear and it's blue and it extends to the horizon in all directions.

And the water is rough. White caps and riptides make a regular appearance. It's not a lake you put a dock in; it's a lake you find safe harbor from, and Lake Michigan storms have sent ships who haven't found one to the cold sandy bottom for centuries. It's vast and blue and beautiful.

The west Michigan shoreline on the Lake varies. Sometimes, there is a beautiful long beach like you can find at Holland State Park, other times there are sandy dunes, like at Sleeping Bear, and sometimes there is an elevated shoreline that requires a homeowner to build a long stair from the house down to a five-foot strip of beach like on parts of the Leelanau Peninsula. And other times, the shore ends at a sandy bluff, hundreds of feet above the lake, commanding a spectacular view of the blue water, sand, and sunset on the one side and green wooded hills on the other.

In a shrewd move, Northlake had extended its city limits all the way west to a sandy bluff overlooking Lake Michigan and developed a second entertainment district there, creatively called the Bluffs.

I found the BeachHead Bar at the north end of the Bluffs. It had a strange sign with a logo I didn't quite understand—a blob of yellow coming to a point across a blob of blue. The building was an old, two-story wood construction that didn't seem like much from the outside, an opinion that changed once I went in.

The BeachHead was a typical northern bar on the inside—a lot of blond wood, TVs of different shapes and sizes, and a couple of keno screens announcing a constant stream of winners. There were tables in the center and a bar along one side, but the crown jewel of the place was the glass wall on the west side that had a clear view from the top of the bluff of Lake Michigan. Beyond the glass was an outdoor deck with all-weather tables and chairs that would seat at least another fifty. No one was out there just then, though, which wasn't a surprise since the nights were getting colder and there was a game showing on all of the TVs inside.

Which leads me to the one huge, terrible drawback about the place.

It was filled with Green Bay Packers fans.

Packers jerseys, yellow scarves, and the odd cheesehead were everywhere. The BeachHead sign suddenly made sense to me. The yellow blob on the left was Wisconsin. The blue blob was Lake Michigan. And the yellow blob, which was a Packer-cheese yellow, was crossing Lake Michigan to the Michigan coast at Northlake. It was a lot of work to get there, but I had to admit it was clever. In a horrible, putrid, Packers sort of way.

A waitress hustled by with a full tray of baskets. "I'm out of tables, but we have a couple of seats at the far end of the bar."

"Can I order dinner there?"

She nodded as she pivoted away between the tables.

As I made my way to the far end of the bar, a cheer broke out as the Packers scored, jumping out to an early lead on the Raiders, dammit. I took a seat, then ordered a beer and dinner. I ended up getting a blackened whitefish sandwich in case you're wondering, and I have to say, environment notwithstanding, if you ever go to the BeachHead, you should order it.

I finished eating around half-time and when the bartender asked if I'd like another beer, I said, "Is Devin here tonight?"

The bartender appraised me. "Don't you know him?"

"My friend recommended this place, and I just wanted to tell him it was exactly what I thought it would be."

The bartender smiled. "An oasis in a sea of Honolulu Blue, right?"

"Something like that. And you can't beat that view."

The bartender barely glanced at the Lake, which shows you can get used to anything. "That's him at the end of the bar. But I'd wait until after the game to say anything."

I nodded. "Then I'll have that beer."

He brought me one and I watched the game, and I waited and I will admit that the final beer I ordered in the fourth quarter tasted the best of all since it was paired with a Raiders come from behind victory and the moans and curses of a green-clad populace.

The place wound down then. Some left right away, some ordered one more round to rail against the Packers' prevent defense, and Devin Wright spoke to his two buddies at the bar, gesturing time and again at the screen.

Devin Wright was medium height, but broad, with a squared off haircut and a groomed and trimmed beard that made his face seem like an angled block of stone. He wore dark jeans that were cleaned and pressed, unscuffed black work boots, and a dark denim Oxford style shirt that strained a little at the arms and shoulders. I'd watched him throughout the night, and he'd seemed a gregarious good sort and, if he seemed disappointed in the loss, that too seemed to be in a good-natured way as opposed to the way, say, a New York Jets fan would act. When his second friend had left and he gestured to the bartender for another drink, I made my way over.

"Mr. Wright? This is a great place."

He smiled. "Devin, please, and thanks."

"I had the whitefish. Fantastic."

His smile broadened. "It better be. I pay to get it straight out of the lake damn near every day." He squinted at me. "I know most of the Packers fans around here. New or visiting?"

"Both. Here for the next month or so."

He pointed his glass at me. "People come up here for the summer, but I think fall is the best time. Good for you. What's your plan?"

"Actually, I'm here for work. I'm a lawyer. I represent Brock Niesen now."

I waited to see how that would go. I have to admit I was surprised when he smacked his hand on the bar and said, "Shepherd, right, right. You left me some messages. I'm sorry, I was downstate for a week then my lodge needed a new pump. What can I do for you?"

"I don't want to bother you here, Devin. If we could just set a time when we could talk—"

Devin Wright waved a hand. "We're here now and this is the best chance you'll have to get me. I need another drink to wash away that last drive anyway."

He ordered one for himself and one for me and when they came, said, "Terrible thing about Brock. Totally got out of hand."

I nodded. "I've been out to the drive-in and saw it."

"I take it you want to know what happened to my U-Store?"

I nodded.

"I wasn't there, but from what I could see, it spread right down those bushes on Kevin's property over to that old fence." He shook his head. "I was after Kevin to split a chain link with me, but he always said he was short. Man's tighter than a...well, he's tight with a buck. Anyway, it spread to a row of units and then it was boom, boom, boom, right down the line until it hit the Carmody place."

He shook his head. "Now that, well, what that family's gone through…And the Tripps, of course." Devin Wright wiped his mustache, then said, "Have you heard about Eli Tripp yet?"

"Only what I've read."

"Best Frost Giant linebacker we ever had and a center fielder to boot. Could've played either one in college but always wanted to be a firefighter and always wanted to live here. Heir apparent to the Chief. We're going to miss him, I'll tell you. And little Liam of course."

"You said 'boom.' Were there actual explosions?"

He shrugged. "There wasn't much left of my motorhome that was parked between the units and the Carmody house. I have to believe the tanks would've made a bit of noise when they went."

"What about the units? Anything explosive in those?"

Devin Wright shook his head. "There's not supposed to be. I tell my renters to be careful what they store, but packrats are packrats. Keeps me in business, I suppose. I don't know what all was in those units. Scooter would have a better idea."

"Scooter?"

"Scooter Derry. He manages it for me."

"I see."

"I think he's gotten inventories from the tenants for the losses they're claiming."

"Are they claiming against your insurance?"

He shook his head. "I only carry insurance on the structures. It's up to them to get renter's insurance on what's in there."

"Has your claim been honored?"

Devin Wright smiled. "U-Stores aren't very expensive to build, Nate. The claim wasn't very large—my adjuster was authorized to cut a check on the spot. Certainly not enough to make me set fire to my own place."

"I didn't say that, Devin."

"No, no you didn't, but you're investigating which, I have to say, I respect. From what I've seen, though, your boy started a fire that got out of control and hurt a lot of folks. Want another beer?"

"No, I've bothered you enough. I appreciate you talking with me."

"Nonsense. If fellow Packers fans can't commiserate over a loss, what's the point?"

I smiled. "I'm afraid I just came here to track you down. And for the whitefish."

"No." He sat back on his stool. "Please don't tell me. A Lions fan?"

I smiled, nodded.

He put his hand to his head in mock sadness. "You were probably rooting for the Raiders, weren't you?"

"Very quietly."

"Ah, well you're always welcome back. Spend time with the good folk and you may see the error of your ways."

I pointed at the deck. "I'll be back for a sunset."

"You make sure you do." He offered me his hand. "I don't know that I can say good luck, but I do hope you enjoy your stay."

I took it. "I will. Thanks again."

Devin Wright got up and joined a table that was still in full swing. I nodded to the bartender and walked out into the crisp Michigan night.

I never saw the punch that smashed into my jaw.

19

I staggered to the side, catching my balance on a trash can, and saw the flash of another overhand fist coming at me. I ducked, tucked my chin to my chest, and felt the punch bang off my shoulder.

I charged, driving my shoulder into a belly, and heard an "oomph" followed by a "Get out of here!"

I kept driving until the man slammed into the outside wall of the bar. There was another "oomph," and I decided that was promising, so I did it again until the man locked his arms around my neck since my head was under his arm. He started to squeeze, and I started to get pissed, so I stepped low underneath him, picked him up, and slammed the middle of his back onto a garbage can.

He howled and released my head.

I thought the garbage can slam would be enough to end this nonsense and let go to drop this guy to the ground, but he found his feet, yelled, and charged, swinging wildly with both hands. I ducked, ducked, then uncorked a short right to his jaw.

I stepped back as the man went down onto his face. I had a chance to take in the back of a green ball cap, a Packer's jersey, and battered work boots with the heels worn down on the outside before a group of people piled out of the BeachHead.

Devin Wright was one of them. "What the hell's going on here?"

I rubbed my jaw, which was starting to hurt. "He jumped me."

"Out of nowhere?"

I nodded. "Said I should get out of here."

The man groaned and rolled over. I recognized the round face and goatee. It was the man who'd accosted me outside Maggie's a few days back. I took a quick look at his belt. I didn't see the pistol he'd been carrying then and felt fortunate.

"Christ Almighty, Tommy!" said Devin. "What the hell are you doing?!"

The man struggled to sit up. One of Devin's friends knelt down and helped him. "He shouldn't be here," Tommy slurred.

"Everyone's allowed to watch the game here, you know that."

Tommy shook his head, put his arms around his knees. "He's sat at the bar all night. All night! And you talked to him!"

Tommy's uneven cadence and half-closed eyes showed he was half in the bag. Correct that, most of the way.

"So you punched him?" said Devin Wright.

"He shouldn't be here! Eli should!"

Devin Wright opened his mouth, shut it, then shook his head. "Get him inside. I'll take him home in a minute."

Even with a man under each arm, it took a moment to get Tommy to his feet. He was still mumbling as they took him in.

"And coffee!" Devin Wright called after them, then turned to me. "I'm sorry, I didn't realize he'd had that much to drink."

I smiled, rubbing my jaw. "He really doesn't like Lions fans, eh?"

Devin Wright didn't smile. "Tommy, that's Tommy Chase, he's been struggling some. He was a childhood friend of Eli's."

"Gotcha."

Devin Wright glanced into the bar, took a deep breath, then put his hands on his hips. "We'll keep him occupied 'til the Sheriff gets here."

"Did you already call him?"

"No, but I figured you'd want to."

"You know he jumped me, right?"

"No question. A couple of the guys saw it."

"Then no need."

Devin Wright stared at me, then nodded. "Thanks."

I shrugged. "These things run hot sometimes."

"You okay to drive home?"

"Yeah. Thanks again for the whitefish and the beer."

"Looks like I owe you another one. Stop by any time."

"After the trial maybe."

"That's probably best."

Then Devin Wright went back into the BeachHead, and I drove back to the condo.

∽

THE NEXT MORNING, Friday, I was sitting with Cyn and Emily in Cyn's conference-dining room. I told them about my conversation with Devin Wright and the separate insurance on the units and the renter's contents before I said, "I'll have Olivia find out the amounts, but it doesn't sound like Devin profited from the fire at all. I get the sense the unit structures don't cost that much."

Cyn nodded. "I did some checking. That seems true."

"His motorhome might have been worth a lot," said Emily.

"For sure. Let's get the roster of renters and we'll see if this Scooter guy who runs the U-Store can tell us who had what in there."

"Will he do it?"

"I got the impression that Devin Wright will let him. If not, we'll subpoena it."

My jaw hadn't bruised overnight, so I didn't mention the extra reason I thought Devin Wright would be cooperative. We were moving on to other witnesses when the doorbell rang. I answered it.

Sheriff Sean Sizemore was standing at the door. I stepped outside and closed it. He had his aviators on and his hat off as he said, "I understand there was a dust-up at the BeachHead last night."

I didn't say anything.

Sheriff Sizemore nodded and took his glasses off. "Devin Wright told me that Tommy Chase got in a bad way."

"I see."

"Said Tommy came after you and forced you to take care of it."

"Okay."

"Anything you want to add to that?"

"I didn't call to make a complaint, Sheriff."

"It's early yet. Are you going to?"

I pointed back into the condo. "I've been working for a while this morning. *If* I had a criminal complaint to file about something, it would be done already."

I realized as I said it that I wasn't taking everyone into account, so I said, "Do I need to worry about my staff?"

Sheriff Sizemore shook his head. "Tommy will behave now."

"Anybody else I need to worry about?"

"What are you saying?"

"I'm saying is there anyone else I need to keep an eye on?"

"I'll do what eye-keeping is needed. But you should know folks up here loved Eli. And they're mad they didn't get a chance to know little Liam."

"I'm getting that impression. Is that it?"

The aviators stayed on me. "I guess so. Take care of yourself, Mr. Shepherd."

"Goodbye, Sheriff."

"What was that about?" Emily said as soon as I shut the door.

I sighed, went back into the conference room, and told them what had happened.

"Why wouldn't you press charges?" said Emily. "Or at least file a report?"

"We already have a problem with the jury pool," Cyn said. "They hate our client and love the victims. If word gets out that Nathan pressed charges against Eli Tripp's childhood friend within a week of arriving, they won't hear a thing he says at trial."

I shrugged. "That was part of it, I guess. But I was thinking more that it was the right thing to do."

"What was?"

"To cut the person in pain a little slack."

Cyn stared at me for a moment before she said, "True," and we went back to work.

~

IT WAS ALMOST noon on Friday when I heard back from Department of Natural Resources Officer Sam Wald.

"You had me sweating, Officer Wald."

"Sorry about that. We had, well, we had an emergency that kept me out for a couple of days."

"No problem."

"And I've been trying to decide what to do with your case."

"How so?"

"I've decided that I have some opinions, but I'm not sure that I want to give them for your client."

"Why's that?"

"I deal with the consequences of careless people all the time. Forest fires that get out of control, animals that are wounded with bad shots or faulty traps, morons who dump invasive animals or plants that run wild."

"Okay."

"So the fact that your client didn't mean to kill the fireman or the kid doesn't mean anything to me."

"I see."

"But I also hunted at his age and did my share of moderately stupid things that I was fortunate enough didn't have tragic consequences."

"There but for the grace of God."

"So that's why, ultimately, my opinion made my decision for me."

"And what's that?"

"I don't think it's likely that a SafeBoom target attached in the way you described for me could've started that fire."

I felt a surge of excitement. "Why's that?"

"It's just not consistent with our experiments and what I've seen. You read our study?"

"I did."

"Then you know that when we tested the debris for ignition—the leaves, dead grass, and such—we put the target on the ground, right in it. The drier it was, the more times it ignited."

"Right."

"But as we increased the dampness of the tinder, we decreased the number of ignitions we had."

"Stands to reason."

"And then, when we put the target on a metal pedestal above the tinder, we didn't have any ignitions once the pedestal got to six feet high. The ammonium nitrate balls just didn't stay ignited long enough to catch anything below it on fire. Now put all that together with the facts of your case, and I just don't think it's likely that the target would have started a fire."

There is a natural tendency when people get good news to accept it at face value and move on. But when you get a favorable opinion from an expert, you need to probe for weaknesses right away because if you don't, you can be sure opposing counsel will, except they're going to do it in front of the jury. So I asked Officer Wald everything I could think of right then.

"Aren't arborvitae extremely flammable?"

"They are. They'll go up like a torch."

"So why isn't it likely that the target ignited the bushes here?"

"Two reasons. First, the height of the target above the bushes. Ten feet is just too far, in my experience, for the target to be likely to set something on fire."

"What about the wood fragments from the movie screen? Could part of the pole or screen have caught fire, fallen down, and ignited the bushes?"

"Have you ever built a campfire, Mr. Shepherd?"

"Of course."

"Do you start it with logs or small twigs and tinder?"

"Gotcha."

"Even if the explosion blew pieces of wood everywhere, which I assume it did, the target materials wouldn't have been able to ignite something that thick."

"So the distance from the bushes to the target was one thing. What's the other?"

"It was April. It was a damp spring. I checked the weather, and it hadn't rained in five days, but there had been plenty of moisture that spring. That has an impact on ignition too."

"What if one of the bushes was dead?"

"Was it?"

"I don't know. Just thinking out loud."

"That would be a factor but, to me, just not enough. The height of the target and the damp conditions make it unlikely, in my opinion, that the target ignited the bushes."

"Do you hold that opinion to a reasonable degree of scientific probability?"

"Yes. It is more likely than not, in my opinion, that the Safe-Boom target did not ignite the arborvitae bushes."

I scribbled a note. "That leaves the million-dollar question."

"What started the fire if the target didn't?"

"Yes."

"I have no idea. And from my understanding, that's not why you called me."

"No, it's not. Will you testify if necessary?"

"I will."

"Great. I'll disclose you as a potential witness and touch base closer to trial. In the meantime, send me an invoice and I'll see that it's paid—"

"—I'm not taking an expert fee."

"But it's perfectly appropriate, Officer—"

"—I'm not going to do that. I'm only testifying because it's a natural offshoot of my research."

"I'd expect to reimburse you for your professional time, Officer Wald."

"No. But if you'd like to make a donation to a state wildlife fund, that would be fine."

"Can you give me some suggestions?"

"I'll email you."

"How much?"

"Whatever you think is appropriate."

"Officer Wald, I really appreciate this."

"I'm not doing anything, Mr. Shepherd. Our research speaks for itself."

"I'll keep you updated with any new information."

"Thank you."

I hung up. So that you know, this is how putting a case together works. One expert can almost never support your whole case. Instead, he or she has a specialized area of knowledge on one thing and it's up to the lawyer to cobble together the whole picture, the whole case, with multiple experts and pieces of evidence for the jury.

Samson Ezekiel Wald was willing to testify that the Safe-Boom target Brock shot probably didn't start the fire. It didn't explain how the fire actually started, which was still a big problem, but it was a start.

I hustled over to tell Cyn and Emily the good news. Cyn was gone, but before I could tell Emily, she said, "Guess who got a big windfall from the fire?"

20

I blinked. "Who?"

"Corey Linden."

"The owner of the Carmody house?"

"Uh-huh. The Carmodys had an option to own, but since the house was destroyed, Linden keeps the money and doesn't have to sell."

"How do we know all this?"

"Olivia. Didn't you see her email?"

"I was on the phone with Wald. Give me the highlights."

Emily checked her screen. "Maura and Noah Carmody moved into the home about four years ago. They signed one of those rent-to-own contract deals—"

"—A land contract?"

She nodded. "So this Linden guy files all the paperwork with the county like he's supposed to, that's how Olivia found it, but get this—during the first five years, Linden still has to carry homeowners' insurance on the house. And there's a specific provision that if the house is destroyed during that time, he has the sole right to the proceeds."

"I suppose that makes sense."

"But he also gets to decide whether to rebuild. And if he doesn't, guess who loses everything they've paid toward a down payment?"

"I see. What did Linden decide to do?"

"No one's sure, but he hasn't started rebuilding."

I nodded, remembering the rubble I'd seen on the site. "Yeah, he hasn't even started the demolition work. Has Olivia found out what the insurance payout was?"

"She has."

"What?"

Emily smiled. "She said you have to call her to find out."

"Praise over an email isn't the same, is it?"

"Not remotely."

"Where are the Carmodys staying now?"

"She didn't say."

I sighed. "I suppose I have to find out, huh?"

"No time like the present, Boss."

I called Olivia and put her on speaker.

"Did you see my email, Shep?"

"Emily just told me. Did you find out what Linden got for a payout?"

"I did."

There was silence on the line. Emily grinned.

"Would you like to tell me?" I said.

"Triple what he paid for it."

"How is that possible?"

"Linden bought the place from his uncle years ago. Since then, construction and home prices have soared across the country in general, in northern Michigan in particular, and especially in the growing town of Northlake."

"How did you learn about the payout?"

"Through the legitimate and above-board methods you trust me to engage in."

"You're sure?"

"I wasn't offended by the initial question. I am by that one."

"Right. Where are the Carmodys living now?"

"Noah is an over-the-road trucker who's gone for a week or so at a time. Maura and the two girls have moved back in with her mom."

"Here in town?"

"Yes. There was a Go Fund Me started for them, for housing and to replace some of their possessions, but they refuse to claim it."

"Don't they need it?"

"From what I can see, they do, desperately. But Noah posted that they can't accept it."

"Why?"

"Because it feels like they're trading on their son's death. He asked everyone to give the money to someone in their own lives who needs it instead."

I looked at Emily. We shared a compartmentalized look that makes people wonder about lawyers. I admired Noah's position. And knew that it was one more thing that was going to make our case more difficult. I saw that Emily understood.

"Man," I said.

"Yeah. Maura hasn't posted anything. From what I can tell from posts by her friends and family, she's struggling."

"Understandable."

"You know how you asked me to keep a general eye on the tenor of the posts in town?"

"Yes."

"It's not good."

"No, I expect not. Anything specific?"

"The nicest ones run along the lines of 'Brock Niesen has always been a troublemaker who deserves to spend the rest of his life in jail.'"

"Got it."

"Kim Tripp, the firefighter's mom, is running a blog with case developments and posting to all the main social media accounts every day. A lot of pictures of her son. Lots of bad things to say about Brock. A lot of 'Amens' and 'likes' in the comments."

"Not surprising." I remembered what Kevin Niesen had said. "Is she calling on people to boycott the Niesens' businesses?"

"She is. The dad's propane business and the Golden Apple Orchard. I can't tell if it's working yet."

"It is according to Kevin Niesen."

"There you go. You've come up a few times too."

"Yeah?"

"Personally, I feel privileged."

"How's that?"

"I've never met a real life carpetbagging, downstate troll before."

"I'm the first one to pass the bar."

"Congratulations. I don't think you're her favorite person."

I moved my jaw back and forth. It was still a little sore. "I don't think she's alone on that. Anything else?"

"Isn't that enough?"

"Sure, but you usually have one more thing."

"Not today. Did you find a gym yet?"

"Sure."

"Is he lying, Emily?"

Emily grinned. "One hundred percent."

"How about you?"

Her eyes widened. "Uhm."

"Well, well, well," I said.

"Things have been moving kind of fast, Olivia," said Emily.

"So's the calendar, Emily. Your goal date, the date *you* set, is the end of this month."

I chuckled and began to write on my notepad.

Emily silently offered me one, then two birds and said, "I don't know that we'll be able to make it to a gym from where we are, Olivia."

"Fine. I'm going to ship you a jump rope, two kettlebells, and a list of exercises. Do you have a back patio or a basement up there?"

"She has a huge patio, Liv," I said and held up a sign to Emily that said, *Hell→You→Creation*.

"Good. Thirty minutes, Emily. You can spare thirty minutes a day."

"Maybe."

"Listen, this was your goal, Emily, not mine. You said you had certain things you wanted to accomplish by your wedding at the end of this month and I'm here to help you do it."

Emily nodded. "Thanks, Coach. I'll get it done, at least until the trial starts."

"That's it! I'll send you some protein recommendations too."

Emily stared at me. "Thanks, Olivia. Hey, the Boss was just motioning to me that he wants a jump rope too!"

"I'm sure he didn't, but good idea. Two it is. Later."

Olivia hung up.

"Judas," Emily said.

"You signed yourself up for personal training," I said. "How is the wedding stuff going by the way?"

"Fine. It'll happen whether the flowers are pink or purple."

"Is that an issue?"

"Apparently. Josh is handling it." Emily smiled. "I'm thinking that this trial might be happening at the perfect time."

At that moment, Cyn came in through the front door, bags of lunch in hand.

"Speaking of which," I said, "why don't we eat and catch up?"

Cyn doled out gyros, chicken shawarma, and Greek salads that were an excellent discovery from Christos' Cafe in the Bluffs district. As we unwrapped, I told them that Officer Wald was on board to testify that the SafeBoom target alone wasn't enough to start the fire under the conditions that existed that night.

"Which leaves us with developing a theory of how it actually started," I said.

"And who started it if Brock didn't," said Emily, taking a bite of shawarma.

Cyn popped a plastic cap on a Greek salad dressing and poured. "So the usual motive for arson is to collect on the insurance money for the property. We have three property owners—Kevin Niesen owns the drive-in, Devin Wright the U-Store, and Corey Linden the Carmody house."

"Kevin Niesen didn't have much insurance," I said. "The screen was old and outdated, and it will cost more to replace than he's going to get."

"Plus, he'd be framing his own son," said Emily around another bite.

"Money can do strange things," said Cyn. "If there's enough of it."

"Devin Wright had insured the U-Store," I said. "But his insurance is limited to the structures, which really aren't that expensive to build or replace, which means there isn't much insurance gold at the end of that rainbow."

"The contents could be a different story though," said Cyn.

I nodded. "A tenant could have had anything in one of those units."

"So Devin Wright doesn't seem to have a motive to burn the units, but one of his tenants might. Which leaves us with Corey Linden."

Emily shook her head. "He got triple the value of the house

and gets to keep the Carmodys' payments over four years besides. That's something."

"It's not nothing," I said.

"I don't think money is enough of a motive if we're pointing at Linden," said Cyn.

"Why's that?" I said.

"With the other two, it's just a matter of burning an unoccupied piece of property for a little cash. That's not hard to justify. For Corey Linden to have done it, he had to have been willing to burn a house with a family in it."

"So he'd have to have a motive to kill them too," said Emily.

Cyn nodded. "Or thought they weren't home. I'm just pointing out that would be a tougher sell."

There was a silent contemplation of case theories and Mediterranean food.

Emily looked up. "Do we have to have an actual theory that someone else did it?"

"We don't have to prove it definitively," I said. "But if we're going to put an expert up there that said the SafeBoom target didn't start the fire, we have to give them some way that the fire *could* have started if we're going to raise reasonable doubt."

She looked back down. "That's what I was afraid of. So what do we do?"

"Our expert disclosure is due today. We disclose Officer Wald as a target expert and Bret Halogi as a fire expert. The judge didn't require reports so for now we can play them off as being on board to keep the prosecution honest. We don't have to call them if they're not necessary. Halogi is still on board?" I said to Cyn.

Cyn nodded. "She's read the file and can talk about the nature of the spread. She's testifying in another case right now, so she'll be here early next week to look at the site."

"Perfect. In the meantime, Emily, get the U-Store tenant

roster from Scooter Derry and see if he knows about any high value items they had in there. Then we'll sic Olivia on their claims to flesh it out."

"What are we looking for, just anything that's plausible?"

"Let's put it this way, if Brock didn't start the fire, then something had to. No one else has found what that was yet, so let's see if we can."

We all nodded, agreed it was a great plan for what we had, and finished our lunch.

It wasn't of course. It was a shit plan. But it was all we had right then, so we started the tedious process of running it all to ground.

21

I could tell you what we did all weekend, but it would bore the ever-loving bejesus out of you. We weren't to the good stuff yet, like preparing witness cross-examinations or the opening statement; it was doing the dozens of little things that go into trial preparation. We started lining up subpoenas, drafting jury instructions, drafting motions *in limine* to keep certain evidence out, and drafting our trial brief. We were double checking everything prosecutor Astrid Olsen had produced so far, but that was difficult because we'd only been on the case for a week, so we constantly felt like we were missing something because we weren't quite immersed enough in the case yet to know for sure that we hadn't.

We fell into a routine, Cyn, Emily, and I. We each used our own condo to work but met in Cyn's dining-war room for mid-morning coffee, lunch, and dinner to take a break, touch base, and re-focus where we needed to. We didn't really come up for air for the next few days.

It was late Monday morning when Dagmar Niesen called me.

"Hello, Dagmar."

"Mr. Shepherd, I'm sorry to bother you."

"It's no bother. And Nate, please. I don't have too much to report just yet, we're still going over the State's case and pulling things together."

"I'm sure of that, but I'm not calling about the case. Or I guess I am but not exactly in that way."

"What do you mean?"

"Kim Tripp, you know who she is?"

"I do."

"She's coming after my business."

"That's consistent with what I've seen of her. What's going on?"

"She's been posting online and telling everyone who'll listen that my son's a murderer."

"I've heard about that."

"But this is new."

"What is?"

"She put up...I don't know how to describe it but it's upsetting. Could you come out here to see?"

Normally, my answer to that would be "no" as a family member's problems aren't nearly as significant as the person's who has been accused of murder, but I had a feeling that this might be one more thing going on in the community that I needed to know about it. "Can it wait until lunchtime? I can come out then."

"That's more than early enough. Thank you."

We hung up. I worked a little longer, told Cyn and Emily I'd be making the lunch run, and went out to Golden Apple Orchard.

∼

IT DIDN'T TAKE a detective to see the problem. I don't know if you've driven in rural Michigan, or in any rural place for that matter, but it's fairly common to drive on two-lane county roads that are only interrupted every mile or so by an intersection controlled by a stop sign. It's also fairly common for people to post local signs at those quiet corners, signs like "Bob's Christmas Tree farm, straight ahead" or "Free eggs, left one mile."

The Golden Apple Orchard did a similar thing. For the three miles leading to the orchard, there were little gold signs, shaped like an apple, saying *Golden Apple Orchard-3 mi*, *Cider and Donuts-2 mi*, and *You Pick-1 mi*.

Or that's what the signs *had* said. Now, in red paint, those signs read, *Home of a Murderer*, *Support a Baby Killer*, and finally, beneath *You Pick* someone had written *Burn a baby or a firefighter*.

When I reached the orchard, I found Dagmar Niesen digging at a new sign. It was a piece of plywood nailed to a four by four on each side and buried in the ground. *A Killer Lives Here!* it said in bold red letters, and beneath it was a printed picture of a weeping fireman bent over a blanket. As I stopped, I realized it wasn't a blanket. It was a blanket-covered body.

I hadn't seen that picture before.

"They must have had an auger," Dagmar said as I approached.

"What do you mean?"

"To get this in so quickly. They must have augured the holes for them to be this big."

I looked down to see what she meant. The holes extended out a good six inches in each direction from the post. I know because it was also filled with concrete.

"Do you have a front-end loader?" I said.

"I have apples falling, Nate. We're using every spare hand and piece of equipment for that."

I nodded. "How about another shovel?"

She looked at me, then nodded. "Back at the shed."

I held out my hand. "Why don't you get it? And a post hole digger if you have one."

She handed me the shovel and climbed into her truck without a word.

I was digging my way around the concrete when she returned.

"We could cut the post off at the ground," I said.

Dagmar Niesen shook her head. "I want it out."

She started digging again, and I started using the post hole digger to remove cylinders of dirt from around the concrete.

"I saw the signs on the way in."

Dagmar nodded. "I wanted to get this out first. I'll pull those after. They apparently go in all directions."

"Did you call the Sheriff?"

"I did. He agreed this sign was a trespass. The others aren't on my property, so there's nothing he can do." She tossed another shovelful of dirt to the side. "But he'll be sure to look into it."

I jammed the post hole digger into the dirt, pulled the handles apart, and lifted another cylinder of dirt out of the ground. "Seems kind of obvious."

"That's what I said."

"And the Sheriff?"

"'Thinking and proving are two different things, Dagmar.'"

"Ah."

We dug a little more, her in flat scoops, me in round cylinders, before she said, "Traffic was down this weekend. A lot. I have a couple of local elementary schools coming this afternoon, so I want to get this out of here before they arrive."

The first four by four was ready to come out so the next five minutes was spent cutting the plywood off the post. Dagmar stared at the picture for a moment, then pulled it off, crumpled it up, and then cut the plywood into sections. The post was loose enough now that we could wobble it back and forth and I could pull it out. I decided that, when I had the chance, I'd tell Olivia that it counted as my deadlift workout for the day.

We pulled the other post out twenty minutes later. Dagmar waved at the concrete-bottomed posts and said, "Leave them there. I'll bring them back with the front-end loader at the end of the day. I just wanted that down." The regular Golden Apple Orchard sign was now clearly visible from the road.

Her phone rang. "Hi, Linda...Good and you?...Good...No?...Why's that?...It's down now...Are you sure, we have the bounce house inflated and extra donuts...No, of course...Yes, I understand...Maybe next year...Sure...Thanks for calling...Bye."

Dagmar Niesen hung up, took off a glove and ran a hand down her long braid. "The elementary schools just cancelled. Both of them. Seems a parent saw the sign on the way in today." She looked at me. "They've been coming here for years."

"Can you stay afloat?"

"I don't know. I have a processing contract for a good part of the crop, but we sell a lot on-site too. Eventually, I'm going to have apples rotting if I can't move them."

"How long can you make it?"

"Until the end of the year. If I sell this crop." She took a deep breath. "So what can I do?"

"About the signs?"

She nodded.

"Do you have cameras?"

"It's an apple orchard, not a bank, Nate."

"Maybe hide some trail cams out here then."

"I have a couple of those."

"And you called the Sheriff—"

"For what that's worth."

"—which will lay the groundwork if something else happens."

Dagmar wiped her forehead with the back of a gloved hand and gave me a faint smile. "That's not very satisfying."

"I'm telling you legally what can be done."

"Sure." Dagmar Niesen stared at the two holes. "I suppose it's going to be like this until the trial."

"I would guess."

"And after, if he's convicted."

"Maybe."

"How is the case looking?"

"We've made some progress, but it is still pretty strong against him." It may seem cruel, but I wasn't going to tell her about our breakthrough with Officer Wald on the targets and risk that news leaking out. Instead, I asked, "Tell me, what do you know about Kevin's efforts to sell the drive-in?"

"Only that he's trying."

"Did he ever discuss the insurance with you?"

"Not really. I kept to the Orchard, and he kept to his propane and the drive-in."

"Did he ever mention whether he got a payout on the fire?"

She thought. "He did. He said it wouldn't be enough to pay for a new screen, but it might let him get out from under the remaining debt on the place." Her head snapped up. "You don't think he's involved, do you?"

"Could he be?"

"No. I don't think so. I mean, the idiot did call the Sheriff on Brock after I told him what he'd done, but neither of us knew what else had happened, that there had been deaths."

I didn't say anything.

Dagmar Niesen's eyes darted back and forth before she said, "No, no, that doesn't make any sense. That man has faults, a lot of them, but he loves Brock. He wouldn't do this to him."

"Okay. I just want to make sure I'm not missing anything."

Dagmar Niesen shook her head. "You're not missing anything there. Kevin has nothing to do with this."

"Alright."

She pulled at her braid again. "I visited Brock over the weekend."

"How is he?"

"Scared. Mad."

"I imagine."

"He can't spend the rest of his life in there, Nate."

I nodded but didn't say anything.

"He's only fifteen."

"I know."

"He didn't mean to hurt anyone."

"I realize that."

"And that doesn't matter? The law doesn't care?"

I paused, then told her the truth. "No. For this type of crime, it doesn't."

She stared. "You need to get him out of there."

"I'm working on it." I pointed. "You sure on the posts?"

"Yeah. You've done enough here. Thanks for helping."

"Thanks for calling me. I needed to see what's going on. Let me know if anything else happens."

Then I climbed back into my Jeep and headed back into town, past signs which, at regular intervals, proclaimed the Golden Apple Orchard to be the home of a murderer.

22

The post hole digging had made my trip to the orchard take longer than I'd expected so the lunch rush was over by the time I stopped in at Maggie's. Maggie herself was behind the deli counter making sandwiches and smiled as I walked up. "Here for the group or just a single today?"

"The group," I said.

"So that's a tuna on sourdough, a lettuce turkey wrap, and ..." She pointed a finger at me, bouncing it, and said, "you're changing it up just a little to a pastrami on a salt bagel with horseradish."

I blinked.

She grinned. "I'm right, aren't I?"

"You need to take that act on the road."

She bowed and got to work on the tuna. "So how do you like Northlake?"

"I'd never been. It's beautiful."

"Been out to the Bluffs yet?"

"Just to the BeachHead the other night."

Maggie stopped cold. "You're not a Packers fan, are you?"

I smiled. "No. I had to meet someone in hostile territory."

"I knew I liked you." She put a slice of tomato on the tuna. "There are better places out there to take in the view."

"Like where?"

"Sunset Shores for one. There are some vineyards with great views too. I'm not a huge wine fan, but some of the grounds are worth the price of admission."

"I'll try to check one of them out."

Maggie started on the lettuce turkey wrap. "I imagine you won't have much time, will you?"

"Not right now, no. But maybe I'll sight see a little after if..." I stopped myself.

Maggie smiled. "I suppose things might get a little heated. Don't worry though, you're always welcome here. This deli is a 'no punch zone.'"

"You heard about that?"

"Word gets around. And Tommy Chase has a big mouth."

"Yeah? What's he saying?"

"That he's going to sue the lawyer who busted up his back. Did you really drop him on a garbage can?"

I shrugged.

"That can't have been easy," she said as she sliced a salt bagel in half. "Tommy's a big boy."

I shrugged again and asked, "He was a friend of Eli's?"

Maggie frowned. "Back to grade school. They kind of went different paths but always stayed close."

"Different paths?"

"You've met Tommy?"

"A couple of times."

"Take all of your first impressions of Tommy, think the opposite, pour them into firefighter's gear, and you have Eli."

"You knew him?"

Maggie nodded.

"I understand he was a very good man."

"The best," she said as she smeared horseradish on the bagel and wrapped it up. She gathered the three sandwiches, added the chips and oranges, and I followed her down to the register.

I almost didn't say it, but coming straight from the Dagmar's orchard, it was at the top of my mind. "Thanks for your courtesy."

Maggie smiled and waved it off. "We've all got jobs to do. We don't need to get threatened while we do them."

"I can't imagine someone threatening you."

"Then you've never been on the business end of a tourist who got her tuna on wheat when she ordered gluten-free sourdough."

"Yikes."

"Exactly. Besides, Brock either did it or he didn't and, either way, I don't think he meant it. People make mistakes sometimes, bad mistakes, but they're still just mistakes."

I paid, Maggie handed me the bag of sandwiches, and I left thinking I needed some Maggies on the jury.

∽

I WAS ALMOST BACK to the condos when my phone buzzed.

"Hi, Mom."

"Don't be mad," she said.

"Should I be?"

"No, you shouldn't. But I know how you are."

"How am I?"

"Obsessed with work before a trial."

"I would have said 'focused,' but, okay. What's up?"

"We're coming up to Northlake!"

"Um, okay."

"I've been after your father to take me up north for the fall festivals for years, but you know the odds of that during hunting season. Well, with his dialysis, the hunting trip's a no-go, but we can squeeze in a nice weekend between treatments."

"How's he doing?"

"Good. The doctor is still hopeful that he might be able to get off the dialysis at the end of the month."

"Which means your fall festival window will have closed. I get it, Mom, but I'm really not going to have time—"

"—Oh, I'm not asking you to sightsee, but I thought maybe you could meet us for a snack at some point Saturday. You have to eat, don't you?"

I looked at the bag of food in the passenger seat. "Sure."

"And don't worry, we found a bed-and-breakfast nearby that'll take all of us, so we won't be in your hair at all."

"All of us?"

"Mark and Izzy are coming too."

"I see. That's this Saturday?"

"That's still almost three weeks from your trial, isn't it?"

I was quiet for just a second too long, so she said, "I know your trial is very important but, after all that's happened, well, the two of us just wanted to see you for a little bit."

"You're playing the death card, Mom?"

"If you say so, dear. So you'll do it?"

"I'll be there. Just tell me where to meet."

"Oh, good. Your father will be very happy."

"I'll see you this weekend, then."

"Are you eating?"

"I have a bag of food right here."

"Don't you lie to me, Nathan Shepherd."

"Wouldn't think of it, Mom."

Then I hung up and entered the condo with lunch and an invitation.

23

When I walked in, Cyn was sitting at the dining room table with a woman I didn't know. The woman had that particular color of hair that had once been black but was now streaked with all shades of gray and white to make it the uniform color of smoke. She had a lean face with fine lines that deepened when she smiled.

"This him?" she said. Her voice was raspy to the point of a croak.

"It is."

"He looks young to be as good as you say."

"I don't know that I'd say anything like that in front of him."

"Oh, right." The woman stood. She wore black boots, black jeans, and a gray t-shirt, and cords rippled in her forearm as she shook my hand. "Bret Halogi," she said.

"Nate Shepherd. Cyn exaggerates."

"Cyn does a lot of things, but that's not one of them. I don't know that it matters here, though. From everything I've seen so far, I'd say you're cooked."

I nodded. "It's a hard case."

"I'm not sure I can help."

"Then I need you to tell me where the prosecution is playing it straight and where they're vulnerable."

Bret Halogi shrugged. "It's your dollar."

"We weren't expecting you until tomorrow."

"It seemed like there was a lot to do."

"There is."

"Let's go then." Bret Halogi grabbed her black jean jacket off the back of a chair.

"To the site?"

She looked at me. It turned out that her eyes were black and capable of an excellent deadpan stare.

"Right," I said. "I'll drive you."

She nodded. "Good to see you again, Cyn. Catch up before I leave?"

"I'll be here. Call when you're done."

Bret Halogi slipped on her jacket. "Let's go, Shepherd."

~

ON THE WAY to the site, I started to tell Bret Halogi what our own investigation had found out so far.

She held up a hand. "I appreciate that, Shepherd, but do you know the biggest mistake fire investigators make?"

"What's that?"

"They interview witnesses *before* they look at the scene and *before* they test the wreckage. It creates a confirmation bias for their findings and, before you know it, you have some poor bastard in jail for arson because the investigator has a preconceived notion of what the scene reveals."

"Fair enough. Should we not have sent you the witness interviews?"

"Don't worry. I didn't read them."

"What do you want to know now?"

"Not much yet. Let me take a look first. Am I going to be able to do my own testing?"

"I'll be able to get us access to whatever evidence the prosecutor preserved, but we're on a tight window. Do we have time?"

"I'll make time."

"What do you know?"

"Your client shot a SafeBoom target, and the prosecution claims it spread east through a variety of fuels until it killed two people."

I nodded. "I have an expert who will say—"

"—Something that I don't care to hear right now."

I smiled. "Right."

We were quiet the rest of the drive.

∾

I TOOK Bret Halogi to the drive-in and walked with her to jagged poles where the movie screen had been. She dropped a large black bag, battered and streaked, then pulled out a camera, a laser measuring device, and a digital recorder. I stood aside and watched her work as she took measurements and spoke into the recorder.

She snapped measurements from the screen poles to the remaining arborvitae hedge on the west and the snow fence on the east. Then she looked straight up and said, "Do we know how high the target was?"

"Between twenty-five and thirty feet."

"How'd the kid climb...oh, there were spikes hammered into the poles." Bret reached out and touched a couple of the blackened metal Ls still sticking out of one of the remaining poles. "Probably to service the screen."

I didn't reply as Bret went back to moving, back and forth

between the poles and where the hedges still stood, her hair billowing back and forth like the smoke she was chasing.

She pointed. "It spread east and left the bushes to the west. That's either from the wind or an accelerant or both."

I nodded.

She put down the laser and used the camera to take pictures before dictating some more. She pulled out some bags and took samples of the bushes.

"Hasn't too much time passed to learn anything?" I asked.

"I can still learn their resin content and what kind of fuel they make."

After she'd taken the arborvitae samples, we tracked east toward the boundary with the U-Store lot where she took more measurements, more pictures, and a sample from the old privacy fence that still stood.

She tapped the temporary orange snow fence. "Can we go over there?"

I nodded. "The owner gave us permission. Let me just text him so he knows." I did.

Devin Wright texted back a thumbs up before I'd even removed the first stake of snow fence. Once I did, Bret Halogi stepped through and immediately walked to where the grass border met concrete. She pointed to a swath of dead grass that continued as a black scorch mark on the concrete pad before it cut off in a straight line. "See this area?"

"Yes."

"This is where the woodpile was. It was piled up between the fence and the outer wall of the first unit."

I hadn't dug into the fire evidence related to the storage units yet, so this was the first I'd heard of the woodpile. I just nodded.

Bret Halogi was drifting back and forth, picture snapping and laser measuring, when I saw a man walk toward us from the office. He wore a green ball cap, worn jeans and work boots, and a t-shirt that told me he wasn't rude, he just had the balls to say what was true. He had a scraggly beard and carried a pop bottle that I estimated to be one-eighth filled with dip spit.

I left Bret and met him.

"Help you?" he said.

"Are you Scooter?"

He spit into the pop bottle and nodded.

"Nate Shepherd. Devin Wright said I could look at the fire site. Did he mention it?"

"Texted me just now. Don't take nothin'."

I shook my head. "We won't be going in any units."

"And stay here in the burn area. Got people in and out most of the day."

"Sure. Did any of the renters make a claim with you?"

"Claim?"

"Against your insurance?"

There's an art to spitting in a dip bottle. Scooter nestled his top lip into the far side of the opening, puckered his bottom lip like he was going to blast a trumpet, then spit into the bottle without leaving a trace of dip on his beard. "Not sure how that's your business," he said.

"If they made a claim for damage to their property, that would tell us what burned and how the fire spread."

Scooter nodded. "Might've. Not sure off hand. I'd have to check the paperwork."

"Would you do that?"

He shrugged, spit. "I'll check with Devin."

"When are you going to rebuild?"

"When Devin says, I guess."

"What's the hold up?"

Scooter spit. "Insurance. Lawyers. You know how it is."

"Any security cameras?"

"Nah. Probably be gone by the time the Sheriff got here anyway."

"When are you here?"

Scooter stared before he spit, then said, "Why would you care?"

"In case I need to stop by after you talk to Devin."

"Sometimes in the morning. Sometimes in the afternoon."

"Ever at night?"

"Nah. Unless there's a problem. Like when some little shit sets three units on fire."

"Right."

"How do you get in, key card?"

"Code. Keypad." He looked over my shoulder. "She about done?"

Bret was measuring and clicking.

"Not sure. Probably."

"Make sure you hammer that snow fence back in when you leave." He spit one more time, then wandered back up to the office.

I went back over to Bret Halogi, who was standing at the far end of where the storage units had been, the part closest to the Carmodys' house. She stepped off the concrete pad to a thin strip of grass and asphalt. "The motorhome was here next to the storage building."

"That's what they say."

She stood. "It was. See the cracking and buckling here, and here."

"Yes."

"That's from the heat." She walked to the boundary between the U-Store and the Carmody house, which was also marked by orange snow fence where the old fence had been and snapped another measurement. "There's not much room between where the motorhome was and the side of the Carmody house.

Between the gas, the debris, and the west wind, I'm not surprised it spread there."

She pulled up a stake, rolled open a section of orange snow fence, and crossed into the Carmodys' yard.

"We don't have permission to go there," I said.

"Neither did the fire," said Bret Halogi and crouched down in the small space between the wreckage of the house and the property line with the U-Store. She snapped measurements, took more pictures, and filled some plastic bags with debris. Then she took out her phone, tapped it a few times, showed me the compass function, then stood facing me, turning a little to the left then a little to the right.

"West," she said. She shifted back. "Southwest."

"Make sense?" I asked.

She nodded. "The house would've been right in line with the wind direction."

She pocketed her phone, put her equipment back in her bag, and strode back to the property line. She took the stake with the fencing attached out of my hand and jammed it back into the ground with one swift jab.

Then she turned back toward the drive-in, pointed, and said, "So the fire starts at the screen and catches the bushes on fire. The wind drives it straight east, toward us, where it catches the wood pile next to the old fence. Then it spreads from unit to unit to unit, right down the line, until it hits the motorhome parked between the last unit and the Carmody house. The motorhome explodes and the Carmody house catches fire."

I nodded. "That's what they're saying."

Bret stared. "It's not far from the motorhome to the side of the house."

"Okay."

Bret Halogi crossed her arms, staring down the row of where the units had been to the drive-in. "But the rest of this would have taken some time. No one reported the original explosion? From the target?"

"I don't know. They haven't given us the dispatch records."

"We need to nail down the timeline."

I nodded. "We're putting that together now."

She strode back toward the drive-in. I followed.

"Where's the report from their fire investigator?"

"I didn't see one in the file."

"There should be one."

"I'll double check."

"It'll have a detailed listing of the structures and the contents that were burned."

"I'm pretty sure there wasn't one, but I'll have Cyn check again."

Bret Halogi glanced at me. "If the State didn't do a report, then we need to find out what was in these units." She pointed at the blackened concrete pad. "The storage building itself wouldn't be a big fire source. Asphalt shingles on the roof could catch, and the timber framing, but the walls were thin metal. They won't burn easily, but they'll transfer a lot of heat and air to allow the fire to spread to what was in the units. Fire is all about fuel, Shepherd. What was in the units is important."

"Got it."

We made it back to the drive-in and replaced the snow fence there. Brett Halogi strode back to the charred screen poles, pushed her smokey hair behind one ear, and stared back down in the other direction before she said, "It's definitely possible that the fire spread from here to the house. There are some things worth exploring, but they're long shots."

"Such as?"

She pointed at the drive-in screen poles. "Exploding targets don't usually cause fires. They can, but if what you say is true about where the target was, that seems like a long drop to the bushes."

"I have a target expert."

"What does she say?"

"He. He says it's unlikely that a target from that height would ignite the bushes."

"I agree. The storage units are close to the property lines on both sides, so close that I'm sure it violates some zoning setback rule."

"Interesting but, legally, that's not going to get us off the hook."

She nodded. "Then my first impression?"

"Please."

"There was a fire that started here on a night with a strong west wind. In a straight line, you had bushes, a wood pile, three storage units, a motorhome, and the Carmody house. I'm not at all surprised the fire spread to the Carmody house, Shepherd. It's pretty logical. And reasonable."

I'd hoped for more, but I couldn't say I was surprised at her opinion. "I needed to know that."

"Right now, I can backstop you to keep the State honest. I'll double check the prosecutor's work but to do that, I need everything I asked for, including the State's Fire Investigation Report. And I'll need access to all of the police debris samples for my own testing. And we need to get to work on a timeline."

I nodded. "Then we'd better get back."

24

Bret Halogi had given me a lot to think about. I was mulling it over as we drove back—the steady path of the fire, the logic of its course, and the fuel it had burned. Given Bret's opinion that the State's case was reasonable, I was thinking about the angles—whether the target started the fire, nailing down the contents of the units, and establishing a hard, evidence-based timeline for what had happened that night—when Bret said, "So when did you join Friedlander & Skald?"

"I haven't," I said, still thinking about how the fire had started.

"Really? That's strange."

"How so?"

"They don't usually work with outside counsel. And Cyn said this is her second case with you."

I nodded. "The first one was kind of a fluke. They hired me as local counsel and then their main lawyer died."

"And this time?"

"Cyn said I was the right one for the case."

Bret nodded. "She must be planning on making you a job offer."

"I don't think so."

She turned her black eyes on me. "I've known Cyn a long time. She doesn't suffer fools or outside counsel."

"I agree on the first and submit myself as evidence of the inaccuracy of the second."

Bret Halogi stared at me, then looked back out her window.

"You've known Cyn a long time?" I asked.

"We grew up near each other."

"Where was that?"

"In the north."

"Minneapolis area?"

She smiled. "Close enough. But then she found law, and I found fire, and we don't get to see each other much anymore. It's always a treat when our paths cross. So, let's go over one more time what you need to get for me."

~

BACK AT THE HEADQUARTERS CONDO, I pulled Emily into the dining-war room after Bret Halogi had left. I dialed Astrid Olsen and put it on speaker.

"Astrid Olsen's office," said a woman's voice.

"May I speak to Astrid, please?"

"Who's calling?"

"This is Nate Shepherd."

"I'm sorry, Mr. Shepherd, Ms. Olsen is not available for y— Ms. Olsen is not available."

"Do you know when she will be?"

"I don't, I know she's quite busy with several cases."

"That's why I'm calling, on the Niesen case."

"I understand, Mr. Shepherd. Is there something I can assist you with?"

"I need to speak to Ms. Olsen about her disclosures."

"I may be able to help you with that."

"There may be some records missing."

"Oh, I can answer that. Ms. Olsen has provided you with all of the documents."

"I'm sorry, you are?"

"Melody, Mr. Shepherd."

"You're Ms. Olsen's assistant?"

"I am indeed."

"Thank you. Is Ms. Olsen saying she's provided me with all the documents she has or all of the documents she thinks I'm entitled to?"

"She said to tell you that you have all of the documents."

"I see. There are some things I'd expect to be here that aren't, Melody. Can I give you a few documents to double check?"

"I'll relay any message you like, Mr. Shepherd."

"Great. We don't have the Fire Investigation report from—"

Emily tapped a name.

"—from Investigator Kurt Vernon."

"Fire Investigation report, check."

"We don't have any medical records or ambulance run reports for any of the alleged victims."

"Victims' medical records and ambulance reports, got it."

"There's no list or inventory of items claimed to have been destroyed by the fire in the U-Store facility."

"U-Store items, right."

"And no internal dispatch records from police or fire showing when they were called to the scene."

"Dispatch records. Was there anything else, Mr. Shepherd?" Melody's voice spilled cheer and light through the phone.

"We also need to arrange for testing on the samples that were taken from the scene."

"I see. You'll need to arrange that with Ms. Olsen directly."

"Fine. When's a good time to reach her?"

"Ms. Olsen prefers that those type of arrangements be conducted in writing. You can email her directly any time."

"I see. I'm beginning to think Ms. Olsen doesn't like me, Melody."

"Oh no, Mr. Shepherd, she's never said that to me at all. That's just her standard practice."

"Thank you, Melody. You've been most helpful."

"I'm so glad. Good afternoon, Mr. Shepherd."

I hung up. "You see what she's doing?"

"Sure do, Boss." Emily grinned. "Want me to compel the crap out of her?"

I nodded. "And subpoena everyone else. Police, fire, ambulance, the U-Store. Get all of those records. Email her a list of what we want for testing and file an emergency motion with the Court so that we get it heard by next week."

"No problem." As she wrote, her phone buzzed. She looked, rolled her eyes, and blew a lock of hair straight up into the air.

"What?" I asked.

She held up her phone, showing a "13" on her text icon. "My mom is texting me every hour with wedding deetz." Right on cue, her phone buzzed again.

I thought. "Speaking of moms, mine just called and told me she's bringing half the family up this weekend. Why don't you shoot down to see yours for the weekend?"

Emily shook her head. "Josh can handle it."

"It's probably the last break we'll get before the trial."

She looked at me, thoughtful. "I do need to calm her down if I'm going to get any work done."

"Do it. Go Friday night and come back late Sunday."

"Are you sure?"

"Positive. Let's just get the subpoenas and the motion out before you go."

Emily looked relieved. "Thanks, Boss."

I nodded. "I'll dig into what we have for a timeline. You confirm what reports we have and compel what we don't."

Her face went hard. "On it."

So that's what we did. Cyn pointed us to all of the files Emily and I needed and left to take Bret Halogi to a late dinner. I went back to my condo and by midnight, I still only had the skeleton of a timeline. Without the more detailed dispatch records, I had to pull references from the basic police and fire reports, which, given the scope of the fire and the resulting deaths, seemed terribly light.

A 911 call had come in at 1:37 a.m. on the morning of April 10th reporting a fire at the drive-in and U-Store. Fire and rescue trucks were immediately dispatched and arrived at the Mission Road site at 1:49 a.m. The Carmody house had collapsed at 1:56 a.m., killing Eli Tripp and Liam Carmody. Later that morning, after a report from his parents, suspect Brock Niesen had been apprehended and arrested.

I was sitting there contemplating how little we'd been given and wondering just what the hell Luke Mott had been doing while he was representing Brock when headlights flashed across my window as Bret Halogi dropped Cyn off at the condo next door. They flashed again as the black car backed out and Cyn went in.

It seemed like there was a lot I didn't know.

25

Friday morning had Emily and I back in front of Judge Roderick for a hearing.

"What am I doing here, Mr. Shepherd?" he said.

"Your Honor, we're seeking to compel production of certain documents and evidence—"

"—Why haven't you attached a summary of the meeting with opposing counsel to work this dispute out?"

"Ms. Olsen has declined to discuss the matter, Your Honor," I said.

"That's not true, Judge," said Astrid Olsen. "We have discussed this matter. In writing."

"In writ—great booberries, Ms. Olsen, that's not the spirit of our local rules and you know it."

Astrid Olsen straightened. "I find that people can misinterpret or misreport conversations to the Court, Your Honor. Written communication speaks for itself. I thought that in a case of this magnitude—"

"—In a case of this magnitude, you can follow our local rules!" Judge Roderick shook his head. "Are you withholding anything, Ms. Olsen?"

"We've given Mr. Shepherd all of the documents he's entitled to, Your Honor," said Astrid Olsen.

"That's not what I asked, Ms. Olsen, and I'm not going to sort this out until you two do what you're supposed to do! Both of you go into the jury room right now and hash this document issue out!"

"Your Honor," I said. "We also need access to the fire debris samples being maintained by the State."

"What? Why?"

"To perform our own testing."

Judge Roderick turned to Astrid Olsen. "Am I to assume there's been no discussion on this either?"

She stood a little straighter. "Your Honor, we advised Mr. Shepherd in writing that—"

"—That's it!" Judge Roderick pointed. "Out!"

As I collected my file, Astrid Olsen still stood there, looking like she was going to say something more.

"Judge?" said a voice from the side of the courtroom.

"What is it, Pierce?"

Mason Pierce was looking at Astrid Olsen as he said, "The parties could agree to record their conversations from here on out. That's just as good as getting it in writing and would reduce any misunderstandings."

Judge Roderick looked back at us. "See, that's what happens when you've actually worked for a living before you spend three years buried in books—you come up with actual solutions!" Judge Roderick hit the bench with his palm. "Mr. Shepherd, Ms. Olsen, and you too, Ms. Lake, if you can get this mess moving—go in the jury room, work this out, record it for all I care on those little phones of yours, and come back here with your agreement that we'll put on the record. Is that sufficient for you, Ms. Olsen?"

"Certainly, Your Honor."

"Get out of here, all of you."
We did.

~

Hearing about the resolution of a discovery dispute is almost as exciting as being behind the customer in line at the hardware store who's arguing with the cashier about being overcharged eighty-six cents for lawn fertilizer so I'll cut to the end—Astrid Olsen swore that she'd given us all of the official records *that she had* from police, fire, and medical. It was clear, though, that there were documents floating around out there that she didn't have, and my sense was that she wasn't worried about that because the people who'd written them had already told her what they knew. We would have to obtain the information from the original sources ourselves.

The one area I pushed back on was for a report from the State's Fire Investigator, Kurt Vernon. Astrid maintained, though, that Investigator Vernon had not written a report and that she wasn't obliged to make him write one just for my benefit.

Astrid then resisted giving us the debris samples that had been collected from the scene, claiming our testing ran the risk of destroying the evidence. We eventually had to take that issue back to the judge, who said that Astrid Olsen better turn all of that evidence over today, that I better return it all intact by the Monday before trial, and that we would both be subject to sanctions, excommunication, and dunking if we didn't comply.

Oh, and in case you're wondering, yes, Astrid Olsen recorded our whole conversation on her phone, and no, that is not usual, even among paranoid attorneys.

I didn't know what to make of it either.

The rest of the day was a whirl of discovery—Cyn went to

the prosecutor's office and the Sable County Sheriff's evidence room to obtain the debris fragments for Bret Halogi's testing; Emily went back to our makeshift office to bombard police, fire, rescue, and the local hospital with subpoenas and document requests; and I went back to the U-Store to track down Scooter Derry to find out just what had been in those storage units.

∼

FOR THE FIRST TIME, I actually went through the front entrance of the U-Store instead of slipping through the snow fence barrier on the side. There was an old touch pad with raised buttons like an old-fashioned phone that sat on a rusty curved pole in front of a chain-link gate. It also had a call button, which I pressed.

No one talked back, but the gate creaked open. Slowly.

The office building was back in the middle of the facility, off to one side. I passed undamaged rows of storage buildings, each three units wide, with chipped painted walls, rolling metal garage-style doors, and asphalt shingle roofs. Near the back of the facility, pop-up trailers and campers and motorhomes were lined up in two neat rows.

I parked in front of the office, a wood paneled, shingled building with long windows on two sides that allowed a view of the parking rows and the units. There were two other cars, a rusted Dodge pickup and a new silver Ford Expedition. I parked my Jeep between them and went in.

Scooter Derry stood behind a wood paneled counter that had probably been built when David Lee Roth was leading Van Halen. He was holding a plastic bottle of Vernor's that was sloshing with brown liquid that wasn't ginger ale. He was talking to Devin Wright, or, I should say, he stopped talking to Devin Wright as I entered.

Devin Wright turned to me. He flashed me a smile that was filled with charm and genuine seeming cheer. "Shepherd!" he said. "Good to see you!"

He looked at Scooter Derry. "That's the Niesen boy's lawyer."

Scooter spit into his bottle. "We met."

"Oh right, right, you both texted me." Devin Wright strode straight over and offered me a squeeze of a handshake. "What brings you here? Checking the scene again?"

"I wanted to check on information with Mr. Derry."

"Mr. Derry? Scooter, are you putting on airs when I'm not around?"

"No, Mr. Wright. I didn't know he was coming."

"Well, murder certainly has priority over my little business. How's the case looking, Nate?"

"I'm still trying to get my bearings, Devin."

Devin Wright chuckled. "See, that's a sign of a good lawyer, Scooter. They don't give you anything unless they have to." His face turned serious. "Tommy hasn't given you any more trouble, has he?"

"No."

"Good. We tolerate a good bit of mischief up here, but you should be able to get a beer and a sandwich without getting jumped."

"I haven't complained any, Devin."

"No, no you haven't. I can't say I wish you luck, but I do hope you come back when things are less…heated."

"Thanks." I pointed a thumb over my shoulder. "I didn't mean to interrupt. I'll wait outside until you're done."

"No, no, we're finished. Right, Scooter?"

"Right." He punctuated it with a spit.

"You'll let me know?"

"I will."

"See you, Nate. Don't forget that beer I owe you at the Beach-Head before you go."

I nodded, and Devin Wright left in his Expedition.

I turned back to the desk. Scooter greeted me with silence and a spit.

"I wondered if you had a chance to look at the contents of the units that burned," I said.

"That's private."

"Did the fire department ask for that information?"

"You'd have to ask the fire department about that."

"But they would have asked you, right?"

"I don't want to get in the middle of a fire and murder investigation."

"That's literally exactly where your facility is—between an alleged fire and a supposed murder."

He jerked a thumb at the Carmody house. "That pile of ash ain't 'supposed.'"

"Do renters have to declare what they store?"

"No."

"And you said you don't have any cameras here?"

"Nope."

"How about a list of items they're not allowed to store?"

Scooter pointed at a plastic bin attached to the wall labeled *Terms for Rental*. I took one of the papers from the pile inside.

"Are your unit walls just metal? Seems like that would make it hard for the fire to spread."

Scooter said nothing.

"Do you have the insurance claims the renters filed with you?"

"Haven't found them."

"Did you give it to the police?"

Scooter stared, silent. I stared back. Scooter spit.

"That's how it's going to be with everything?"

Scooter spat again.

"Thanks. I'll talk to you soon."

As I left, I thought it was clear that I was going to get stonewalled, by the prosecutor and the town. Normally, I'd be able to use subpoenas and motions and discovery to force people to comply with the process. I was still going to do all of that—in fact, Emily was doing it right now—but the problem was that all of that took time, and I was running out of it. I was just over two weeks away from trial and there were still some answers I needed to prepare our case.

I needed reinforcements. So I made a call to make sure they were on the way.

26

"Couldn't wait to see me, Shep?" said Olivia.

"What do you mean?"

"Brad and I are on the road right now." Dr. Brad was her rock-climber boyfriend who practiced cardiology in his spare time.

"You're already coming up here?" I said.

"Are you kidding? This one drags me all over God's creation to climb rocks. When he heard I'd be working on a case that was just a stone's throw away from Sleeping Bear Dunes, he couldn't get packed fast enough."

"There aren't any rocks there."

"No, but there are dunes and bluffs and trails and, unfortunately, he's actually been listening to me so 'cross-training' has entered his vocabulary."

"Careful what you wish for, Liv."

"Don't I know it. Why the call?"

"You know how you said you may need to have your feet on the ground up here to investigate?"

"Sure. I was thinking the week before trial."

"Can you move it up?"

"What's happening?"

"I'm getting stonewalled, and I don't have time to unstone it with paperwork."

"So you need an unstoning expert?"

"Looks that way."

"Or you need *the* unstoning expert."

"I need the expert."

"Lucky for you, I packed extra. I had a feeling things might be going that way. Monday soon enough? Brad and I have plans through the weekend."

"That's plenty, Liv. Thanks. I'll have Cyn arrange for a place for you to stay."

"Brad already booked us a VRBO house north of you. I think it might be better if people don't necessarily know I'm part of the team."

"Good idea. Word's been traveling fast. Send me the bill."

"Done."

We hung up. I was still under the gun, but I felt better about my odds of finding out what I needed with Olivia fully on the job.

It was late afternoon when I got back to Cyn's condo and found her standing on the porch talking to Emily.

"What's this?" I said.

"Emily was just telling me that she thinks she changed her mind about going home." Cyn would never go so far as to frown, but her arms were crossed.

"Are the subpoenas done and delivered to the process servers?" I asked.

Emily nodded. "Yes, but I can still get started on—"

"—That was the only thing that needed to be done in the next 48 hours. Go home."

Emily scowled. "Don't force the patriarchy on me by making me tend to my wedding."

"I don't care how you spend your time, but we're at a natural break point. We've just sent out a bunch of things to a bunch of people for a bunch of information we don't have. Their responses are going to shape our case. Preparing before we know what those facts are is a waste of time and might predispose us to reach the wrong conclusions.

Emily frowned at me.

I smiled. "And, from a purely selfish perspective, I don't want your mother to kill me."

Emily looked an appeal to Cyn.

Cyn shrugged. "Nathan's in charge of the case. And he's not wrong."

Emily's phone buzzed from her pocket.

"Who's that?" I said.

Emily didn't check. "Spam."

I grinned.

"Fine." She turned and went back toward her condo.

"Sunday night," I said.

"Sunday afternoon."

"Sunday night."

"Bye."

Her door shut.

I turned to Cyn. "What about you?"

"I'm flying back to Minneapolis."

"Getting some time at home?"

She shook her head. "Partnership meeting tomorrow."

"You don't Zoom that?"

"Sometimes. The timing works out here."

"They have you attend those?"

"Some key employees, yes. I'll be back Sunday too."

"Good. Safe travels."

Twenty minutes later, Emily was pulling out of the driveway.

I felt better that her bag must have already been packed. Cyn followed five minutes after.

I sat in the family room of my condo, went to make some dinner, and realized I had nothing to eat. I decided to go into town for a bite before getting back to work.

~

I'M SIMPLE, I would have just picked up a sandwich from Maggie's, but it closed mid-afternoon. There was a Meijer and an IGA on that side of town, but I honestly didn't feel like making anything, so I kept going down Main Street, skipped past a couple of fast-food restaurants and three brew pubs, then whirled the steering wheel to grab an open spot when I saw the sign for *Thai Garden*.

The street was busy, most of the spots were full, and the lights inside showed a packed house. The hostess told me that she was sorry but there would be an hour wait for a table but that, yes they did indeed serve takeout that I could order from the app, wait by the bar, and have my food to go in about twenty-five minutes.

I thanked her, stepped aside, and struggled for a couple of minutes to load the app, then ordered. Once dinner was in the hopper, I found a place at the bar, ordered a beer, and waited.

I hadn't had much downtime. It was good to take a breath. I didn't think about the case specifically, but instead, just let it bounce around in there a little.

I had finished my beer and was considering another when a voice said, "I'm glad to see you're branching out."

I turned to find Maggie next to me. It took me a beat to recognize her out of context—styled short black hair, long earrings, and a dark shirt and jeans instead of her green "Maggie's" uniform—but there was no mistaking her smile.

I smiled. "I didn't have a choice. My usual place had the audacity to close for the night."

"Kids today. No work ethic."

I nodded. "Do you know a man can't even get a good pastrami sandwich this hour of night?"

Maggie shook her head. "You'll have to plan ahead and order extra. What'd you get here?"

"Spicy green papaya salad, Pad Thai, and green curry chicken."

"All for you?"

"I thought I'd live the high life."

"I'm surprised to see you out and about."

I pointed. "Just waiting for some takeout."

She nodded. "It's worth it."

"Is it always this crowded?"

"During the summer and fall tourist season. It's not too hard to get a table here in the winter."

"I suppose not."

"Will you be here that long?"

I shook my head. "I'd guess three weeks or so."

She smiled. "Almost a month? I'd better order more pastrami."

"Our table's ready, Maggie," said another voice I knew. "Who's this?"

Devin Wright walked up. He'd traded his denim oxford out for a black one, and his beard looked newly sharpened as he put a hand on her shoulder.

"I was just chatting with a new regular customer, Devin."

Devin Wright did a double take, and his face went from grim to a smile. "Shepherd! If you're a regular, then you must have good taste." I got the old squeeze handshake again.

A whiskey appeared on the bar. Devin Wright took it, sipped, and said, "Do I need to be jealous?"

"I don't know," said Maggie. "Nate, are you planning to try to convince me to take on a partner and expand to a second location in Glen Arbor?"

"I'm afraid my money's all tied up in pork bellies."

Maggie held out her hands. "There you go, Devin."

"That's not what I'm doing, Maggie." He smiled. "How dare you?"

"Hmph. Is that a prospectus in your pocket or are you just happy to see me?"

Devin Wright gave his whiskey a casual wave. "Good ideas and good money make good partners, Maggie."

"If I were looking, I'm sure that would be true, Devin." She turned back to me. "Where's the rest of your crew?"

"They took the night off. My associate, Emily, is getting married at the end of the month, so she has a few details to finish up."

"You all are a long way from home, aren't you?" said Devin, sipping.

"Not really, no."

"I'm sure things are different up here than what you're used to downstate."

I smiled. "The pastrami is better up here certainly."

Maggie smiled and tipped her head.

"Did you find what you were looking for at the U-Store the other day?" Devin said.

"Not really, no."

"What was it? Maybe I can help."

I thought, decided it was no secret, then said, "I'm trying to find out what was in those units that burned."

Devin nodded. "The contents? Why's that?"

"So I can trace how the fire spread."

"Seems fairly obvious, doesn't it?"

"It is. I'm just checking all the boxes."

"That's good business, I suppose?"

"Scooter wasn't very helpful."

Devin smiled. "No, I don't imagine he would be, but he might not know much. People can be private about that sort of thing up here."

Maggie laughed. "Tommy Chase hasn't been. He's been telling everyone who'll listen that the Mission Road Fire screwed up his biggest job."

"How so?" I said.

"He had some supplies, flooring I think, in there. Now he can't do the job until the replacement floor comes in."

Devin Wright swirled his whiskey. "Did Tommy say who the job was for?"

Maggie nodded. "John Warhelm's place over at the Bluffs."

Devin Wright winced. "Ouch."

"What?" I asked.

"I can't imagine John took the delay well."

"Who's John Warhelm?"

"Someone with enough money to be used to getting what he wants," said Devin, shaking his head. "That's Tommy, though. It's always something with him." He smiled and pointed at me over his whiskey. "As Shepherd knows."

"So Tommy is in construction?" I asked Maggie.

"Construction's too strong a word," she said. "Carpet installs, painting, clearing land, whatever he can find. Anyway, I'm sure he'd tell you all about it if you asked.

"I'm not so sure," I said and made a show of rubbing my jaw.

Maggie laughed again. "That's right, you two have met. Well, all of Northlake isn't like that, Nate."

"I'm sure."

"Are you here by yourself?" said Maggie. "You're welcome to join us."

Devin Wright looked far less enamored with the idea than

Maggie, but to his credit, he gave me an easy smile and said, "Please do. My treat."

Right then, the bartender deposited a bag onto the bar. "Here's your dinner, sir. Do you need anything else?"

"No, thanks," I said, picked up the bag and stood. "Looks like I'm all set," I said to Maggie. "Thanks, though."

"Lunch tomorrow?"

I smiled. "I'd say the odds are high."

Devin Wright gave my hand a quick shake and said, "Good to see you, Shepherd," and before I could say "You too," he had one hand on Maggie's back and was guiding her to their table.

I left them to their date or their expansion discussions, and I believe that I wasn't any more sure of which one it was than they were.

27

I followed up my Friday night takeout with Saturday morning coffee and work. I was reviewing photos of the Mission Road site—the drive-in to the U-Store to the Carmody house—when Bret Halogi called me.

"Bret, good timing. I was just looking at the photos."

"Now's a good time then? I wasn't sure since it's Saturday."

"Every day between now and trial is a good time."

"You said you have an expert who will say that it's unlikely that the SafeBoom target started the fire at the drive-in?"

"Yes."

"I agree with her."

"Him. But I thought you didn't have an opinion about whether SafeBoom targets can start a fire?"

"I don't. I have an opinion on what set the bushes on fire."

I sat up. "What?"

"Gasoline."

"What do you mean?"

"I mean the ammonium nitrate from the SafeBoom target didn't set those arborvitae bushes on fire. Gasoline did."

"How do you know?"

"From samples taken at the drive-in. There were traces of gasoline on the movie screen fragments and the bushes. That was consistent with the burn pattern too. I believe the gasoline was used to set the bushes on fire and from there it was off to the races."

"Stupid question, but there's no gasoline in a SafeBoom target, right?"

"Of course not."

"Just making sure. So this is a source totally separate from the SafeBoom target, right?"

"Right. Someone used gasoline to start the fire on the bushes."

"Why haven't I heard about this?"

"Because there's no fire investigation report. I found it by looking at the debris sample directly and cross-checking with the State's lab testing."

"Okay. How certain are you that gasoline was used?"

"Ninety-nine percent."

"Based on the testing?"

"And based on the fact that they found a plastic cap with gasoline on it."

"What?"

"It was in the debris they collected from the site. Looks like the cap was from a gallon of milk. I'd say that's how the gas got there."

"So that's how the initial blaze started. What about how it spread?"

"I haven't gotten that far. Do you have a list of the storage unit contents for me?"

"Not yet."

"I need that. I'll run my own tests on the rest of these samples, but I wanted to let you know about the gasoline right away."

"Thanks, Bret."

"No problem. Get me the contents."

As she hung up, I gnawed at the new problem. The Safe-Boom target didn't start the fire, gasoline did. But who used the gas? Kevin Niesen? Could he have used the vandalism to start a fire on the screen, not knowing it was his own son who'd done it? But there was no clear motive for that since the insurance wasn't enough to replace it.

I didn't know how it fit together, but I could see the first glimpse of a defense in the case. If I could break the initial chain of causation, if I could show Brock didn't start the original fire, none of the subsequent damage, or the murder, could be laid at his feet.

I was still gnawing at it when I went to pick up my lunch.

~

"Pastrami, rye, Swiss, mustard, hot?" said Maggie, pointing.

I smiled. "Please."

"I carry a wide variety of other sandwiches, you know."

"I'm sure."

"Branching out wouldn't hurt you."

"I'm sure it wouldn't, but you've already got this one half built."

Maggie smiled. "I know a lost cause when I see one."

"Ouch. How was dinner?"

"Great. I tried a *new* dish. You should've joined us."

"I didn't want to third wheel your date."

"It wasn't a date."

"Does Devin know that?"

Maggie wrapped the sandwich with three expert folds and a flip. "I know that, and that's all that matters, isn't it?"

"I suppose that's true."

"He's trying to talk me into expanding. I don't want to manage another location, and I don't want a partner, but he's a good customer, so I thought I'd humor him. On the business discussion."

"Got it."

"Sides. If you say salt and vinegar chips and an orange, I might scream."

I put a finger to my chin. "Fine. Salt and vinegar chips and an apple.

She shook her head and grabbed them. "He had some thoughts on your case, Devin did."

"Oh?"

"He wondered if you were going to be able to show what had burned in the units."

"Why?"

"Curious, I think." She rang me up. "And concerned."

"Concerned?"

Maggie nodded. "That some hotshot downstate lawyer was going to figure out how to get Brock off the hook."

"Why does he care?"

"Those deaths hit us hard up here, Nate. All of us."

Maggie smiled as I paid but it didn't reach her eyes just then.

"I'm only trying to figure out what happened, Maggie."

She nodded. "Okay." The full smile returned. "We're closed tomorrow. What are you going to do?"

"Starve probably. Have a good weekend."

"You too."

PART IV - POSITION

28

Late that afternoon, I made my way up to the North Hills Farm Winery to meet my family. I did indeed go up and down some hills until I found the entrance, which led me up another hill, a steep one, to the long, flat building that sat at the top.

Now you might be thinking that Michigan is a land of ice and snow and that northern Michigan is even icier and snowier, so how can there be wineries up there? I can only tell you that the northwest corner of the Lower Peninsula of Michigan has a strip of land near Lake Michigan where the lake creates a zone that is perfect for growing grapes. I don't know all the whys and wherefores, but I can tell you that there are a bunch of vineyards in the region that produce good grapes that turn into good wines, especially whites, and that I'd just arrived at one such place.

I parked in the half-full grassy area and walked over to the building. I skipped the part that housed the tanks and barrels and walked through the official tasting room to an outdoor sitting area that overlooked the hills and the vineyards. It faced north, so the sun was setting on our left but the crisp air and the sharp, late light on cultivated fields and northern woods was beautiful.

"Hey, Shepherd!"

A woman with a shock of wild blonde hair stood and waved from a set of wooden Adirondack chairs and a rough-hewn table. I went over to my sister-in-law Izzy and received a hug, followed by a hug from my mom, a handshake from my dad, and a nod from my brother Mark. Mark, Izzy, and my mom had little flights of wines in front of them while my dad had a water.

"You've lost weight," said my mom.

"Mom, it's barely been two weeks."

She shook her head. "You're not eating."

"I am. There's plenty of great food up here."

She raised her chin. "That doesn't matter if you don't eat it."

I'd fought that battle and lost enough times to say, "Make the trip up, okay, Dad?"

"Don't change the topic to me, Son."

"Can't a son ask after his pop?"

"Not to get out answering his mother's questions, no. Your turn."

My dad's skin wasn't as tan as usual, but he'd gained some weight since the last time I'd seen him, and he looked stronger, almost back to normal.

"What'd they say last week?" I asked.

My dad gave me a glare.

"His kidney function keeps improving," my mom said. "There's a good chance they'll take him off dialysis at the end of the month. If he behaves."

My dad raised his water to me.

"How was the walking around today?" I asked.

"Fine," he said.

"What'd you see?"

My mom and Izzy jumped in and were in the middle of

describing the strip of shops in downtown Northlake when our server, a woman who looked to be in her twenties, said, "How did you like the sampler? Did you find something you like?"

"I'll have a glass of this one!" said Izzy.

The server nodded. "The Pinot Blanc. Excellent."

After she'd gone around the table, the server said, "And you, sir?"

I'm not much of a wine guy so I looked at Izzy. "What do you think?"

Izzy tapped each glass. "Yes, no, yes."

I smiled. "I'll take one of those."

The server stared at me for a moment, then nodded. "The Riesling. Another water for you, sir?"

"Please," said my dad and the server left.

As she was walking back to the main building, which was behind my parents, I saw a woman get up from another table, go over to the server and grab her arm, then point at us. When the woman saw me looking at her, she dropped her hand and turned her back but, judging from the head bobs, she was still talking to the server.

The server nodded, then disappeared into the building. My family's backs were still to her, so they didn't see the woman as she scurried back to her table.

There was more conversation with my family about the downtown shops, including one that featured wooden bowls of all sorts, which my mom found particularly enthralling, before she said, "You've been up here for two weeks, Son. Is there anything we should see?"

I didn't think burned out drive-ins and ruined storage units would be high on the chamber of commerce list of attractions, so I said, "I've mostly been working on the case, Mom."

"Right," she said but clearly didn't understand how I hadn't had time to open my eyes to my surroundings.

"How's the case going?" said Izzy.

"Fine. Busy."

"Are you going to win?" said Mark.

I paused. "This is going to be a tough one."

I was spared a discussion of arson by our server. She brought a tray of drinks and handed them out. "Would you mind if I cash you out?" she said. "I'm about to go off shift."

"Sure," said Mark. "I've got it, Dad."

The server handed Mark the electric pad and Mark stuck his card in.

"Oh wait, Nate didn't get his drink," said Izzy.

"I'm sorry," said the server without looking at me. "Let me check." She looked at the pad. "I didn't enter it, I'm sorry." Again, she didn't look at me. "Would you like me to reopen it?" she said to Mark.

"I won't miss a Riesling, Mark," I said.

"Sure?" he said.

I nodded as I looked past the server to where a woman, the same woman, was talking to what looked like a manager. And pointing at me. The manager's face was a mask.

Mark paid, the server left, and we sat and talked for another half hour.

A new server never made her way over.

We reached the point where we had to decide whether to find a new server for another drink or leave. My dad, although he wouldn't admit it, was getting tired from the day, so they decided to pack it in. I was just as glad because I knew a new server wasn't coming and I don't think they'd noticed. They asked if I wanted to join them for dinner, but I'd decided they were going to have a better experience without me and begged off for work.

"Well, this was wonderful," my mom said on the way out to our cars.

"Very scenic," I said.

"There's one good view after another out here," said Izzy.

"What's the plan tomorrow?" I asked.

"Your father wants to get a view of the Lake over on the Bluffs, then I'd like to stop at one of the orchards up here and load up for the trip home. I've been checking all these reviews, but it's so hard to tell which ones are good when you haven't been there."

Out of habit, I started to say I'd been working too much to sightsee, but then I smiled and said, "Actually, I know a great place."

29

I was supposed to meet Olivia the next night, Sunday, at Cyn's condo to strategize on getting her going on the case. After my last few experiences in town, though, I changed plans, texted her, and drove twenty-five minutes north to meet her in the town of Glen Arbor.

Glen Arbor is located on Big and Little Glen Lake and, if you haven't seen it, the water is what can only be described as Caribbean Blue. It's also a great base of operations if you're going to explore the Sleeping Bear Dunes National Lakeshore. Which, of course, Dr. Brad and Olivia had.

I met Olivia at Art's Tavern, right there on the main drag. Given the time of day and the season, it wasn't too busy, so I spotted the bleached white hair and half-mirrored glasses right away. I joined her.

"No Dr. Brad?" I said as I sat.

"He left. He's on call tomorrow so we hit the Dunes Hiking Trail early."

"Yeah? How was that?"

"The guide says it's hilly with all sand and no shade as you cross nine hills and the dune plateau. Apparently, it's hot and exhausting with no water except for Lake Michigan itself."

"And?"

Olivia grinned. "It was glorious."

"I imagine so."

"The guide was incomplete though."

"Oh?"

"Yeah, it said to take water, sunscreen, hat, shoes, and a snack."

"That sounds pretty thorough."

She shook her head. "It didn't mention that you should take a weighted backpack for the best workout."

"That does seem negligent of them."

"Fortunately, we planned ahead."

"Thank goodness."

"You should've come."

"You know I would have if I wasn't working."

"Lies flow so easily from your lips." She pointed around the bar. "So why the location change? You know I would've come down to your place."

"I'm starting to become known in Northlake."

"Aren't we full of ourselves."

I told her about getting protested by Kim Tripp, getting popped by Tommy Chase, and getting ignored by our server the night before.

Olivia pursed her lips. "You may be right."

"I'm pretty sure I am. I think you'll have better luck if people don't see us together and you keep your base up here."

We took a quick break to order smoked trout dip and grilled whitefish sandwiches, then she said, "Sounds like my first priority is to find out what was in those U-Store units."

I nodded. "I've made no headway on that. Devin Wright is the owner, but I think the manager, Scooter Derry or the tenants are our best bet. I've subpoenaed the information, but it's going to take too long, and I haven't had time to independently dig into things."

Olivia nodded. "I'm on it. I also have some info for you on the drive-in. Kevin Niesen has sold it."

"He has? I hadn't heard."

"It just happened."

"Who's the buyer?"

"An LLC. I haven't had time to track down who owns it or find what they intend to do with the drive-in property yet. That's not the interesting part though."

"What is?"

"Niesen was still carrying a mortgage on the property. A small one but still on file."

"Not a surprise."

"No. But he paid it off right before the sale."

"Okay."

"With proceeds from an insurance payment. Which appeared to be enough for him to accept a lower sales price and get out from under the property."

"How in the world did you find that out?"

"The real estate agent community is a generous one."

"You're a real estate agent now?"

She sipped her lemonade. "I certainly can appear to be."

Our smoked trout dip came, which was delicious in case you're wondering.

"That has to be a coincidence, right?"

Olivia shrugged. "It could be."

"It's his own son that's on the hook."

"He is."

I thought. "But it ties in with expert testimony I'm developing."

"How so?"

"I've got an exploding target expert who'll say that it was unlikely that the SafeBoom target Brock shot set the bushes on fire. And I have a fire expert who'll say that the fire in the bushes was accelerated with gasoline."

Olivia's eyebrows arched over her glasses. "Kevin Niesen had already put the drive-in up for sale when Brock blew a hole in the screen, right?"

I nodded. "That's why he did it."

"So now Niesen is stuck having to fix the screen if he wants to sell it."

"Which will be expensive."

"But maybe if the whole screen is gone—"

"—He could just use the insurance money to knock down his mortgage instead."

Our whitefish sandwiches came. We ate a few bites, thinking.

"It's not nothing," I said. "But I'm not sure it's something."

"Are you sure?" said Olivia. "All you have to do is raise doubt. Motive and causation might get you most of the way there."

"But it's his son. I think the jury's going to want more."

Olivia chewed, then said, "If this theory is true, Kevin Niesen didn't mean to frame his son for murder. He just meant to teach his son a lesson and get some insurance money for a screen. The deaths were an accident."

"I would need to put him there, at the drive-in. We already know there's no security footage. Can you look into it?"

"Done. So it sounds like Kevin Niesen's whereabouts and the contents of the U-Store are my first priorities?"

"Please. What's new on social media?"

"Kim Tripp is posting six or seven times a day to anyone who'll listen. Judging from the number of comments, she's gaining traction."

I nodded. "Any calls for vandalism or violence?"

"What do you mean?"

I told her about the vandalizing of the orchard and about my run-in with Tommy Chase.

Olivia looked thoughtful. "She's been calling for a boycott of the propane business and the Orchard. She's figured out that the Orchard sells its apples to an outfit called Midwest Fruit and is pressuring them. She's definitely trying to hurt them financially."

"From what Kevin and Dagmar tell me, it's working."

Olivia looked thoughtful.

"What is it?" I asked.

"Some of her posts are pretty provocative."

"How so?"

"Slogans like 'the fires of hell aren't hot enough for a baby killer,' animations of Brock and his parents laughing in front of flames, a cartoon lawyer—who bears a striking resemblance to one of the people at this table—walking into court with a bag overflowing with cash and bills falling out of his pockets."

"I see."

"And the word 'evil' gets thrown around a lot."

I nodded. "So no direct calls for violence but plenty of incendiary comments. Sorry."

"The pun is excused. It was the best word to describe it. I'll keep you posted."

We finished our sandwiches and were waiting for the bill when she said, "Your dad seemed to handle the weekend okay."

"Oh, did you see him?"

"Brad and I stopped by their B&B last night."

"That's a little bit of a drive."

"Not that far."

I took the check. "So Dr. Brad just happened to come up with you this weekend for some hiking on the same weekend that my dad just happened to take his first trip away from home, eh?"

"Coincidences are funny that way."

"Dr. Brad didn't happen to take dad's vitals, did he?"

"You know Pop would never allow that."

"But if anything went wrong, his cardiologist would just happen to be a stone's throw away?"

Olivia shrugged. "I guess I never thought of that. Your parents are on the way home today, right?"

"Should be heading back now. Just like Dr. Brad."

"Huh. We all set?"

I put the signed check back in the plastic folder with the pen. "We are."

"Thanks for dinner."

"Sure. Thank Dr. Brad for me."

"For hiking with me? I suppose, but he's the one who's lucky."

We left.

∽

I WAS STILL DRIVING BACK to Northlake when my mom called.

"Hey Mom? Are you on the way—"

"Nathan David Shepherd, what's wrong with you?"

This, as you may imagine, was not a good sign.

"A lot of things, I expect."

"Don't you play smart with me, young man."

"Mom, could you narrow it down a bit?"

"We went to Golden Apple Orchard today like you suggested—"

"Oh good! Did you get the apples you were looking for?"

"Of course we did, it was an orchard. And some cider too.

And we met Dagmar Niesen who is just the most lovely woman."

"Good."

"We were only going to buy a bag or two, but there was no one there even though it was a glorious afternoon, and their hayrides were empty, and there was no line for cider, and so we ended up with a couple of bushels of Honeycrisp and Gala and a special Golden apple that's like no apple I've ever tasted before."

"Sounds like quite the haul."

"I'll be baking pies 'til Christmas and the grandkids will have apples in their lunches. And don't try to distract me! Nathan, there was no one there!"

"I figured. That's why I sent you. And because of the apples of course."

"Because of this case you're working on?"

"Yes."

"What in the world is it? Dagmar assumed I knew, and it seemed rude to ask."

I paused, then said, "Her son is accused of starting a fire that killed a young firefighter and a child."

"Did he mean to? Kill them?"

"No, but it doesn't matter if he set the fire on purpose."

"Did he?"

"I'm sorry, Mom, but I really can't talk about it."

"How are you going to explain it to a jury if you can't explain it to your mom?!"

I smiled. "I think it's possible that something or someone else started the fire, but I'm still working on it."

"Sounds like you better work harder."

"I'm trying, but I'm busy being scolded by my mother for something."

"Right."

"And I still don't know what that something is. Are you mad I sent you to the Niesen's Orchard?"

"Of course not! That poor woman needs all the help she can get and these apples, well, I'm going to make Shirley Dalrymple absolutely weep with envy when I put those Goldens in a tart."

"Then you're mad at me because...?"

"Is it true that you've only been to see that boy once?"

I blinked. "What?"

"Have you only been to see Brock Niesen one time since you've been up there?"

"Well, yeah, since I met him, I've been investigating—"

"—Nathan, we raised you better than that."

I have to be honest; I've been on the receiving end of the blunderbuss from my mother a few times and more often than not I've deserved it, but it had been years, and I still didn't really understand what she was so fired up about.

"It's going to be a tough case, Mom, but I'm putting together the best defense I can given—"

"—I'm not talking about your case! I'm talking about your client!"

I still didn't get it. "What do you mean?"

"The boy is fifteen! And he is in jail, an *adult* jail if I understand it correctly, isolated and alone and probably scared out of his mind."

"Right, that's why I'm working all the angles on the case to give him the best shot at getting out of there."

"You need to help take care of that boy, Nathan David. All of him."

"Mom, I'm his lawyer, not his guardian."

"Don't you lawyer up with me, young man! Dave, here, you talk to him."

There was a clatter and some mumbling and then my dad said, "Hello, Son."

"Hi, Dad. How're you feeling?"

"Fine. Your mother and I weren't Cade and Olivia's guardians."

I didn't say anything. Neither did he.

A moment later, I heard their voices, faintly.

"What did he—?" said my mom.

"He understands," said my dad.

"Oh good." Her voice became louder again. "Well, honey, we're about to hit the turnoff here, so I better pay attention so that we don't end up in Grand Rapids."

"Dad let you drive?"

She cackled. "Dr. Brad's orders."

"Olivia said they stopped by yesterday?"

"Oh yes, it was nice to see them. He really is a charming young man."

"He is."

"All right then, we're going to go. I'll text you when we get home. And thanks for pointing us to such a lovely orchard."

"Sure, Mom."

She hung up.

I stared at the phone.

When Cade and I were freshmen in high school and Olivia was a sophomore, something happened to them. They don't talk about it so it's not my place to tell you here, but Cade and Olivia ended up on their own, in part because Cade has always presented as larger and older than his years and in part because Olivia has always been Olivia, even back then.

We'd always been friends, Cade and I in particular, but after that we began to see more of them. I remembered food drop-offs from my mom that morphed into regular meals at our house. I remembered my dad being late because he'd stopped after his shift to replace a headlight on Olivia's car or to show Cade how a tripped circuit panel worked. And I remember that was the year when holidays and Sundays at our house increased by two.

I remembered that Cade and Olivia were on their own, but they were never alone. My mother, my father, and Sheriff Warren Dushane were always there, and they had worked a long time to pick up the pieces.

And the law had nothing to do with it.

As soon as I arrived back at the condo, I opened my laptop. The first available time for me to see Brock Niesen was the next morning at 7:30 a.m.

I took it.

30

I'd just reserved my time with Brock at the Sable County Jail when Emily burst into my condo without a knock.

"How are things, Boss?"

"Hey! I didn't expect you 'til later tonight."

She blew one of her bangs up out of her eyes. "If I'd stayed any later, my mom would've had nine more things for me to do, so I made a break for it."

"You abandoned Josh?"

Emily waved a hand. "He has everything under control. The man's a saint. And the luckiest man in the world, of course."

"That goes without saying."

"That better not have been sarcasm, Boss."

"My comment was totally and utterly genuine, Emily."

"Seriously, what's going on with the case?"

"Seriously, is everything okay with the wedding?"

Emily flopped down and dropped a backpack next to her. "My mom's freaking out that I might not make the rehearsal dinner." She ticked off a finger. "She also insisted on another fitting for my dress because Olivia's pre-wedding workout plan apparently works too well. Aunt Clare isn't talking to Aunt Ellen so now the family seating is all jacked up and Mom didn't care for my suggestion that we just cut all the collateral family who can't behave. And Dad keeps pissing her off by offering me money to elope."

I smiled. "And Josh?"

"Is the best. He's taken care of everything that I care about."

"Tell your mom not to worry about the rehearsal dinner. Even if the trial isn't quite over, you can go."

Emily's eyes grew hard. "Don't do that."

"Do what?"

"I'm a trial lawyer just like you."

"I know that."

"I'll handle my responsibilities here."

"I know that too."

"Don't take them away. I'll manage my mother."

"Done."

"Besides, you're going to let me do the closing."

I smiled. "No, I'm not."

"The experts then?"

"I'm handling their fire expert. You'll have some of the U-Store tenants for sure. Probably a first responder."

She shook her head. "That's not enough."

"You're going to be busy handling all the causation briefing and arguments."

Emily sat up straight. "We have a causation defense?"

"I think we might."

I told her about my call from Bret Halogi and how she thought the fire at the drive-in was caused by gasoline rather than the SafeBoom target.

Emily saw where I was going right away. "So if Brock didn't start the fire, he didn't commit the murder."

"Right."

"But that would mean, what, that his dad did it?"

"Maybe. It looks like he had a motive."

I told her about his sale of the drive-in and how the insurance payment just happened to cover the remaining balance on his mortgage.

"But his own son? Would he do that?"

"I have Olivia on it. I think we're going to have to put Kevin Niesen at the scene for the jury to believe he could have done it."

"For sure." Her eyes lit up. "Causation arguments like this are tricky. We're going to have to show a complete break in the chain to get Brock off the hook."

I nodded. "If his act combines with another act to cause the death, he's still guilty. We'll have to show that he didn't contribute to the Carmody house fire at all."

Emily nodded, thinking. "So we have to show that he didn't start a fire at all with his SafeBoom target or that the fire he started went out."

"Basically."

She stood. "And here I thought you were just lounging around up here unsupervised while we were gone. I'll get to work on the law."

"Thanks."

As Emily turned to go her phone rang. She looked at it and swore.

"Mom?"

"Sixth time since I left."

"Whatever you need."

"Just the peace and quiet of a murder trial, Boss." She answered the phone and left.

From what I could hear, there was a budding orchid emergency.

～

Cyn arrived back a little later. Emily and I had decided to eat dinner on our own, so I was cleaning up the remnants of chicken thighs and rice when there were three sharp raps on the front door. As I let her in, she strode to the dining room table and said, "I assume you have time to talk?"

"Just finished dinner. Want anything?"

"I ate on the way."

Cyn sat down at the table, so I joined her. "How'd your meeting go?" I asked.

"That's what I wanted to talk to you about."

"Sure." We sat. "There were some developments while you were gone. I can email the Firm if they want a status update."

She lifted a red eyebrow but shook her head. "No. It's not that. They know the case is well in-hand."

"I don't know if I'd go that far."

"I would."

"You know best. So what's up? Is there a problem?"

"No, Nathan. The opposite in fact. Why are you smiling?"

"I haven't been called Nathan this many times in one day since grade school."

She cocked her head.

I waved her off. "Long story. What is it?"

"The partnership at my firm discussed a number of issues. One of them was expansion."

"Oh?"

She nodded. "They're adding several attorneys. One would be based in the Midwest."

"Which state?"

"Any one of eleven. Where the attorney has his or her home base is not particularly relevant."

"So what does this have to do with our case?"

"Nothing. It has to do with you and whether you'd be interested."

"In joining Friedlander & Skald?"

"Yes."

"I don't have a national level practice, Cyn."

"The firm wouldn't be interested in your practice, Nathan. It would be interested in you."

"To do what?"

Cyn shrugged. "You know what I do?"

"Yes."

"That."

It was my turn to raise an eyebrow. "Drop in as a hired gun to try cases?"

"We prefer trial specialist to hired gun. But yes."

"Murder?"

She shrugged. "Cases with high stakes that justify our fee. Murder is certainly one that comes up."

Cyn's face was a green-eyed, calm, unreadable sea.

I nodded. "So win the case, get a job offer?"

She shook her head. "The firm knows what we're up against here. They were simply discussing options as part of our planning. And my opinion carries some weight."

I smiled. "They let you pick who you work with?"

She didn't smile as she said, "Yes. And I'd like you to consider it."

My smile broadened. "To quote a good legal assistant friend of mine, who says you can afford me?"

Cyn's face remained serious. "We can." Then she told me what they paid. "That's the base. There are stipends and bonuses for travel. And wins. Again, as you know."

I blinked. "Did you say—?"

"I did." She stood. "Consider it, please."

"I will. Thanks."

She nodded. "I saw your updates to the file on the plane. You're meeting with Brock in the morning to follow up on the gasoline theory?"

I was too stunned by the money to add that I was also checking in on him, so I just said the easiest thing. "Yes."

"I'll see you tomorrow when you get back."

She left, and I sat there for a while, not thinking about the case.

31

I returned to the Sable County Jail proudly managed by Sheriff Sean Sizemore early Monday morning. It was far busier than I expected, and it wasn't until I recognized the looks of angry wives, disappointed parents, and consoling friends that I realized that this was when the bill for the sins of the weekend came due.

I followed a guard down a hall, which was if anything more spotless than it had been the last time I'd been there, as he led me to a room where Brock Niesen waited. His limbs seemed longer and his hair shaggier than the last time I'd seen him. His acne was worse, his face more pale, and the dark smudges under his eyes a deeper black. He sat, slouched back, arms crossed, and only looked up for a second before he ducked his head back down.

"Hey, Brock."

He gave me a little salute.

"How're you doing?"

"Like balls in a bag."

I have to admit, I had no idea what that meant, but I decided it was bad. "Are they treating you okay?"

He looked at me. "I'm in jail, genius."

"Are you still in isolation?"

He nodded.

"How often are you out?"

Brock shrugged. "Once a week, I think. It's hard to keep track exactly."

"By yourself?"

He nodded again.

"Outside?"

"If there's no lightning."

"What can I get you?"

He looked up. "A phone."

"That's not allowed."

He put his head back down. "Then why did you ask?"

"Do you like books?"

"Not really."

"If they let me bring you some, I will."

He shrugged again.

"If there's anything else you need, let me know."

Brock didn't respond.

"And if they give you phone time and you want to call, just—"

"—I call my mom."

I nodded. "If you ever can't reach her then."

"Sure. These talks are so fun."

I couldn't blame him. I hadn't really reached out in a social way since I'd arrived in Northlake, so I shouldn't, and didn't, expect googly-eyed appreciation from my first attempt. Still, I had to start somewhere.

"There's been a development in your case," I said.

"Yippee."

"At trial, I'll be putting on experts to talk about the fire. We have a theory about how you didn't cause it."

He looked up.

"I have one guy, a DNR officer, who will say that a SafeBoom target won't start a fire, or at least that it's not likely to start a fire when it was placed so high above the bushes. I have another expert, a fire investigator, who will say that the bush fire was started with gasoline."

Brock scowled. "That matters?"

I nodded. "You shot the SafeBoom target, right?"

He nodded.

"We have evidence that the target didn't start the fire, the gasoline did."

"And because I shot the target...I'm not responsible for the gasoline?"

"That's the theory."

Brock looked confused. Causation arguments do that to people all the time, so I continued.

"There's a thing called causation in the law. You have to do the thing that causes the harm, or in this case, the death, to be found guilty."

"You're saying that because I shot the target, and the target didn't start the fire, they won't find me guilty?"

"That's what we'll argue to the jury."

"That could actually work?"

"It could. Nothing's guaranteed, but I've seen Officer Wald testify before and he's very effective. He did some great research showing that SafeBoom targets won't ignite the bushes in a situation like this. I think the jury will listen to him."

Brock's eyes had a light to them I hadn't seen until then. "That seems crazy but, if that's the law, okay."

"There's a down-side."

"What?"

"I have to investigate your father."

The scowl again. "What for?"

"Someone had to have started the gas fire. He's the most likely suspect since he got the insurance money from the screen being destroyed. We have to provide evidence that your dad, or someone, whoever, put the gas there at the drive-in."

Brock shook his head. "Wait, I thought you said I wasn't responsible because I shot the target?"

"Right. It looks like the fire was started with gasoline so whoever did that would be the one on the hook. That's why we need to prove that your dad or someone else was there."

Brock's confused look was back as he said, "But I used the gasoline."

"What?"

"But you said that's okay because I shot the target."

"What do you mean you used the gasoline?"

"I put it next to the target."

My stomach dropped. "You put gasoline next to the target?"

"Yeah."

"Why?"

"I wasn't sure if I had enough SafeBoom to put a hole in the screen, so I taped the gasoline to it."

"Did you use a plastic milk gallon container?"

"How did you know that?"

"The lid…it doesn't matter."

"But I shot the target, not the gas container. So we can still argue that I didn't mean to hurt anybody, right?"

"No, Brock."

"But you said—"

"—Forget everything I said."

Brock's face fell. He recrossed his arms and his eyes seemed darker for having been lit up a moment before.

"I was assuming someone else doused the bushes in gasoline and lit it," I said. "The fact that you lit it when you blew up the target means it's not a defense. It's just more potential evidence that you…it's more evidence that we have a problem."

"So I'm still screwed."

I gathered myself and showed him a calm face. "It just means I have to keep working on other angles is all. I'll be back in a couple of days."

"Why?"

"To see how you are."

I stood and summoned the guard.

Brock didn't look up as I left.

∾

I LEFT the jail with nothing. Nothing in my hands, nothing in my case, no defense, nothing. Even my conversation with the guard left me nothing—no Brock couldn't have a phone; no he couldn't have electronics; no, he couldn't be taken out of isolation; no, he couldn't have more time outside; no, he couldn't have additional visitors besides his family or me.

It didn't get better in the car. I called Officer Wald. I asked him if it was possible for a SafeBoom target to ignite gasoline. He said not every time but often enough. He asked why that was relevant. I asked him, hypothetically, what would happen if a gallon of gasoline were taped to twenty-five pounds of SafeBoom in circumstances like our case. Officer Wald said that could easily ignite arborvitaes.

I thanked Office Wald, told him I wouldn't be calling him at trial, and asked him to send me his final bill.

I called Bret Halogi next. She wasn't in so I left her a message that we'd had a new development that I'd tell her about when we spoke. Technically, the other side can't get communications between an attorney and his expert, but with important—or damning—evidence, I was always cautious, i.e. paranoid.

Finally, when I'd pulled back into my condo driveway, I texted my oldest nephew, Justin. He was in high school that fall. I asked him what someone his age would do to pass the time if he wasn't allowed electronics, a phone, or sports equipment, and didn't like to read.

The request seemed even dumber when I wrote it out like that, but I sent it anyway.

There was a small truck in front of Cyn's condo. Two guys were loading monitors and boxes. I went over as Cyn walked out. I pointed in question at the guys.

"We're two weeks out," she said. "I've rented us an office next to the courthouse."

The two weeks comment must have shown on my face.

"What?" she said.

"Our defense theory is sunk."

"Why?"

We stepped away from the men and the truck before I said, "Brock strapped the gasoline to the SafeBoom. Wald can't help us and is out."

Cyn's face didn't twitch, but she crossed her arms.

"Right."

Cyn blinked once, then said, "So what's our theory?"

"I have a call in to Halogi. I haven't called Olivia yet to have her stop figuring out where Kevin Niesen was that night. And, honestly Cyn, I'm not sure yet."

Cyn nodded. "Grab your stuff. You and I can go to the office right now."

32

Our new workspace was on the third floor of an old brick building in downtown Northlake right next to the courthouse. It had one office, which Cyn insisted I take, and a large common area with workstations for Cyn and Emily at either end with a large war room table in between. The three of us were sitting at the war room table, my phone in the center on speaker as we spoke to Olivia.

"So you can stop the search on Kevin Niesen's whereabouts that night," I said.

"You're sure Brock started the fire?" said Olivia.

"Yep. I talked to Officer Wald on the way over here. The SafeBoom could ignite the gas, and we know the gas started the fire."

"So now what?" said Emily.

"I still think our best shot is to try to find a break in causation between the drive-in and the house, then argue that the deaths weren't Brock's fault."

Emily shook her head. "It's going to be pretty tough to find a definitive break in the chain, Boss."

"It doesn't have to be definitive," I said. "It has to be probable. Liv, any luck on finding out the contents of the storage units?"

"No luck, Shep."

I swore.

"Just my skill."

I took a deep breath. Emily giggled.

The phone stayed silent until I said, "What did you find, Liv?"

"I'm glad you asked. So the first unit was rented by Benny Bird of Benny Bird Barbeque. He apparently competes on the barbeque circuit and stored his equipment there."

"What kind?"

"He claims a smoker, a tent, and a trailer were all destroyed."

"Doesn't seem super flammable."

"No, but the cords of wood he had stacked along the side of the unit were."

"Along the side—that was his wood piled by the arborvitaes?"

"Yep."

"Okay. What about the second unit?"

"That was rented by your friend Tommy Chase. He used his unit as storage for his business."

"I understand his work is a little all over the place?"

"It is from what I can see. In this case, he claims he had some flooring in there."

"Let me guess, the flooring was wood?"

"Raw planks. It went up like matchsticks."

"Great. And the third unit?"

"The third belonged to Naomi Hoppel. She's an older woman who'd just made the switch to assisted living and so her family had put all of the things from her house in there after she moved."

"All of the things?"

"Furniture, knickknacks, and all the other things you accumulate over forty-odd years in one house."

"How full?"

"To the brim, according to her claim."

"Sweet Jesus, it's like the whole thing was tinder."

"Pretty much," said Olivia. "Then outside Mrs. Hoppel's unit was the motorhome, which belonged to Devin Wright, which we already know exploded and spread the fire to the Carmody house."

We were all quiet for a moment. "Seems like a pretty logical row of dominoes, doesn't it?"

"It does," said Olivia.

"Liv, do you have a list of the contents of the U-Store units that's admissible?"

"The lack of trust in that statement is concerning, Shep."

"But hardly uncalled for."

"True, but in this particular case, unjustified. They've all filed claims loss forms that you'll be able to use. I'll send them over to you."

"Anything strike you in the claim forms?"

"Not particularly for the units, no. Devin Wright made a claim for his motorhome that was pretty significant, but since the vehicle was only two years old and the way prices have gone up, he lost his ass buying a new one. Which he already has."

"So no motive to torch the motorhome?"

"It doesn't look like it."

"Keep checking the others?"

"Of course."

Olivia cleared her throat.

"Great work," I said.

"Thanks, Shep."

I tapped my pen on the table. "All right, we know what kind of fuel was in and around the storage units. Let's talk about time.

Have we received any responses to our subpoenas that give us a better timeline?"

Cyn nodded. "We've received the dispatch reports and the fire department records. At 11:31 p.m. on April 9th, 911 received multiple calls reporting an explosion but no location. We have nothing then until 1:37 a.m., when a man named Patrick Dabbs called 911 reporting a fire on Mission Road, which he described as involving the Lakeside Drive-In and the U-Store lot."

"Not the house?" I asked.

"He didn't mention the house in the call. The fire department was dispatched and arrived at the scene at 1:49 a.m. The engines focused on the Carmody house, and Maura Carmody and her two daughters were removed by 1:54 a.m. The house collapsed at 1:56 a.m. Eli Tripp and Liam Carmody were later found to have been in the house at the time of collapse."

I nodded. "So we have almost two and a half hours from the time Brock blew up the screen to the time the house collapsed. We need to fill in that gap best we can. I'll talk to Halogi to see if that makes sense timing-wise for the spread of the fire. Olivia, can you check on where this Patrick Dabbs was that night?"

"On it, Shep."

"Emily, how are you coming on the motion to keep Brock's high school bonfire out?"

"Just finishing it up. I'll email it to you today and we can get it filed tomorrow."

"Great. Liv, anything happening on social media?"

"Kim Tripp is posting even more. She has some mini-virals going on. I wouldn't be surprised if they start picking it up downstate on traditional media. On the plus side, I don't think anyone has associated me with the lousy troll of a downstate lawyer who's made his gibbering, slobbering way into town."

"Slobbering?"

"She's upped her meme game."

"That's to be expected," said Cyn. "We often have that problem when we come in from the outside."

"Any tips for how to handle it?" I asked.

"Yes. Win."

I raised an eyebrow. Cyn didn't smile.

"All right," I said. "We can't create any doubt about Brock blowing up the screen and starting *a* fire. Let's keep looking at everyone and everything between the drive-in and *the* fire."

"So we don't have anything?" said Emily.

"Not yet, no."

"Then what's our theory of the case? What's our plan?"

"Right now? To cross-examine everyone to create reasonable doubt."

"That sounds like winging it."

"You make it sound so half-assed."

"Isn't it?"

"Yes, but you don't have to make it sound that way." I stood.

"Where are you going?"

"To my office to look for the other half."

Although Olivia chuckled before she hung up, Emily shook her head and muttered something about a whole-ass mess as I shut the door.

33

I was staring at the new dispatch records which gave us the skeleton of our timeline when Bret Halogi called me back.

"What's the problem?" she said.

"How did you know there's a problem?"

"When a lawyer calls me and doesn't say why, it means there's a problem he doesn't want a record of."

"There's a problem. My client is responsible for the gas." I told her what Brock had done.

Bret Halogi was quiet for a moment before she said, "My understanding is that the exploding target will sometimes detonate the gas."

"That's my understanding too."

"Often enough that we can't eliminate that as the cause."

"That's also my understanding."

"And that makes it likely that your client started the fire that ignited the bushes."

"Right."

"So that eliminates your primary theory of the case."

"It appears that you understand completely."

"Am I still on the case?"

"Yes."

"So you want me to examine every other link in the chain that eventually leads to the Carmody house?"

"Exactly."

"I've looked at it some, but I'll need to do more."

"I've been able to get a preliminary list of the storage unit contents that we know of so far. Cyn is sending it now."

"That will help. I have ash and debris samples from each unit already. They're limited, but I'll confirm the state investigator's testing." She paused. "This is going to require a lot of extra work, Shepherd. And expense."

"I understand. Spend the time and the money. And send me an interim bill if you need to."

"No, Friedlander & Skald is good for it. I just wanted to make sure you knew."

"Thanks. We also have a more detailed timeline from the dispatch reports. It looks like we have an explosion at 11:30 p.m., a 911 call reporting the fire at 1:37 a.m., fire on the scene at 1:49 a.m., and collapse of the Carmody house at 1:56 a.m."

"You'll send those to me?"

"They're on the way."

"I assume the Carmodys called in the fire?"

"No. It was a man named Patrick Dabbs."

There was silence at the other end of the line.

"What is it?" I said.

"Something's been bothering me. I don't think it's relevant to what caused the fire but, based on this timeline, it's bothering me more."

"What's that?"

"You mentioned the SafeBoom explosion at 11:30 p.m. I think it's also likely that at least one of the gas tanks in the motorhome exploded too."

"Makes sense."

"Even if it didn't, the fire itself would have generated flames, light, noise from the units collapsing, all that stuff."

"Okay."

"No one was at the drive-in so it's possible the fire could have spread to the U-Store units before anyone saw it. But by the time all of the units were on fire, it would have been visible for anyone to see. And if a motorhome exploded right next door—"

I sat back as what she was saying sunk in. "—It should wake you up, even if it is the middle of the night."

Bret Halogi nodded. "So why were the Carmody children still in the house?"

We were both quiet for a moment.

"Would it have been a normal explosion?" I finally asked.

"I don't know what you mean by 'normal,'" she said.

"I mean it would have made a noise, a boom. It wouldn't have been a silent whoosh or something?"

"There would have been plenty of noise when the tank went up."

We were both quiet a little more.

This time, she broke the silence. "Like I said, it probably doesn't have anything to do with causation—"

"—But it's definitely something I need to check. Thanks, Bret."

We hung up and I went back out into the common room to Emily and Cyn.

"I just talked to Halogi," I said.

"And?" said Emily.

"She agrees we're screwed on the gasoline and will look for something else to try to break the chain after that."

Emily blew a bang up into the air.

"She also brought something up that I think is important, but I'm not sure how it fits."

"What?"

"When she heard the dispatch timeline, she pointed out that it would have taken time for the fire to consume the U-Store units and time for the fire to spread to the Carmody house."

Emily frowned. "Right."

"And that the last part of that would have been noisy. Especially if the motorhome tank blew."

It took Emily two seconds. "So why were the Carmodys still in the house?"

"Exactly."

Emily thought. "But does it matter? Whatever it was probably isn't going to excuse Brock, or whoever started the fire."

"You're probably right. But we don't have much and I think we should know. What do the run sheets we just received say?"

We both turned to Cyn.

Her fingers flew over keys before she scrolled and said, "The paramedic run sheet just says that when the rescue squad arrived, they treated Maura Carmody and the girls for smoke inhalation and burns, then took them to the hospital."

"Do we have any medical records for Maura Carmody and the girls?"

Cyn shook her head. "We subpoenaed them. We got a letter from hospital counsel that we're not entitled to them without Mrs. Carmody's signed written authorization."

"I can research whether that's true—" Emily said.

"—Don't bother," I said. "It is. I had to go round that course during my old firm days. If she doesn't consent in this circumstance, we don't get them."

"What do you think they show?"

"I have no idea."

I thought. "But I do have another one for our investigator."

∾

A COUPLE OF DAYS LATER, I was working in the office when I received a text from Olivia. As I headed for the door, I told Emily I was leaving.

"Where to, Boss?" "To talk to a paramedic."

Emily's eyes widened. "You're going to Eli Tripp's firehouse?"

"No. I'm desperate, not suicidal. But firemen do have to eat."

34

Northlake has a couple of the national chains scattered about, but by all accounts, Laramie's was the best specialty grocery store and butcher shop in town, so it was the perfect place for me to stock up my condo for the things I'd eat during the trial. And, if it just so happened that a certain creative and thorough investigator had figured out that it was also where the local firehouse bought its grub, well, what greater testament to quality can you get?

I waited in the parking lot, which had a steady stream of ten to twelve cars at any one time, until a rescue vehicle, a small ambulance type, pulled in and parked. I gave the two men in their blue uniforms a little time, then went in.

The store wasn't too big, about a double unit in a strip mall wide, with metal aisles of groceries on one side and a butcher's counter on the other. I saw one blue uniform disappear down an aisle of breads while another waited in line at the butcher counter. He looked young, in his twenties maybe, with short red hair, freckles, and the unusual tan line right across the nose of someone who spent a good amount of time outside with a ball cap on.

I stepped into line behind him just as the man behind the counter said, "Are you here to pick up the order, Grant?"

The paramedic nodded. "For the week, yeah."

"I don't think it's quite ready, let me check." The man disappeared into the back.

"A whole week for a firehouse?" I said. "I can't imagine that bill."

The paramedic turned, revealing the name *Ferris* stitched onto his shirt and I silently praised Olivia once again for her skills.

Grant Ferris was one of the paramedics on the Carmody run.

He grinned and nodded. "It's not too bad divided twelve ways."

"Is that how many are on your shift?"

Grant Ferris nodded. "Give or take." He grinned. "Never hurts to make more, though. It won't go to waste."

"I bet not. What if you have a run while you're cooking?"

"That's why we do everything low and slow. It's pretty rare to get a fire that keeps us out long enough to ruin a good pork butt or chili."

Grant Ferris's smiled faded.

"Right," I said. "The Carmody fire."

He nodded. "It ruined…a lot of things."

"I'm sorry for what you lost."

"Thanks." Grant Ferris looked into the back, but the butcher hadn't returned.

"But you did save Mrs. Carmody and the girls."

He shook his head. "We can't take credit for that."

"What do you mean?"

"That was all Sasha."

It took me a moment to place the name. "The oldest daughter?"

Grant Ferris nodded. "If it wasn't for her, Mrs. Carmody and Felicity would be—"

"—Here you go, Grant," said the butcher as he came back carrying a big box. "It's the usual plus the extra ground chuck you ordered. Need anything else?"

"No, thanks, Rip."

Grant Ferris turned, holding the box in both hands, nodded to me and went to meet his partner.

"See you next week," said Rip and turned to me. "Now what can I help you with, si—"

Rip of Laramie's Specialty Goods and Butcher Shop stopped, pulled his head back, and said, "You're the lawyer."

"I'm *a* lawyer. Could I have six of the bone-in chicken thighs, please?"

"I'm sorry, but we're out."

I stared at the little bin filled with them under the glass, then pointed. "I'm sorry, I meant those there."

"Those are reserved for an order. Sorry."

"How about the breasts next to them then?"

"We're out of those too."

I nodded. "Is there anything under the glass that's not spoken for?"

"I don't believe so, no."

"Expecting a new shipment?"

"Not anytime soon, no."

I nodded. "I expect I'll have more luck at a bigger chain then."

Rip stared. "They tend to care less about the local market. Thanks for stopping by."

I walked to the door. Grant Ferris had deposited his box in his partner's cart and was pointing at me as I left.

I didn't really blame any of them.

I was an outsider after all.

I WAS STILL THINKING about what the paramedic had said about Sasha Carmody and wondering where I was going to find chicken as I pulled into one of the street parking spaces in front of our rental office.

A woman stood in front of our door, holding a sign.

"Justice for Eli! Justice for Liam!"

Kim Tripp had found where we worked.

I thought about parking around back, decided it was too late, and opened the door. Kim Tripp increased her volume.

"Justice for Eli! Justice for Liam!"

I made eye contact with her, nodded, and walked past.

Kim Tripp with her mousy-brown hair, red plastic glasses, and cropped jeans, stepped closer and shouted louder, her face twisted in fury.

"Justice for Eli! Justice for Liam!"

Some spittle hit my shirt, not with insult or intent, but as a by-product of passion and rage.

I've mentioned that this section of Northlake has a strip of shops. People on the sidewalk were stopping now, watching.

I opened the door and went in. The door muffled the sound but didn't mute it completely. I heard "Justice for Eli! Justice for Liam!" as I walked up the stairs.

∾

"HAVE you met our new welcoming committee?" said Emily.

"I did. When did that start?"

"Right after you left. Word travels."

"Everywhere, apparently." I told her about Laramie's. "I'll run to another store tonight if you need anything."

"Thanks, I'll send you a list."

"I did get one thing there."

"I thought you were shut out?"

"Not from the store. From Grant Ferris, the paramedic who treated Maura Carmody and her girls."

"What?"

"Maura Carmody didn't get them out of the fire. Sasha did."

Her eyes widened. "The daughter?"

I nodded. "How old is she? Eight?"

"Yes."

"What does the run report say?"

Emily pulled up the run report and spoke as she scanned it. "Adult woman and two minors treated for smoke inhalation, burns, and disorientation at the scene before being transported to hospital for further evaluation."

"Disorientation," I said.

Emily pressed her lips together. "It was the middle of the night. Her house was on fire. That can be disorienting."

"But there's an explosion, the house catches fire, and Maura Carmody doesn't call 911 or get her kids out of the house. Her daughter does."

Emily thought, then said, "It's strange for sure. But I don't know if it matters."

"Me either. But we at least have to know why. We have to get those medical records."

Emily shook her head. "You already said the law's pretty clear. I checked and you're right—we don't get Maura's records unless she consents or we have reasons that don't exist here."

I thought. "The hospital objected to our subpoena. Let's file a motion to compel them to produce the records."

"Are you sure? It's not the best look."

"Are you suggesting the town's opinion of us might drop?"

"Fair."

"Let's see what happens."

35

A few days later, on the Friday morning ten days before trial, Judge Roderick called us in for a final pretrial and a hearing on our motions. Emily and I were there early because I'm paranoid like that. We were the only case on the docket, so the courtroom was empty as we took a seat at the defense table. A moment later, the judge's door opened, and staff attorney Mason Pierce walked out.

Emily walked over as he sat at his desk on the side of the courtroom. "Everything okay with the jury instructions I sent over?" she said.

His faint smile stayed. "Could I open them? Yes. Will the judge use all of them? I can't say."

"Anything else we need to know about the judge's preferences?"

"I'm sure he'll tell you."

"Have you worked for him long?"

"About two years."

"Is this your first job?"

"My first *law* job."

Emily smiled. "Your hands don't exactly say paper pusher."

Mason Pierce smiled back. "This seemed like a better option. How about you?"

"I've been doing this for about a year. I was a prosecutor for a couple of years before that."

"Which one do you like better?"

"I like trying more cases as a prosecutor. I like getting paid more in private practice."

"For sure. I think that's my next step."

"Yeah?"

Mason Pierce nodded. "I've been interviewing."

"You won't regret it." Emily looked at me. "Much."

I saluted.

The court reporter and the bailiff walked in, so Emily came back and took her seat.

"I'm hurt," I said.

She grinned. "So let me do the open."

"I'll get over it."

Astrid Olsen arrived one minute before the hearing was to start, a move I had come to be sure was more designed to avoid a conversation with me than a reflection of her busy schedule. She nodded to Mason and the bailiff, ignored me, and took her seat. A moment later, the bailiff said, "All rise."

Judge Roderick emerged from his office and took the bench. "Counsel, identify yourselves for the record please."

We stood and we did.

"So are we going to trial?" he said.

"We are, Your Honor," said Astrid Olsen.

"Have you made a plea offer, Ms. Olsen?"

"No."

Judge Roderick straightened his glasses with his thumb and forefinger. "Why not?"

"The State does not believe this case lends itself to a plea deal, Your Honor."

"The State has an obligation to conserve resources, doesn't it?"

Astrid Olsen straightened. "The State also has an obligation to expend them where appropriate, Your Honor."

"Make an offer."

Astrid Olsen paused, kept her eyes on the judge, then said, "The State offers defendant the opportunity to plead to one count of arson and two counts of murder."

Judge Roderick looked at me. "Counsel?"

I raised an eyebrow. "So Ms. Olsen is offering my client the opportunity to plead guilty to the crimes she charged him with?"

Judge Roderick looked at Astrid Olsen.

"Yes," she said.

He looked back at me.

"I can't recommend that, Judge."

"Even if it affects sentencing?"

"Even if."

"One of you is going to be disappointed." He straightened his glasses again. "Fine. Let's go through these motions. I'll give both of you an opportunity to revisit this plea issue at the end of the hearing."

That, by the way, is judicial foreshadowing, and it's never good.

Judge Roderick opened a file folder. "Let's start with your motion to change venue, Mr. Shepherd. Am I to understand that you are not enamored with our small town?"

"Northlake is delightful, Your Honor," I said. "But we believe that circumstances have developed in such a way that a fair trial here would be problematic."

"You don't think I can run a fair trial, Mr. Shepherd?"

"I know you can, Judge. But the jury pool is being inundated with materials on social media which—"

"—which we can ask them about during jury selection.

There's no guarantee the jurors are even on social media, Mr. Shepherd. Do you have an Instagram account, Pierce?"

"No, Judge," said Mason Pierce.

"See, there's one and we're not even picking jurors yet."

"Judge, there has also been vandalism to the Niesen family's property and organization of a boycott—"

"I assume the vandalism was done by one person."

"I can't make that assumption, Judge."

"Do you have proof otherwise?"

"No."

"The Court finds that there are no factors enumerated in the Rules which warrant a change of venue here. The Court further finds that the defense motion is untimely and made after the Court's deadline."

"Your Honor, that deadline passed before we entered an appearance in the case."

"Brock Niesen was represented by counsel before you came on the case, wasn't he, Mr. Shepherd?"

"He was."

"And that attorney, Luke Mott, lives here and practices locally, doesn't he?"

"He does."

"The Court presumes that he was just as competent as you, Mr. Shepherd, and as a lifelong resident of Northlake, has at least as much knowledge of the venue as you've accumulated these past two weeks. Motion to transfer denied."

Judge Roderick flipped to another set of papers. "Next, we have a defense motion to exclude evidence of prior acts. Ms. Olsen, what's this about?"

"Your Honor, last year the defendant was convicted of trespassing and criminal damaging. The defense seeks to prevent us from mentioning it to the jury at trial."

"That was a juvenile proceeding, wasn't it?"

"It was, Your Honor."

"How is that relevant?"

"The defendant damaged a landowner's property by burning it."

Judge Roderick did the glasses straightening thing. "Mr. Shepherd?"

"Your Honor, my understanding is that my client was at a bonfire party with a bunch of other teenagers."

"Mr. Shepherd's client started the fire, Your Honor," said Astrid Olsen, "And it damaged the landowner's property."

I shook my head. "If that's a criminal pattern, then high schools across the state are filled with serial arsonists, Judge."

Judge Roderick frowned. "Was a structure damaged, Ms. Olsen?"

"No, Your Honor."

"I'm inclined to see Mr. Shepherd's point unless you have something more."

Astrid Olsen straightened, then glanced over at me, the first time she'd even come close to making eye contact that day, before she looked back at the judge. "It's not the similarity in damage we're interested in, Judge. It's the similarity in ignition."

She stopped.

When the pause stretched on, Judge Roderick flipped his hands out. "Which was?"

"The defendant ignited the bonfire with gasoline."

The judge looked at me.

"That's about as common as it gets, Your Honor. It's hardly a criminal pattern that should be allowed into a murder trial."

Astrid Olsen shook her head. "The fire scorched the landowner's ground and spread to some nearby brush. The fire department was eventually called and they, along with a fortunate rainstorm, were able to douse the blaze before we had an out-of-control forest fire. The defendant has a history of starting fires with gasoline that burn out of control."

"It was a homecoming campfire with half the student body in attendance, Judge."

"It goes to state of mind, Your Honor. The defendant knew what could happen to a gasoline fire that spreads out of control. He'd done it before."

"The two situations are nothing alike, Judge."

Judge Roderick raised a hand. "I'm denying the defense motion to keep this evidence out. But as you know, Ms. Olsen, that doesn't necessarily mean the evidence comes in. This is just a preliminary ruling, and I share Mr. Shepherd's concern that this evidence could unduly prejudice the jury. However, I also see how it may be relevant depending upon the context of how the evidence is presented. Mr. Shepherd, you may renew your objection at trial if Ms. Olsen attempts to admit this evidence."

He flipped another stack of papers and said, "If there are no other issues—"

"Your Honor," said Astrid Olsen, "the defense has attempted to subpoena Maura Carmody's medical records."

"What medical records?"

"From the night of the murders."

"What?" Judge Roderick scowled. "What possible relevance could that have?"

Astrid Olsen shook her head. "None that I can see, Your Honor. The Hospital's counsel hasn't had time to respond yet, so I've prepared a motion to quash that subpoena, which we filed this morning." She handed me her brief and held another up to the judge. "May I?"

He waved her up and took the papers.

"What possible justification could you have for seeking Mrs. Carmody's records, Mr. Shepherd?"

There was no way I'd reveal the reason until I knew if I was going to use it, so I said, "To get a full picture of what happened that night, Judge."

"Mrs. Olsen, am I correct that none of the charges you've brought stem from an injury to Ms. Carmody?"

"That's correct, Your Honor. They stem from the death of her son Liam, the death of Mr. Tripp, and the intentional destruction of a swath of properties."

Judge Roderick shook his head. "I'm not seeing it, Mr. Shepherd."

"Judge, Mr. Tripp and Liam Carmody died in the collapse. We're entitled to information that would shed light on the events leading up to the collapse."

"Just what information about the collapse would Mrs. Carmody's medical records have?"

"I don't know yet, Judge, because I haven't seen them. But if she's going to testify, I should be able to look at records that could contain Mrs. Carmody's narrative of the facts."

Judge Roderick turned to Astrid. "Do you intend to call Mrs. Carmody, Ms. Olsen?"

"Not if I can help it, Your Honor. She's been through enough."

"It sounds like she won't be contributing to the narrative, Mr. Shepherd."

"Maybe not, Judge, but the records might contain information from her, given close in time to the events, that are relevant to the case."

"What possible relevance could these records have to her house burning down?" said Judge Roderick.

"Judge, my client's freedom is at stake. I should be allowed to exhaust all avenues of discovery."

"No, you shouldn't, Mr. Shepherd. The subpoena for Mrs. Carmody's medical records is quashed, and the discovery denied. Mr. Shepherd, I know you didn't have a chance to respond in writing. You may file a motion for reconsideration if you wish. But given our proximity to trial, I suggest you spend your time more productively. Do we have anything else?"

We handled a few minor trial details dealing with timing and filings before he said, "Last thing then, jury selection. Have you read our local procedure, Mr. Shepherd?"

I glanced at Emily, who nodded.

"I haven't yet, but Ms. Lake has, Judge."

"I expect you to be familiar with it."

"Ms. Lake is, and I will be."

"And I expect your questions to be submitted to me by next Wednesday."

I looked at Emily.

"May I?" she said.

"Please."

Emily stood. "Judge, am I correct that we won't be able to ask any questions of the jury at all?"

"That's right, Ms. Lake."

"What if there's additional information that we need?"

"Ms. Lake, I was a prosecutor for twenty years before I donned the robe. I know how to follow up on a problem area. I suggest, though, that you spend some time and attention in crafting your proposed questions."

"No questions at all, Judge?" I asked.

Judge Roderick straightened his glasses and leaned back in his chair. "I imagine this is where you tell me how important it is for an attorney to establish rapport with a jury during voir dire, isn't it, Mr. Shepherd?"

The fact is that's exactly what I was thinking. Voir dire is the time when the lawyers, well, usually the lawyers, question potential jurors to determine if they can serve. More importantly, it's a lawyer's only chance to have an actual conversation with the jurors, to discuss the case and, well, yes, to build rapport. It appeared that Judge Roderick didn't agree with that sentiment, so I said, "I just want to make sure we can follow up on any relevant areas, Judge."

Judge Roderick shook his head. "We don't have some big Lansing or Grand Rapids jury pool here, Mr. Shepherd. We have a bunch of hard-working folks who need to get back to what pays the bills and I'm not going to engage in some downstate nonsense where we spend a week picking a jury. No one here has that kind of time. So you give me your questions, Ms. Olsen will give me hers, and I'll synthesize them so that we get to the heart of the matter. I'll take a break before you have to make your challenges so that you can give me any follow-up inquiries and *if* I think they're worthwhile, I'll ask them. Is that a problem, Mr. Shepherd?"

"Not at all, Judge."

"Good, because Ms. Olsen has found it to be acceptable, sixty-four times, is it?"

"Sixty-seven, Your Honor."

"With no complaints?"

"Not from me, Your Honor."

"And more importantly, no overturning on appeal, is that right?"

"That's right."

"There you have it. Ms. Lake, I look forward to your questions."

"We'll both be working on it this weekend, Judge," Emily said.

"Right. See you in ten days, people."

With that, Judge Roderick stood and left.

Astrid Olsen had her file and was halfway to the door when I called to her. "Astrid."

"What happened with—wait, do you want to record this?"

She looked over my shoulder at where I knew Mason Pierce was sitting.

"Not this time. What's your question?"

"What happened with Maura Carmody that night?"

When she didn't reply, I said, "If it's not relevant, I'm not going to bring it up, but I need the full picture."

Astrid Olsen stared at me. "She doesn't have to give that information to you."

"Then you tell me. I'll accept your representation of what happened."

She didn't blink. "You heard the judge. I don't have to give you that information either."

It was my turn to stare back. "Just like you didn't have to give me your Fire Investigator's report?"

"My Fire Investigator didn't make a report. Was there anything else?"

"I guess not."

She turned and left without another word.

I turned to Mason Pierce. "Does she handle all of her cases like this?"

Mason Pierce stared at me for a moment, then said, "No."

"Is it the downstate thing or something else?"

"Something else. See you next week, Mr. Shepherd. You can email me the copy of your jury questions, Ms. Lake." Then Mason Pierce picked up his file and went into the judge's office.

"You sure are charming them, Boss," Emily said.

"I noticed."

"Hope you have better luck with the jury."

"Me too."

"Or we're pretty much screwed."

I couldn't disagree with her.

36

The last week before trial is a sprint. I try to get into my trial routine—get up at the same time, go in at the same time, eat the same thing morning, noon, and evening. The same philosophy applies to the case materials; we spend time organizing every document, every piece of evidence, every statement, so that we can grab it when we need it. The point is to control the things you can control, so that you are ready when a thing you can't control—a witness's lie, a judge's ruling, or an attorney's ambush—springs at you from out of the tall grass.

I'd forgotten how much easier that part of the process was when I was working with Cyn. Her instincts for organization were unmatched and that skill had only been honed by her life trying one case after another. She was remarkable, she was cool, and she made every task go twice as fast.

Which was a good thing. Because in the week before the Brock Niesen trial, there was more than one tiger hiding in the grass.

Cruel Sentence

I WENT to see Brock Niesen at the Sable County Jail on the Monday before trial. I told him what to expect at trial, made arrangements to get a couple of suits for him from his mom, and generally let him know what our strategy was, which, at that moment, took alarmingly little time.

Brock responded with arm-crossed nods and no eye contact.

When we were done, I said, "Here," and slid five thin paperback books across the table.

"I told you I don't like reading books," Brock said.

"They're not books, exactly. They're manga."

"Manga?"

"Ever try it?"

He shook his head.

"My nephew Justin is your age. He said a bunch of his friends like this one."

Brock peeked at the table. "*One Piece*?"

I nodded. "The adventures of a teenage pirate captain who gains special powers after eating a Devil Fruit."

"Sounds stupid."

I shrugged. "It's the most popular series out there. Thought it might help pass the time."

He picked one up. "There's pictures, like a comic."

"That's what manga is. The series has been going for a long time so there's plenty more if you enjoy it."

Brock shrugged. But he didn't put down the book.

⁓

CYN AND EMILY were deep in conversation when I entered the office. They stopped abruptly and looked at me.

When they didn't say anything, I did. "What's up?"

Emily glanced at Cyn, who remained impassive.

"What?" I asked again.

"We don't have a strategy!" said Emily.

"We have a strategy," I said. "We're going to poke holes in the prosecutor's case, remind the jury that the State has the burden of proof, and argue that there is reasonable doubt."

"But we don't have an alternative explanation for how the fire started."

"Not yet, no."

"We have to have another explanation if we're going to win."

I pressed my lips together, nodded, and said, "There might be a reason for that."

"A reason for what?"

"That we don't have an alternative explanation for how the fire started."

"What?"

I waited.

Emily's smart. It didn't take long. "Because Brock's the one that started the fire?"

"That would be one reason why there's no other explanation."

"But we need another story to win."

"I'm not going to make something up, Emily."

"I don't mean that, I mean…I hate to lose!"

"You and me both. I'll make use of whatever evidence they put in, poke holes in it, call it into question, and hopefully cultivate doubt."

"Does that actually work?"

"Sometimes," said Cyn.

"Rarely," I said. "But it's what we have. For now."

Emily accepted the explanation but didn't look satisfied. I didn't blame her.

I wasn't either.

I spoke to our fire expert Bret Halogi on Tuesday afternoon. "Tell me something good, Bret."

"That's one way to keep this call short."

"Ah. Tell me what you've learned then."

"I'm double checking the evidence samples from each fire source. Since we know Brock used gasoline, I'm focusing on the wood pile, the storage units, and the motorhome."

"Learned anything so far?"

"I've learned that, so far, the evidence supports what the prosecution says burned along the way to the Carmody house."

"What about what burned in the Carmody house?"

"What do you mean?"

I paused, knowing what I could be unleashing. "Have you looked at the source of the fire in the Carmody house?"

"Some. Not in detail though. I was focusing on seeing if I could break a link in the chain of the fire on the way there."

"What if the Carmody part of the fire started in the house? Could we tell?"

"We could have back when it happened. It would be harder to tell now."

"Can you check?"

"Sure. Why?"

"Because of what you said before—Maura Carmody and her children should have been out of that house long before it collapsed. I've just been prohibited from getting to her medical records and now I've learned that it was the oldest daughter that led them out of the fire."

"Interesting."

"And I'm getting the impression the prosecutor knows what happened but isn't saying."

I heard the scratch of a pen before Bret Halogi said, "So an innocent explanation would be they were confused by the fire—"

"—And the explosion."

"And the explosion. Another would be that there was an independent carbon monoxide or gas leak in the house. And the most sinister one is that someone did it on purpose. There's no evidence of foul play, is there?"

"Only the insurance payment to the landlord." I had another thought. "And the fact that the husband was out of town. Neither of which proves anything."

"I'm not going to speculate on something like that, Nate. Not with a woman who's lost her son."

"I don't want you to, Bret. But I'd like you to look at whether the fire in the Carmody house could have started independently."

"You know if there was a gas leak in the house and your client's fire ignited it, he's still not off the hook, right?"

"I know. Could you check though, please?"

"We don't have much time."

"We'll pay the extra charges."

"I don't mean that, I mean I may not find anything. And I still have to work on the chain from the drive-in to the house."

"I realize that. But I have to exhaust everything."

"I'll get on it."

"Thanks."

~

I WENT to see Brock on Wednesday morning and no, I'd never visited a client that many times in the week before trial. I'd also never had a client who was fifteen before.

"Did you bring more?" He said before I sat down.

"More what?"

"Of the *One Piece* manga books?"

"You didn't seem that interested in them last time."

He sat back in his chair, folded his arms. "Figures."

"Fortunately, I didn't pay attention to you." I slid five more books across the table.

Brock sorted through them. "*The Oath*, *The Crap-Geezer*...you got the next five!"

"Wouldn't do to get them out of order."

"How many are there?"

"Around one hundred and three. The one hundred and fourth is out next month. Are they as good as Justin said?"

"Better!"

And Brock told me all about it.

~

OLIVIA CALLED me later that afternoon. "I have a better handle on what was in the storage units."

"Really? How?"

"With documents that you might be able cross examine people with if they don't admit to it."

"Then I might thank you."

"You will. Storage Unit No. 1 belonged to Benny Bird and so did the wood pile. The wood was for his barbeque smoker, and he stored it outside both to season it and because there wasn't room to put it in the unit, which was filled with his competition smoker, trailer, tent, and accessories. He's claiming a complete loss, and that it cost him another barbeque grand championship, whatever that is."

"Alright. I assume it still looks like the insurance is negligible?"

"Right. The smoker's custom built, but he made it himself so the value's sketchy. Not much there."

"And no one's going to believe he set fire to the wood he was storing to burn in his smoker."

"Exactly. Storage Unit No. 2 belonged to Tommy Chase. He mostly lost flooring supplies."

"Like what?"

"Carpet, padding, but more importantly wood flooring. A lot of it."

"I think you'd mentioned that?"

"I did, but it turns out this was a special order. Patagonian Rosewood. He was going to do some big job up at the Bluffs for a guy who was going to redo his whole first floor in deluxe wood until, poof."

I remembered my conversation with Devin Wright and Maggie the week before.

"John Warhelm," I said.

"What?" said Olivia.

"The big job was for a guy named John Warhelm. Sorry, should have told you that. So sounds like it would have been a lot of flooring?"

"Literally tons."

"Did Tommy have the flooring insured?"

"No, Tommy Chase appears to be a fly-by-the-seat-of-your-pants guy. His business isn't licensed, he's not insured or bonded, and he'll tell anyone who'll listen that losing this wood almost put him under."

"So no motive there?"

"Not even a little. It looks like he might have lost his friend and his business in the same fire."

"And Storage Unit No. 3?"

"The Naomi Hoppel Unit. Tell me, Shep, are you familiar with scrapbooking?"

"A little."

"Knitting?"

"Never done it, but sure."

"How about quilting?"

"I've seen them."

"Well, it appears that Naomi Hoppel engaged in the most flammable hobbies known to woman and stored the fruits of her decades of labor, along with a house full of old wooden furniture that she couldn't take to an assisted living facility, in Storage Unit No. 3."

"Sweet Jesus."

"Yep. The fire would've blazed through there like a desert wind. Right to the motorhome."

"And I assume Mrs. Hoppel's goods weren't insured?"

"You can assume that none of it was even insurable. She'll get a few hundred dollars."

"You can't insure memories, I suppose."

"No, you can't."

"So, plenty of fuel for the fire at each stage."

"Yes."

"And no motive for anyone else to start one."

"That's what it looks like. There is an upside though."

"What's that?"

"You now know who *not* to point the finger at."

"I guess I do."

We were both silent for a moment. Olivia was a good enough friend, and investigator, to let me.

"Along those lines," I said.

"Yeah."

"I need you to look closer at the Carmodys."

"At what, exactly?"

"At anything. Everything."

"Out of something more than desperation?"

"Something's not adding up." I told her about the delay getting out of the house, about my conversation with the paramedic, about being shut out on the medical records, and Astrid Olsen refusing to talk about any of it.

"Do you really think something's there?"

"I don't know. But I need to check."

"We need to be careful with this."

"Don't worry—the last thing I'm going to do is point the finger at a bereaved mother."

"Unless you have something."

"Unless I have a dead bang something."

"Understood. I'm on it."

"Thanks, Liv. How's scenic Glen Arbor?"

"Beautiful. I have to come back when I can actually see it."

"You're the best."

"True. Looks like you're going to need to be too on this one."

"That's my impression."

"Don't screw it up. Bye."

∽

That's where we were on Thursday, scrambling to prepare a defense for a trial only four days out. You never feel like there's enough time even under the best of circumstances and this? This definitely was not those circumstances. That day we were just keeping our heads down and plowing ahead—Cyn methodically organizing, Emily writing like the wind, me putting together cross-examinations, each of us squeezing every moment out of the day.

We were considering a group order for dinner when we got word of the fire.

37

By the time I reached the Golden Apple Orchard, the main barn was gone. The flashing lights of two firetrucks revealed firefighters training hoses on a smoldering pile of rubble. As I hopped out of my Jeep, the water from one of the hoses dribbled out, looking like nothing so much as a guy falling short of peeing out the campfire.

The wreckage still radiated heat as another hose kept its stream trained on the jagged beams and charred planks that was all that was left of Dagmar Niesen's primary building—the place where the caramel apples and donuts and cider concessions were sold, where full baskets of her specialty golden apples were displayed, where families could grab empty bushel baskets to go pick their own. The centerpiece of her commercial operation was gone.

The surrounding buildings still stood: her warehouse, her vehicle garage, her specialty gift shop. But the barn was the hub of the Golden Apple experience, and there was nothing left of it but wreckage and ash and smoke.

Dagmar Niesen stood off to one side—tall, straight, arms crossed—staring at the wreckage. Her jeans and flannel were smudged, her thick work gloves covered in black, and her blonde-white hair sprinkled with ash. I made my way around the trucks to her.

"Are you hurt?"

She didn't look at me. "I couldn't get anything out, nothing that mattered anyway. The equipment was all too heavy."

"How did it start?"

She shook her head. "It was going when I got here." She turned to the firetrucks. "It was over by the time they did."

"What do you mean?"

"They didn't show up until the whole thing was gone." She pointed as another hose ran out of water. "And all they did was spit on the ashes." She punctuated it by doing the same.

Two new tanker trucks pulled up. A firefighter who was already there went over and, after some gesturing and talking to the tankers, walked over to us.

"Dagmar, I'm sorry," the firefighter said.

"Took you long enough, Rolf," she said.

"We had another call tonight. We were re-filling when yours came in."

"Convenient."

"Not at all. But true."

She stared at him now for the first time. "You waited until my building had burned, Rolf."

The firefighter stiffened. "We would never do that, Dagmar."

"Yet there it sits."

He shook his head. "You can't fight a fire without water. Do you know how it started?"

"No."

"Our investigator will be out in the morning then."

"Ours will be here tonight," I said.

The firefighter looked at me for the first time. "This is a possible crime scene."

"It certainly is."

"We need to investigate this without the scene being disturbed."

"Then I suggest you get your investigator out here right now."

He stared at me for a moment. "You're the lawyer."

"I am. I take it you're Chief Rolf Hagen. I'd hoped we wouldn't meet until next week."

"This scene can't be disturbed," said Chief Hagen.

"It won't be. It'll be investigated. I hope you participate."

Chief Rolf Hagen walked away. I watched as one tanker was used and the other drove away. When the hose started again on the smoking barn-pile, Dagmar Niesen turned to me and said, "You need to get back to work on my son."

"I will. I'm going to wait until Bret Halogi gets here."

"You already called her?"

I nodded.

"I can tell her everything she needs to know," said Dagmar. "But my son only has you."

I realized that what she said was true and nodded. "Call me if you need anything."

"I won't." She looked back at the ash pile. "I still have the trees."

I texted an update to Bret Halogi, who replied she was on her way, and headed back to the office, leaving Dagmar Niesen standing in the smoke.

∞

Cyn and Emily were still at the office when I returned.

"Is Dagmar okay?"

"She is. The orchard isn't." I explained what I'd found.

"I called Halogi," I said to Cyn. "I assume that's okay?"

Cyn thought, then said, "An initial investigation is worthwhile to see if there is a connection to the case. I'm sure the firm will pay for it. Talk to me before Bret does anything else though."

I nodded. "The Orchard's in trouble."

"How so?"

"People were boycotting, and the crowds were down as it was. It's going to be almost impossible for them to sell there for the rest of the season."

"I imagine so."

"Will the firm or the family or whoever is paying for the case help?"

"I have no idea, Nathan. I, and you, have only been engaged to defend a murder."

"Right. Emily, fire up that change of venue motion again."

"Sure, Boss. Why?"

"If Bret Halogi finds this was intentional, we're going to argue Brock can't get a fair trial in the place where people are setting fire to his orchard."

"Do you think the judge will buy it?"

"No. But we have to try."

∼

THE NEXT DAY, Friday morning, I went to the Sable County Jail to see Brock Niesen for the last time before trial. He was waiting for me in the room. He was slumped in his chair, arms crossed, and he didn't look at me as I came in.

I dropped five more *One Piece* manga books on the table.

His reaction was nothing like it had been two days before. In fact, there was no reaction. At all.

I didn't think that word of the fire could have gotten to him overnight in the jail but clearly I was wrong.

"Hey, don't worry," I said as I sat. "Your mom is fine."

He looked up. "What's wrong with Mom?"

"Nothing. The fire was only to the barn. She's fine."

Brock sat up, eyes wide. "What fire? What happened?"

Apparently, he didn't know about the fire, so I told him.

"She's okay though?" he said.

"Yes. I saw her. Mad, but okay." I didn't tell him about his mom's suspicion that the fire department had delayed, both because I didn't know if it was true and because Brock had enough on his plate.

"I bet." He looked up. "How is she going to sell for the rest of the season?"

"She was still working on that."

Brock shook his head. "This is our busiest time. We sell a lot of our crop by people picking their own and make even more on the concessions. Things were tight as it was."

If his mom hadn't told him about the boycott, I certainly wasn't. Instead, I said, "I'm sure she'll figure it out."

"But she's okay?"

"Don't worry, she's okay." Ready to change the subject, I pushed the manga books farther across the table. "Here are the next five."

Brock slumped back in his chair. "Don't want 'em."

"Really? You seemed to enjoy the last ones."

He crossed his arms and shook his head.

"C'mon," I said. "I'm dying to hear what *The Crap-Geezer* was about."

Brock didn't budge.

"And here," I picked up one of the new volumes. "*The Legend Begins*. Maybe that really gets things going."

"Look inside," he said.

"Well, I think it'll be more fun if you read it."

"No look inside. At the first page."

I raised an eyebrow, then leafed through it. "Okaaay."

"See when it was written?"

"Um, yeah, in Japan, 1997."

"Before I was born."

"Sure, but pirates are always good, right? Especially pirates with special powers."

"He's been writing them for more than twenty-five years."

"Yes."

"Longer than I've been alive."

"By a good bit, yeah."

"But not as long as I'll be in prison."

Ah.

"We don't know that, Brock."

"They say I'm a murderer, right? That I started a fire that killed the firefighter and the little kid. So I should be locked up for the rest of my life."

"We're fighting it."

"Yeah, who did it then?"

"What do you mean?"

"If I didn't start the fire, who did? Because you already told me that if I started the fire, then I'm responsible."

"We don't have to show who started the fire, Brock. We just have to create doubt that you did."

"No one's going to believe that! See this...'" He held up Book 15, *Straight Ahead*. "I haven't read it yet, but it's going to have a good guy and a bad guy and a beginning and a middle and an end, and I'll enjoy it because it will have an explanation. Even *I* know we can't go in there and say, 'Wasn't me.' No one's going to believe that!"

"The burden's on the State to prove that what it says is true, Brock. It's not on us to prove how it happened."

"But we have to! Or nobody's going to believe us."

I was quiet because arguing the burden of proof was not

going to help here. And also, because I was afraid Brock was right.

Brock kept going. "I was reading the first book for, I don't know, the third time because there's nothing else to do in here and because it was good. And I started reading the page that described when it was written, and I realized that it was written all the way back in the 1900s and then I realized that even though they didn't put the English version out for another *six* years, it *still* came out before I was born. And then I realized that even though that was a long, long time ago, all that time, from then until now, is still shorter than the time I'm going to be in prison. I'll read all one hundred of these books in less than a year and I'll still have years and years and years and years to go."

He flipped the book back at me. "He could write another hundred books, and it still won't be enough."

"We're looking at everything, Brock."

He looked up. "Can you tell me we have a chance at all, Nate?"

"Yes."

"Is it small or big?"

Brock was in a bad place, but I couldn't lie to him. I had to see if we could work our way out of this instead.

"It's small, Brock, and it'll be hard to do, but it's there. Do you want to hear what we're going to do?"

For the first time in all our meetings, I had his attention.

"Yes. Please."

So I spent the next hour with him explaining it all—the evidence, the experts, and how we were going to attack them. I didn't give him everything. There were options, potential paths, that I kept to myself, even from Cyn and Emily out of the superstition that giving it voice might speak it into the prosecutor's mind. But I told him a lot and within fifteen minutes, he was invested and asking questions and following along.

By the end of our time, I think he got it. And I think he felt just the smallest bit better. Brock would never take the stand so it wasn't the most efficient use of my time three days before trial, but I knew that Monica and David Shepherd would have approved.

When I left, the sullen look was still there, but the frantic one was gone.

And he kept the books.

I WAS DRIVING from the jail to the office when Oliva called.

"Liv, I was just about to call you."

"Great minds. You first."

I told her about the fire at the Orchard.

She swore, then said, "I can't say I'm surprised. The social media rhetoric is bad. Kim Tripp keeps fanning the flames, but it's burning on its own now. Turns out literally."

"I had a thought this morning."

"Congratulations!"

"Cade still has his airstream, right?"

"Sure."

"How do you think he'd feel about camping in a scenic orchard up north for a week or so?"

"I think if it came with an opportunity to whoop ass, he'd have it hooked up before you hung up."

"Good. I'm pretty sure I can get him paid too."

"You've got enough to do. I'll call him as soon as we hang up."

"Thanks. Why'd you call?"

"I waded through the ownership records of the LLC that bought the Lakeside Drive-In."

"Oh, right. I'd forgotten. Anything interesting?"

"Only if you think Devin Wright is interesting."

"Really?"

"Really."

"That *is* interesting."

"I thought so. Especially when you consider that he bought the drive-in at a depressed price."

"You've given me something to think about, Liv."

"Careful. You're driving."

"Thanks."

"I'll call Cade. Bye."

∽

It wasn't quite lunchtime, but I figured I'd stop at Maggie's and get us all sandwiches on the way into the office. I was between the coffee rush and the lunch crowd, so Maggie was the only one working behind the counter when I arrived.

"Nate Shepherd," she said with a smile.

I smiled. "Maggie…I don't know your last name."

She tilted her head. "It's Day, thank you for asking, Mr. Shepherd. Will it be breakfast or lunch? You have the look of someone who's been up so I'm going to guess lunch for three?"

"Right again, Maggie Day. And a large coffee, please."

"Looks like you could use that first. Drink it while you wait?"

I smiled. "Thanks."

She poured me a cup, slid it into a cardboard holder, and passed it over the glass.

"It'll take me a moment to switch out the lunch trays. That okay?"

"No problem."

I sipped the coffee, which was just the right amount of scorching hot, and watched her work and thought about Brock.

"You're quiet this morning," she said.

I looked up. "Sorry. Preoccupied."

"Ah. Is it almost time for your case?"

I nodded. "Monday."

"I bet you'll be glad when it's over."

I smiled. "That depends."

Maggie nodded. "I suppose it does. We'll all be glad."

Maggie had never really talked about the case itself.

"Yeah?"

She nodded. "It's been hard. On everyone."

"I bet. Did you know either of them?"

Maggie kept her eyes on the trays as she unwrapped lettuce, then three types of cheese slices. "Everyone knew Eli. I know Maura and Noah better." She looked up. "She's had a hard time."

I had lost a wife, but a son? "I can't imagine."

"Will she have to testify? Maura?"

"I don't know. Maybe."

Maggie nodded and focused on a tray of peppers, then pickles. "She'll be a wreck."

I nodded, but I didn't say anything.

"How do you do it?"

I raised an eyebrow. "Represent defendants? Everyone has a right to—"

"No. Immerse yourself in all that pain all the time?"

I thought.

"I'm sorry," said Maggie, her eyes still down.

"No, it just isn't what people usually ask. I guess I would say that I know people who do harder things."

She looked up, nodded. And a man came in the door.

"Hey, Maggie! Serving lunch?"

Maggie smiled. "Just set things up, Trent. Be right with you."

"Cool. You hear someone took a torch to the Niesen place last night?"

Maggie looked at me, then said, "No."

"The main barn at the orchard, I guess."

"Was anyone hurt?"

"No."

"Good."

"Would've served the bitch right though."

"Trent."

Trent raised his hands. "No one was hurt, no one was hurt. But maybe it'll put her out of business."

"Trent, stop it."

"I'm just saying, then she wouldn't be able to pay to defend that murdering piss-ant of hers."

"Trent, I have other customers." Her hands flew as she wrapped the sandwiches.

"What? He don't mind, do you?"

I smiled at Maggie and said to Trent, "You think the kid did it?"

"Hell yeah, he did it. Too bad we don't have the death penalty anymore."

"Even for a kid?"

"A kid who killed a baby? That fire's nothing compared to the one he has waiting for him."

Trent stopped as I paid and took the bag from Maggie.

"If you send me your order, I can bag lunches for you in advance," she said.

"I think I will, Maggie. Thanks."

"I can't wish you good luck."

I smiled. "A good lunch is enough."

She smiled back. "Good lunch."

∽

When I arrived at the office, Cyn said, "How was Brock?"

"A little rough today," I said as I handed out the lunches. "I had to tell him about the fire and our case strategy."

"That would do it," said Emily.

"Speaking of both," I told them about my idea for hiring Cade to "camp" in the Orchard and about Devin Wright buying the drive-in.

Cyn nodded. "We'll pay for Cade."

"Great, thanks," I said.

"I'm not sure the Devin Wright purchase is something," said Emily. "But it's not nothing."

I nodded. "I thought the same."

"All that and still time to stop at Maggie's?" said Emily, as she held up her bag.

"I was doing some jury research."

"And?"

"One potential juror looks forward to our client spending an eternity in hellfire."

"Excellent."

"A more sympathetic one wonders how we can do what we do."

Emily gave a thumbs up. "Super."

Cyn gave me a calm, green stare. "We don't get paid because what we do is easy."

"True. Tell me what you want, and I'll order us trial lunches from Maggie next week."

PART V - SHOOT

38

On the Monday morning of trial, one hour before we were supposed to start, Emily and I were in Judge Roderick's office sitting in front of his desk. Astrid Olsen was in the chair on my other side while Mason Pierce tried, unsuccessfully, to blend in by the wall.

We were arguing.

"Judge," I said. "Someone burned Dagmar Niesen's barn down. I don't know how much more evidence you need."

"Evidence?" said Astrid Olsen. "All I've heard is speculation this morning, Your Honor."

Judge Roderick looked at me. "Do you have evidence that the barn fire was intentionally set, Mr. Shepherd?"

"Yes, Judge. My investigator found evidence of the use of accelerants."

"I didn't see an affidavit attached to your amended motion."

"I just learned on the way here, Judge. I can have it to you by this afternoon."

"This is a delay tactic, Your Honor," said Astrid Olsen. "We have a panel of potential jurors waiting outside right now."

Judge Roderick snapped a look at her. "I'm aware of the

Court's schedule, Ms. Olsen. You say you have evidence that accelerants were used, Mr. Shepherd?"

"Yes, Judge."

"Do you have evidence that someone besides Ms. Niesen used them?"

"Excuse me, Judge?"

"I understand that accelerants were used, Mr. Shepherd. Do you have evidence who used them?"

"Not yet, no."

"Then if there is no evidence that someone at large burned down the Niesen's barn, I don't see how it supports your motion to transfer venue, particularly at this late date."

"But Judge, why would Mrs. Niesen burn down her own barn? It's crippled her."

Judge Roderick straightened his thick brown glasses. "Mr. Shepherd, I know you understand the burden of proof. Ms. Olsen has the burden of proving that your client started the fire that killed Eli Tripp and Liam Carmody. But you're the one coming into my court with an untimely motion claiming that your client is unable to get a fair trial in our jurisdiction because his mother's business was intentionally burned down, so you have the burden of proving that to me. I'm willing to accept your representation that your expert's affidavit is on the way and I'm willing to delay trial this morning so that I can consider the affidavit if, and only if, your expert also has an opinion, to a probability, regarding who started the fire. Does he?"

"She, Judge. And no, she doesn't. There's no way she could."

"Then your renewed motion to transfer venue is denied."

I shifted gears. "What about the additional jury questions we submitted then, Judge? Will you be asking those?"

Astrid Olsen shook her head. "We renew our objections to questions regarding the Golden Orchard fire, Your Honor. They were submitted late—"

"—The fire happened after the deadline!" Emily said.

Judge Roderick raised his hand. "Ms. Lake."

Emily literally bit her lip. "Sorry, Your Honor."

"But more importantly, they aren't relevant to this proceeding. They're simply designed to elicit sympathy for the defendant and his family."

Judge Roderick looked at me.

"Judge, we believe those questions will more accurately reveal the potential jurors' predisposition than questions about where they work and whether they're married."

"I agree, Mr. Shepherd. To a point. Proposed additional questions 1 and 2 are allowed. Questions 3 through 7 are not. Anything else?"

"No," Astrid and I replied.

He looked back and forth between us. "Then let's seat a jury. This morning."

~

VOIR DIRE IS the process where the potential jurors are interviewed to see if they can fairly hear the case and follow the law. That's the grand idea, anyway, but what each side is really trying to do is get as many people as possible on the jury who are going to see the case their way.

Usually, the attorneys ask the questions. This makes it easy to follow up on a topic but, more importantly, it lets us talk to the jurors, get to know them, and helps us figure out who we might be able to build a rapport with. We're wrong sometimes, of course, but it helps us make the choice of who to include and who to exclude. The other side's doing the same thing, so we don't always get who we want, but we usually get some.

Judge Roderick didn't allow any of that. He put twenty people in the jury box and ran through his own list of questions

—marital status, employment, reasons they can't serve, their own encounters with the legal system—all of which I assume he used for just about all of his cases.

He was concise, I'll give him that. He blew through the preliminaries quickly and efficiently and I'm sure he saved time compared to when the lawyers run the process. It was also clear that he was taking advantage of the opportunity to build rapport with potential voters. Effectively, I might add.

Then Judge Roderick asked questions specific to our case. Two members had lost a child. Both thought it would affect their ability to hear the case and were excused. Three had experienced a house fire or had the fire emergency squad come to their house. Two thought they could still hear the case fairly, but the one who had lost her home completely to a kitchen fire did not and was also excused.

That led the judge to people who had met Eli Tripp or knew him personally. More than half of the people raised their hands. The one who had met Eli when he pulled her father-in-law out of a smashed car using the jaws of life and the one who had dated him at Northlake High School were excused. The ones who had seen him play football for the Northlake Frost Giants, who had met him at the Northlake Bass Fishing championships, or had worked with him at the Big Brothers Big Sisters of Northlake all thought they could stay impartial.

Yes, having all of that come out during the questioning was just as bad for us as it sounds.

Fewer people knew the Carmodys. One woman used the same daycare for her kids and so knew how hard all of this had been on the surviving children and the parents. Judge Roderick allowed the woman to explain how hard it had been for her to tell her own four-year-old that Liam Tripp had gone to heaven before he excused her from serving. One man knew Noah Carmody because they'd worked for the same long-haul trucking outfit. He was excused, more because he was scheduled to be on the road that week than because he knew Noah.

That was the extent of people who knew the Tripps or the Carmodys directly. One woman raised her hand and explained that she didn't know Eli Tripp, but she did know Karen, his mother. When Judge Roderick asked if it would affect her, the woman said she didn't think so but then looked down. When Judge Roderick asked her why she hesitated, she admitted that she had stood with Karen outside Laramie's and that she may have, at one point, held a sign and shouted for justice for Eli, but it was just that one time. Judge Roderick thanked her and excused her without asking us.

Which led Judge Roderick to ask whether, even though they didn't know the families personally, the potential jurors had heard about the Mission Road Fire and the deaths of Eli Tripp and Noah Carmody.

Every hand went up.

Judge Roderick nodded and observed that this was a small town and word of such things would naturally get around and that this had been reported on a little more than what they all were used to in this pleasant corner of the state. He asked who could put aside what they'd read in social media or seen on the news or heard around town and decide the case solely and only on the evidence these fine lawyers presented to them in this courtroom.

All but two raised their hands. Judge Roderick questioned the two. One couldn't get past the thought of little Liam Carmody dying in that fire. The other thought Brock Niesen was a delinquent and wondered where his parents were. Both were excused and Judge Roderick turned to the question of Brock, his mother Dagmar Niesen, and his father Kevin Niesen.

Most of them had gone to the Lakeside Drive-in at one time or another, but no one knew Kevin directly. Not quite as many had gone to the Golden Apple Orchard, but a few of them knew Dagmar and all of them had a favorable impression of her with one lady in particular mentioning that she must be heartbroken at what her son had done. The lady was excused.

Only one person had heard of Brock Niesen before the events of the Mission Road fire, but unfortunately, that man's son had been suspended for two baseball games because the boy had attended a bonfire party that Brock had been behind. I only had to stand for Judge Roderick to cut off the irate dad's comments, but enough came out that everyone on the panel was aware that Brock had some kind of history and all in all may not have been a *good kid*.

After that juror was excused, the judge called us up, took any proposed follow-up questions, and I mentioned that he hadn't asked our proposed questions about the fire at Golden Apple Orchard. To his credit, the judge agreed and asked if any of them had heard about the vandalism at the Golden Apple Orchard, including the signs and the fire. It turned out word had gotten around and most of them had. Everyone said that they could still be impartial. One older gentleman raised his hand and asked if Brock had been in jail when the fire at the Orchard was set. The judge thanked the gentleman for his service, excused him, and told the jury that it was conclusively established that Brock did not start the fire at the Golden Apple Orchard and that Orchard fire was not to play a role, at all, in their deliberations in this case.

Finally, Judge Roderick explained that while Brock Niesen was a juvenile, he was being tried as an adult, and asked if everyone could assess the evidence presented to them and reach a verdict without regard to Brock's age. When one woman raised her hand and asked if that meant an adult sentence would be imposed on Brock, Judge Roderick told her that the jury should not consider the potential sentence since that was his job but simply assess the evidence presented to it by both sides as to whether a crime had been committed. When she muttered that she sure hoped so, the woman was excused.

When the jurors all agreed one more time that they would limit their deliberations to the evidence presented, Judge Roderick had Mason Pierce take them back to the waiting area and told us that since he'd already discharged anyone with an obvious prejudice, we could go ahead and use our peremptory challenges to pick our final jury.

Cyn and Emily and I all huddled with Brock around our grid, deciding which of the potential jurors we would get rid of with our peremptory challenges. After we'd made our first pass at it, I motioned for Dagmar Niesen, who'd been sitting in the first row, to join us. I explained what we were doing and asked if she had any insights on any of the potential jurors.

She did. We had already flagged a handful of people, but Dagmar took the red pen out of my hand and checked one, two, three, jurors right across the grid.

When I nodded and asked why, she said, "Comment at the grocery store, post to Facebook supporting the Orchard boycott, and a complete jackass."

"Good with those?" I said to Cyn and Emily.

"Yes," said Emily.

"As long as they're after these two," Cyn said, pointing.

"Agreed. Brock, how about you? Any other thoughts?"

Brock was wearing a blue suit that had probably fit three months ago but was now the slightest bit short at the sleeves. I'd asked Cyn to replace it, but she declined saying she thought that poor fit actually made him seem younger.

I had to agree as Brock tugged down at one sleeve and stared at the grid. He looked young. Young enough that he could be facing fifty years in a little cement room. Maybe even seventy.

"I don't know, Nate," he said finally. "They all seemed kind of mad."

There was no hiding that part. All of them knew about Eli and Liam's deaths. I'd caught more than one judgmental or skeptical or distrustful look in our direction as Judge Roderick asked his questions. I'm sure that seemed mad to Brock.

"We just need people willing to hold the State to its burden."

"They all think I did it."

"I don't think that's true, Brock."

"You think I did it."

At the defense counsel table before opening statement is no place to express doubt, so I said, "I don't think you did it, Brock, and I don't think the State can prove it."

Brock tugged at his suit sleeve again and looked down. "What you guys said is fine, I guess."

We all nodded, and I set our preferred order of challenges.

We used all but one of them. Astrid Olsen passed the last three times with hers. In the end, we had a jury that cut both ways. There were two guys who hunted and shot sporting clays and had even shot exploding targets themselves—they might think that no one in their right mind would think a SafeBoom target could lead to murder or might be angry that basic gun safety hadn't been followed. There were three parents of teens and preteens who might sympathize with a careless teenage Brock or be unable to look past little Liam's death. There was a young man whose parents had divorced who might understand Brock's pain or might view a divorce as no reason to blow things up. They were all like that, each with a factor that could push them either way. I suppose that's the point of the whole exercise so I would have felt okay about the jury except for one unavoidable, ever-present thing.

They all knew of Eli Tripp and Liam Carmody. Every one of them. It was too small a town for it to be otherwise.

Once they were sworn in, Judge Roderick thanked the remaining panel members for doing their duty, excused them, then said to the jurors who'd been selected, "Why don't we take a ten-minute break and when you come back, we'll have opening statements."

39

"Murder is not an accident," said Astrid Olsen.

She was wearing a pale suit the color of sea ice that mirrored her eyes. Her white-blond hair was pulled back in a long braid as she stood straight in front of the jury, hands on the lectern, her trial notebook in front of her.

Her voice quavered when she said the word "murder."

She cleared her throat and said it again.

"Murder is not an accident."

This time, her voice was clear.

"Murder is when a person purposefully starts a chain of events that kills someone. And doing certain things are so bad, so evil, that if a death results, it's murder.

"Arson is one such act. If you commit arson—if you purposefully set fire to or destroy the property of another and that fire results in death, the person who started the fire is guilty of murder."

Astrid pointed at the bench.

"Judge Roderick will give you the rules and the law at the end of the case. It's my job right now to tell you what the evidence will show. And the evidence in this case is going to show that Brock Niesen purposefully and deliberately set out to destroy his father's movie screen at the Lakeside Drive-In on Misson Road. Brock Niesen purposefully and deliberately mixed twenty-five pounds of SafeBoom exploding target mix, over *twenty times* the recommended amount, then strapped a gallon of gasoline to it for good measure. Then he purposefully and deliberately climbed the drive-in screen and wedged his explosive into the support frame. Then Brock Niesen went back across the street and deliberately took aim through the scope of his Savage AXIS rifle and purposefully shot the target, blowing a hole in the screen and sending a gasoline fireball into the bushes right below, setting them on fire.

"After setting off his bomb, Brock Niesen left. He left and he let that smoldering bush fire burn. And burn it did. There was a strong west wind that night, like we get here, that pushed the flames along the bushes to the U-Store facility next door, where it burned through a pile of wood and then through three storage units in a row, one, two, three, until it grew and it spread to a motorhome on the other side, a motorhome that exploded and spread the fire further."

Astrid Olsen paused, all nervousness gone. She stood there waiting, the eyes of every juror on her.

"The fire spread to the home of Noah and Maura Carmody. To the home where they lived with their three children, Sasha, Felicity, and little Liam."

She paused again. The jury waited.

"That fire spread and consumed their home. Maura was able to pull her two daughters to safety. But her husband Noah wasn't home that night; he was gone, driving his route overnight like he did every week, so Maura was all alone trying to save her children. She was overcome with smoke when she emerged with the girls. By then, the fire department had arrived and Eli Tripp, a decorated fire veteran, sprinted in to find little Liam."

She looked at each juror now.

"The evidence will show that Eli Tripp found little Liam. Because the evidence will show that Eli Tripp was holding Liam Carmody in his arms when the roof collapsed on them both."

A juror gasped.

"That's why this is murder." Astrid Olsen pointed. "Brock Niesen destroyed the drive-in screen on purpose that night. The evidence will show, without a shadow of a doubt, that Brock Niesen purposefully created an explosive of SafeBoom and gasoline, purposefully shot the explosive with his rifle, and purposefully blew a hole in the movie screen. What he intended after that point isn't relevant. Because he set off his bomb on purpose and because the fire he started killed Eli Tripp and little Liam, Brock Niesen murdered them. Under the law, it's no different than if Brock Niesen had sighted Eli Tripp and little Liam in the scope of his rifle and pulled the trigger himself. For that reason, at the end of this trial, we will ask you to find Brock Niesen guilty of arson and guilty of the murders of Eli Tripp and little Liam Carmody."

Astrid Olsen stood there, comfortable now under the jury's collective gaze, then nodded and took her seat.

I stood and took my place in front of the jury. Their eyes snapped back to me and the best look I got was skepticism. I searched for a neutral face, but all I found was anger and grief and scorn as I started.

"Ms. Olsen just presented you with a pretty long daisy chain. To get from where she started—Brock Niesen damaging his father's movie screen—to where she wants you to go—Brock Niesen murdered Eli Tripp and Liam Carmody—she makes one assumption after another after another. But she's not allowed to ask you to leap from one end of the chain to the other. She's not allowed to ask you to assume that any part of what she just said is true. It's Ms. Olsen's job to prove everything that she just said to you, every single solitary thing, beyond a reasonable doubt."

The faces held their original expressions.

"The judge will explain to you at the end of the case that the State has the burden of proof, that the State has to prove every element of its case beyond a reasonable doubt. We don't have to put on any evidence at all. Ms. Lake and I could sit there and not call a single witness, not ask a single question, and if the State doesn't provide evidence supporting every link in the chain that's required to support a conviction, then it hasn't carried its burden and Brock Niesen can't be found guilty."

I waved. "Of course we are going to ask questions, and we're certainly going to cross-examine the State's witnesses. But I ask you to remember that the State carries the burden here, and that you view all of the State's evidence and witnesses through that lens. I'm asking that of you because it's important. Ms. Olsen or a witness or an officer may try to shift the burden to us, to ask us to prove who caused the fire that burned the Carmodys' house and tragically, horribly, killed Eli Tripp and Liam Carmody. But that's not how this works. It's up to the State, it's up to Ms. Olsen, to prove that Brock Niesen caused the fire that resulted in the deaths of Eli Tripp and Liam Carmody and to prove it beyond a reasonable doubt. It's not up to us to prove anything."

If their faces were any indication, I was making no headway. Zero.

"So why is this important? It's vitally important because Ms. Olsen isn't asking you to go from A to B. She's not asking you to find that Brock Niesen fired a gun and killed Eli Tripp with a bullet. No, she's asking you to find Brock Niesen guilty of murder by going from A to B to C to D to E to F. She's asking you to find that Brock Niesen shot a target, which caused some bushes to catch fire, which caused a fence to catch fire, which caused a wood pile to catch fire, which caused Benny Bird's storage unit to catch fire, which caused Tommy Chase's storage unit to catch fire, which caused Naomi Hoppel's storage unit to catch fire, which caused a motorhome to catch fire, which caused the Carmodys' house to catch fire, which caused the death of Eli Tripp and Liam Carmody."

I shook my head.

"That's a long chain. That's a fragile chain. That's a daisy chain held together by the most delicate stems. And Ms. Olsen has the burden of proving that every single solitary link in that chain happened beyond a reasonable doubt. If there's even one break, in one link, her case fails.

"You're not going to hear any testimony, none at all, that Brock Niesen intended to hurt Eli Tripp or Liam Carmody that night. And you're certainly not going to hear any testimony that he wanted to kill them. No, Ms. Olsen only gets you there with a daisy chain of causation and we don't think she can meet that burden beyond a reasonable doubt. That's why at the end of the case, we'll ask you to return a verdict of not guilty. Thank you."

Maybe a third of the faces had gone to neutral and a couple of scornfuls had gone to skeptical. I decided to judge that as progress and sat down.

Emily pushed a notepad toward me where she'd written, "Can we break the chain somewhere?"

I kept a straight face, nodded to her, and wrote a *?* underneath.

"Thank you, Mr. Shepherd," said Judge Roderick. "Ms. Olsen, you may call your first witness."

Astrid Olsen stood. "Thank you, Your Honor. The State calls the defendant's father, Kevin Niesen."

40

I stood. "May we approach, Judge?"

He waved us up.

I leaned close so the jury wouldn't hear us. "Judge, we renew our objection to compelling Mr. Niesen to testify against his son. We further object to any specific testimony from Mr. Niesen regarding any communications he had with his son as privileged."

Astrid Olsen lifted her chin. "As we briefed, Your Honor, Mr. Niesen has knowledge of a number of things that don't arise from his relationship with his son, making his testimony relevant. Further, although I know Mr. Shepherd spends a great deal of time practicing in other states, *Michigan* does not recognize a parent-child testimonial privilege which would prevent Mr. Niesen from testifying about his communications with his son."

Judge Roderick looked at me. "I know you know she's right about the law."

I shook my head. "The parent-child privilege should be recognized by the Court, Judge. If a minor, a child, can't talk to his father, who can he talk to?"

Astrid Olsen sniffed. "He can't talk to *anyone* about murdering someone. Except his lawyer."

Judge Roderick leaned forward. "You will address your arguments to me, Ms. Olsen. And, you, Mr. Shepherd, have made your record for the Court of Appeals. Objection overruled." He waved us away.

As I returned to my seat, Kevin Niesen was waiting by the gate to come forward. He wore what I now took to be his golf casual work clothes—a quarter-zip pullover, dress pants, and loafers, with his sole concession to court seeming to be switching out his khaki pants for black. When Astrid Olsen directed him to the stand, he hurried up, glancing at his wife, his son, and the jury along the way. His sunglasses fell down out of his hair as he sat. He caught them and hastily stuffed them into a pocket as he was sworn in.

"State your name please?" said Astrid Olsen without preamble.

He leaned forward. "Kevin Niesen."

"You don't want to be here today, do you Mr. Niesen?"

"Of course not."

"Because it's your son's trial?"

"Yes."

"How about because Eli Tripp and Liam Carmody are dead?"

"Yes, yes, of course. That too."

"For the record, you are Brock Niesen's father?"

"I am."

Astrid strode to the exhibit table and returned with a rifle. "I'm handing you what's been marked as State's Exhibit 49. Do you recognize it?"

Kevin Niesen didn't touch it. "I think so."

"Take it, please, and inspect it."

Kevin Niesen reached halfway, stopped, then continued and

took the rifle. He checked the action to make sure it was empty, glanced at it, then handed it back. "There."

"Do you recognize this rifle?"

"Yes. It's my son's."

"Please state the brand and type for the record."

"It's a Savage AXIS chambered for 270 Winchester."

"How do you know it's your son's?"

"I helped him buy it three years ago for deer hunting."

"Do you know the specs for this gun?"

"Some of them."

"You would agree with me that it fires a round at approximately three thousand feet per second?"

"Approximately, yes."

"You've fired that weapon with your son?"

"I have."

"Who taught him to use it?"

"I did."

"I see it has a scope on it. Who taught him to use that?"

"Me."

"Have you seen him hit a target from fifty yards?"

"Yes."

"Many times?"

"Yes."

As Astrid Olsen walked the rifle back to the table, she said, "What is your marital status, Mr. Niesen?"

"I'm divorced."

"From whom?"

"Dagmar Niesen."

"That's the defendant's mother?"

"Yes."

"On the morning of April 10th, did you receive a call from Dagmar Niesen?"

"I did."

"And so the record is clear, you were divorced when you received that call?"

"We were."

"What did she say?"

"She asked me to speak with my son."

"Why?"

"Because he had something to tell me."

"What happened next?"

"There was an argument."

"Between whom?"

"Dagmar and Brock."

"How do you know?"

"I could hear them."

"What was the nature of the argument?"

"She wanted him to get on the phone and he refused."

"What happened next?"

"Dagmar got back on the phone and told me that Brock had blown a hole in my movie theater screen."

Emily and I had gone back and forth about how to handle this conversation. Technically, it was hearsay, and we could fight it, but it was probably encompassed by a couple of exceptions which would allow it in and if that seems confusing, that's because it is and lawyers screw it up all the time. The bottom line was, I knew Astrid had plenty of other evidence that Brock was the one who shot the SafeBoom target and I wanted to spend as little time as possible talking about it so I decided not to object. Ultimately, if we were going to win this case, we had to attack the things that happened after Brock shot the target, not before.

"We should clear up a couple of things for the jury. What movie theater are you talking about?"

"The Lakeside Drive-In."

"On Mission Road?"

"Yes. I am, I was, the owner."

"For how long?"

"About fifteen years."

"And so when you say that Mrs. Niesen told you that your son had blown a hole in your movie theater screen, that's what she was talking about?"

"Yes."

"Did she say how Brock put a hole in your screen?"

"By shooting a SafeBoom target."

"How did she say she knew?"

"She said she caught him coming home with the gun, then found the empty SafeBoom packaging in the garbage."

"What did you do then?"

"I told her to put him on. He refused."

"Then what did you do?"

Kevin Niesen paused, then said, "I called the police."

"Why?"

He looked down. "I wanted to teach him a lesson."

"I see. Tell me about your call."

"I called the Sheriff's office. I reached the dispatcher. I told them that I was the owner of the Lakeside Drive-In and that my screen had been vandalized and that I knew who had done it."

"What did the dispatcher say?"

"She asked me to hold, so I did. I waited a couple of minutes and then Sheriff Sizemore picked up. I know Sean and that surprised me so I joked about getting a flunky this early in the morning."

"What time was it?"

"Six-ish."

"A.M?"

"Yes."

"What did he say?"

"He didn't joke back. I should've known right then."

"What did the Sheriff say?"

"He just said, 'You know who damaged your screen?' I said, 'Yes. And I want you to take him in to scare him.' 'I'll take him in,' he said. 'Who was it?' 'Brock,' I said. Then Sheriff Sizemore told me that he'd be right over. I told him Brock was at his mom's and that I'd meet him there." Kevin Niesen stopped. "I didn't know."

Astrid Olsen ignored him. "What happened next?"

"I went to Dag's, to my ex-wife's. When I got there, Sean was leading Brock to his car in handcuffs." He gave a wry smile. "I thought that was good at the time."

"Then what happened?"

"Sean, Sheriff Sizemore, nodded to me and drove away. Then Dagmar came flying out and gave it to me pretty good." He looked down. "She had wanted me to talk to Brock, not have him arrested by Sean. She didn't approve of my methods. At the time, I thought it was the right thing to do."

Kevin Niesen looked more embarrassed than upset.

"Did you speak with your son at the station?"

"I did. Sean was holding him in an interview room, and he suggested that I go in and get Brock to admit what he did, and then, he, Sean, would go in and scare him. I thought that was a good idea, so I went in and asked Brock what he did. He didn't tell me, he just sulked like teenagers do. So I told him that his mom had told me what he'd done and I lit into him pretty good. And that's when he said, 'I'm not moving with you to f'ing Indiana.'"

"What does that mean?"

"I'm moving to Indiana. Brock usually spends summers with me. He didn't want to go."

"How does damaging your screen change that?"

"Who knows what kids think. I think he thought—"

I stood. "Objection, Your Honor."

"Sustained."

Astrid nodded. "Did Brock ever tell you how he thought damaging the screen would prevent you from going to Indiana?"

Kevin Niesen nodded. "Eventually, he said 'I guess if you can't sell your theater, you'll have to stay here for the summer.'"

"What did you do next?"

"I came out and told Sean. He asked if I was sure that Brock had done it. I said yes and told him the stupid kid was trying to keep me from moving away. Sean asked me if Brock had done it on purpose. I said if blowing up twenty-some pounds of Safe-Boom was on purpose then yes. Then that's when all hell broke loose."

"What do you mean?"

"Sean told me to follow him, led me into the room with Brock, and read Brock his rights, which I thought was a nice touch. Then he said that he was holding Brock on suspicion of murder and when I asked what the hell he was talking about, Sean said that two people had died in a fire that was believed to have started at my drive-in. I said you've got to be fu—you've got to be kidding me and he told me I should get Brock a lawyer and then all this business started."

"To be clear, Mr. Niesen, your son Brock blew a hole in your movie screen on purpose, right?"

I stood. "Objection, Your Honor."

"Sustained."

"Let me say it another way, Mr. Niesen. Your son told you that he blew a hole in your movie screen so that he wouldn't have to move to Indiana with you for the summer, right?"

Kevin Niesen sat there.

"Answer the question, Mr. Niesen," Astrid Olsen said.

Kevin Niesen still sat there.

"Mr. Niesen," said Judge Roderick.

"Yes," Kevin Niesen said finally. "He did."

"No further questions, Your Honor."

When Astrid Olsen took her seat, I stood.

"Mr. Niesen, you were trying to sell the Lakeside Drive-in on April 10th, true?"

"That's true."

"You'd had listed it for sale since the end of the previous season, right?"

"That's right."

"And as of April, you still didn't have any offers, did you?"

"Not yet, no."

"One of the obstacles to selling the drive-in was that its screen was outdated and didn't comply with more modern building codes, wasn't it?"

"I don't know that I'd say that. It's a good theater that's served this town for many years."

"Since the 1950s actually, right?"

"More or less, yes."

"Mr. Niesen, I'm handing you what's been marked as Defense Exhibit 82. That's a printout of an email to you from the listing agent for the Lakeside Drive-In, isn't it?"

Kevin Niesen looked at it and frowned. "It is."

Cyn popped the email up on the screen without my saying a word.

"In that email, your agent says that the most recent potential buyer 'has concerns that the screen doesn't meet current wind standards given that we're so close to Lake Michigan,' doesn't he?"

"That's what the email says."

"Mr. Niesen, you said you called the police to teach your son a lesson, right?"

"I didn't mean it to be this harsh, but yes."

"You also called the police so you could make an insurance claim for the screen, didn't you?"

"Excuse me?"

"You called the police on your son so that no one would suspect that you set fire to your own screen, right?"

Kevin Niesen frowned. "I'm not sure I follow the question."

"Well, it would be pretty suspicious if the rickety-old, out-of-code screen that was preventing you from selling the drive-in suddenly caught fire, wouldn't it?"

Astrid Olsen stood. "Objection, Your Honor. Mr. Niesen has never been accused of starting this fire."

"Goes to bias, Judge," I said.

Judge Roderick thought. "Overruled."

"You made an insurance claim for the damage to your screen, didn't you, Mr. Niesen?"

He glanced at the jury. "Yes."

"You reported to the insurance company that your son, Brock Niesen, started the fire, didn't you?"

"I don't believe I put that in the claim form."

"No, you told the insurance investigator, didn't you?"

"I don't remember—"

"—I have the transcript of the interview right here." I held up a paper. "Are you going to make me read it to the jury?"

Kevin Niesen glanced at them. "I did tell the investigator that Brock had started the fire, yes."

"As a result, he didn't investigate you, did he?"

"Objection," said Astrid Olsen.

I turned to her. "Well, it's true."

"Overruled," said Judge Roderick.

"Because of what you told him, the insurance investigator didn't investigate you, did he?"

Kevin Niesen shifted in his seat. "Not that I'm aware of."

"You received an insurance payout for the damage to the drive-in, right?"

"A small one, yes."

"You then turned around and used that money to pay off the remaining balance on your mortgage, didn't you?"

"I don't recall that that's exactly how it went."

"Fair enough, Mr. Niesen, I mean it has been almost two months. Tell you what, here's a copy of the insurance check that was issued to you, Defense Exhibit 84, and here's a copy of the receipt for your last payment on your mortgage made one month later, Defense Exhibit 85, and here's a copy of the release of mortgage filed a month after that, Defense Exhibit 86."

Kevin Niesen sorted through the hard copies of the documents as Cyn put them up on the screen for the jury.

"How did you get these?" he said.

"From the prosecutor's file, from your wife as part of the divorce settlement, and from the registrar of deeds. Back to my original question, the insurance pay out was almost exactly the balance of your loan, right?"

He looked back and forth between the papers before saying, "They're pretty close."

"And after you paid that mortgage balance and after the screen was gone, you were able to sell the drive-in, weren't you?"

He looked up. "That's not why."

"Mr. Niesen, the drive-in sold after you paid the mortgage and the screen was gone, right? Just last month?"

"Yes, but—"

"You had reduced the asking price, right?"

"Yes, but—"

"And you had no note to worry about when you sold it, right?"

"Yes, but that doesn't mean—"

"It's up to the jury to decide what that means, Mr. Niesen."

"I care about my son, Mr. Shepherd."

"No one said you didn't, Mr. Niesen." I took the exhibits

back, then said, "Your divorce with Dagmar became final at the end of last year, right?"

"That's right."

"Your plan was to move to southern Indiana, wasn't it?"

"For a fresh start, yes."

"You said Brock didn't want to go there for the summer, right?"

"Change can be hard sometimes."

"You didn't have to make him go to Indiana, did you?"

"I want to spend time with my son."

"You could come up here for the summer, couldn't you?"

"I have a business in Indiana."

"You're running that business from up here right now, aren't you?"

"Yes."

"You still have a propane business up here, don't you?"

"Yes, but it's easier to run all of that from down there."

"Easier for you?"

Kevin Niesen made a face. "Who else would I mean?"

"How about your son?"

"He's just a kid. It's easier for him to move than me."

"I see. And easier for him to take the blame for things, right?"

Astrid Olsen stood. "Objection, Your Honor! There's no basis to claim Mr. Niesen had anything to do with the fire!"

"I didn't claim anything of the sort, Judge."

"Sustained. Move along, Mr. Shepherd."

"Mr. Niesen, you had potential criminal exposure in this case, didn't you?"

Kevin Niesen scowled. "I don't know what you mean."

"You bought Brock the gun, didn't you?"

Astrid Olsen stood. "Objection, Your Honor. This is outrageous!"

"Goes to bias again, Judge."

Judge Roderick straightened his glasses. "You have a very limited window here, Mr. Shepherd."

I looked back to Kevin Niesen. "You bought Brock the gun, right?"

"To hunt, yes."

"You bought him SafeBoom targets in the past, didn't you?"

"To practice for hunting, yes."

"You are one of his custodial parents, right?"

"Right."

"So you're in charge of deciding how to safely store his hunting rifle, aren't you?"

Kevin Niesen glanced at the judge. "He wasn't living with me when he did this!"

"Ah, right. But I assume they were using the same safety practices you set up when you lived there. As his father."

"I...I don't know."

"You didn't check, did you?"

"After I left, no."

"Did Ms. Olsen mention to you any criminal liability you might have for your son's actions?"

"She said, she said she appreciated my cooperation as a witness."

"I see. And I suppose you could be sued for money in a civil case too, couldn't you?"

"I don't know about that."

"So it would help protect you, help protect your money, if you paint Brock as an incorrigible, uncontrollable teen, wouldn't it?"

Astrid Olsen stood. "Objection!"

"Overruled."

Kevin Niesen straightened. "I don't know. You'd have to ask my lawyer."

"So you've hired a lawyer to defend yourself against the claims stemming from the Mission Road Fire?"

"I have. It would be stupid not to."

"Yes, it would. But you've refused to pay for a lawyer for your son's defense, haven't you, Mr. Niesen?"

"What? What do you mean?"

"I mean that you haven't paid a dime for your son's legal defense, have you?"

Kevin Niesen shifted, paused, then said, "Brock made his own bed here."

"So the answer is you haven't paid for your son's lawyer, right?"

"That's right."

"Only for your own."

Kevin Niesen glared. "Yes."

"Thank you." I nodded to Judge Roderick and sat down.

I noticed Brock as I did—his arms crossed, slouched back, glaring at his dad. I put one arm around the back of his chair, handed him a pen, and whispered, "Sit up and nod as if I'm telling you something important, then write whatever you want on this pad."

He nodded fiercely, sat up, and started scribbling as Astrid Olsen said, "Mr. Niesen, you didn't start the fire at your drive-in, did you?"

"Absolutely not, no."

"And although you didn't know what Sheriff Sizemore was going to do, you told him the truth about what your son did, didn't you?"

"I did."

"You don't have any doubt that your son, Brock Niesen, blew the hole in your screen and started the fire to avoid going with you to Indiana?"

I stood. "Objection. Asked and answered."

"Just making sure we didn't lose the thread of his testimony after all those topics on cross Your Honor."

"Overruled. For this question, Ms. Olsen."

"Mr. Niesen?"

Kevin Niesen shook his head. "No, unfortunately, I don't doubt that."

"Thank you."

Brock made three explanation points on his pad. He'd written *He sold me out to cover his own ass!!!*

I nodded. I realized that the testimony I'd just elicited from a father would be very hard for a son to hear.

I stood. "Mr. Niesen, you just said you believe Brock started the fire at your drive-in?"

"I'm afraid so."

"You don't know anything about how, or even if, that fire spread to the Carmody house, right?"

Kevin Niesen thought. "No, no I suppose not."

"And since we're summarizing things here, let me make sure I have this straight—you called the police to report your son, interrogated your son for the police at the station, used the information from that interrogation to make an insurance claim for yourself, used the insurance money to pay off your mortgage, sold the drive-in, then hired a lawyer for yourself but not for your son, is that right?"

Kevin Niesen straightened and frowned. "I don't know that I'd say it like that."

"No? Why don't you tell the jury which thing I said wasn't true?"

Kevin Niesen looked at me, looked at the judge, then looked at the jury.

I waited. He shifted.

"Would you like me to have the court reporter read that back to you?"

"No." Kevin Niesen glared at me. "No, it's all true. You just made it sound...I just wouldn't have said it that way is all."

"I see. I can't imagine why your son didn't want to go to Indiana."

Astrid Olsen leapt out of her seat. "Move to strike!"

"Mr. Shepherd!" said Judge Roderick. "You will keep your editorial comments to yourself. That comment is stricken from the record."

They were both right—my comment was inappropriate and should have been stricken. But Brock's face was now calm, and he nodded thanks as I sat.

Kevin Niesen was excused. He tried to make eye contact with Brock on the way out. Brock stared straight ahead. Dagmar, on the other hand, stared at her ex-husband the whole way out.

"Ms. Olsen, who is your next witness?" said Judge Roderick.

"Your Honor, the State will call Sheriff Sean Sizemore."

"Fine, let's take a short break and then put him on the stand."

41

Sheriff Sean Sizemore took the stand wearing his dress uniform and holding his broad-brimmed hat so that it didn't mess his slicked back hair. He put his hat on the flat rail, put his folded aviators on the brim, and nodded to Astrid Olsen.

After swearing him in and introducing him as the thrice elected sheriff of Sable County, Astrid Olsen said, "Sheriff Sizemore, how were you involved in the events of April 10th?"

"It actually started on the evening of April 9th."

"How so?"

"Between 11:31 and 11:35 p.m., my office received multiple phone calls to report an explosion."

"How many?"

"Fourteen, I believe."

"What did your staff do?"

"None of the reports indicated a location, just that it was loud and, in some cases, shook the windows. The calls were scattered over a large enough area that it was difficult to determine where to go, so dispatch advised my deputies on patrol of the event and advised them to be aware."

"How many units were out that night?"

"I had three deputies patrolling."

"Were you out there?"

"Not yet, no."

"What happened next?"

"I received a call sometime after 2:00 a.m. from one of my deputies that two victims had died in a fire and that the source of the fire was suspicious. I went to the scene at Mission Road as fast as I could."

"Why?"

"Because a death in a suspicious fire can result in significant criminal charges and I handle the investigation of suspicious deaths in our county personally." He looked at the jury. "We don't have many deaths like that in Sable County and I take my responsibility to protect our citizens seriously."

Astrid Olsen nodded agreement. "What did you learn when you arrived at the scene?"

"I learned that Eli Tripp and Liam Carmody had been killed in the Mission Road Fire."

"What did you do then?"

"I coordinated with Fire Chief Rolf Hagen who was also on the scene. He advised me of the path that the fire had taken, that the fire was suspicious, and that he already had his fire investigator, Kurt Vernon, on site."

Sheriff Sizemore turned to the jury again. "Arson investigations require the utmost cooperation between fire and police personnel, so as Investigator Vernon began inspecting the source of the fire, I began by interviewing witnesses."

"Who did you interview?"

"I spoke to Devin Wright, the owner of the U-Store facility. I determined that his facility did not have security cameras that would assist us in the investigation. I then spoke to the 911 dispatcher, who provided me with a transcript of the call reporting the fire."

Astrid Olsen approached Sheriff Sizemore. "Sheriff, I'm handing you a document that has been marked as State Exhibit 3. What is that?"

"The transcript of the 911 call I reviewed that night."

"What did you learn?"

"I learned that the caller had seen the bushes of the Lakeside Drive-In and material outside the U-Store facility on fire when he drove by."

"When was that?"

"His 911 call came in at 1:37 a.m. Fire trucks were dispatched at 1:38 a.m."

"Who was the caller?"

"Patrick Dabbs."

"What did you do next?"

"I went to Mr. Dabbs' house to interview him regarding what he saw."

"Did you speak to Mr. Dabbs that night?"

Sheriff Sizemore shook his head. "He did not answer his door or phone."

"Did that concern you?"

"No. It was the middle of the night."

"What did you do next?"

"I went back to the Mission Road site. By then, the fire was under control. I then coordinated with Investigator Vernon and my forensic team to start identifying and cataloging evidence."

"Were you treating this as a homicide?"

He looked at the jury. "We were treating it as a tragedy. The fire crew, Eli's crew, was pretty shaken up. My team worked to make sure we didn't lose any evidence. None of us, my team and Investigator Vernon, were sure yet about the cause, but we were treating it as suspicious, just in case."

"What happened next?"

"We were on the scene throughout the night and any law enforcement staff that hadn't been working overnight came in that morning. I was still at the Mission Road scene when my office patched a call through from Kevin Niesen."

"What did Mr. Niesen tell you?"

"He told me that he believed his son Brock had blown up his screen at the drive-in that night."

"That's the defendant, Brock Niesen?"

"Yes."

"What did you do?"

"I immediately went to Brock Niesen's house. His parents consented to my taking Brock Niesen to the station. Once there, Kevin Niesen questioned his son before I did. Kevin Niesen then indicated to me that Brock had used a high-powered rifle to detonate a SafeBoom target on the movie screen. I then read Brock Niesen his Miranda rights and detained him."

"What did you do next?"

"I obtained and executed a warrant to search Brock Niesen's home."

"What did you find?"

"We found the Savage AXIS .270 rifle."

"That would be State's Exhibit 49?" Astrid held up the rifle from the evidence table.

"Yes. We also found packaging for twenty-five pounds of SafeBoom targets."

"That would be State's Exhibit 50?" She held up plastic wrapping and pouches.

"Yes. We also found an empty gas can."

She held up a plastic red gas container people use for lawn mowers. "State's 51?"

"Yes."

"What did you do next?"

"I went back to see Investigator Vernon and told him what I'd learned. He then determined—"

I stood. "Objection, Your Honor."

"Please limit your testimony to your findings, Sheriff," said Judge Roderick.

Sheriff Sizemore nodded to the judge. "Certainly, Your Honor. Investigator Vernon then spent some time on the drive-in theater grounds. When he returned, he told me that his findings supported a conclusion that the Mission Road Fire had started at the drive-in."

"Did the two of you arrive at any other conclusions?"

"Yes. When I advised him of the multiple calls reporting an explosion at 11:31 p.m. the night before, we concluded that it was in all likelihood the sound of the SafeBoom target being detonated."

"It can be that loud?"

"Twenty-five pounds? Absolutely. I also asked Investigator Vernon if that timing made sense for the spread of the fire. When he said it did, I acted on this information and arrested Brock Niesen on suspicion of arson and murder. Your office then took over from there."

"Thank you, Sheriff Sizemore." Astrid Olsen sat.

I stood. "Sheriff Sizemore, you never told Kevin or Dagmar Niesen that you wanted to talk to their son about a murder, did you?"

"I wasn't obligated to."

"So you didn't tell them, right?"

"Mr. Niesen called me, Mr. Shepherd. I responded to that call."

"That's right. And you never told either of them that you were interviewing their fifteen-year-old son on suspicion of murder, did you?"

"I had no such obligation."

"Sheriff Sizemore, I'm perfectly happy to keep asking this question until you answer it, but I think we're going to irritate everyone in this courtroom. So, let me ask you, for the fourth time now—you didn't tell the Niesens that you were interviewing their minor son related to a murder, did you?"

Sheriff Sizemore glanced at the jury. "No, I did not. I didn't have to."

"You did not tell them that fire had consumed other buildings on Mission Road, did you?"

"No. I didn't have to."

"You did not tell them that two people had died that night, did you?"

"No. I didn't have to."

"When you took Brock Niesen to the station, you told his father Kevin to go in and get him to admit to damaging the screen, didn't you?"

"I did."

"You let Kevin believe that you were just going to scare him, didn't you?"

"I can't say what Kevin Niesen believed."

"You lied to Kevin Niesen so he would elicit information from his son, didn't you?"

Astrid Olsen stood. "Objection, Your Honor. It's well-established that officers can use deception to obtain confessions."

I put my hands out. "Exactly, Judge. And the jury also gets to know when an officer has told that lie to obtain an arrest."

"Overruled," said Judge Roderick, but he shot me a look and turned to the jury. "Members of the jury, it is permissible for officers to deceive suspects in order to obtain a confession or to obtain information relevant to an investigation. Sheriff Sizemore doing so in this case does not undermine his credibility as he testifies as he is now under oath and is required to tell the truth."

I turned back to the Sheriff. "So, Sheriff Sizemore, you lied to

Kevin Niesen to trick him into getting information from his son, didn't you?"

He looked at the jury. "I take my oaths seriously, both my oath to protect the citizens of our county and my oath to tell the truth now." He looked back at me. "Yes, I led Mr. Niesen to believe that I had taken Brock in to scare him, and I allowed Mr. Niesen to confirm that Brock had indeed blown up the movie screen that night. Eli Tripp and Liam Carmody deserved no less."

"Got it. You lied to Mr. Niesen then and you're telling us the truth now, right?"

Sheriff Sizemore stiffened. "That's right."

"So that we all have it straight, you will lie to arrest Brock Niesen, but you won't lie to convict him. Do I have that right?"

"I won't," said Sheriff Sizemore through gritted teeth.

Astrid Olsen stood, just a little late. "Objection! Move to strike."

"Overruled," said Judge Roderick. "You've made your point, Mr. Shepherd. Move along."

I nodded. "Sheriff, you said a moment ago that Eli Tripp and Liam Carmody 'deserved no less.' You would agree with me that Eli Tripp and Liam Carmody deserve no less than a thorough and complete investigation of their deaths, wouldn't you?"

"Absolutely."

"You mentioned that as part of your thorough and complete investigation, you went to the home of Patrick Dabbs, the witness who called in the fire?"

"I did."

"But he did not answer the phone or the door that night, did he?"

"That's right."

"You didn't go back and talk to Mr. Dabbs later that day, did you?"

Sheriff Sizemore scowled. "No, I didn't need to."

"Right, because you'd tricked the Niesens into giving you information—"

Astrid Olsen stood. "Objection, Your Honor!"

I looked at Astrid. "Isn't deception a trick?"

Judge Roderick pursed his lips. "Overruled. But I believe I've told you that we've had enough on that score, Mr. Shepherd."

"Let me say it another way, Sheriff. Because you found out" —I made air quotes around 'found out'—"about Brock Niesen, you never went back and talked to Patrick Dabbs, did you?"

"It didn't seem necessary, no."

"Because you believed you'd found the source of the fire, right?"

"I had found the source of the fire."

"You also didn't retrace Patrick Dabbs' activities that night, did you?"

Sheriff Sizemore scowled. "That wasn't necessary, no."

"So you did not learn that Mr. Dabbs was at the BeachHead until 11:35 p.m. on the night of the fire, did you?"

"I don't know how that's relevant."

"I can see that. Cyn?" A receipt from the BeachHead Bar & Grill popped up on the screen. "We've blocked out the credit card number, but that's Patrick Dabbs' name there, right?" Cyn highlighted it for the jury.

"Yes."

"That time in the corner says 11:35 p.m., April 9th, right?"

"It does."

"And my goodness, the receipt shows that he had five Jack Daniels and Cokes, doesn't it?"

Sheriff Sizemore wobbled his head with impatience. "Along with an order of nachos, yes."

Astrid Olsen stood. "Your Honor?"

Judge Roderick nodded. "Are we getting to a point, Mr. Shepherd?"

"We are, Judge, yes. Sheriff Sizemore, since you didn't talk to him, you also didn't learn that after Mr. Dabbs left the BeachHead, he went to Pappy's and stayed until 1:30 a.m., did you?"

Judge Roderick nodded. Astrid Olsen sat.

"No," said Sheriff Sizemore. "So what?"

Another receipt popped up on the screen. "That's a receipt for Patrick Dabbs again, from Pappy's this time, right?"

"Yes."

"It was generated at 1:30 a.m.?"

"Yes."

"And goodness, it's for three more Jack and Cokes, right?"

Sheriff Sizemore shook his head. "Yes, Mr. Shepherd, it is, and if your point is that Mr. Dabbs should have been pulled over for DUI then the answer is yes, but we can't catch everyone."

"That was *not* my point, Sheriff Sizemore. I'm sure you do the best you can with your limited resources."

I stepped away, toward the jury. "See, as Ms. Olsen has pointed out more than once, I'm not from around here, so I had to get a map of Northlake to see where all of these places were."

A map appeared on the screen. "That dot is the BeachHead, that's Pappy's, and that's Mr. Dabbs house. Is that a true and accurate depiction of where those places are located, Sheriff?"

He studied the screen. "Yes."

"There aren't many roads out that way, so Mission Road is really the only logical way to go from the BeachHead to Pappy's, isn't it?"

"That's right unless you went far out of your way."

"And Mr. Dabbs only lives a couple of minutes from Pappy's, right?"

"That's right."

Another red dot appeared on the screen. "That's where the Lakeside Drive-In is, right?"

"Yes."

Another dot. "And the U-Store?"

"Yes."

Another dot. "And the Carmody house?"

"Yes."

"Right on Mr. Dabb's route from the BeachHead to Pappy's, true?"

Sheriff Sizemore now saw where I was going. "Yes."

"In his 911 call, Mr. Dabbs said he saw flames in the bushes of the drive-in and along the west side of the U-Store, didn't he?"

"He did."

"So if he cashed out at the BeachHead at 11:35 p.m. and drove over to Pappy's right away, he would have passed the drive-in a little before midnight, wouldn't he?"

Sheriff Sizemore stared. "You'd have to ask him."

"I agree, Sheriff Sizemore. Someone doing a complete and thorough investigation would have to ask Mr. Dabbs when he saw the fire. You never did, though, did you?"

The muscle in Sheriff Sizemore's jaw twitched. "It wasn't necessary once Brock Niesen was arrested."

"See now, as Brock's lawyer, I think it was. The way this fire spread from one place to another, and the time it took, is a crucial aspect of this case. And you never asked Mr. Dabbs when he actually passed the drive-in, did you?"

He shifted. "I did not. It wasn't necessary."

"Sheriff Sizemore, you're not a fire investigator, are you?"

"No, I'm not."

"You will defer to fire experts in this case as to the manner in which the fire started and spread, won't you?"

"I will certainly defer to Chief Hagan and Investigator Vernon on those issues."

"And to anyone else who has actual qualifications related to fire investigation and who has tested the debris in this case, right?"

"If their opinion is reasonable, yes."

"Well, Sheriff Sizemore, you're not in a position to determine what a reasonable fire opinion is because you have no qualifications, do you?"

"I have no formal training, no."

"Your training is in criminal investigation, right?"

"That's right."

"So going back to your investigative training, it's reasonable to assume that if Patrick Dabbs left the BeachHead at 11:35 pm and went straight to Pappy's, then he likely passed the Drive-In between 11:45 and 11:50 p.m., isn't it?"

Sheriff Sizemore shook his head. "We don't know that Mr. Dabbs went straight there."

"No, Sheriff Sizemore, *you* don't know that Mr. Dabbs went straight there. *I* know because I asked the bartender at Pappy's what time he arrived."

Astrid Olsen stood.

I raised my hand. "Let me ask you a hypothetical question, Sheriff. I want you to assume that, if necessary, Dani Petrikowski will come in and testify that she was working as the bartender at Pappy's that night, that Mr. Dabbs entered the bar at approximately midnight, and ordered three Jack and Cokes over the next hour and a half before leaving at 1:30 a.m. after Dani cut him off. Do you understand these hypothetical facts?"

The jaw muscle twitched. "Yes."

"Given those facts, it is reasonable to assume that Patrick Dabbs passed the drive-in between 11:45 and 11:50 p.m., isn't it?"

"Assuming all that is true, yes."

"So when he reported to 911 that he saw the fire in the

bushes and on the west side of the U-Store, that was where the fire was at a little before midnight, right?"

"Maybe."

"It wasn't where the fire was at 1:37 a.m. when he made the 911 call, right?"

"You'll have to ask him."

I looked at the jury. "No, *you* should have asked him, right?"

Sheriff Sizemore glared.

I waved at him. "I think we both know the answer to that. Given what he drank that night, you're not surprised that Mr. Dabbs waited until after he was home to call in the fire, are you?"

"Objection. Speculation."

"Sustained."

"So we've established that you didn't interview Patrick Dabbs, the witness who called in the fire. You also didn't interview people who made insurance claims as a result of the fire, did you?"

"Why would I do that?"

"Besides the fact that insurance fraud is the number one motive for arson?"

Astrid Olsen jumped up. "Objection."

"Sustained."

I kept going. "Benny Bird made an insurance claim for the loss of his barbeque equipment. You didn't interview him, did you?"

"No."

"Tommy Chase made an insurance claim for the loss of his work supplies that were destroyed. You didn't interview him, did you?"

"No."

"Naomi Hoppel made an insurance claim for the loss of her crafts and furniture. You didn't interview her, did you?"

"No."

"Devin Wright made an insurance claim for the destruction of his motorhome. I know you asked him about video cameras. But you didn't ask him about his motorhome claim, did you?"

"No."

"Corey Linden made an insurance claim for the destruction of the house he rented to the Carmodys. You didn't interview him, did you?"

"I did not. None of those were necessary."

"As part of your complete and thorough investigation, you did not interview anyone with a financial interest in the fire because you had interviewed and arrested Brock Niesen, right?"

"Yes. Because he did it."

"Brock Niesen didn't file an insurance claim as a result of this fire, did he, Sheriff?"

He scowled. "No. That wasn't his motivation."

"On that we can agree, Sheriff, because Brock Niesen did not have a financial interest in this fire, did he?"

"Objection," said Astrid Olsen.

I turned to her. "Really? Are you going to present evidence that he did?"

"Overruled," said Judge Roderick. "Address your arguments to me, Mr. Shepherd."

I nodded and turned back to Sheriff Sizemore. "Sheriff, Brock Niesen did not have a financial interest in this fire, did he?"

"No, but as I said, that did not appear to be his motivation."

"Sheriff Sizemore, did you interview Maura Carmody?"

Sheriff Sizemore blinked. "No. Why would I do that?"

"I would think that would be part of a thorough and complete investigation."

He shook his head. "She'd been through enough."

"I realize it would be difficult, but it was necessary, wasn't it?"

"I don't see how. We knew that your client started the fire."

"I know that was your assumption, yes, but there were other things that needed an explanation, weren't there?"

"Like what?"

I paused.

What I was about to do could blow up our case far worse than twenty-five pounds of SafeBoom ever could, but at that point, I had a client who had unquestionably started a fire when he destroyed his dad's movie screen, a fifteen-year-old client who was going to spend not years, but *decades*, in prison. My duty right then was to investigate every single piece of the case. If I'd been able to get the medical records, or if Astrid had told me what had happened, I might not have said what I said next. But I hadn't and she hadn't, so I did.

"Like why Mrs. Carmody and the kids were still in the house. Did you ask her?"

Astrid Olsen objected, there was a yell behind me, and twelve jurors snapped their heads around to me.

Judge Roderick banged his gavel, once. "Enough! Mrs. Tripp, you will maintain decorum or will be asked to leave. Ms. Olsen, your objection is overruled. And Mr. Shepherd, you have the narrowest of windows here."

I nodded, ignored the jury, and stared at Sheriff Sizemore, who was giving it right back. "Sheriff Sizemore, according to your testimony, there was an explosion of SafeBoom right there at the drive-in at 11:30 p.m., an explosion that prompted fourteen calls to your office. There was a fire at the drive-in and the west side of the U-Store at midnight, and eventually, at some point—according to your joint investigation—a motorhome blew up before the Carmody house caught fire, and the firetrucks arrived with sirens blaring. So my question to you, Sheriff, is, did you ever ask Mrs. Carmody why, with all of that commotion, the Carmodys were still in the house?"

It was easy to see that Sheriff Sizemore was angry. It was just as easy to see that he'd never thought of that before.

"No," he said.

"I'm sure, in fact I'm certain, there's a good explanation for it. Wouldn't it be part of a thorough and complete investigation to find out what that explanation was?"

Sheriff Sizemore gnawed at the inside of his cheek. "Yes."

"No further questions."

Astrid Olsen was on her feet before I sat down.

"Sheriff Sizemore, there was not a single shred of evidence that you're aware of that indicated Mrs. Carmody played a role in this fire, was there?"

"None."

"Do you find it as reprehensible as I do for Mr. Shepherd to suggest that?"

I stayed seated. Slings and arrows were a byproduct of my gambit.

"I do. Mrs. Carmody, and her son, are the victims here."

"Are you at all surprised that the people Mr. Shepherd mentioned filed insurance claims?"

"Of course not. His client destroyed their property. That's what insurance is for."

"You did not find any evidence that any one of them was involved in setting any aspect of this fire, did you?"

"No. None."

Astrid Olsen pointed at me. "Mr. Shepherd claims he has evidence that Mr. Dabbs observed the fire shortly before midnight instead of at 1:30 a.m. Does that change anything?"

He shook his head. "Not really. If anything, it's just more evidence of his client's guilt."

"How so?"

"It shows the fire started after his client blew up the Safe-Boom target and gasoline at 11:30 p.m."

"Finally, Mr. Shepherd implied that you were dishonest when you spoke to Brock Niesen's parents."

I stood. "Objection, Your Honor, mischaracterization. I did not imply it. I said that he lied."

Judge Roderick frowned but said, "Sustained."

Astrid Olsen did not look at me as she said, "Mr. Shepherd said that you lied when you spoke to Mr. and Mrs. Niesen."

He stared at me. "He did."

"Why did you do that?"

Sheriff Sizemore turned to the jury. "Eli Tripp and Liam Carmody were dead. I had a suspect in custody. It is well-established law enforcement protocol to encourage a defendant, or his parents who are witnesses, to provide us with information leading to solving the crime and making an arrest. Including telling lies. Eli and Liam deserved it."

Astrid let that sit there for a moment, then said, "Nothing further, Your Honor."

I stood. "Sheriff Sizemore, Eli and Liam deserved a complete and thorough investigation into their deaths, didn't they?"

I could see the war on his face, but Sheriff Sizemore said, "Yes."

"I think you and Ms. Olsen misunderstood me. I'm not suggesting that Mrs. Carmody had anything to do with setting her house on fire. I'm asking if you ever investigated whether something happened that night that made it difficult for the family to leave?"

He shook his head. "That's ludicrous."

"So the answer is 'no?'"

"The answer is 'hell no.'"

"Thank you, Sheriff. No further questions."

42

"That was a bold strategy," said Cyn when we were back at the office that night.

"I don't hear approval in that statement," I said.

Cyn shrugged. "Most of it was sound. You upset the jury with the Carmody line of questioning though."

"Showing the Sheriff had missed another significant part of the investigation seemed important," I said.

"I understand," said Cyn. "But it came off as if you were pushing some blame onto Mrs. Carmody for her son's death."

I shrugged to hide my wince. "Judgment call."

Cyn nodded. "It was."

"It wasn't all bad," said Emily. She doled out bags from a drive-thru. Blind ordering from a car was becoming the best chance we had of getting service outside of Maggie's. "You made Sizemore look sloppy. And Niesen look like an asshole."

I gestured to Cyn who was methodically unfolding her sandwich and creasing the wrapper to make a plate. "Niesen is a self-centered narcissist, which explains Brock's behavior but doesn't excuse it," she said. "And Nathan did a good job of showing that Sheriff Sizemore was sloppy and had gaps in his investigation.

But unless we fill those gaps with information, it's not going to be enough to exonerate Brock."

"Right." I sat down myself. "Today we created a two-hour window where someone else could have acted and showed a bunch of people with a motive to do it—"

"—But we don't have any proof yet that says anybody did," said Emily.

"Exactly. I'm going to call Olivia and let her know where we are."

"And ask for a miracle?"

I sighed. "Reluctantly. She'd never let me forget it."

"Before you do, who did Astrid say she's calling tomorrow?"

"The U-Store witnesses for sure—Benny Bird, Tommy Chase, and Naomi Hoppel. I'm not sure who else."

Emily nodded. "I'm taking Bird and Hoppel, right?"

I'd been thinking about it on the way back to the office. "I think I have to Emily."

"Why?"

"I've put us in this situation. If an opening, comes up, I need to exploit it."

Emily stared. "I can exploit with the best of them."

"I know. But I need to do it."

She looked down. "Okay, Boss. Go work some magic with Olivia."

I went to my temporary office and called her.

"How'd it go?" she said.

I told her.

"Shep, I'm never going to tell you your business—"

"—You always tell me my business."

"I always tell you your personal business because you need my guidance. I never tell you your *legal* business."

"I actually think that's true, Liv."

"I know it's true. Just like I know you overextended yourself on Maura Carmody with the jury today."

I sighed. "I did. But isn't this where you save my ass by revealing some information that you've miraculously discovered?"

"You know it doesn't work like that."

"A guy can dream. Your information on Patrick Dabbs and Pappy's was effective today. Thanks."

"It was just leg work."

"Leg work that the Sheriff didn't put in."

"I never skip leg day, you know that."

"I do. The three U-Store renters are testifying tomorrow. Do you have anything new?"

"No shortcuts today, Shep. All three seem to have stored their moderately valuable and extremely flammable belongings in the units for perfectly plausible reasons and none of their insurance claims seem out of whack either. You're just going to have to grind it out one question at a time."

"Can you keep looking?"

"Always. There's also been some action on social media you should know about. Kim Tripp has organized a pressure campaign against Midwest Fruit."

"And they are?"

"A company that processes a variety of fruits, including apples, for things like juices, pie filling, and other ingredients in the industrial food complex. The Golden Apple Orchard sells a large portion of its crop to it."

"Mrs. Tripp disapproves?"

"She wonders, publicly and often, if Midwest Fruit knows it is supporting a murderer's defense. She's been at it for a while, but the trial seems to have added juice to the campaign, and I don't apologize for the pun."

"How much juice?"

"Some of the companies Midwest sells to have noticed, as has the star of a modestly rated reality TV show."

"Any other sunlight to sprinkle?"

"Other than my disposition, no."

"Thanks, Liv. Everything okay up in Glen Arbor?"

"No worries. Staying up here was the right call."

"Definitely. I'll talk to you tomorrow."

We hung up. I'd only been half joking about expecting a miracle discovery from her. She'd saved my ass more than once in a case and my derrière was certainly endangered now, but it looked like I was going to have to do what she said—grind out simple cross examinations, find basic signs of reasonable doubt, and hope I could build enough of a case to win.

I put the saying about hope and empty hands out of my mind and went to work on my cross-examinations of the U-Store tenants.

∾

It was about nine when my phone buzzed.

"Mom? Is everything okay?"

"Yes, dear, are you done for the day?"

"Sure."

"Are you lying?"

"Of course not."

"I'm sorry, I just never know when to call."

"Now's fine. What's up?"

"We got good news today. Your father's been taken off dialysis!"

I sat back. "That is good news! So it's all done? No more?"

"That's it and I don't have to tell you how pleased your father is. I think sitting still for four hours was worse for him than the needles."

"That's great, Mom! Thanks for telling me."

"I knew you'd want to know. How much longer are you up there?"

"The rest of this week. Maybe the beginning of next."

"How is that boy, Brock, doing?"

"He's holding up."

"I can't imagine what Dagmar is going through, watching that. She must be so worried."

"She is, but she's managing."

"Are you eating?"

"Every day."

Her sniff of skepticism crossed the state from cell tower to tower. Technology is amazing.

"I'll know you're lying when you come home with your shirt hanging off your shoulders."

"It's not like that, Mom."

"Says you. And make sure you take plenty of water if you go out on the sand dunes."

I can't tell you what maternal calculus led my mother to warn her son against the danger he would face if he wandered out onto the coastal sand dunes of northern Michigan without water while he was in the middle of a trial because I decided the better course of action was to say, "I will."

We hung up. I felt the release of concern I hadn't realized I'd been holding for the last few months for my dad. And it brought home to me, again, how lucky I was, especially after the testimony I'd heard from another father that day.

In the quiet of the office, I heard another phone conversation.

"I can't tell you when I'll be home, Mom," Emily said. "How would I know that there's a baby's breath shortage?...Fine, add the lilac...Well, why did you suggest it then?...Mom, I can tell you both that Astrantia is lovely and that I have no idea what it is...I'm serious, you pick. I don't care...You're wrong, Mom, a boy's life is more important than what's going to fill a flower place setting...I told you; I don't know. My boss is calling for me, I have to go...Yes, we're still working, I told you we're in trial. Bye."

I decided it was a good time to go out and get a bottle of water as Emily hung up.

I grinned. "I *am* an ogre."

Emily shook her head. "Do we ever get to just try cases?"

"No," I said.

"Sometimes," said Cyn from her station.

Emily looked at us and shook her head.

Then we all went back to work.

43

The first witness Astrid Olsen called the next day was Benny Bird. Yes, that was in fact his real name; yes, he was the owner of Bird's BBQ; and yes, he too believed it was a sign that the good Lord had put him on this earth to smoke meat and give people something delicious to eat.

Benny Bird was a heavy-set guy with a reddish blond buzz cut, a reddish face, and a reddish goatee that didn't hide his smile when he spoke. He told Astrid how he'd started barbequing as a hobby, how he'd found that he had a gift for it after he won some local competitions, and how he'd climbed the rungs of the barbeque ladder to a grand championship. After that win, he'd started a seasonal business here in Northlake that let him feed others to feed his family, which truly was a blessing.

I glanced at Emily, who shook her head. No one, and I mean no one, would believe that Benny Bird had anything to do with the fire that night.

That was borne out when Astrid Olsen said, "Now, Mr. Bird, was that your wood piled outside the U-Store?"

"Yes, Miss Olsen, yes it was." Benny Bird curled his lips into his goatee and bowed his head. "And I'm very sorry about that."

"Why are you sorry, Mr. Bird?"

"It was cherry wood, you see, and I was awfully excited because cherry wood is expensive, but the Tolliver Orchard just up the way, they were getting out of the growing business because they couldn't keep up with the cherry prices out of Turkey, so Len Tolliver sold his orchard and uprooted hundreds of trees before the dozers came. He told me I could take as many as I wanted. Now Miss Olsen, it's rare to get that much cherry wood and even rarer to get it for the price of your labor, so I went out with my buzz saw and my son and we cut as many logs as we could carry. Let me tell you, when you use that cherry to smoke a pork butt, you have something special, especially with my rub because I add just a little bit of—"

Astrid Olsen may have been stiff, but she knew enough to smile as she said, "So you had to store some of the wood outside of your unit?"

Benny Bird didn't even notice the interruption. He just smiled and nodded as he said, "My smoker and trailer take up most of the inside of the unit and we had so much wood there was no way it would fit. Besides, it still needed to season and the good Lord's sun and rain is the best way to do that. So I talked to Scooter—"

"—That's Scooter Derry, the manager of the U-Store?" said Astrid.

"That's right. I talked to old Scoot, and he said I could just stack it right alongside and only charged me another twenty dollars a month. So me and my boy, we just stacked it all, in nice, neat rows, from the side of the unit all the way over to the fence."

"That's the wood privacy fence between the U-Store and the Lakeside Drive-In?"

"That's the one, Miss Olsen. We filled that whole area."

"How much wood was there, Mr. Bird?"

"Oh, I'd say it must've been eight rows wide and five feet high." Benny Bird's voice cracked. He put a hand to his mouth, cleared his throat, and said, "And there's not a day goes by that I don't think about it, Miss Olsen." His voice cracked again.

"Think about what, Mr. Bird?"

"Think about how greedy it was of me to take all that wood and stack it all up right there like kindlin'. How, if I hadn't done that"—his voice cracked—"how if I hadn't done that, little Liam Carmody would still be alive." A tear leaked from the corner of his eye as he turned to the jury. "I'm just so, so sorry."

"No one here thinks this is your fault, Mr. Bird."

"That's kind of you, Miss Olsen. But I don't always feel that way."

I'm sure Astrid Olsen had other questions for Benny Bird. She was smart enough not to ask them. "No further questions, Your Honor."

Here was my problem—Benny Bird had been out on the barbeque competition circuit since I'd arrived in Northlake and had only come back for this one day between competitions out of a sense of duty and a deep respect for the legal system. I hadn't been able to talk to him, at all, about what he knew, which very well might be absolutely nothing. And Astrid Olsen had just made it so that the jury would not tolerate me wasting any of their time or keeping Benny Bird from his divine purpose. I mentally crossed off almost all of my questions and stood.

"Mr. Bird, when did you first stack that wood next to the unit?"

Benny Bird looked up and said, "I do believe Len pulled his trees in spring the year before, so I'd say that it was cut and stacked by early last summer."

"Was it dry enough to burn without an accelerant?"

Benny Bird nodded. "It had sat out for almost a year. I was going to start using it this summer, but of course, now it's nothing but a pile of ash." His eyes grew wide. "I'm sorry, I don't mean to say that me losing the wood was important. I found more, for sure."

"We all understand, Mr. Bird. No one took it that way."

"Thank you, Mr. Shepherd. I just had plans for a specialty cherry wood tenderloin that I'd been tinkering with."

I smiled. "Pork or venison?"

Benny Bird grinned. "See now, you've hit right on it, Mr. Shepherd. I planned to do both. I'd cook the pork myself all summer but then, when hunting season came around, I'd set up my smokers so that hunters could come in every Saturday and smoke their own venison tenderloins."

"Like a class?"

"More of a time for like-minded folks to gather and if they laughed and learned a little about smoking, all the better."

"I've never heard of something like that."

"Well, you know I can't take credit for it. Tommy was the one who had that idea."

"Tommy?"

"Tommy Chase, the guy who rents the unit next to me. We'd see each other now and again at the unit, and when he asked me what the wood was for, I told him and he said how he'd love to put some tenderloins on my smoker and, bam, the smoke your own idea came right after. He saw the appeal right away."

"Oh?"

"Yeah, Tommy knows his woods, although he puts them on floors instead of using it to cook. Told me he'd wished he known all that cherry was available at the orchard, but by the time he'd checked, it was too late."

I was running out of time with the jury. "What did you lose in the fire, Mr. Bird?"

"All of the cherry wood, but I can't complain since all that cost was my time. My smoker was damaged, but steel and cast iron doesn't burn. The trailer I use to hall it was shot and one—no, two plastic tents in there. Maybe a couple of coolers of spices and rubs and such."

"Was there anything else in the unit?"

"No, Mr. Shepherd, that's about all."

"Thanks, Mr. Bird, that's all I—"

"—So you smoke yourself then?"

I stopped. "I do."

"I'll make sure to send you some of my pork rub."

I smiled. "That's very kind. Thanks." I sat down.

"Ms. Olsen?"

"No further questions, Your Honor."

"That was rude of me," said Benny Bird. "I'll send some to you too, Miss Olsen."

She gave a stiff nod. "Thank you, Mr. Bird."

With that, Benny Bird was excused from the stand.

"We'll take a ten-minute break and come back," said Judge Roderick and excused the jury.

∽

I WAS HUDDLING with Emily and Cyn about our approach to the next witness, Tommy Chase, while Dagmar Niesen was leaning over the rail talking to Brock. She'd done the same thing during every break the day before—talk to him quietly, often reaching out to touch his shoulder. Brock had been a typical sullen teenager every time I'd met with him, and he was not much different now except that he listened to her, and he nodded, and once, he put his hand on hers.

Dagmar knew these might be some of the last times she would have access to her son. It appeared that Brock was realizing the same thing.

A shriek went up from the back of the courtroom and yes, that's exactly what the sound was. I looked. Kimberly Tripp was standing there, holding out her phone as it blared, "That's why today at Midwest Fruit—"

"—Mrs. Tripp?" Mason Pierce stood and, even from a distance he loomed over the courtroom. "Please take your phone outside."

"Of course, Mason," she said, and killed the sound. Then she looked at Dagmar Niesen with a light in her eyes that her red plastic glasses could not contain. "Check your emails," she said to Dagmar, then pushed out the big double doors. There was another shriek, more gleeful than the first, and then a "They're doing it!" as the doors swung shut.

I looked at Dagmar, who was already looking at her phone. Her lips curled inward.

"What is it, Mom?" said Brock.

"It's nothing, Son," she said, and put it in her pocket.

"Mom?!"

"Your trial is what's important. Let's concentrate on that."

"You know I can't now!"

Dagmar looked at me.

I nodded. "Best to know what we're dealing with."

She looked back to Brock. "Midwest Fruit has cancelled our apple contract. But don't worry, we'll be fine."

For the first time, I saw real concern on Brock Niesen's face. "They buy most of our crop, don't they?"

"There are plenty of people that need apples, Son. Let's keep our eyes on the ball here."

I went back to talking with Cyn, and Dagmar tried to distract Brock by telling him how their dog Chet was doing.

Her soft voice seemed to calm Brock down and he didn't seem to notice when she shot a glare over her shoulder at the courtroom door.

Then I put the Golden Apple Orchard's plight aside and concentrated on Tommy Chase.

44
———

After the break, Astrid Olsen called Tommy Chase into the courtroom. He wore black pants, faded at the seams, with a blue Oxford shirt that strained to button at the neck and the belly. He lumbered in slowly, like someone who'd hurt his back, which I suppose he had. He put a hand on the back of each pew as he passed, as if for balance, and when Mrs. Tripp patted his hand, he nodded and smiled.

Tommy Chase settled into the witness chair with a sigh, ran both hands over the hat-line on the back of his hair, then swore to tell the truth, the whole-truth and nothing but the truth so help him God.

His eyes wandered around the courtroom until they found me. I did my best poker face. His eyes jerked away.

"Could you state your name for the record, please?" said Astrid Olsen.

"Tommy Chase."

"What do you do for a living, Mr. Chase?"

"I'm in construction."

"What kind?"

"Flooring mostly."

"Do you rent a storage unit out at the U-Store on Mission Road?"

"I do. I mean, I did. It's gone now."

"Gone how?"

"It burned down in the fire that kid started."

As I stood, Astrid Olsen raised one hand and said, "Mr. Chase, you're only allowed to testify to things you know so, to save Mr. Shepherd and the Court time, let's be clear, you didn't see Brock Niesen start any fires, did you?"

"No. But isn't that why we're here?"

"Judge?" I said.

Judge Roderick nodded. "Mr. Chase, you will limit your testimony to things you actually witnessed. Members of the jury, you will disregard Mr. Chase's conclusory statements as they are not evidence."

As I sat, Astrid Olsen said, "Mr. Chase, what did you use your storage unit for?"

"Work supplies, mostly."

"Like what?"

"Flooring and such. Usually, I would have things delivered direct to the site, but there are always excess materials when you're laying a floor, so I'd take what was left and put it in the unit."

"Why would you do that?"

"Because then a job might come up later where I could use the remnants. Happens more than you think."

"I see. And did you lose anything in the Mission Road Fire?"

"I sure did. All the inventory I had stored in my unit."

"And what did that consist of?"

"I had some carpet and padding that I lost. I had some tiles that survived, but they're covered in smoke and such. The worst was the rosewood flooring though." He shook his head. "I lost all of it."

"Tell me about that."

"I was doing a job over at the Bluffs. Or I was going to do a job, I should say. I had an install for an entire first floor of Patagonian Rosewood. Beautiful stuff. The renovation was running behind though and the homeowner didn't want to keep all that flooring at his home. So I'd stashed it at my unit until they were ready for me."

"Who was the homeowner?"

"Mr. Warhelm."

"That's John Warhelm?"

"Yes."

"What happened to the rosewood flooring?"

"It went up like a candle."

"It's flammable then?"

"I mean, it's wood."

"Did you lose it all?"

"Every last plank. Most expensive bonfire ever."

"Is it a costly material?"

"Very. It's a pretty rare wood, but it burns like any other."

"Speaking of which, we heard from Benny Bird earlier today."

Tommy smiled. "Ol' Benny had quite the barbeque."

"What do you mean?"

Tommy's smile faded. "I didn't mean anything, really. His stuff went up like mine."

"He mentioned that he had stacks of cherry wood outside the unit?"

"He did."

"You saw it before the fire?"

"I did. That's all gone too, and that's a damn, excuse me,

that's a dang shame. It had finally seasoned, and Benny was going to use it to smoke us some pork butts."

"Benny said you knew that was good wood?"

"Sure. Cherry wood is right up there. A shame the kid screwed that up too."

I stood. "Move to strike, Your Honor."

"Sustained. The jury will disregard that last comment. Mr. Chase, keep your editorializing to yourself."

Tommy Chase nodded. "Yes, sir."

"And you saw where the wood was stacked?"

"Yes."

"Where?"

"Right between the drive-in fence and the unit, real tight like."

"If the fence were on fire, it would be touching the wood?"

"Well, the woodpile was certainly stacked along the fence if that's what you're asking."

"And you had wood flooring stacked in your unit?"

"I sure did."

"How much?"

"Enough to cover the first floor of Mr. Warhelm's house."

"Can you describe it more than that?"

"Well, it's a big house. I'd say I had it stacked waist high, and it covered more than half the unit."

"And it was a total loss?"

"Every last bit of it."

Astrid Olsen nodded and scrolled through her tablet. Then she put it down, folded her hands on the lectern, and said, "That's not the only thing you lost in the fire, is it?"

"No, no it's not."

"What else did you lose in the fire, Mr. Chase?"

"My best friend, Eli Tripp."

"How did you know Eli?"

"We grew up together. Played football and baseball together." He looked past Astrid Olsen to where Karen Tripp sat. "Mrs. Tripp gave me a lot of Lunchables growing up."

"How about more recently?"

Tommy Chase scowled. "I haven't had any Lunchables recently, no."

"No, Mr. Chase. I mean Eli. Did you see him more recently? Before he was killed?"

"Oh, yeah, right. Sorry. Not as much as before, of course. He was always taking shifts to fight fires, and I was working too, but we still went out some, yeah."

"You said Eli was always taking shifts to fight fires. Did he enjoy it?"

Tommy Chase nodded. "That's all he ever wanted to do, ever since we were little. Took his qualifying exam right out of high school, took a training course at Northlake CC—"

"—That's Northlake Community College?"

"Right. And was hired almost straightaway. There was a time I tried too but"—he looked down at his belly—"I'm not quite built for carrying things up a ladder."

"How has Eli's death impacted—"

I stood. "Your Honor, may we approach?"

Judge Roderick didn't look surprised as he waved us up.

"Judge," I said. "This testimony is becoming a victim impact statement that's more appropriate in a sentencing hearing."

Astrid Olsen stood stiffly. "He had a relationship with one of the victims, Your Honor."

"I agree with Mr. Shepherd, Ms. Olsen. You've had some leeway to explain their relationship. Let's keep it to the alleged crimes right now."

Astrid Olsen nodded without looking at me as we returned.

"One last thing, Mr. Chase. Have you met Mr. Shepherd before?"

He looked down. "I have."

"Tell me about that."

"I ran into him outside the BeachHead a few weeks back."

"It was a little more than that, wasn't it?"

"I guess."

"What happened?"

"I punched him."

"As he came out of the bar?"

"Yes."

"What happened then?"

"We scuffled a bit."

"I see. Care to tell me why?"

"I…well, I…I'd had a bit to drink and a Thursday night football game is one of the times I might have seen Eli so I guess I was missing him and…well, Mr. Shepherd here from downstate and all, got me thinking that the Niesen kid, or whoever did it, might get away with it and…well I'm not proud of it, but it sort of got the better of me."

"By 'it' got the better of you, you mean your temper?"

"Yes. And Mr. Shepherd there did too, if I'm being honest."

"Thank you, Mr. Chase. No further questions."

I'd had no intention of asking Tommy Chase about our fight after he'd sucker punched me, but Astrid Olsen didn't know that, so she'd decided to be proactive. "Drawing out the sting" is what lawyers call it when you bring up something on direct that the other side might ask about on cross so that the jury will continue to trust you. I hadn't planned on bringing up any of that nonsense at the BeachHead, but since Astrid had, I needed to address it.

I stepped forward. "Hi, Mr. Chase."

"Hi."

"You and Ms. Olsen were talking about our run-in at the BeachHead a couple of weeks ago, right?"

"That's right."

"You punched me as I was walking out of the bar after the Packers game, right?"

"I did."

"I didn't press charges, did I?"

"No, you didn't."

"I suppose you could argue that a Lions fan might deserve a whoopin' for being in a Packers bar on game day, couldn't you?"

A couple of jurors smiled.

"I believe you gave as good as you got. But yes."

"Devin Wright is the owner of the BeachHead, isn't he?"

"He is."

"He also owns the U-Store?"

"He does. I mostly dealt with Scooter though."

"That's Scooter Derry, the manager?"

"Yes."

"You talked to Scooter Derry and Devin Wright about making an insurance claim for the loss of your building supplies, didn't you?"

"I did. I didn't really know what was involved with doing that. Or who to call even."

"You said that your unit was filled with rosewood flooring planks?"

"Patagonian Rosewood, yes."

"Stacked about waist high and taking up half your unit or so?"

"That's about right."

"And you said it was the most expensive bonfire ever?"

Tommy Chase nodded his head. "Sure was."

"How much was the flooring worth?"

He paused. "About twenty grand."

"That is expensive. And you made an insurance claim for that loss, didn't you, Mr. Chase?"

"I tried to."

"What do you mean 'tried to?'"

"The U-Store insurance denied it. My insurance only allowed a partial claim."

"Which part?"

"For my carpet remnants and pads and such. A few tools."

"What about the rosewood flooring?"

He shook his head again. "My insurance company wouldn't cover it because I didn't have a receipt and because technically it wasn't mine. It was Mr. Warhelm's."

"That's the man who owned the home it was for?"

Tommy Chase nodded. "He's the one who replaced it, eventually. I was lucky; he could have sued me for the loss, which I never could have paid, but he said the fire wasn't my fault."

Nothing. Tommy Chase had nothing. The only thing he'd given me was a chance for some humor about him jumping me coming out of the bar and I wouldn't have gotten that if Astrid hadn't brought it up in the first place. He'd confirmed his unit was full of hardwood flooring that spread the fire toward the Carmodys' house and that he had no financial motive to burn it. In fact, the fire had almost ruined him financially and probably would have if this Warhelm guy weren't so understanding. My cross had added nothing to our defense. In sophisticated legal terms, I'd screwed the pooch.

There was only one thing left to do.

"No further questions, Judge," I said.

Astrid Olsen stood. "So the jury is clear, Mr. Chase, you didn't receive any insurance payments worth twenty thousand dollars for the rosewood flooring that was destroyed, right?"

"Not a cent."

"How much did you receive as a result of the fire?"

"About seventeen hundred dollars."

"Thank you, Mr. Chase."

As Judge Roderick dismissed us for lunch, I watched burly Tommy Chase shuffle out of court.

"At least you kicked his ass," said Emily.

I shook my head. "Not when it mattered."

45

The gallery of the courtroom was still full and while it could have been my imagination, it seemed to me that Kim Tripp and her sister were camping out by the door, conspicuously waiting for us to pass.

"Maggie's dropped our order off," said Emily, holding up a bag. "Where do you want to go?"

I knew Brock was having a hard enough time keeping it together. Subjecting him to the Tripps, or even all the other onlookers in general, wasn't going to help.

I went over to the side desk. "Excuse me, Mason?"

Mason Pierce looked up. "How can I help you, Mr. Shepherd?"

"Is there someplace in the courthouse we can eat?"

"Sure, there's the deli on the first floor or the coffee stand by—"

"—We have food. Is there a room anywhere that's not being used? Somewhere more private?"

"All five of you?"

"If you can."

He nodded and stood. "This way," he motioned and made his way toward a side door near the bench.

I said something to Cyn who snapped something to Emily, who gestured to Brock and Dagmar, and we all followed Mason Pierce through a door he barely fit through.

We came out into the general hallway but a little farther down and to the side from the main entrance. Given the crowd, I was glad.

We turned a corner and followed Mason Pierce down another hall. We rounded another corner and came face to face with Astrid Olsen.

Astrid stopped, her eyes locked with mine, then darted away instantly to Mason. She stared at him for a moment, then turned and walked in the other direction. Mason watched her go, then looked at me. "It's just up this stair."

"Have I offended her in some way, Mason?"

"Why would you say that?"

"I've tried cases against people who couldn't stand me who've been more willing to talk."

"Atti's been burned by a defense lawyer before." Mason stopped, frowned, and I could tell, instantly regretted saying it. "I shouldn't have said that."

I waved. "I won't mention it. And it'll keep me from wondering what I did."

Mason led us up a narrow stair to a landing with a small door. He took out a key and, in a way that reminded me of a half-giant leading a boy wizard into a secret chamber, opened it.

We were on the second level of the library, directly under the dome where the light streamed in through arched windows. A small circular table sat in a nook between two arches. There were only two chairs, but the raised stone landings in the arches on either side provided window seats for the rest.

"Here you go," said Mason. Two hardcover books and a

smooth, round gray stone sat on the table; Mason swept up the books and pocketed the stone. "This is the service entrance. No one will bother you up here."

"But where will you eat?" I said.

"The judge and I have to take care of other matters during the break anyway." He smiled. "Take your garbage down with you. They don't empty it up here."

"Done. Thanks, Mason."

He nodded and left.

It was a little awkward, spreading out between the table and the window seats, but it was far better being surrounded by books and arched windows than rubberneckers and protestors.

Emily had doled out the sandwiches (all correct from Maggie, by the way), and we had started to eat when Dagmar's phone buzzed. She excused herself and went back out onto the landing to take the call while Cyn and I agreed, without saying it directly in front of Brock, that I had to do better this afternoon, or we were in serious trouble.

I was going through my questions for the next witness with Emily when I heard, "But it will all just rot!" and then another sound that I was pretty sure I recognized.

I gestured to the others, including Brock who I told to stay there, and went out onto the landing to check on Dagmar.

She straightened, wiped her eyes, and hung up, all in one surprisingly swift motion.

"Lawyers," Dagmar said with one last swipe.

"We do have that effect. Usually not until we present the bill."

She half-smiled. "I'm sure he'll send me one of those too."

I pointed at her phone. "Something related to this?"

"No. Well, yes, but no. It was my business lawyer. He confirmed that Midwest Fruit is pulling out of our contract today. We had five years left and they're technically in breach, but my lawyer says that this"—she waved at the courthouse—"falls into some sort of morality clause or adverse publicity clause or screw-the-little-guy clause that gives them an argument that they can do it without notice. If we sue, we might win—years and hundreds of thousands of dollars from now."

I had spent time in a big civil firm. I knew exactly what she meant and thought she'd summarized it fairly accurately. "How bad is it?"

I think her lip trembled, but it was gone before I could be sure, and her eyes became blue ice. "I have apples on the ground, in my bins, and in my bushels. They'll rot before this is sorted."

I nodded. I understood, in the abstract, yes, but I understood. "How leveraged are you?"

"Enough that this will sink us."

I stood there next to her for a moment, just standing, then said, "I can tell Brock you had to go if you need to tend to this."

"My son needs your support, Nate. Not me. Just give me a moment."

I nodded and watched as the emotion drained from her face and she became the implacably hard pillar of support I'd seen all week.

"All right," she said. "I've wasted enough time. I don't want Maggie's BLT to go to waste."

We went back into the library. Dagmar told Brock that his uncle had almost tipped his tractor mowing a ditch, and I pulled out my sandwich.

Good Lunch! was written on the wrapper.

I would need it.

∼

Cruel Sentence

NAOMI HOPPEL WAS the little old lady who had rented the third storage unit and when she appeared in court, it turned out she was indeed little and old and dressed like a lady attending a tea party. She testified clutching, and I kid you not, a small pink handbag from which she extracted a tissue more than once. She told the jury how she'd had to move out of her home of forty years after Larry had died and that, while the place her kids had found for her was quite nice, what with the common area and the meal delivery and all, it couldn't hold all of the things from her house and certainly couldn't hold all of the memories of her life with Larry. And while she knew that an insurance company wouldn't put much of value on the things she had stored in her unit—from the armoire that had been her grandmother's to her father's roll-top desk to scrapbooks she'd done with her kids and grandkids and now two great grandkids, thank you very much, along with all of those quilts that had been in Mary Roscoe's house when she'd passed that revealed so much about the history of Northlake—well, there were some things you can't put a price tag on or make an insurance claim for because memories are more important than money, as she told her grandkids every chance she got, which wasn't nearly enough.

And yes, it was all flammable and she was not surprised that it had burned like the devil himself. And she felt partially to blame for how big the fire had been because not the day before, she'd gone with her grandson to add a vintage rocker and a butter churn she'd found at the Frankfort flea market and stuffed them right into her storage unit even though it was so full they barely fit.

She unclasped her handbag with a snap and pulled out another tissue to dab her watery eyes. "If Mr. Bird and Mr. Chase hadn't helped, I don't know that my Zachary would have been able to squeeze them in at all."

"And all of your things were destroyed, Mrs. Hoppel?"

The dabbing was furious now. "It all burned, dear. Along with that poor sweet boy."

"Thank you, Mrs. Hoppel."

I stood and stepped into the pink-clad minefield.

"Mrs. Hoppel, I'm Nate Shepherd. I represent Brock Niesen."

"Miss Olsen told me you might ask some questions."

"Only a couple. You say you were there the day before the fire?"

"Yes. I had to wait until Zachary got off work, he hired on with the concrete plant in Manistee so it was later than I'd like, but he's the only grandson with a truck so beggars can't be choosers."

"And the wood pile was there that day, on the far side of the unit?"

Mrs. Hoppel clucked and shook her head. "Yes, it was. I tried to get Mr. Bird to get rid of it. I mean it was home to so many mice that would run from his wood pile to my quilts and eat a hole through them. Do you know how fast a mouse can ruin a quilt?"

"I imagine pretty fast, Mrs. Hoppel."

"Quick as a blink, young man."

"So it was late when you were there, at your unit?"

"Later than I'd like. I had to wait until Zachary finished his shift, then he had to drive to my house here in Northlake, then we, well he, had to load the rocker and butter churn into his truck and then by the time we got there, to the U-Store that is, it was Grand Central Station in our row. Mr. Bird was blocking one side of the aisle, hooking up his trailer with that barbeque contraption, and Mr. Chase was blocking the other side with a truck, so we settled in to wait for them to finish."

"I see. Did—"

"—Mr. Bird was concentrating on switching out his smoking contraptions, who even knew that you need more than one of those monstrous things, and Mr. Chase had one of those big supply trucks with the roll-up back, you know the type, angled right across my unit. Mr. Chase is a good boy though. He came right over and made small talk—he never fails to ask about my granddaughter, if you ask me he was sweet on her in high school—and then asked what we were doing. When he heard we only had two things, he said he'd be unloading for a while yet, so he pulled his truck right out of the way, got Mr. Bird, and the two of them helped Zachary move my things around so that the rocking chair and butter churn would fit inside. They really are sweet boys, all of them."

"Thank you, Mrs. Hoppel, that's all—"

"Oh," her eyes brightened, and she pointed a tissue filled hand at me. "Miss Olsen said that you would want to know about insurance."

"—That's not necess—"

"I had several valuable pieces in there. I'm sure I could get two hundred dollars for the armoire. And I had at least four, no six, other primitive furnishings that were worth at least one hundred dollars."

"—Really, Mrs. Hoppel—"

"One hundred *each*. Of course, the quilts and scrapbooks were far more valuable." She started dabbing her eyes again. "But only to me."

Getting a dear, sweet old lady off the stand without seeming to bully her is more difficult than threading a cross-stitch needle in the dark. Especially when she's killing you.

"Thank you, Mrs. Hoppel. I don't have—"

"Listen to me prattle on." She dabbed. "You wanted to know about insurance. My daughter handled the claim for me. She says they might pay as much as two thousand dollars. That's a lot but hardly enough for your memories, is it?"

"No, ma'am. Thank you, Mrs. Hoppel, that's all I have."

"Nothing else?" She sniffed. "It's not like the movies, is it?"

I smiled. "No, ma'am, it isn't."

I sat down. Judge Roderick dismissed her, then dismissed us and the jury.

We'd made no progress that day. In fact, things had gotten significantly worse.

46

"Things are worse," said Emily.

"Yes," I said.

The three of us sat there, eating quietly in the office. Emily folded her sandwich wrapper with a thump on each crease as she said, "Piles of wood, carpet remnants, flooring, and old furniture."

"Don't forget the quilts."

"The quilts! How could I forget dearly departed Mary Roscoe's collection of legacy quilts!" She shook her head in disgust. "All of it flammable and not a bit of it worth burning."

Cyn was alternating between whatever she was doing on her computer and precise bites of a grilled chicken caesar. "Today was a setback."

"Ya think?" said Emily.

"Sending a report?" I asked.

Cyn nodded. "You have enough to do. I'll update the Firm."

"Let me know if they want to have a call."

"They won't right now. They know how these things go."

"How can you be so calm, Cyn?" said Emily. "I'm used to this one's placid positivity—"

"Thanks?" I said.

"—but we just got our ass handed to us today and you haven't even twitched."

Cyn kept typing. "We get paid to try cases, not to win them."

"You don't want to win?"

"Who said that?"

"You just did!"

Cyn turned to Emily. "If you want to be the trial lawyer you say you do, you'll have to develop a more subtle understanding of what people say. And don't."

Emily's head jerked back.

"Nathan did all that he could with the information we received today. What we need is more information we can use, which is what I assume he is going to work on right now."

I nodded. "As soon as we're done, I'm calling Olivia and Bret Halogi to see what we can do."

"And to answer your other question, Emily Lake, I want to win every winnable case. And I do."

As Cyn turned back to her computer, I stood. "I'm taking the paramedics tomorrow."

"I thought you were going to let me do it?" said Emily.

"With all that's happened, I need to take them."

"You said that when you took the rental witnesses back! And it couldn't have gone worse today!"

Cyn stopped typing, turned, and stared. "Yes, Emily, it could have."

She kept her green gaze on Emily a beat longer, then went back to typing.

When Emily looked back to me, I said, "If things go sideways tomorrow, I'm going to be the face of it."

Emily didn't look happy, but the air went out of her, and she nodded and said, "Sorry, Boss."

"Don't be. Trials are trials."

I went into my office to call Olivia.

"How'd it go today, Shep?"

I told her. In detail.

"Ouch."

"On top of that, Dagmar Niesen lost all of her contracts for her orchard."

"I saw that online. Kim Tripp hasn't been able to stop posting about it. Can Dagmar fight it?"

"Not according to what her lawyer told her today."

"One thing at a time, I guess. So, it was really that bad today?"

"The prosecutor even made Tommy Chase jumping me seem endearing."

"To be fair, you had it coming for being in a Packers bar."

"Right. And every one of those rental units was filled with very cheap and very flammable crap."

"How can I help?"

"I'm not sure. We didn't get much new info today. Mrs. Hoppel said all three of them were there the day before unloading things into their units. And Chase said that the homeowner, John Warhelm, is the one who might have received the insurance payment to replace the wood flooring that was worth twenty grand or so. Maybe dig into that?"

"Seems thin."

"It's all thin, Liv."

"I'm on it. Let me know if something else comes up?"

"Always. Thanks."

We hung up. I went to call Bret Halogi, had a second thought, and called Cade instead.

"What's up?" he said.

"How are things going at the Orchard?"

"I need more jobs sitting by a firepit in a lawn chair in front of my camper, sipping whiskey while holding a shotgun and looking at the stars."

I chuckled. Subtlety had never been Cade's strong suit. "Is that a deterrent?"

"No sign of spray painters and fire bombers today."

"Good. Dagmar got some bad news today." I told him about the cancellation of the apple contracts.

Cade was quiet a moment, then said, "There are an awful lot of apples over here, man."

"So I understand."

"That's a shame. Need anything else from me?"

"Don't think so. Can you stay through the weekend though?"

"Planning on it."

"Thanks."

"Dream job, brother."

We hung up, and I dialed Bret Halogi.

"Hi, Nate. Am I still going to testify Friday?"

"Yes. I'm going to cross-examine their fire witnesses tomorrow. Thought I'd fill you in on what happened today and get your thoughts."

"Great. Shoot."

I told her about Benny Bird, Tommy Chase, Naomi Hoppel, and the contents of their units.

"That, as we say in the industry, is some flammable shit."

"That's what it seemed like to me," I said.

"They confirmed the cherry wood pile was against the fence?"

"Yes." I heard her pen scratch as she took notes.

"And that the carpeting and flooring was in the second unit?"

"Yes."

"How much flooring did he say?"

"Enough to cover half the unit waist high."

"Hardwood?"

"Patagonian Rosewood."

"And junk in the last one?"

"I don't think Mrs. Hoppel would describe it like that."

"I'm sure she wouldn't. Let's say things that were valueless to an insurer and flammable to a firefighter?"

"Accurate."

She was quiet for a moment, then said, "Nate, this all totally tracks with the fire spreading across these units. And Mrs. Hoppel said her unit was filled with this stuff?"

"Enough that her grandson and two more men had to shift things around to make room."

"If that's true, it's no leap for the fire to spread to the motorhome. And by no leap, I literally mean—"

"I got what you meant, Bret."

"—no leap. Those flames would've licked right across. Then boom.

Now we were both quiet.

"Any suggestions for their fire expert?" I asked.

"Get specifics. He didn't make a report so force him to commit to how it spread at each stage. I'll start re-looking at the samples and lab results tonight, but so far everything you've said has made sense."

I tapped the desk. "You said the flames would've licked across Mrs. Hoppel's unit, then boom? You're sure?"

"About the flames?"

"About the boom."

"Certain. Does it matter?"

"For what I'm going to ask tomorrow it does. Can I assume it was loud?"

"I can testify that, to a probability, it was loud."

"Enough to shake windows?"

"Nearby?"

"Yes."

"Yes."

"I'll call you tomorrow night."

"I'll be waiting."

We hung up. Then I tried to focus on my cross-examination of the fire witnesses.

The image of things collapsing in flames was not helpful.

47

The next day, Astrid Olsen told the story of the Mission Road Fire. First, Astrid called the 911 operator to establish that she'd received the call from Patrick Dabbs at 1:37 a.m. on April 10th. The operator dispatched two trucks at 1:38 a.m., and they arrived at the scene by 1:49 a.m., which the operator believed was a swift response time for a small community.

Next, Astrid called Fire Chief Rolf Hagen. Chief Hagen was a big blond Viking of a man with unruly hair and a flushed red face that looked like he'd just come from fighting a fire. Although he was in his late forties, he looked like he'd have no trouble running a coiled hose up a ladder, smashing a door with an axe, or carrying an unconscious person on his shoulder. He wore his dress uniform for court and, unlike Sheriff Sizemore, did not seem entirely comfortable on the stand, which he explained by stating that it was only the second time he'd actually had to testify in court despite a lifetime of service fighting fires in Northlake.

After he confirmed being dispatched to the Mission Road Fire, Astrid Olsen asked, "What did you do when you arrived at the scene, Chief Hagen?"

"As we pulled up, I could see that the U-Store facility and the Carmody house were active burns, so I called for more trucks before we even stopped. I also told dispatch to call for as many tanker trucks as they could pull from the surrounding districts."

"Why is that?"

"This area was outside of town. There were no hydrants, and no creeks or ponds we could pull from. It appeared that we were only going to be able to use what we brought with us."

"What did you do next?"

"The Carmody house was the only dwelling, so we set up there. As one team was prepping the hoses, another went to the house. Hauser and Tripp broke down the front door—"

"—That's firefighters Clay Hauser and Eli Tripp?"

"Yes. They broke down the door but before they could go in, Maura Carmody stumbled out with two children who I later learned were her daughters, Sasha and Felicity."

"What happened next?"

Chief Hagen raised his chin. "Hauser picked up Felicity and led Mrs. Carmody and Sasha to the paramedics. Tripp ran inside."

"The burning house?"

"The burning house."

"Why?"

"Because Mrs. Carmody said her son was still inside."

"That's little Liam?"

"Yes."

"Was it safe to go in the house?"

"No fire is safe, Ms. Olsen."

"Did you believe there was time for Firefighter Tripp to get Liam out?"

"That doesn't matter. Our job is to go in."

"And Eli Tripp did?"

"Yes, he did."

Cruel Sentence

"Was that the right decision?"

"One hundred percent."

"What happened next?"

"At 1:56 a.m., the Carmody house collapsed."

"Had Eli Tripp and Liam made it out?"

"I wasn't sure at first. I was hoping that Tripp had made it out the back."

"Did you eventually learn what happened?"

"Yes."

"What?"

"Eli Tripp and Liam Carmody were in the house when it collapsed."

"How do you know that?"

"I found their bodies."

"You personally?"

"Yes."

There was a muffled sob from the back of the courtroom. Judge Roderick looked back there but didn't say anything. Astrid Olsen paused and let the sound filter through the courtroom. I watched the jury, who were torn between Chief Hagan and Kimberly Tripp.

Eventually, Astrid Olsen said, "Don't you have firefighters to do that?"

"I am in charge of my men, Ms. Olsen. I'm charged with their safety."

"For the record, is there any doubt that you found Eli and Liam?"

"None. We made a positive identification after the blaze was controlled."

"Tell me about controlling the fire."

"As I mentioned, we had limited access to water. We received support from surrounding communities and refilled our own tankers and eventually the blaze at all three structures was controlled by 4:24 a.m."

"All three structures—that's the Drive-In, the U-Store, and the Carmody house?"

"Yes."

"Did you have an opinion that night as to the cause of the fire?"

"Not at that time, no. I called in Kurt Vernon to investigate, along with police forensics."

"Did you have an opinion as to the direction the fire had spread?"

"Yes. That was clear. The fire had spread west to east, from the Drive-In to the U-Store to the Carmody house."

"Why was that clear?"

"There were significant winds out of the west that night of fifteen miles per hour with gusts to twenty-five. We could see it, the fire, pushing east as we were fighting it. Also, by the time we arrived, the fire at the Drive-In had virtually died out while the fire in the east section of the U-Store lot and the Carmody house was still raging."

"Were you involved in the investigation that night, Chief Hagen?"

"Other than recovering the bodies of Eli Tripp and Liam Carmody, no."

"Why is that?"

"Kurt Vernon was taking the lead with the fire investigation. And I had other tasks."

"Such as?"

"We exhausted a lot of resources responding to this call. I had to assess our equipment status and get us back to full readiness as quickly as possible."

"Why is that?"

"There's always another fire, Ms. Olsen. We have to be ready."

"Your equipment was not the only thing you had to assess, was it?"

"No. I had to assess and manage my men."

"They were exhausted from fighting the fire, I assume?"

"That wasn't a problem. Losing a brother was. I had to evaluate how they were doing."

"How were they doing?"

"About how you'd expect."

"Which was?"

"Not well." Chief Hagen paused before he said, "We don't begrudge the sacrifice, Ms. Olsen. But that doesn't mean it's easy."

Astrid Olsen nodded. "Was there something else you had to do that night while Kurt Vernon was investigating the fire?"

"Yes."

"What was that?"

"I had to tell Mrs. Tripp that her son had passed."

"Did you?"

"Yes. I went to her house. I was there for some time."

There was another sob, just quiet enough that Judge Roderick did not acknowledge it. But we all heard it.

"Was Eli Tripp a good firefighter, Chief Hagen?"

"The best, Ms. Olsen."

"Did he make a mistake going into that burning building to try to save Liam Carmody?"

"Absolutely not."

"Did he do anything wrong at all? By that I mean, was there something else he could have done that would have made the rescue successful?"

"He did everything right, Ms. Olsen. He just ran out of time."

"No further questions, Your Honor."

I stood.

"Chief Hagen, I believe you said that when you arrived on the scene, the fire was focused on the east unit of the U-Store and the Carmody house, do I have that right?"

"You do."

"Patrick Dabbs made the 911 call at 1:37 a.m. indicating the bushes at the drive-in and the west end of the U-Store were on fire. That's not consistent with what you saw when you arrived twelve minutes later at 1:49 a.m., is it?"

"We just agreed that the east end and the Carmody house were on fire when I arrived, Counselor."

"That's right. Based on your experience as a firefighter, it's more likely that Mr. Dabbs observed the fire sometime before midnight, isn't it?"

"I couldn't say when Mr. Dabbs saw the fire."

"Based on your decades of experience fighting fires and your knowledge of the conditions that night, it's certainly reasonable to say that the fire took more than an hour and a half to spread from the west end to the east end of the U-Store, isn't it?"

Chief Hagen thought. "That's reasonable, yes. I'm not sure how it's relevant, but that's a reasonable assumption."

"So there was a significant delay in calling in the fire, wasn't there?"

"That's possible. I couldn't say for sure."

"The fire didn't spread from the wood pile on the west end, through all the units, through the motorhome then the Carmody house in twelve minutes, did it?"

"No, the fire probably didn't spread that far, that fast."

"So it's likely there was a delay in calling in the fire, right?"

"It's likely there was some delay, yes. I can't say how much."

"That's fine, Chief Hagen. You mentioned Kurt Vernon was the fire investigator on this case?"

"He was."

"You didn't personally investigate how the fire ignited and actually spread, did you?"

"It seemed pretty apparent."

"Sure, but Mr. Vernon is the one who actually did the scientific leg work to reach that opinion, right?"

"He did."

"You would defer to a fire investigator regarding the causes of ignition and spread in this case, wouldn't you?"

"I would defer to Mr. Vernon on those issues."

"You would defer to anyone who scientifically analyzed the evidence on the scene, wouldn't you?"

"I suppose I would have to know their opinion first."

"Well, you didn't conduct a physical examination of debris left in U-Store units, did you?"

"I examined the debris of the Carmody house."

"We'll get to that. You didn't examine the debris of the U-Store units, did you?"

"No."

"You didn't examine the debris of the motorhome, did you?"

"No."

"You did examine the structural remains of the Carmody house but that was limited to a search for Eli Tripp and Liam Carmody, right?"

Chief Hagen stared. "For their bodies, yes."

"You didn't conduct any scientific testing on the structural remains of the Carmody house, right?"

"That's right."

"Or the U-Store units?"

"That's right."

"Or any other area subjected to fire that night."

"That's right."

"So you have no scientific basis to object to the findings of Kurt Vernon or any other investigator, do you?"

"Only what I observed that night."

"Which did not include scientific testing, correct?"

"That's right."

"Speaking of what you observed, did you speak to Maura Carmody that night?"

"I did not. I was managing the fire, and she was gone to the hospital by the time I was done."

"So you didn't have the opportunity to evaluate her, right?"

"No, our paramedics took care of her."

I nodded. "Chief Hagen, you mentioned that by the time you'd arrived on the scene, the motorhome was already burning, didn't you?"

"That's right."

"There was evidence that the motorhome had exploded, wasn't there?"

"That's the conclusion Investigator Vernon reached. It was borne out by the scattering of debris that I saw."

"That would have been loud, wouldn't it?"

"I wasn't there. I can't say."

"You've heard motor vehicles explode, haven't you?"

"I have. I didn't hear this one."

"We can agree that motor vehicle explosions are usually loud, can't we?"

Chief Hagen stared before he said, "I'm not sure what you're getting at, Counselor."

"I am asking whether you and I can agree that motor vehicle explosions are usually loud. Can we?"

Chief Hagen glanced that the jury. "Usually, yes."

"Thanks, Chief Hagen. That's all I have."

Astrid Olsen stood. "Chief Hagen, it's ludicrous for defense counsel to blame Maura Carmody for not waking up and getting her children out of the house after the explosion, isn't it?"

I stayed standing. "Objection and move to strike, Your Honor. I didn't say that at all. Ms. Olsen did."

Astrid Olsen pressed her lips together.

"Sustained and granted," said Judge Roderick. "The jury will disregard that last statement from the prosecutor."

Astrid Olsen turned back to Chief Hagen. "Chief Hagen, you were on the scene of the fire for hours?"

"I was."

"You observed the fire?"

"I did."

"Although you did not perform any testing, you did not observe anything that led you to doubt Investigator Vernon's findings that this fire started with the explosion of a SafeBoom target and gasoline at the Lakeside Drive-In, did you?"

"I did not."

"Thank you."

I stood as Astrid Olsen sat. "So the jury's clear, Chief Hagen, by the time you observed the fire, it had already engulfed the U-Store units, the motorhome, and the Carmody house, right?"

"That's right."

"You didn't *observe* how it got there, did you?"

"No. I observed its consequences."

"Thank you."

As Chief Hagen left, he stared at me, nodded to Astrid, and stopped briefly to put a hand on Mrs. Tripp's shoulder, who nodded as she wiped her nose with a tissue.

Great.

"Next witness, Ms. Olsen?" said Judge Roderick.

"The State calls paramedic Grant Ferris, Your Honor."

48

Grant Ferris seemed even younger in his dress uniform than he had at Laramie's grocery store. He removed his hat to show his red hair had been newly trimmed and the freckles and mid-face tan line made him look more like a kid who'd just come in from playing ball than a paramedic who saved lives, which shows just how deceiving looks can be.

The young paramedic spoke quietly with a tremor in his voice until Astrid asked him to speak up. He told the jury about growing up in Northlake, about training to be a paramedic, and about the three years he'd been on the job before Astrid asked whether he was one of the responders to the Carmody fire.

"I was."

"What did you do?"

"We were the first rescue unit there so our job was to handle the first people in need of assistance."

"And did you fulfill that role?"

"I did."

"How?"

"Shortly after we arrived, firefighter Hauser helped guide

Mrs. Carmody and her two girls out of the fire. He brought them to me."

"What did you find?"

"They had varying degrees of smoke inhalation, Mrs. Carmody's a little worse than the girls. They also had minor burns. The girls were scared as you might imagine."

"I'm sure. What happened next?"

"It was pretty chaotic, with new engines arriving and all of the noise and sirens and things that go along with fighting a fire. I'd barely started to evaluate them when the west side of the house collapsed."

"Is that when Eli Tripp and Liam Carmody were killed?"

"I believe so, yes, but I was focused on Mrs. Carmody and the girls. I continued to evaluate them, provide supportive care, and then, about 2:16 a.m., we decided to transport them from the scene to the hospital."

"That's about twenty minutes after the house collapsed?"

"Yes."

"What happened next?"

"We proceeded to the emergency room at Northlake Hospital and transferred care to the emergency staff there and returned to the fire."

"Did you treat anyone else that night?"

"No. Unfortunately, there weren't any other survivors."

"Were you involved in the recovery of the fatalities?"

Grant Ferris looked down. "I was."

"Had you ever been involved in that process before?"

"No. This was the first time."

"The first time recovering a firefighter or a civilian?"

"Both," he said quietly.

"What did you do then?"

"I helped transfer El—I helped transfer the bodies then returned to the firehouse for a debriefing."

"A debriefing?"

"The Chief and the Lieutenant were there to discuss all of our findings and logs so that a complete report could be made."

"Did you discuss your findings with them?"

"Yes."

"Did you discuss the events of the evening with anyone else?"

He nodded.

"You need to answer out loud, Mr. Ferris."

"Yes."

"Who?"

"A counselor."

"There was a counselor there too?"

He nodded again.

"Out loud, please, Mr. Ferris."

"Yes, there was a counselor there that night that the union provided."

"You spoke to her?"

"I did." Grant Ferris was still looking down. "Eli had played ball with my oldest brother."

"Thank you, Mr. Ferris. No further questions."

I stood. "Would you like to take a break, Mr. Ferris?"

His head snapped up. "No. No, thank you."

"That was a very difficult night for everyone, wasn't it?"

"Yes. Very."

"As part of your duties as a trained paramedic, you evaluated Mrs. Carmody and the girls, right?"

"I did."

"You mentioned smoke inhalation and minor burns?"

"Yes."

"Who had the burns, all of them?"

"No. It was primarily Sasha."

"Primarily Sasha or only Sasha?"

Grant Ferris shifted. "I guess only Sasha."

"Sasha was the only one you treated for burns, right?"

"That's right."

"According to your run report, those burns were on Sasha's hands, weren't they?"

"That's right."

"I assume you also evaluated them for shock?"

"We always do with victims of a traumatic accident or fire."

"Was Maura Carmody exhibiting signs of shock?"

Grant Ferris thought, then said, "Yes."

"You hesitated there."

"I was just remembering. Yes, she showed signs of shock."

"According to your run report, Maura Carmody was disoriented, wasn't she?"

"She was. That can be a sign of shock."

"It can, sure. Was it here?"

Astrid Olsen sprang to her feet. "Objection, Your Honor. What possible relevance can this have?"

I shrugged. "This case is all about Liam Carmody's death, Your Honor. I should be allowed to ask questions about the events surrounding it."

Judge Roderick took those brown glasses between his thumb and forefinger, staring as if he were trying to use the lenses to burn me like an ant. But he said, "Overruled. But keep to the immediate events, Mr. Shepherd."

I caught a glimpse of Astrid Olsen's glare as I turned back to Grant Ferris. "Mr. Ferris, in your professional opinion as a paramedic who has treated accident victims many times, was Maura Carmody's disorientation a sign of shock?"

The courtroom was silent. Grant Ferris looked from Astrid to the jury then me as the silence stretched on.

"I'm not sure," he said finally.

"Were you unsure at the time?"

"Yes."

"Why?"

"There was an element of grogginess that seemed…like more."

"Your Honor!" said Astrid Olsen.

Judge Roderick was staring at Grant Ferris. "Overruled, Ms. Olsen."

"Did you evaluate her for other sources of her disorientation?"

"We're pretty limited in the field."

"Sure. Did you do that limited evaluation?"

"I did, but I really couldn't tell much. I mean, we can't do blood tests or anything."

"What would a blood test show?"

Astrid's hands were clenched at her sides. "Your Honor! This is outrageous."

"It's not, Ms. Olsen," said Judge Roderick. "But the objection is sustained."

"You said you took Mrs. Carmody and the girls to the emergency room, right?"

"I did."

"Of course, the hospital has the ability to run blood tests, doesn't it?"

"Objection!" Astrid Olsen was just staying on her feet now.

"I'm sorry I have to ask, Your Honor, but the State won't give me Maura Carmody's hospital records."

"Sustained. Let's keep this to what this witness knows, Mr. Shepherd."

"Yes, Your Honor. Mr. Ferris, when you handed Mrs. Carmody off to the emergency room staff at Northlake Hospital, I assume you described her disorientation?"

"Yes."

"Did you recommend that they do blood tests?"

"Objection!"

"I'm only asking what he actually did and said, Your Honor."

"Overruled," said Judge Roderick.

I stepped closer. "Mr. Ferris, did you recommend to the ER staff that they do blood tests on Mrs. Carmody?"

"Yes."

"To investigate her disorientation and grogginess?"

"Yes."

"And like me, you don't have access to Mrs. Carmody's hospital records, so you don't know what the results of those tests were, or even if they were done, correct?"

"That's right."

"Mr. Ferris, you said Sasha was the only one of the three with burns, is that right?"

"That's right."

"And you said those burns were on her hands, correct?"

"They were."

"Did Sasha tell you how she got them?"

Astrid Olsen's palm smacked the desk as she stood. "Your Honor, when is this going to end?"

"With this question, Judge," I said.

Judge Roderick stared at me with barely contained intensity, but he said. "Overruled."

"This is hearsay, Your Honor," said Astrid Olsen.

I shook my head. "It's a present sense impression and an excited utterance, Judge."

"The objection is overruled, Ms. Olsen."

I turned to Grant Ferris. "How did Sasha tell you that she burned her hands, Mr. Ferris?"

Grant Ferris looked miserable as he said, "Getting to her mom's room."

"Thank you, Mr. Ferris. No further questions."

Astrid Olsen strode around the table until she was five feet in front of him. "Mr. Ferris, are you surprised that a woman who barely escaped from a house fire was in shock?"

"No, of course not."

"Are you surprised that a woman suffering from smoke inhalation was disoriented?"

"No."

"Are you surprised that a mother who had just rescued her daughters from a burning building was groggy?"

"No. No, ma'am."

"And for the love of God, the news of the death of your four-year-old son could certainly trigger shock, disorientation, and a grief reaction on a level most of us can't even understand, can't it?"

"Certainly, yes."

"There's no evidence that you're aware of that Maura Carmody mixed up a SafeBoom explosive, taped it to a gallon of gas, and blew it up with a high-powered rifle, is there?"

I didn't bother to stand on that one. "Objection, Your Honor."

"Sustained."

"Are you as offended as I am that counsel—"

"—Objection, Your Honor."

"Sustained. Ms. Olsen?"

Astrid Olsen raised her hand and literally took a deep breath before she said, "Mr. Ferris, the shock of smoke inhalation, the fear of escaping a fire, and the trauma of losing a son can all cause disorientation, can't they?"

"Yes. Yes, Ms. Olsen. Of course."

Astrid Olsen was rigidly calm as she went back to her seat.

I stood. "Mr. Ferris, you testified that the bodies of Eli Tripp and Liam Carmody weren't recovered until a couple of hours after you took Mrs. Carmody to the hospital, right?"

"That's right."

"So while Maura Carmody was in your care, did anyone tell her that her son had died?"

Grant Ferris looked down. "No. We didn't know for sure yet."

I nodded. "To be fair, I suppose she could have come to that conclusion when the house collapsed, right?"

"She could have except..." He shut his mouth, blushed, and looked down.

"Except what, Mr. Ferris?"

Silence.

"Mr. Ferris? Except what?"

Grant Ferris exhaled. "Except she wasn't aware of that either. That's why I was so concerned."

"Thank you, Mr. Ferris."

I sat down.

When Astrid Olsen gave a stiff shake of her head, Judge Roderick dismissed Grant Ferris from the stand and announced a one-hour break for lunch. The moment the jury was out of the room, Astrid Olsen charged over to my table, locking eyes with me for what I believed was the first time. She leaned in close, her words more hiss than whisper.

"You miserable shit. You're going to make me call her now. You're going to make her live through it again when she's barely hanging on as it is."

I pulled back, saw Astrid's face, and realized the truth. "You know what happened to her. You *know* and you didn't share it. This is on you, Astrid. *You* did this to her."

She blanched for a second before fury overtook her again as she whispered, "I'm going to *bury* you with her, do you hear me? I am going to bury you in her pain."

Astrid stepped back and raised her voice so the rest of my table could hear.

"And I'm going to put your client in a concrete box for the rest of his life."

49

We went up to our library hideaway for lunch. To be honest, we were kind of a somber group. Brock and Dagmar whispered as they unwrapped their sandwiches, while Cyn quietly ran me through the exhibits the State's fire investigator was going to use next.

Emily seemed particularly irritated and didn't have any comments on the morning testimony, which was unusual. She was frowning as she received one text, then another, then another.

She rolled her head and exhaled. "Be right back."

As the door snicked shut, I asked Cyn, "Know what that's about?"

"Her mother has concerns about whether beef wellington can get soggy."

"Ah."

"And I believe that she's uncertain about our strategy."

"Tell her to join the club."

"The jury is curious."

"Curious with reasonable doubt?"

"Curious to know what you're implying."

I nodded.

"If you don't deliver something, they're going to be angry."

"I know."

"Furious."

"I'm open to ideas."

Cyn's mouth ticked. "I provide structure for the man, or woman, with the ideas."

"Mr. Shepherd?"

Brock and Dagmar were looking at me.

"Yes, Brock?"

"Why was the prosecutor so angry with me this morning?"

"She wasn't mad at you, Brock. She was mad at me."

"Because you blamed Mrs. Carmody?"

"Is that how it seemed to you?"

Brock nodded. "Sorta, yeah." His shaggy hair, which had started the day combed, was falling into his eyes.

"Then yes." I leaned forward. "This afternoon is going to be hard, Brock. I'm going to need you to keep a straight face and, if any of it gets to be too much, just look down and write on the notepad."

"Write what?"

"Whatever you want."

"Okay. Why?"

"The fire expert is going to testify."

Brock tilted his head. "Okay?"

"He's probably going to end his testimony with the pictures."

"Oh?" His face fell as he realized what that meant. "Oh."

Dagmar Niesen put her hand over her son's and squeezed.

※

KURT VERNON WAS a fireplug of a man who strode into the courtroom like he was marching through snow. His brown blazer was open because there was no way he could have buttoned it, and his tie didn't hide the fact that the top button of his white oxford shirt was open too. He gave a squinting assessment of the entire room as he plopped into the witness chair, then waved at Astrid Olsen that she could begin.

"State your name, please, sir?"

"Kurt Francis Vernon."

"What do you do?"

"I'm the fire investigator for Sable County."

"How did you—"

"—I was a firefighter for twenty years here in Northlake, I took my certification exam, got licensed and all that, and have been on the investigating side for eighteen years now. It's all there on my resume."

Astrid blinked, then said, "Did you investigate the Mission Road Fire that occurred on April 9th and 10th of this year?"

"Sure did."

"Describe your involvement for us please."

"Rolf called me that night—"

"—That's Fire Chief Rolf Hagen?"

"Yeah, right. Rolf called me in for a multi-alarm, multi-structure, multi-fatality fire. I started my investigation that night."

"What did you find?"

"A mess. When I got there, the crew on the ground didn't know if we had multiple ignitions or if it was all one blaze. I don't blame 'em because they were trying to fight it without access to hydrants, so they had their hands full. Once I started looking, though, it was pretty clear we had one blaze."

"How so?"

"We had a heck of a lot of wind that night out of the west—fifteen miles per hour with gusts to twenty-five—and the fire had progressively burned everything out just like you'd expect from west to east. It didn't take a genius to see."

"Could you explain that a little more, please?"

He waved. "When I got there, the drive-in was about burned out, the wood pile was smoldering down, the U-Store building was still burning some, while the Carmody house was still going strong. West to east, just like you'd expect with a strong west wind."

"I see. What did you find as you started your investigation?"

"While the fire was active, I couldn't do much except observe. Once it was controlled, I took samples and pictures, starting with the drive-in."

"What did you do next?"

"The sun had finally come up, and the fire was under control, although the debris was still hotter than—it was still pretty hot, but I was able to see the burn pattern clearly in the light of day. I was just starting to take my samples at the drive-in when Sean called me to say—"

"—That's Sheriff Sizemore?"

"Yeah. We had coordinated while the fire was still poppin' and he was going to go interview the witness who'd called it in, so I actually turfed Sean a couple of times until he texted me to pick up my damn phone. It was a good thing too since he'd had a break in the case already."

"What was that?"

"That boy's pop—"

"—You're pointing at the defendant Brock Niesen?"

"Yeah, that tall drink of water slumping behind the table right there. His pop had called to say he, meaning the kid there, had plunked an exploding target on the drive-in screen and Sean asked if I could verify any of that real quick. So I hopped right over to what's left of the screen and I see the bushes right below are burnt and I start circling out and I eventually find some little balls of unexploded ammonium nitrate and a milk jug cap besides."

Astrid Olsen handed him two plastic baggies. "I'm handing you what's been marked as State's Exhibits 11 and 12. Are those—?"

"—Yeah, that's what I found. And the milk gallon cap smelled like gas too, so that's what put me on the track that the kid had done more than just blow up the SafeBoom target. He'd rigged up a little something extra to make sure there was a fireball too."

"What did you do next?"

"I called Sean right back and told him we had the little fu— the little bast—we had the guy."

"After you told Sheriff Sizemore about the ammonium nitrate balls and the cap, what did you do next?"

"Then I got down to business tracing the cause and origin of the fire. By this point, we knew there were fatalities, so we all had to turn square corners to make sure we put the kid away."

"Tell us what you found, Investigator Vernon."

Then he walked the jury through it. He started with the SafeBoom target. He showed the jury a sample SafeBoom target, how it came in two separate packages of black ammonium nitrate balls and white aluminum powder, and how you mixed the two together in a plastic container until you had a gray mix ready to go boom when you shot it.

"Of course, that brain surgeon over there made twenty-five pounds of it and then filled one of these with gas and taped it to the side," Investigator Vernon said as he slapped a gallon plastic milk container on the stand.

"Would that cause an explosion?" Astrid Olsen asked.

"A huge one. And the gas would cause a fireball."

He then explained how that would be more than enough to ignite the arborvitae bushes, which were so filled with sap and dry tinder that they would go up "like candles on the devil's birthday cake." Given the strong west wind, the fire had spread right down the line of bushes and—with a somber shake of the head—he pointed out that if the wind had shifted just a few degrees, that might have been as far as it went. But it didn't, and instead it caught the decrepit old privacy fence and the wood pile stacked against it.

"It was seasoned cherry wood," said Investigator Vernon. "And it burned hot and hard just like Benny Bird had hoped. Just at the wrong place and the wrong time."

He explained that although the U-Store building had metal siding, it had a timber frame and an asphalt shingle roof that sat atop tar paper and plywood, which was more than flammable and had caught fire from the monstrous cherry wood bonfire that was burning alongside it. There hadn't been much to consume in Benny Bird's unit, but when it spread to the middle unit where Tommy Chase's hardwood flooring and carpeting was stored, the blaze had more fuel and, when it hit Naomi Hoppel's unit filled with quilts and old wood furniture and all manner of stitchery for tinder, the fire was in business again.

"Even with the metal walls separating the units?" asked Astrid Olsen.

Investigator Vernon nodded. "The walls didn't go all the way to the ceiling so there was an easy updraft connecting them. Between that gap and the west wind, it was like there was no barrier at all."

As he discussed each stage, he showed the samples he'd taken. He had a sample of burnt arborvitae, a sample of cherry wood ash, some twisted plastic, some partially consumed carpet padding, and a scorched sample of cloth.

"The material in Mrs. Hoppel's unit was all tinder and fuel," said Investigator Vernon. "By then the storage unit was collapsing and it did, right into the motorhome outside." Investigator Vernon's face became somber for the first time. "That caught it, of course, and when the gas tank and cooking propane tanks blew, it scattered burning debris onto the Carmody home, some of which, once aflame, would have been very hard to extinguish. It's an old house, built in 1922 with two layers of shingles on the roof and old wood siding on the exterior walls. The wind fanned those flames, and their house caught."

He explained what happened to the house, but there wasn't much to it. The west side of the house caught fire, it spread, and eventually, the house collapsed and was consumed.

Investigator Vernon then showed pictures he'd taken of each step, of each section of the Mission Road Fire, then a few taken at an angle so the jury could see how the burn went in a dead straight line from the drive-in to the smoking wreckage of the Carmodys' house.

"Investigator Vernon, as a result of your training and expertise and as a result of your investigation of the scene, were you able to come to a conclusion as to the cause of the Mission Road Fire?"

Kurt Vernon squinted. "Are you asking me if I was able to tell what caused the fire?"

"Yes."

"Yeah. The fire was caused by the SafeBoom target and gasoline bomb that kid blew up."

"You're pointing at the defendant, Brock Niesen?"

"Yes."

"Do you have an opinion as to how the fire spread?"

"Like I said, the wind pushed it in a straight west to east so that it ignited and consumed everything in its path."

"All the way to the Carmody house?"

"Once that kid put gasoline on the arborvitae bushes, the fire just spread from fuel source to fuel source until it found the Carmodys."

"All that way?"

Kurt Vernon nodded. "There was nothing to stop it. In fact, it just grew."

"Mr. Vernon, you know that Brock Niesen is on trial for murder—"

"Good."

"—so this is important. I want you to assume that Brock Niesen blew up the SafeBoom target—"

"—Not hard since his dad told us he did."

"Did the detonation of the SafeBoom target start a fire?"

"No question, yes."

"Did the fire started by Brock Niesen spread directly to the Carmodys' house?"

"Yes. It was all one fire. Only the fuel sources changed."

"Did the fire started by Brock Niesen directly and proximately cause the deaths of Eli Tripp and Liam Carmody?"

"Yes."

"Can you say that to a reasonable degree of scientific probability?"

"I can say it to a one hundred percent certainty." He pointed at the picture on the screen of the black swath running from one property to the next.

Astrid Olsen nodded. "Mr. Vernon, you were also involved in the recovery of Eli Tripp and Liam Carmody?"

Kurt Vernon squinted. "I was."

"For the record, there's no question they were killed in the fire when the roof collapsed?"

"None."

"You found them?"

"Once the rubble had cooled. And with the help of his brother firefighters and Chief Hagan, of course." He started to speak, stopped.

"What is it, Investigator Vernon?"

"We thought at first that we'd only found Eli. We continued

to search the rubble for Liam but then I was the one who realized what had happened."

"And what was that?"

Investigator Vernon stared at Brock as he said, "I suspected Eli Tripp had covered Liam with his body when the roof fell. I flipped the body over, carefully and saw that it was true. Eli died holding Liam."

Then Investigator Vernon looked down, clicked a button, and a picture appeared on the six-foot screen of Eli Tripp wrapped in a charred embrace with Liam Carmody.

A juror gasped. Another cried out.

And Kimberly Tripp screamed.

Judge Roderick banged his gavel. "Ms. Olsen. Take that down please."

"Why?" said Investigator Vernon. "That's what they looked like." He pointed at Brock. "That's what he did."

He withstood it for a moment. Then Brock Niesen began to cry.

50

In case you're wondering, there was nothing wrong with what Astrid Olsen did. She'd disclosed all of Investigator Vernon's pictures as exhibits and she was entitled to use them. I'd seen the photos, and I'd warned Brock about them, and I'd even shown them to him in advance. But I didn't know for sure if she would use them, or how, since using a graphic autopsy or accident photo is always a risk, where you have to walk the line between convincing the jury of the justice of your case and offending them.

Astrid Olsen had used the horrific photo in the most effective way possible. She didn't warn the jury that the picture was coming. Instead, she'd shocked them with it, giving them a brief look, just a glimpse, that would fuel their nightmares for weeks. As she took it down, I knew she'd never show it to them again.

It had done its job.

That didn't mean that Judge Roderick liked what it had done to his courtroom. He asked for quiet, then decided a short break was in order. Ten minutes later, when everyone was back in the courtroom and Kurt Vernon was back on the stand, Astrid Olsen said that she had no further questions for him.

I stood and got to work.

"Mr. Vernon, I'm handing you what's been marked as Defense Exhibit 92. You know what that is, don't you?"

He took it, glanced. "It's a form."

"It's a fire investigation form from the State of Michigan, right?"

"If you say so."

"You know that, don't you? As a fire investigator?"

"I know the paper pushers in Lansing are always spitting out something like that."

"So are you telling the jury that you're *not* aware of the form the State suggests you use in fire investigations?"

Kurt Vernon waved a hand. "I know about it."

"I've looked all through the file in this case, Mr. Vernon. I can't find the State form you filled out for the Mission Road Fire."

"That's because I didn't use one. Like you said, it's a suggestion."

I held up the form. "It seems pretty helpful—twenty-one pages to help organize witnesses, describe the structures that burned, list categories of what burned, describe your testing."

"I don't need bureaucratic paperwork to solve fires."

"So you didn't generate the State form in this case, right?"

"I just said that."

"In fact, you didn't create any written report of your findings, did you?"

"I didn't need one."

"How do you keep track of all these things then?"

"I fought fires for twenty years and have investigated them for eighteen. I know what I'm doing."

"You mentioned your resume earlier. You don't have a scientific degree, do you?"

"No. Don't need one."

"No degree in chemistry or biology, right?"

"No. I'm a field guy."

"No time working or training in a lab, right?"

"You don't fight fires in a lab."

"So when you need a sample analyzed or need scientific testing done, you send it out to a lab, right?"

"That's right."

"And you rely on their analysis when reaching your conclusions, don't you?"

"Along with my own findings, yes. It's not like downstate up here, Counselor. We have to manage our resources so, yes, I send things out."

"It makes sense—"

"I'm glad you think so."

"—to rely on people with trained expertise in an area, doesn't it?"

"Sure. That's why they brought me in."

"And why you send samples out to a qualified lab, right?"

"When necessary, yes."

"You sent samples out to the lab in this case, didn't you?"

"I did."

"Of the debris from the different stages of this fire, right?"

"That's right."

"It appears that you sent four times as many samples from the drive-in site as you did from any of the other sites. Do I have that right?"

"Yes."

"I assume that's because you believed that's where the fire had started."

"I *know* that's where the fire started."

"Because Sheriff Sizemore told you about his conversation with Kevin Niesen, my client's dad?"

"Yes, your client's father provided us with very valuable information, which I then verified with my investigation."

"You testified earlier that you received the call from Sheriff Sizemore just as you were beginning to take samples. Is that right?"

"Yes."

"And you then focused your investigation on the drive-in site, where you found the ammonium nitrate—"

"—Yes, yes. I found the ammonium nitrate balls and the container cap that smelled of gasoline, which confirmed what Sheriff Sizemore had learned from your client's father."

"That call from Sheriff Sizemore steered your investigation, didn't it?"

"I wouldn't say 'steered.' It provided me with information that assisted my investigation."

"Once you received the call from Sheriff Sizemore, you paid less attention to the other sites of the fire, didn't you?"

"I wouldn't say that, no."

"You didn't take as many samples from the other sites, did you?"

"I don't recall."

"No. Why don't we go through your sample inventory then." Cyn popped the document up on the screen. "It says right here that—"

"—Yeah. I see that. I didn't take as many samples from the other sites."

"And you didn't send as many samples out for laboratory testing from the other sites, did you?"

Investigator Vernon glanced at his inventory that was standing six feet tall on the screen. "No, I didn't. But it wasn't necessary because now we had a fire source."

"Mr. Vernon, a fire can have more than one source, can't it?"

"There's no evidence of that here."

"Let's take this one question at a time, Mr. Vernon. First, a fire can have more than one source, can't it?"

"Yes, but—"

"—And a prudent investigator should analyze the evidence to determine whether there was more than one source for a fire, shouldn't he?"

"That didn't happen here."

"Again, that's not what I asked. A prudent investigator should—"

"—Yes, an investigator should always check for any source of a fire."

"And there can of course be more than one source of a fire, can't there?"

"Yes, but that's not—"

"—I didn't ask what you think happened here yet, Mr. Vernon. I asked if there can be more than one source of a fire?"

"Sometimes."

"So, yes?"

"Yes. Theoretically."

"And to determine whether there was another source for a fire, you have to examine all of the potential sites and sources carefully, don't you?"

"Not necessarily, no."

"Explain to the jury when an investigator *doesn't* have to examine a potential site and sources carefully."

"When the initial event clearly encompasses or caused it."

"So for example, if a bomb flattened surrounding buildings?"

"Right."

"We didn't have an event like that here, did we?"

"How do you mean?"

"The SafeBoom target wasn't powerful enough to reach the other buildings, was it?"

"No, but—"

"—So you had a duty to carefully investigate each site of the fire to make sure it was caused by the initial fire, right?"

"Yes. And I did."

"Very good. So I see you took eight samples from the drive-in area for testing?"

"Which found the traces of the gasoline, yes."

"I see." I nodded to Cyn who popped a slide up that showed *Drive-In—8*.

"Now, Mr. Vernon, I did not see any samples sent in from the wood pile. Is that right?"

"It was sitting right next to the fence!"

"Sure. But you didn't test any of the ash, right?"

"Why would I?"

"So you didn't, did you?"

"No, of course not."

"There was a lot of ash, wasn't there?"

"There was a lot of wood."

Wood Pile—0 went up on the screen.

"You sent in two samples from Mr. Bird's unit, right?"

"Right."

Bird—2 appeared on the screen.

"One was identified as asphalt and the other wood?"

"From the roof and the framing, yes. And no accelerants were found."

"You believe the primary things consumed in the first unit were the roof and framing, true?"

"Yes. That's how it spread to the second unit, Mr. Chase's."

"And I understand from your earlier testimony that you believe that the primary fuels consumed in Mr. Chase's unit were the carpet and the hardwood flooring, right?"

"That's right."

"Mr. Chase testified there was quite a bit of the Patagonian Rosewood in there, is that your understanding?"

"Yes. That amount of wood flooring would have burned with enormous intensity."

"Similar to the wood pile?"

"Not exactly the same but similar, yes."

"You sent in two samples from Mr. Chase's unit, yes?"

"Yes."

Chase Unit—2 appeared on the screen.

"One was a carpet fragment?"

"Yes."

"The other a piece of plywood?"

"From the roof, yes."

"Both revealed traces of varnish, didn't they?"

"Yes. From the flooring burning. It generates an enormous amount of toxic fumes. Fortunately, no one was nearby."

"From there you believe the fire spread to Mrs. Hoppel's unit, right?"

Kurt Vernon nodded. "There was so much fuel in there and the flames so high that the structure walls around that unit collapsed."

"And you sent in two samples from Mrs. Hoppel's unit?"

"We recovered a quilt fragment and the remains of a chair leg."

Hoppel Unit—2 appeared on the screen.

"You said there was so much fuel in Mrs. Hoppel's unit. And yet you only chose to take two samples?"

Kurt Vernon smirked. "You're suggesting Mrs. Hoppel is an arsonist?"

"No, I'm suggesting that a reasonably careful investigator would know that all of those things could present a fire risk and would evaluate them."

The smirk didn't leave. "A reasonably careful fire investigator would see that a massive fire had barreled down on the Hoppel Unit driven by a stiff west wind and set all of its many flammable contents ablaze."

"The roof collapsed on the Hoppel Unit, but not on the other two, right?"

"Right. There was so much fuel in her unit that it burned inside out. The heat caused some of the lighter stuff, paper, cross-stitch fragments, to float away."

"And it's your testimony that the flames from the Hoppel Unit spread to the motorhome?"

"And blew it up, yes."

"You only took one sample total there, right?"

"Right."

Motorhome—1 appeared on the screen.

"And if I'm reading your lab requests right, you didn't take any samples from the Carmody house, did you?"

"We were recovering more important things from the Carmody house."

"There were all sorts of fire sources in the Carmody house, weren't there?"

"Not that were likely, no."

"In general, fires can start from faulty wiring, can't they?"

"In general, not here."

"They can generally start from a grease fire in the kitchen, can't they?"

"In general, not here."

"They can start from the furnace, the hot water heater, an active curling iron, dryer lint, a gas leak, right?"

"Counselor, that's asinine."

"Mr. Vernon, watch your language in my court," said Judge Roderick without any real heat. "And answer the question."

"Yes, Your Honor." Kurt Vernon rolled his head back to me.

"Yes, those are all possible sources of house fires, along with a dozen more, none of which happened here."

"You didn't inspect for any of those dozens of other causes, though, did you?"

"I didn't have to! There was a massive fire right next door with a prevailing west wind!"

"So the answer is no, you did *not* investigate any other source of a fire in the Carmody house?"

"Of course not! There were even explosions for Chri—for Pete's sake!"

As *Carmody House—0* appeared on the screen, I asked, "Can we assume the motorhome explosions were loud?"

Now Kurt Vernon rolled his head all the way around his neck. "They weren't quiet."

"And there were at least two?"

"I believe the gas tank and a propane tank exploded, yes."

"The Carmody house was only seven minutes from collapsing when the fire department arrived. Is it safe to say the explosions occurred at least ten minutes before the fire department arrived?"

Kurt Vernon actually thought about that one. "I'd say at least ten minutes earlier."

"At least fifteen minutes earlier?"

"Probably."

"Twenty?"

"That's possible, but I couldn't swear to it."

"So we can agree the motorhome explosions occurred at least fifteen minutes before the fire department arrived?"

"Yes."

I picked up the sample State Fire Investigation Form. "Mr. Vernon, the State's Investigation form has a section for the investigator to list his findings for every room of a structure that burned. Are you aware of that?"

"I know what's in the form."

"It has blanks for the investigator to list what the room is made of—the floor, the ceiling, the walls, right?"

He sighed. "Yes."

"And it has a blank, right here, for contents, doesn't it?"

"Yes."

"Because the contents of a room are a key to why it burns, right?"

"Sure."

"That's part of what investigating a fire entails, isn't it?"

"It can be."

"You didn't record the contents of the Bird Unit, did you?"

"I already told you, Counselor, I didn't use that form."

"You didn't record it *anywhere*, did you?"

"No."

"That's not good investigative practice, is it?"

"It's irrelevant."

"So you're telling the jury it's *good* investigative practice?"

He glanced at the jurors. "It's not ideal. But it didn't matter here."

"You didn't record the contents of the Chase unit, did you?"

"No. But it didn't matter."

"You didn't record the contents of the Hoppel unit, did you?"

"No. But it didn't matter."

"You didn't record the contents of the Carmody house, did you?"

"I know the most important contents of the Carmody house—the bodies of Eli Tripp and Liam Carmody."

"So you didn't bother to make a written record of any of your findings, did you?"

"I didn't have to, Counselor, since it was clear your client started a fire that burned down the Carmodys' house."

"You determined what happened the moment you got the call from Sheriff Sizemore, didn't you, Mr. Vernon?"

"No, I determined what happened the moment I found the ammonium nitrate balls and the milk jug cap."

"And after that, you didn't spend much time on the rest of the structures, did you?"

"I didn't have to. It's silly to think I would."

"No further questions, Your Honor."

Astrid Olsen stood.

"Does paperwork fight fires, Mr. Vernon?"

"No."

"Do you have any doubt how this fire was started?"

"No. It was started when that boy blew up an exploding target to stick it to his old man."

"Do you have any doubt how this fire spread?"

"No. It went from the bushes to the wood pile to the units to the motorhome to the Carmody house, driven all the way by a strong west wind."

"Is there any question that there was sufficient fuel to burn along the way?"

"No. This was all a tinder box."

"Even though you didn't write it down?"

Kurt Vernon shrugged. "It's my understanding that the owners have testified to the contents, just like they told me."

"They have. And that's enough for you?"

"It should be enough for anybody."

She popped a picture up on the screen. The jury winced, but it was just a picture of the blackened swath of debris that stretched unbroken from the Drive-in to the Carmody house. "So, based on your decades of experience fighting and analyzing fires, what happened that night?"

"That boy, Brock Niesen, started a fire that killed Eli Tripp and Liam Carmody."

"Now Mr. Shepherd asked you about all sorts of other possible causes for these downstream fires. Have you seen any evidence that any of them are true?"

"None."

"Thank you, Mr. Vernon."

I stood. "Mr. Vernon, you didn't look for other causes, did you?"

"I didn't need to."

"So you didn't?"

He stared. "I didn't. Because the cause was clear."

"Thanks."

Judge Roderick dismissed Kurt Vernon and we broke for the day.

51

Emily was quiet all the way back to the office, giving no more than nods as Cyn and I talked about the fire witnesses the State had called that day.

"I think you established the timing with Chief Hagan," said Cyn. "You can argue there was a good two-and-a-half-hour gap when the fire was working its way east."

"For whatever that's worth," I said as I opened the office door. "I felt like we established that Vernon was half-assed with the investigation once he heard about Brock, but we still have to—"

"—We didn't establish anything," said Emily quietly.

I blinked. "Really? I felt like we got him to admit that his mind was made up once he got the call from Sizemore."

"*We* didn't establish that. *You* did."

Ah.

"I was the one who met Ferris at the grocery store, Emily, and I was always going to take Vernon since he was their expert, and I had to take Chief Hagan because it turns out he's important for—"

"—So I can only handle a witness if they're *not* important?"

"I didn't say that."

"How am I supposed to learn if I don't do it?"

"We didn't hire you," said Cyn.

Emily and I both turned. Cyn was still standing as she opened her laptop and said, "My firm hired Nathan because we won an impossible case where our client admitted to killing a man. We wanted that expertise and experience here." She looked at Emily with green-eyed calm. "Brock Niesen's life is not a training ground." Cyn turned back to her computer and began tapping keys. "We should focus on our work."

Emily opened her mouth, then shut it, before turning to me and saying, "Then I'll go pick up dinner."

She left.

"That was a little harsh," I said.

"Some truths are. Your call is in five minutes. Do you still have Bret Halogi's number?"

I nodded. "Thanks."

～

FIVE MINUTES LATER, I was on the phone with our fire expert Bret Halogi. I started to take her through the testimony of Chief Hagan, when she said, "Never mind that, tell me about Vernon."

"I did what you asked and took him through his theory of how the fire spread from site to site."

"Tell me what he said, exactly."

So I did. I took her from bushes to woodpile to the smoker unit to the hardwood flooring unit to the unit stuffed with quilts, furniture, and scrapbooks. I told her about how we'd shown the jury where he'd taken samples, like the drive-in, and where he hadn't, like the ashes from the remains of the cherry wood pile.

Bret Halogi swore.

"What?"

"I've been studying this, and it was bugging me and I couldn't figure out why. Do you have the exhibits in front of you?"

"I can pull them up."

"Look at the pictures of the wood pile."

"Got them."

"What do you see?"

I wasn't sure what Bret Halogi was getting at as I said, "Charred, black logs here and there but mostly gray ash."

"Right. A lot of it."

"That makes sense. Everyone said it was a pretty big pile."

"Go to the pictures of the second unit."

I did. It was still partially standing, but the east wall, the one the Chase unit shared with Mrs. Hoppel's unit, was twisted and collapsed. The remaining interior walls and the ceiling were smoke-stained, black, and charred. Twisted black rolls that made bizarre shapes like abstract art from the home of Edward Scissorhands lined one wall.

"Right. I see the fire damage and the collapsed wall and… those shapes are rolls of carpet and pad, right?"

"Exactly. What don't you see?"

I stared, then stared some more.

"I'm sorry, Bret. I don't see what I don't see."

"Think of the wood pile, Nate."

I did. Then, "Sweet Jesus, Bret, the ash!"

"Right, Nate. How much wood flooring did Chase say he had stashed in there?"

"Half the unit, waist deep."

"Patagonian hardwood burns hot, no different than cherry. And it leaves ash."

The cement floor of the unit was stained and there were twisted carpet roles and melted padding and scattered fragments of wreckage and debris littering the place.

But there were no piles of ash.

"That much flooring would weigh thousands of pounds, Nate. It would leave a lot of ash."

I remembered Vernon's testimony. "He, Vernon, didn't take any samples of wood flooring from that unit. It was carpet fibers and some roof." I frowned. "Both samples did show varnish residue from the flooring burning though. That's what Vernon assumed anyway."

"It doesn't make sense."

I've told you more than once that I'm not particularly handy. But I knew someone who was.

"Bret, can I call you right back?"

"I'll be here."

I hung up and speed dialed.

He picked up. "Son? Aren't you in trial?"

"I am, Dad. Is it too late?"

"Not at all. I was just out in the shop. Your mother has finally let me come out here without a babysitter since dialysis is done."

I felt a slash of guilt. "Is it official?"

"Last Monday."

"That's great news! Congratulations!"

"I don't know that's something to congratulate me for, but it is good to know I don't have to be hooked up to that infernal thing again. I assume you didn't call about the old man's kidney function though."

"Right. You installed the hardwood floors at the lake house, right?"

"I did. At our old house too."

"Is it varnished when you buy it?"

"They sell all sorts of prefab things these days, like the vinyl or poly-something-or-other that looks like wood but isn't."

"No, I mean actual hardwood flooring. Like say, Patagonian Rosewood."

"The law must be paying pretty good these days."

"It's not for me. It's related to the case."

"Hmm. Well, if it's the real deal, like actual premium hardwood flooring that you're installing, you have to sand and finish it after you install it because you're going to nick it up and scuff it when you're putting it in."

"Assume it's actual premium hardwood that's going into the first floor of a fancy pants house."

"Then it should be unfinished. You'd install it, then you'll have a few days of sanding and buffing and cleaning, and then you'll put your treatment on it, whether it's oil or sealant or whatever's best for that particular wood."

"You're sure?"

"Did I say it?"

"Thanks, Dad. That really helps."

"You going to make it home to watch the Lions game this weekend?"

"Probably not. But the week after for sure."

"I'll see you then."

"Try not to rewire any sump pumps in the meantime."

"No. I have had my eye on updating the circuit breaker box though."

"I'll be happy to represent Mom at her murder trial."

"No one will convict her."

"Love you, Dad."

"You too, Son."

I called Bret Halogi back. "They don't apply the sealant until after the floor's installed."

"So the varnish, or whatever it was, didn't come from the wood?"

"Flooring can be pre-treated, but it's unlikely with this floor."

"I need to know if I'm going to offer an opinion."

"Right. On it."

"But listen, treated or untreated, if that wood flooring burned, there would be ash. A lot of it. And I don't see it. I can't believe I missed that."

"We were all taking everyone at their word for what was in the units."

"Here's the important part—without that wood flooring, I don't think there was enough fuel for the fire to spread."

"Explain."

"We have a raging fire with the cherry wood pile. That spreads to the roof and to the shingles and to Benny Bird's unit. But remember Benny's unit mostly has a smoker and other things made of metal and plastics and it's not that full."

"Okay."

"But remember, the interior walls don't go all the way up to the ceiling and there's enough fire in Benny's unit and on the roof that it's not hard to justify it spreading to Tommy Chase's unit and all that wood flooring."

"I'm with you."

"But if there's no flooring in there, there's not nearly as much material to burn and what's there is harder to ignite."

"What about the carpet?"

"That has a much higher burn point than the wood. And we also know that the fire didn't spread to Mrs. Hoppel's unit from the roof."

"How?"

"Because the roof is still there over Tommy Chase's unit and it's not that burnt. The working assumption has been that the heat from Benny's wall and the dying flames on the roof ignited the wood flooring, which was more than enough to spread up over the gap in the interior wall to Mrs. Hoppel's tinderbox."

"But if the wood flooring's not there—"

"—It becomes much harder to spread."

I thought. "Unless you helped it along with varnish."

"Unless you helped it along with varnish."

We were silent.

"That doesn't make a lot of sense," I said finally.

"Maybe not. Or maybe we don't know enough yet."

"We don't have much time."

"Then we best get moving. I'll work on the fire science of what we just said from my end. But we'll need more hard facts if I'm going to testify to it."

"On it. Thanks, Bret."

We hung up. I knew who to call next.

"Finally," said Olivia. "I have news."

I went from talker to listener. "What?"

"Corey Linden, the owner of the Carmodys' rental house? He's sold the property."

"To who?"

"Devin Wright."

I digested that. "Really."

"Really."

"So he's grabbed the drive-in on one side and the Carmody house on the other?"

"Yep."

"Do we know why?"

"The plans aren't clear yet."

"Let me guess, both sales are below market."

"They have to be. A burned-out theater and a rubble pile of a home aren't the most attractive properties."

"This just keeps getting more interesting. I'm not sure how it fits with my news."

I summarized the day's testimony but spent more time on my meeting with Bret.

"Wait, the wood flooring *wasn't* there?" said Olivia.

"Halogi thinks there wasn't enough ash," I said. "And if that unit isn't full of wood, it's less likely the fire spreads to Mrs. Hoppel's unit."

"Without a little help, got it. Shep, that seems awfully thin."

"It is. If only I knew a crack investigator who could help me."

"I've trained you well."

"But I'm not sure why Tommy Chase would lie about the wood being in there. We already know he didn't get any of the insurance money for the flooring. That went to the homeowner."

"What was his name?"

"John Warhelm. So if Warhelm, not Chase, gets the insurance, what motivation would Chase have to get rid of the wood?"

"You're not thinking criminally enough, Shep."

"Thanks, I think?"

"Let's assume the wood wasn't in there. Let's assume instead that Chase has taken it out. After the fire, he doesn't get the insurance proceeds, but he still has the wood that is supposedly gone."

"So what, he could sell it?"

"Or use it on another job."

I thought for a moment. "That seems like a lot of work for Chase. He doesn't exactly strike me as the industrious type."

"You'd be surprised how much people will work for what they think is a shortcut."

"I suppose. The value doesn't make sense to me either."

"How so?"

"Patagonian Rosewood is a good material, but the value for the lot was still only about twenty thousand dollars."

"You and I both know that's a lot of money to some."

"True. But stealing and arson money?"

"It's more than what's in a gas station cash register and yet…"

"I hear you, Liv. But it just doesn't quite fit, not enough for me to go into court with guns blazing. Especially now that you're telling me that Devin Wright is buying the adjoining properties at fire-sale prices. Literally."

"I'm on it, Shep. I'll see if our good Mr. Chase has had any suspicious jobs or sales lately. And you said John Warhelm was the guy who owned the house it was supposed to go in?"

"That's him."

"I'll see what we know."

"I hate to say it, Liv, but I'm probably going to get the case by Friday. Maybe even tomorrow afternoon."

Liv laughed, a sound I genuinely enjoyed. "Just another opportunity to prove my brilliance to you. Check your phone at lunch. If I don't have anything yet, we'll talk either way tomorrow night."

"You're the best, Liv."

"I know."

We hung up, but before I could switch gears, my phone buzzed again.

"Cade! Is everything all right there?"

"The Orchard is fine."

"Still sipping whiskey by the campfire?"

"I am. I cleaned my shotgun tonight."

"How industrious."

"You know, a man sitting in front of an air stream sipping whiskey has time to think."

"I take that back."

"About many things."

"Cade, I appreciate the call, but I have to get back to—"

"—But mostly about George Washington."

I sighed. "I honestly can't wait to hear the connection."

"You know George was a farmer?"

"Yes."

"Did you know, he became one of the country's largest whiskey distillers?"

"Vaguely."

"Do you know why?"

"I hope you'll tell me."

"Because it was a way to make his crops shelf stable."

"What do you mean?"

"Corn and rye sitting in a whiskey cask doesn't go bad."

"Do you have a history channel hook up out there or something?"

"Hard cider's become pretty popular now, don't you think?"

My head was still in wood flooring and fires so, to be fair to Cade, it took me longer to get there than it should have but I did get there. "Cade, you can't swing a dead cat without hitting a distillery up here."

"That's what I thought. Traverse City is littered with them."

"Have you talked to Dagmar?"

"Not yet. Thought I'd run it by you, see what you thought."

"I think Dagmar has no traditional buyers for her apples right now. I don't know if she's even thought of that."

"I'll talk to her then, see what she thinks. Later."

"Bye."

Dagmar Niesen's business was, well, none of my business, but I could see what the trial of her son and the collapse of her orchard was doing to her. I hoped Cade could help her. I also had an unreasonable desire to see them thwart Kim Tripp's plan to destroy Dagmar's life.

Thoughts of the orchard left as Cyn came into my office carrying a clear-topped plastic box and a pair of chopsticks.

"Mongolian Beef," she said, and put it down.

"Emily's back? I didn't hear her come in."

"Just a minute ago. You've been burning up the phones."

"Let's get her in here, there've been some developments."

Cyn sat down and crossed her legs. "Let's wait until after we eat."

I raised an eyebrow as I unsheathed and split the chopsticks.

"We had a discussion," Cyn said.

"Ah. Do I want to know?"

"I told her that a boy's life was at stake and that there are certain things only lead counsel can do."

"Okay."

"I also told her that I have never examined a witness in court, but I believe I can fairly say that I've been instrumental in winning cases for our clients."

"You can say that again. She's right, though. I could give her more witnesses."

Cyn shrugged. "We hired you for *your* judgment, Nathan. If you believe you needed to take those witnesses, you did. This isn't the case for training. So what's happened?"

I told her about Bret's theory and about Olivia's investigation. Her green eyes lit up. "That sounds like an avenue toward doubt."

"It sure does. We don't have enough yet to sling around with the jury though."

Cyn nodded. "We're only going to have one shot with this."

"I agree. Especially with what Astrid is going to throw at us tomorrow."

"Maura Carmody?"

"Maura Carmody."

"How are you going to handle that?"

"Carefully."

"You know best."

We ate long enough for me to be jealous of Cyn's impeccable chopstick skills. Then, she pursed her lips.

"Thoughts?" I asked.

"Not about that, no."

"What then?"

"I've been reporting our progress to the Firm. They'll be

interested in Halogi's theory. They're also interested in something else."

"What's that?"

"Your interest in the partnership we discussed."

I smiled. "I've been a little busy."

"I know. I also know you multi-task. Like when you discuss a plan to save an orchard that's not really part of your job."

"I speak that loud?"

"You do. So?"

"Let's get through the trial first."

"Of course. But how are you leaning?"

I sat back.

"The thought of working with your firm, and you, is appealing."

"But?"

"There has to be a but?"

Cyn stared. "But?"

"I'm not sure if the nomadic lifestyle is."

Cyn nodded. "Thank you.

"Think Emily has had enough time to digest your words and her meal?"

"Yes."

"Then let's get her in here and get ready for tomorrow."

PART VI - EXPLODE

52

Early on the morning of the fourth day of trial, I went to Maggie's to pick up a coffee. Three workers—two guys and a woman sporting yellow *Northlake Masonry & Seawall* t-shirts—were in front of me in line, joking with far too much laughter and enthusiasm for the hour. One of the guys and the woman nodded to me as they left, and I stepped forward.

"Good morning, Ms. Day," I said.

Maggie smiled. "Good morning, Mr. Shepherd. Coffee for you or the group today?"

"Just me, please."

"Large, black, coming up." As she went back to the carafe, she said, "Any change to the lunch order?"

"How could I change such a 'good lunch?'"

She smiled over her shoulder. "I'm glad you've liked it. How many more days, do you think?"

"Probably through at least Monday. I'll let you know."

"I'll be here." She came back to the counter, slipping the cup into a sleeve.

"Can an ignorant downstater ask you a question?"

"Sure."

"Where can I find John Warhelm?"

Maggie's smile vanished and she pressed the lid onto the cup with deliberate focus. "Why would you ask that?"

"His name came up last night."

"As part of your case?"

"Peripherally. Not directly."

Maggie was quiet as she rang me up and still quiet when I paid. Finally, as she handed me my coffee, she said, "I don't know, Nate. I'm too busy working to golf at the Bluffs."

I nodded. "Too bad. Thanks anyway."

As I walked to the door, Maggie said, "Good lunch, Nate."

"Thanks, Maggie," I said, and texted Olivia as soon as I was out the door.

~

I MET WITH EVERYONE—Cyn, Emily, Brock, and Dagmar—in the library landing where we ate lunch.

"This is going to be bad this morning," I said.

"Why?" said Brock.

"Maura Carmody is going to testify. It's going to be hard to hear."

Brock nodded, eyes wide.

"I want you to sit there and try to keep a straight face. It's okay if you look down. But don't react to anything she says, okay?"

He nodded again. Dagmar put a hand on his.

"And I want you to remember—you didn't do this, okay? You didn't kill her son. No matter what gets said, you need to believe that you didn't kill her son. Are you with me?"

"Yes," his voice cracked. He cleared his throat. "Yes."

"Say it."

"I didn't kill her son."

"Again."

"I didn't kill her son."

"Do you believe that?"

"Yes."

"Then let's go."

∽

When the jury was seated, Judge Roderick said, "Ms. Olsen, you may call your next witness."

Astrid Olsen looked directly at me as she said, "Your Honor, the State calls Maura Carmody."

The courtroom door opened and Maura Carmody slipped through. She looked to be in her early thirties with black hair that hung straight down to her shoulders. Although a splash of freckles across her nose made her look young, her shoulders stuck out sharply beneath her blouse and her pants swung loose from her legs.

Maura Carmody stopped and grabbed the back of a pew in the back row to steady herself. She looked very thin, very frail, and very afraid.

Before anyone could move, Mason Pierce was over to her. "Right this way, Mrs. Carmody," he said with that quiet voice of his and offered her his arm. I've mentioned how tall Pierce is; he's also wide, and the contrast between them made Maura seem even more fragile. Her mouth twitched in a ghost of a smile, and she clasped his elbow with both hands as he gently led her down the aisle, through the gate, and up to the witness chair.

"Thank you," she whispered as Mason Pierce returned to his desk.

This was not good. At all.

Every eye was on her and Maura Carmody seemed to feel it as she sat straight, hands in her lap, and looked down at the rail in front of her. She glanced up briefly as she was sworn in and whispered her oath, but then her eyes returned to the rail.

"Mrs. Carmody, I'm the prosecutor, Astrid Olsen. We've met before."

"I remember." Her voice was soft.

"We're going to have to ask you some questions about the night of the fire."

"I'm afraid I don't know very much."

"That's okay, you just tell us what you know, okay?"

"Okay."

"And if you need to take a break, just tell me and we will, all right?"

"I will."

"And we'll just get through this as quickly as possible."

"Fine."

"First, let me say how sorry I am for the loss of your son."

Maura Carmody didn't flinch or move or twitch. She just stared at the rail and said, "Thank you."

"Do you know how the fire in your house started, Mrs. Carmody?"

"No."

"Did you use the stove to cook that night?"

"No. I microwaved chicken nuggets and fries for the kids."

"Did you iron anything?"

"Not that night, no."

"Were you having any electrical problems?"

"Not that I knew of, but Noah handles all that."

"When did you first learn that your house had caught fire that night?"

"When Sasha woke me up?"

"That's your oldest daughter?"

Maura Carmody kept staring at the rail. "Yes."

"What happened?"

"She told me there was a fire and that we needed to get out."

"What did you do?"

"I think I led Sasha and Felicity out the front door. I went to go back in for Liam, but a fireman pulled me back and another one went in after him."

"You think?"

"It's a little fuzzy. Then a paramedic helped us and took us to the hospital."

"Oh? Do you remember that?"

"A little. Sasha had burns on her hands."

"When did you learn about Liam?"

Maura Carmody stared at the rail. "A doctor and a nurse told me."

"I see. What happened next?"

"I was upset. They gave me some medicine that helped me sleep."

"Were your daughters with you?"

"They slept with me in the hospital. I didn't tell them about Liam until later."

"Mrs. Carmody, part of this trial has to do with when things happened. Did you hear any explosions that night?"

Maura Carmody shook her head. Her eyes didn't leave the rail.

"I'm sorry, you need to answer out loud."

"I didn't hear anything, no."

"Not at all?"

"No."

"Could you tell the jury why for me, please?"

She nodded. "Noah is an over-the-road truck driver."

"Noah is your husband?"

"Yes. I get nervous when he's gone, and I have trouble sleeping so the doctor prescribed me some medicine."

Astrid Olsen nodded. "To help you sleep?"

"Yes."

"Did you take some that night?"

"I did. After I put the kids to bed, I took...one and...and it didn't seem like it was working...so I took another one."

"I see."

"So I didn't hear anything." Maura Carmody frowned. "I think Sasha came in and said she heard a boom, but I told her it was just thunder and she should go back to sleep."

"When was that?"

"I don't know."

"And then later she came in and woke you up again?"

Maura Carmody nodded. "That's when she said there was a fire."

Astrid Olsen stepped closer. "Mrs. Carmody, you didn't want to be here today, did you?"

Her eyes never left the rail. "No."

"Why?"

"It's difficult for me to come out."

"To court?"

"To anywhere."

"I'm sorry we had to ask you to do that today, but there were some questions about what happened that night."

"Did I answer them?"

"*I* think so." Astrid Olsen looked at the jury and then looked at me. "But Mr. Shepherd might have some more questions for you anyway."

Astrid Olsen sat down, staring at me all the way, daring me to ask a question.

The jury was watching me too.

I stood.

"Mrs. Carmody, I'm Nate Shepherd. I represent Brock Niesen. Would you like to take a break?"

"No, thank you."

"We've never met before, have we?"

"No, we haven't."

"I didn't ask you to come here today, did I?"

"You didn't, no."

"I take it from what you said that you don't know anything about how the fire started in your house, is that fair?"

"No, I don't. Only what the fire department told my husband later."

"And you don't have any knowledge about what time the explosions occurred, right?"

"That's right."

"Or even if they did occur?"

"I didn't hear them, no."

"Mrs. Carmody, you were renting your house from Corey Linden, right?"

"That's right."

"Did he let you out of your lease after the fire?"

Maura Carmody nodded, eyes on the rail. "Corey didn't blame us for the fire or anything. I know we didn't have to pay rent anymore. A few days ago, he wanted us to sign something that made it official so he could sell the land."

"He sold the land to Devin Wright, the owner of the U-Store?"

"I believe that's right, yes."

"Thank you, Mrs. Carmody. That's all I have."

"You're welcome."

Astrid Olsen stood. "Mrs. Carmody, you said 'Corey Linden didn't blame us for the fire or anything,' do you remember that?"

"Yes."

"Who do you blame for the fire?"

I stayed standing and said quietly, "Objection, Your Honor."

Judge Roderick frowned. "Sustained. Mrs. Carmody, you do not—"

"—Myself," said Maura Carmody. She looked up at Judge Roderick. "I blame myself."

"No!" came a voice from the back of the courtroom.

Judge Roderick glared at the back and rapped his gavel, once, then looked at Astrid Olsen. "Are you done, Ms. Olsen?"

"Yes."

He glanced at me. I shook my head.

"The jury will disregard that last statement," said Judge Roderick. "It was an impermissible opinion from a lay witness"—he paused then said gently—"which was unsupported by the facts."

Maura Carmody's eyes returned to the rail.

"You may step down, Mrs. Carmody."

She did, and where she'd been tentative walking in, she moved quickly to get out as she strode arms crossed, eyes down between the counsel tables and down the aisles.

Kim Tripp stood from her seat and tried to hug her. Maura Carmody stepped to the side as if she were a snake and hurried out the door.

Astrid Olsen caught my eye as we turned back to the judge. She was smiling.

"Let's break for lunch everyone," said Judge Roderick.

53

I ducked outside and called Olivia.

"Well hello, sugar-pie," came a southern drawl.

"Uhm, what?"

"Can't bear to be apart for even a morning now, can you? Well, you're just going to have to wait a teensy bit longer and then I'll be back."

I looked at the phone, stared at Olivia's name, then said, "This should be good."

"I have met the most marvelous gentleman, Mr. Warhelm, and told him all about our plans to redo our floors and do you know he has just redone his?"

I grinned. "How fortunate."

"Isn't it just? I told him how wonderful it was to get away from the Texas heat up here at our place in Leelanau but how frustrating it can be to find help when you're so far from home."

"It certainly is."

"Yes, I know, oil money can't solve everything, but it certainly helps. See now, Mr. Warhelm agrees with me. How sweet."

My grin broadened. "Do you need me to even say anything?"

"No, you just keep that credit card limber, and I'll be home this afternoon. Mr. Warhelm is going to show me what he did and I'm certain I'm going to come back just chock full of ideas."

"I'm counting the minutes."

"You surely should be. 'Bye-bye, sugar-pie."

I chuckled as I hung up. I heard a voice and saw that Dagmar had joined me outside. She was on her phone.

"No, there's nothing wrong with it," she said. "It's actually one of the best harvests we've had in years...Our contract fell through at the last minute...Midwest Fruits...Probably, but that will take years in court and I've got bushels now...I have those, yes.... All of those actually.... I'll wait to hear from you then.... Thanks, you too."

Dagmar Niesen hung up, saw me, and gave a weak smile. "Your friend Cade had a good idea last night."

"The distilling?"

She nodded. "I've been calling all morning."

"Any luck?"

"I'm not getting straight 'no's,' exactly. Most of them have contracts for their capacity, but some could use a little more."

"That's something."

"It's not nothing, but it's not enough of something. Yet. And I've gotten a few recommendations from them for other places to try so I'll keep calling." Dagmar jerked a thumb over her shoulder at the courtroom door. "Was that as bad as it seemed?"

"I think so, yes."

"That poor girl."

"Yes."

"She doesn't deserve what's happened."

"No."

"Neither does my son."

"I agree."

"Are you going to be able to win this?"

"I'm going to try."

Dagmar stared at me for a moment longer then looked back at the door. "My apples are rotting on the ground, Nate. I have a chance, a small window, to get them out before they go bad, but if they're on the ground or in the crate or in the warehouse too long, they'll go all the way bad."

I nodded.

"My son is rotting in that jail."

"I know."

She was quiet for a moment. I couldn't reassure her that everything was going to be okay because there was a good chance it wasn't, so I said, "Sounds like we both have a small window."

"We need to fit through it," she said.

"Agreed. Ready to head back in?"

Dagmar gave me a thin smile. "I have another call to make."

I left her to it.

∼

I THOUGHT there was a chance I'd get the case that afternoon, but Astrid Olsen had a series of foundation witnesses to put on, witnesses who would verify that the hard evidence she needed all came in. It's boring stuff, but the way she did it was interesting. She established the chain of custody with Brock's gun and the gas cap and the SafeBoom packaging, obtained testimony from the lab tech who tested the debris from the arborvitae bushes, the smoker, the roof, the carpeting, the quilts, and the furniture, and the coroner who'd officially identified and pronounced Eli and Liam. She did it quickly and concisely, giving the jury a reminder of all of the evidence without diluting the power of Maura Carmody's performance.

Then Astrid Olsen rested her case.

There was a little time left in the day, but Judge Roderick let the jury go early. Once they were gone, I had Emily argue the motion for directed verdict of acquittal, which didn't appease her at all since we both knew it would be denied, which in fact it was, right there from the bench. Judge Roderick asked if we'd be done with our case the next day. I told him it was possible but probably not. He asked who we were calling, and I told him for sure our expert Bret Halogi but that after that I wasn't sure. He said he expected me to give Astrid a heads up if that changed overnight and I said that I would.

Then we all left and went back to the office to see if we had anything more to add to our defense.

~

"WELCOME HOME, SUGAR-PIE!" said a voice as I opened the office door.

Olivia stood there in loose, flowing white yoga pants, a tan dressy tank top, if there is such a thing, and oversized brown sunglasses, grinning and holding two bags of food. "Oh, and you brought guests! I do wish you'd called ahead to let me know we were having company, but fortunately, I bought extra."

"Good evening, dear," I said.

"Dear? Don't be so formal. Call me what you always do."

"I'm afraid I've forgotten."

Olivia flipped her hand lightly. "Your sweet light, of course."

Emily grinned. "Sounds like him."

"Aren't you just a dumplin'," Olivia said to her.

Olivia gave up the bags and as, we divvied things up around the table, I said, "So what did Miss…?"

She put her nose up in the air. "Olivia Perry-Snow. Of the Fort Worth Perry-Snows."

"Of course. Where has Ms. Snow—?"

"—Perry-Snow."

"Perry-Snow—"

"—And it's Mrs."

"What did *Mrs.* Olivia *Perry*-Snow of the Fort Worth Perry-Snows do today?"

"I might have had brunch at The Bluffs Golf and Tennis Club."

"You got in?"

"Please. Challenge me, sugar-pie."

"What did you find out?"

Olivia dropped the accent and smiled. "First, that John Warhelm has a hard time resisting a certain type."

"What type is that?"

"Me. Especially me with oil money."

"Okay."

"And second, that he loves to show off his home on the bluffs of Lake Michigan. It was recently renovated, you know."

"You don't say."

"I do. He was especially proud of the first floor."

"Oh? Why's that?"

"Because he just had a brand-new hardwood floor put in. Must be three thousand square feet of it."

"That floor wouldn't happen to be Patagonian Rosewood by any chance?"

Olivia leaned forward and pushed a finger onto the table. "It would not."

She was smiling. And silent.

"What was it?!" said Emily.

Olivia smiled at her. "Zebrawood."

That meant nothing to me. I stared at Olivia as she sat there grinning. Emily looked as lost as me. Cyn, though, sat back and crossed her legs.

"Interesting," she said.

"It gets better," said Olivia. "He said it was supposed to have been finished last spring, but his first shipment, *of zebrawood*, was lost in a fire by his contractor."

I still wasn't seeing the source of Olivia's satisfaction. "Okay. So it was zebrawood not rosewood in Tommy Chase's unit. How does that make a difference?"

"Would you like to tell him?" said Olivia to Cyn.

"You're doing just fine," said Cyn.

"Thank you." Olivia turned back to me. "Zebrawood is one of the rarest, most cherished woods in the world. It's from an endangered tree that's only found in East Africa and it's very, very hard to get."

"Okay."

"Like illegal to import hard to get."

Olivia had my attention.

"Why would he tell you that?" said Emily.

Olivia smiled at her. "Because only a man who's very rich and very powerful would be able to get it. Sure, you might find zebrawood on the dash panel of an old luxury car or on the wall of an old manor home, and you can certainly find plenty of imitations. What you won't find, unless you are an extra-special man, is a large amount of raw wood to be used for a floor."

"Because of the import restrictions?" I said.

Olivia nodded. "Which makes it very, very, expensive."

"How expensive?"

"For the amount he had, multiple six figures."

I tapped the desk with my pen. "That changes our calculus."

"It certainly does."

"What did you learn about how he got it?"

Olivia shook her head. "I convinced him that Ms. Perry-Snow has more than enough money to afford it, but he wouldn't spill. He said he'd exhausted all of his connections getting a second shipment after his first was destroyed in the fire and wouldn't reveal anything except to say that the second batch had cost him even more than the first. I assured him that oil families are used to solving scarcity problems with piles of cash, but he wouldn't budge."

I smiled. "Maybe you're losing your touch."

"No."

"Just a theory."

"A poor one."

"Let me try a better one. We have six figures worth of exotic wood—"

"More than six figures."

"—More than six figures worth of exotic wood, which supposedly burned in the fire."

Emily nodded. "Except Bret Halogi says it didn't."

I nodded. "Because there's no ash. And with this new value, it suddenly makes a lot more sense why Tommy Chase would steal the wood."

"That's definitely more than the gas station cash register," said Olivia. "And more than enough to justify using a fire to cover it up."

Cyn's fingers were flying on her keyboard. "There's a problem with that theory."

"What?"

"Time."

"What do you mean?"

"He didn't have enough time." Cyn turned her laptop screen toward us. "Here's a general calculator to figure out how much wood covers your floor. For the square footage we're talking about, that was literally thousands of pounds of wood planks. I don't see how he had enough time to move all of that flooring before the fire got to his unit."

Emily slumped back in her chair. "Especially when you factor in that he'd have to hear about the fire, get to the unit, then move wood."

I sat up. "That's because the wood wasn't there that night."

"What do you mean?" Emily said.

"The wood had already been moved." I pulled out my notes from the trial and found the page. "Mrs. Hoppel's testimony. She was at the unit the night before. So was Tommy Chase with an empty truck. He wasn't dropping the wood off—"

Emily grinned. "He was picking it up!"

"And then the fire happened the next day," I said. I tapped my pen. "He couldn't have known that was going to happen, though."

"That doesn't mean he couldn't take advantage of it," said Olivia. "It's a crime of opportunity."

"Maybe. But if there wasn't a fire, what was he going to do with it?"

"Maybe it was finally time to install it." Olivia swore. "I didn't think to ask Warhelm."

"No reason you would." I tapped faster. "There are a lot of gaps here."

"There are four of us," said Cyn.

"Right. Emily, check the police reports for the days before and after the fire."

"On it, Boss. What am I looking for?"

"Break-ins reported at the U-Store. Olivia, let's assume Tommy Chase stole the wood and used the fire for cover. See if you can figure out what he did with it. There has to be a small market for illegal East African wood, and I'd suspect it's not local."

Oliva nodded. "It may take a while to move it, so he may even have some of it still. I'll check both."

"Perfect. Cyn, I need subpoenas."

Cyn nodded. "Who?"

I told her who and for when.

Cyn's fingers flew. "You know we're technically not giving them time to comply."

"I know that, and you know that. Let's see if they do."

"One of them will."

"Yes, but I'm hoping to give him enough information that he'll come anyway. Will you serve them?"

"Yes."

"Get Cade's help if you need it. I'll call Halogi right now and prep her for tomorrow. Every one good?"

Emily pushed her hair back. "You know, Devin Wright has taken advantage of the fire at least as much as Tommy Chase."

"True."

"And just because Chase stole the wood doesn't mean he set a second fire."

"No, it doesn't. But I keep coming back to one thing."

"What?"

"There was no varnish on that wood. And the inside of Tommy Chase's unit was covered in it."

Emily processed. "Chase still would have had to find out about the original fire and come back to act on it."

"Yes."

Emily stared at me for a long moment before she shook her head. "How the hell are we going to prove all this?!"

I grinned. "We'll see."

54

We all scattered, and I received a call late that night and two more early the following morning. Emily found something I thought would work, Olivia hit not one but two home runs, and Cyn was a subpoena-serving marvel. I'm not going to tell you what they told me in the calls because none of it mattered unless we could get it entered into evidence at court.

But if we could? Well, if we could, I thought for the first time that we might have a chance.

I'd done my job—Bret Halogi was as prepared as she could be and I got done with her in time to make one more call to a reinforcement for Cyn, who was gleefully happy to give it.

I hung up the phone and entered the courthouse.

∽

I WAS JUST ROUNDING the corner to the courtroom when I heard yelling.

"What do you mean your case is over? I haven't testified yet!"

It was the voice of Kimberly Tripp.

I hung back as Astrid Olsen said, "Mrs. Tripp, as I said before, you're not a witness."

"What do you mean I'm not a witness! My son has been killed!"

"Yes, but you have no knowledge of the circumstances of his death."

"No knowledge?! Who do you think identified his remains! Who do you think has to live with an empty chair at family meals? At Christmas? At—"

"—Of course, Mrs. Tripp. But that's not relevant to the circumstances surrounding his death."

I winced at that before Mrs. Tripp screeched, "Not relevant! You're saying me losing my son is *not relevant*?"

"Not to the jury's determination of whether Brock Niesen is responsible for your son's death, Mrs. Tripp, no. You don't have knowledge of the facts surrounding the fire."

"I know my son is dead!"

"Yes, Mrs. Tripp, but fortunately you didn't witness it."

"I wish I had! At least then he'd know I was there for him."

"Mrs. Tripp, if there's a conviction, you'll be able to testify in the second phase and give a victim impact statement before sentencing."

"If there's a conviction? *If* there's a conviction?!"

I should have just let her go and keep distracting Astrid, but I was just coming off a trial with a client chewing on me like that and I'm afraid I actually had sympathy for her, so I walked up to Astrid and said, "Excuse me. Can I talk to you for a moment about today?"

Mind you, Astrid had pretty much refused to speak to me for this whole proceeding except to threaten me with Maura Carmody's testimony. But at that moment, she said, "Of course, Nate. Excuse me, Mrs. Tripp. We can talk again at the break."

Kimberly Tripp glared at me, but she'd shouted herself out with Astrid and went into the courtroom as we walked away.

Astrid didn't say thanks, but she did nod in appreciation as Mrs. Tripp walked away, then said, "What is it?"

I handed her copies of the subpoenas. "We may be calling these people today. They're all on both of our witness lists."

As she leafed through the subpoenas, she frowned, which deepened with each new page.

"These two have already been called."

"They're a precaution."

"You didn't give us time to respond."

"There have been some developments."

Astrid Olsen stared at me, any good will from saving her from Kimberly Tripp gone. "I'm not going to be blindsided ag— I'm not going to let you blindside me, Shepherd."

"There are no new witnesses on there, Astrid. You could have called them too. You did call them too."

"What are you angling at? Going to make something up like you did with Maura Carmody?"

I shook my head. "I didn't make anything up with Mrs. Carmody. There was an unexplained delay that you wouldn't give me the explanation for."

"A delay that had nothing to do with the fire that killed her son!"

This conversation was becoming unproductive. I tapped the subpoenas. "This does. I'll see you in there."

I left her re-reading who we might be calling and went into the courtroom.

None of my team was there. Not Cyn, not Emily, not Olivia. Neither were the people they were going to see or the one I had called. Even Dagmar Niesen was missing, although I had nothing to do with that. No, the only person sitting in there was my expert,

Bret Halogi, dressed in black, her smoke-colored hair floating around her black frame glasses. It was just going to be her and me to start the day, to lay the groundwork for everything else we had to do.

The deputies brought in Brock, Judge Roderick brought in the jury, and we went to work.

∼

I LED Bret Halogi through her qualifications—academic credentials that included undergrad in chemistry and biology at the University of Minnesota; advanced degrees in laboratory science and fire safety protection from the Universities of Wisconsin, Toronto, and Oslo; certifications as a forensic and scientific fire investigator in five states; and practical experience fighting and then investigating fires for more than twenty-five years.

"Dr. Halogi, did you review certain things at my request in this case?"

"Yes. I examined all the samples taken by Investigator Vernon at the sites of the Mission Road Fire."

"And when you say you examined the samples, do you mean you examined them personally?"

"Yes."

"You didn't send them out to a lab?"

"No. I performed the laboratory examination personally as I've been trained to do and have done for more than twenty-five years. I also inspected the sites of the Mission Road Fires."

"In fairness, your examination of the sites took place five months after the fire?"

"It did, yes."

"Did you also review Investigator Vernon's report?"

"I couldn't."

"Why is that?"

"Because he didn't make one. In fact, he didn't even record his findings in any format that's recognized as appropriate by any organization."

"Dr. Halogi, Investigator Vernon has already testified to the jury about the results of his investigation."

"Calling it an investigation is generous. What he's done is given Ms. Olsen and the jury a series of conclusions without supporting them with underlying data."

"Could you explain that please?"

"Yes. By Investigator Vernon's own admission, he received a call from Sheriff Sizemore about Brock Niesen before he began his physical examination of the sites and well before any laboratory findings were available. He then oriented his investigation to confirming Sheriff Sizemore's theory rather than objectively investigating the fires and their spread."

"What evidence do you have of that, Dr. Halogi?"

"Investigator Vernon spent the majority of his time examining the drive-in. He took eight samples of debris in the drive-in and the arborvitae bushes. He documented finding the ammonium nitrate balls and the milk jug cap. He confirmed the presence of gasoline as an accelerant in the bushes. All of that was designed to provide evidence to demonstrate how a fire started at the drive-in and support Brock Niesen's arrest."

"Isn't that what he's supposed to do?"

"No. Mr. Tripp and Liam Carmody weren't killed by the fire in the drive-in; they were killed by the fire in the Carmody house. As a result, Investigator Vernon needed to continue to meticulously document and analyze the fire at each site where it occurred. Unfortunately, though, once Investigator Vernon had sufficient information to support the cause of the drive-in fire, he simply provided a cursory conclusion that the fire had spread all the way down to the Carmody house with very little scientific data to back it up."

"But Investigator Vernon took samples from additional sites, didn't he?"

"They weren't enough. He only took two samples in each area and didn't follow up on any of the information provided by those findings. He also did not carefully examine the subsequent fire sites and did not provide data to support his conclusion that the original drive-in fire had spread down the line."

"Have you done that, Dr. Halogi?"

"I have."

"Based on your education and experience as a fire investigator, your laboratory examination of the debris samples, and your inspection of the site in this case, do you have an opinion regarding the Mission Road Fire?"

"I do."

"What is that opinion?"

"First, that it should not be called the Mission Road Fire. It was the Mission Road *Fires*."

"I see. What other opinions do you hold?"

"Second, that the fire started by Brock Niesen's detonation of the SafeBoom target did not spread to the Carmody house."

"What is the basis for that opinion?"

"An actual examination of the evidence. Would you like me to explain?"

"Please."

"It's my opinion that the SafeBoom fire stopped at Bennie Bird's unit, the first unit in the U-Store. It's easier to show you with pictures, if I may."

"Go ahead."

Bret Halogi hit a couple of buttons and a picture of a pile of ash and charred logs came up. "This is a picture of the remains of the wood pile fire between the drive-in fence and the U-Store building. As you can see, there is a significant amount of ash, debris, and charred logs sitting there."

"I see it."

"You can also see the scorch marks going up the side of the building and the partial destruction of the west side of the roof."

"I do."

"And while a portion of the roof is burned through, the walls to Mr. Bird's unit remain standing."

"I see it." I peeked at the jury. They were watching.

Bret Halogi continued. "You recall that Investigator Vernon conjectured that the fire spread along the roof and through the internal timber framing until it ignited the contents of Mr. Chase's unit, which included a substantial amount of hardwood flooring."

I nodded, keeping an eye on the jury. "I remember. What was the amount?"

"Like everything else, Investigator Vernon did not record the actual amount of wood flooring that was supposed to be in the unit. But I understand Mr. Chase testified that the flooring was stacked waist high across half the unit."

I nodded. "That's what he said, Dr. Halogi."

"Here is a picture of the inside of Mr. Chase's unit after the fire." She used a laser pointer as she said, "So you see here, these charred tubes and chunks?"

I nodded. "Yes."

"Those are charred carpet remnants and pads. You see that they are discernible as rolls because their burn point is higher than wood and they melt as well as burn. Do you see how they are scattered throughout the floor of the unit?"

"I do."

"You see also that the common wall with Mr. Bird's unit is still intact while the opposite wall, the one shared with Mrs. Hoppel, has buckled and collapsed. This isn't surprising given the amount of material that was in Mrs. Hoppel's unit."

"The quilts and furniture and such?"

"Exactly. Now with the collapse of the wall, you can see that the roof over Mr. Chase's unit has sagged significantly but has not collapsed."

"I see it."

"Now, those all set the general picture, but that is not the most important part of this picture."

"What is the most important part of the picture, Dr. Halogi?"

"The floor. Do you see it? Here and here and here?" She circled areas of concrete floor with the laser pointer.

"I do. Why is that significant?"

"Because you can see *the floor*. See here? Concrete. And here? Concrete. And here? Concrete. Concrete, concrete, concrete." Every time she said the word, she circled a different section.

"Why is that significant, Dr. Halogi?"

"Because we can see the concrete! If wood flooring in the amount claimed by Mr. Chase and assumed by Investigator Vernon had actually been burned, then the floor should be covered in ash and charred remnants."

"How can you know that Dr. Halogi?"

"First, science. As anyone who's sat around a campfire knows, burnt wood leaves behind ash, even more if the fire is extinguished by water before it burns down as happened here. Second, Investigator Vernon took two samples from Mr. Chase's unit. Neither demonstrated the presence of wood. Third and finally, we have an example from this very set of fires."

She tapped a button, and a picture of the cherry wood ash pile appeared alongside the picture of Tommy Chase's carpet rolls and concrete floor. "See the difference?" she said.

"I do."

"One is what was left after a large amount of wood burned. The other, the picture of Mr. Chase's unit, shows, in my opinion, an area where a large amount of wood did *not* burn."

"Dr. Halogi, this seems like a pretty simple analysis."

"In some ways, it is."

"If it's so simple, how could Investigator Vernon, and everyone else involved, miss something so obvious?"

"It's why every inch of a fire site must be examined, Mr. Shepherd. Unfortunately, if you reach a premature conclusion based on law enforcement or witness reports, details are often missed. It's also another reason why detailed fire inventories, like the form the State provides, are so important—to remind the investigator of areas he should be checking."

"So, if I understand you correctly, you believe that the evidence does not support a conclusion that there was a large amount of wood flooring present in the Chase unit?"

"That's correct."

"And why is that significant?"

"Without that wood, there wasn't enough fuel for the fire to spread through the Chase Unit to the Hoppel Unit."

"But Dr. Halogi, we know that the Hoppel Unit eventually caught fire."

"Yes, we do."

"Do you have an opinion regarding how that occurred?"

"I do."

"What is that opinion?"

"Someone started a second fire with—"

Astrid Olsen leapt up. "Your Honor! Objection!"

"Basis?" said Judge Roderick.

"This theory was not disclosed by the defense."

He looked at me. "Mr. Shepherd?"

"Your Honor, Ms. Olsen entered into a stipulation with my predecessor, Attorney Luke Mott, to waive the exchange of expert reports." I held up a piece of paper. "And if I'm reading this email chain correctly, Judge, it was Ms. Olsen's idea."

Judge Roderick turned back to her. "Ms. Olsen?"

"That's true, but the defense didn't have an expert at the time."

"But you did?"

To her credit, Astrid Olsen didn't flinch. And she told the truth. "Yes."

"And you did not produce a report from your expert to Mr. Shepherd?"

"No, but everyone knew—"

"Overruled. You may continue, Mr. Shepherd."

I turned back to Bret. "What is your opinion regarding how the second fire started, Dr. Halogi?"

"Someone started a second fire using an accelerant."

"Do you have an opinion regarding what that accelerant was?"

"Yes."

"What?"

"Varnish."

"And so the jury understands, varnish is flammable?"

"Very."

"How do you know varnish was used as an accelerant in the Chase unit?"

"Both of the two samples Investigator Vernon took had traces of varnish on it."

"How do you know this?"

"The lab Mr. Vernon used found it. I confirmed the presence of varnish myself."

"So both labs found the varnish?"

"Yes."

"How could that be used to set a second fire?"

"One of two ways. It could be used to ignite materials in the Chase unit, which then spread to the Hoppel unit in the way Investigator Vernon originally theorized. Or, more likely, varnish could be spread over the gap between the roof peak and the metal wall directly onto Mrs. Hoppel's things and ignited. I think that's the most likely scenario."

"Do you hold that opinion to a reasonable degree of scientific probability, Dr. Halogi?"

"I do. The fire started by Brock Niesen did not spread to the Carmody house. A second fire was created using varnish as an accelerant between Mr. Chase's unit and Mrs. Hoppel's. That fire is the one that spread to the Carmody house and killed Eli Tripp and Liam Carmody."

"This next question is very important from a legal standpoint, Dr. Halogi. Did the fire from Brock Niesen's SafeBoom target combine in any way with the fire set in the Chase unit?"

"It did not."

"How can you tell?"

"There wasn't enough material to burn in the Bird and Chase units. And you can see from the roof that it didn't spread that way either. There simply wasn't enough damage over to those two units to support a finding that the drive-in fire continued to spread."

"Dr. Halogi, I have to ask again—how could this be missed?"

"You can't let a police investigation influence a fire investigation, Mr. Shepherd. It will blind you. You have to follow the fire."

"Thank you, Dr. Halogi. That's all I have."

As I sat down, Cyn came into the courtroom, slipped into the front row beside Dagmar, and nodded.

Astrid Olsen stood.

"Dr. Halogi, you weren't on the scene the night of the fire, were you?"

"No."

"You weren't on the scene the week after the fire either?"

"No."

"In fact, you didn't visit the scene until almost five months after the Mission Road Fire, right?"

"The Mission Road *Fires*."

"We'll get to that in a moment. You didn't visit the site until five months later, did you?"

"That's correct."

"You'd agree with me that the people on the scene during and immediately after the fire were in the best position to investigate it, won't you?"

"I agree that they had the best *opportunity* to investigate it. I don't agree that they did."

"Before we get to your little theory about a second fire, let's be clear about something for the jury—there is no question that Brock Niesen blew up a SafeBoom target and gasoline, is there?"

Bret Halogi sat there, unconcerned. "I agree that there was evidence that a SafeBoom target containing ammonium nitrate and aluminum powder was detonated at the Lakeside Drive-in and that a fire occurred in the arborvitae bushes that was accelerated by gasoline."

"Which Brock Niesen detonated?"

Bret Halogi shrugged. "I don't have an opinion on who did it. I have opinions about the fires."

"So you won't even admit to the jury that Brock Niesen started a fire?"

"That's exactly what I was talking about, Ms. Olsen. The criminal investigation shouldn't drive the scientific investigation. The findings are the findings."

"So if the jury heard testimony that Brock Niesen detonated the SafeBoom target, you wouldn't dispute it?"

Bret Halogi shook her head. "That's not part of my engagement, Ms. Olsen, so I wouldn't take a position one way or the other."

"Fine. Speaking of engagements, you're being paid to testify here today, aren't you?"

"I'm being paid for my time, yes."

"You're being paid to say that there was a second fire, aren't you?"

"No. I was paid to analyze the case and offer my opinions, whatever they were."

"Mr. Shepherd wouldn't have called you to testify if your opinions were negative, would he?"

"I don't know what Mr. Shepherd would do, but I agree it would be foolish for him to put me on the stand if I supported your case, just like it would be foolish of you to put someone on who supported the defense."

"Let's get to these opinions that you were paid for—"

"—I'm not paid for my opinions, Ms. Olsen. I was paid for my time to review the case."

"Fine, let's get to these opinions you reached while the defense was paying for your time. You are totally guessing that there was no wood in the Chase Unit, aren't you?"

"I'm not guessing. I'm saying that there's no scientific evidence that there was wood flooring in the Chase Unit."

"No evidence? Mr. Chase has testified that it was there and made an insurance claim when it was destroyed. That's certainly evidence for the jury, isn't it?

Bret Halogi shook her head. "That's not scientific evidence, no."

"So the jury should just ignore the evidence that contradicts you?"

"No. There is no *scientific* evidence that contradicts me because there is no *scientific* evidence to support your claim that wood flooring burned in the Chase Unit."

"That's based on your examination of the site five months later, isn't it?"

"It's based on the photos Mr. Vernon took the day after the fires and the debris samples he collected. Neither of them indicate the presence of wood ash that would be left by the destruction of the amount of flooring Mr. Chase claims was there."

Astrid Olsen rolled her eyes. "And the jury is just supposed to believe that there is no evidence of fuel for a fire that they know destroyed the U-Store units and the Carmody house?"

"No. The jury should understand that there is no scientific evidence to support that the fire spread the way you said it did, Ms. Olsen."

"Let's talk about what *you've* said, Dr. Halogi. You say there was no wood flooring in the Chase Unit."

"I said that there's no scientific evidence that there was wood flooring in the Chase Unit, yes."

"You theorize then that the original fire, the one set by Brock Niesen, could not have spread through the Chase Unit to the Hoppel Unit, is that right?"

"My opinion is that based on the fuel available and the time that elapsed, yes, the original fire at the drive-in died out."

"You say that the fire in the Chase Unit that spread to the Hoppel Unit was accelerated by varnish, right?"

"The sample taken by Inspector Vernon revealed the presence of varnish, yes."

"Wood flooring can have varnish on it, can't it?"

"Theoretically, I'm sure some does. There was no evidence of the presence of pre-varnished wood here."

"Mr. Chase could have been storing varnish there in the unit, couldn't he?"

"I've seen no evidence to indicate that."

"It's possible though, right?"

"Many things are possible. I haven't seen any evidence."

Astrid Olsen turned to the jury. "Dr. Halogi, let's explore this second fire theory of yours further. Who set this second fire in the Chase unit?"

Bret Halogi shook her head. "I don't know."

"Why would someone set fire to the Chase and Hoppel units using varnish?"

"I don't know."

"So Dr. Halogi, you're saying some mysterious person magically appeared at the U-Store and, for reasons you don't know and I can't fathom, saw a fire that you say was dying out, and used varnish to start a second fire and that it was this second fire that killed little Liam Carmody?"

"I'm saying that the scientific evidence shows that the second fire killed both Liam Carmody and Eli Tripp, yes."

"A second fire that just happened to be set for reasons you don't know by a person you can't identify?"

"That's what the science indicates, yes."

Astrid Olsen turned back to Bret Halogi. "How incredibly convenient. You can't prove any of that, can you?"

"I've been very careful to limit my opinion to the science of this fire, Ms. Olsen. And I'm saying you don't have scientific evidence to prove that this fire spread the way you said it did."

"Science needs to be based in reality, though, doesn't it, Dr. Halogi?"

"Always."

"On that we can agree then. No further questions." Astrid Olsen sat.

I stood. "Dr. Halogi, so the jury is clear, your opinion is that there is no evidence that wood flooring burned in the Chase Unit, correct?"

"That's correct."

"And that without that fuel, the fire from the drive-in would not have spread to the Hoppel Unit and from there to the Carmody house?"

"That's right."

"And there is no question that the sample taken by Investigator Vernon indicates varnish was present in the Chase unit?"

"That's right."

"And varnish is an accelerant?"

"Correct."

"You're not saying how it got there?"

"No."

"Or who did it?"

"I am not."

"Thank you."

Astrid Olsen stood. "Dr. Halogi, there was a strong west wind that night, right?"

"Yes."

"Assuming what you said was true, isn't it possible that the wind could have spread the fire from the wood pile to the Hoppel unit?"

Bret Halogi thought for a moment. "There's no evidence of that."

"Isn't it possible?"

"Not to a scientific probability, no."

"It's possible though, isn't it?"

"Possible, but not likely."

"No further questions."

"You may step down, Dr. Halogi," said Judge Roderick. "Mr. Shepherd, you may call your next witness."

I looked back at Cyn. She nodded. I turned back to the judge.

"Your Honor, the defense calls Patrick Dabbs."

55

Cyn left the courtroom and returned with Patrick Dabbs, who hadn't planned on being in court that day. He wore an open flannel jacket with a t-shirt, worn jeans, and work boots. As Cyn led him down the center aisle, he took off a Kodiak ball cap and smoothed down hair that was a couple of days out from a wash. He sat down and looked around, nervous, before the bailiff swore him in.

"Could you state your name please?" I said.

"Pat Dabbs," he said, leaning forward. "Most people call me Dabber." He looked around again. "What exactly is this about again?"

"Do you remember the Mission Road Fires, Mr. Dabbs?"

"Back last April?"

"That's right."

"Am I in trouble? I didn't have nothin' to do with that."

"No, no, Mr. Dabbs. You called 911 that night. Do you remember?"

"I do remember that I called, yes."

"I just want to ask you about that."

"Oh." The relief on his face was visible. "Okay, then."

"Do you remember what you said?"

"Not really, no."

"Let me refresh your recollection then."

I hit a button on my laptop and the 911 call played.

"Oh, right, right," said Patrick Dabbs.

"That's you on the call, right Mr. Dabbs?"

"Yep. Saw it when I went from the BeachHead to Pappy's."

"When was that?"

"Well, Devin closes the BeachHead at midnight during the week so sometime before that."

"Did you drive straight over to Pappy's?"

"Yep. Me'n a couple of the boys thought we'd finish up there. It's close to home for me."

"Did you drive down Mission Road?"

"I did."

"Is that when you saw the fire?"

"Yep. Wasn't too big though. Not like it got."

"Why didn't you call right away?"

Patrick Dabbs looked down. "Thought it'd be best if I waited 'til I got home."

"Because you'd been drinking?"

Patrick Dabbs nodded. "It didn't seem like the smartest thing to call the Sheriff right then."

"Sure."

"And the fire wasn't that big."

"No?"

"No, it looked like it was just some bushes and wood."

"I see."

"And I figured someone must know about it. People burn stuff all the time."

"They do?"

"You know when they're clearing things out and such."

"Right. So why did you call 911?"

"Got to thinking about it when I got home. Realized it was a little late at night to be burning so thought I'd better call to make sure." He straightened. "Good thing I did too."

"Oh?"

"Yeah, they might not have saved Maura and those girls if I hadn't."

I nodded. "You said you and a couple of boys were going from the BeachHead to Pappy's?"

"That was the plan, but it wound up just being me."

"Who else was supposed to go?"

"Jimmy Ringel, but his old lady got on him to come home. And Tommy said he might go, but then he figured he best get home since he had to work the next day."

I stopped, turned, and looked at Astrid Olsen. "Tommy Chase?"

"Yeah."

"You were with Tommy Chase at the BeachHead?"

"We didn't meet on purpose or nothin'. We were all just there."

"And Tommy Chase was going to go with you to Pappy's?"

"He talked about it, but then he told me that he called it a night."

"When did he tell you that?"

"A few days later. Maybe a week? Not sure exactly. Whenever the next time was we were at the BeachHead. Things were a little hectic around here for a while."

"I bet. Mr. Dabbs, what did Tommy Chase tell you, exactly?"

Patrick Dabbs shrugged. "I don't really remember. Just that once he got in his truck, he was too tired to go. He bought me a drink since he'd left me hangin' though so we're all good."

"He left you hanging because he didn't show up at Pappy's when he told you he'd go?"

"Yeah. But like I said, we're good."

"I don't have any more questions, Mr. Dabbs. Thanks."

Astrid Olsen stood. "Mr. Dabbs, you were drunk the night of the Mission Road Fire, weren't you?"

Patrick Dabbs shifted in his seat. "I'd had a few, but I was fine."

"Eight Jack and Cokes is more than a few, isn't it?"

"I don't know that it was that many."

Astrid Olsen looked at the jury. "We do. We've already seen your receipts from the BeachHead and Pappy's that night and it was eight."

"I don't remember it being that many."

"Your memory of that night is a little hazy, isn't it?"

"It's been a while, I guess."

"It's been a while and you were intoxicated, weren't you?"

"Maybe some. Not bad though."

"Bad enough that it affected your memory though, right?"

"I wouldn't say that."

"You don't remember how many drinks you had that night. That's a poor memory, isn't it?"

"I don't know that I'd ever remember how many drinks I had that long ago."

"That's a good point. Do you see Tommy Chase at the BeachHead often?"

"Sometimes, yeah. We both go there."

"You just said you don't know that you'd ever remember how many drinks you had that long ago."

"Right."

"That's because it's been a while and because you go there often, right?"

"That's true."

"So it's hard to remember how many drinks you had on a particular night, right?"

"Yeah."

"And you said you often see Tommy Chase there at the BeachHead, don't you?"

"Yeah."

"You can't be sure that you saw him on this night, the night of the Mission Road Fire, can you?"

Patrick Dabbs cocked his head. "I thought I did."

"But you can't be sure, can you?"

Patrick Dabbs didn't answer.

"Because you see him there so often, it's hard to remember which night it was, right?"

"I guess you're right. I guess I can't say for sure."

"This is the first time you've told anyone that you saw Tommy Chase at the BeachHead the night of the Mission Road Fire, isn't it?"

"I guess, yeah."

"In all the time since the Mission Road Fire, that's never come up?"

"No."

"You've never told anyone that?"

"No. Why would I?"

"No further questions, Your Honor."

I stood.

"More?" said Patrick Dabbs.

"Just a couple. Mr. Dabbs, Sheriff Sizemore never talked to you about your 911 call or the Mission Road Fires, did he?"

"Not that I remember, no."

"Before today, Ms. Olsen never asked you about your 911 call or the Mission Road Fires, did she?"

"No, not that I recall."

"Before today, Ms. Olsen never asked you about seeing Tommy Chase that night, did she?"

"No, sir, she didn't."

"In all the time since the Mission Road Fires, who has talked to you about what you did that night?"

"Just that lady sitting there at your table."

I pointed to Cyn. "You're talking about Ms. Bardor from my office?"

"Yep."

"If anyone had ever bothered to ask you, would you have told them what you just told us?"

"Sure. Why wouldn't I?"

"That's all, Mr. Dabbs. Thanks."

Astrid Olsen stood. "Mr. Dabbs, you refused to come to the door when Sheriff Sizemore came to see you the morning after the fire, didn't you?"

"I...I don't recall that."

"He's testified that he knocked, and you didn't answer. Do you dispute that?"

"No. I sleep pretty deep."

"Especially after eight Jack and Cokes?"

"I don't know. In general, I guess."

"No further questions, Your Honor."

"Thank you, Mr. Dabbs. You may step down."

As Patrick Dabbs left, I turned on my phone to check for texts. I had one. From Emily.

"Do you have another witness, Mr. Shepherd?" said Judge Roderick.

"Yes. The defense recalls Sheriff Sean Sizemore."

Astrid Olsen scowled as Judge Roderick scanned the courtroom.

"I don't see him," he said.

"It's my understanding he's on the way up, Judge."

"Let's take a morning break then."

So we did.

56

Astrid Olsen came right over. "You sandbagged me."

I shook my head. "We both blew that one, Astrid. You never talked to him. I didn't talk to him 'til last night. If we had, this case might have gone a different way."

"This case is going the same way, Shepherd. And so is your client."

I shrugged. "Seems like Mr. Dabbs had answers to some of the questions you asked Dr. Halogi."

She glared. "Pat Dabbs' testimony doesn't change anything. Everybody up here knows that you can find Dabber at the BeachHead or Pappy's or The Loon any day of the week. To an outsider it might matter, but people *from here* know he's a drunk."

"Okay." I started to walk away.

"Why are you calling Sheriff Sizemore?" she said.

I smiled. "Outsider reasons."

Then I went to get a drink of water before we came back in session.

I met Emily and Sheriff Sizemore in the hall.

∽

"Sheriff Sizemore, you are still under oath," said Judge Roderick.

"Yes, Judge," said Sheriff Sizemore, tucking his sunglasses into his shirt pocket.

"Thanks for coming back, Sheriff," I said.

"Certainly."

"Sheriff, did you investigate anything last night?

"Yes."

"What?"

"Emily Lake of your office advised me that Tommy Chase was using a new storage unit on the other side of town. She stated that your office believed that there may be evidence in it that was related to this case. Since we had never inspected that unit, I agreed to look."

"What did you find?

Astrid Olsen stood. "Objection!"

"Nothing related to this case," said Sheriff Sizemore.

"Basis, Ms. Olsen?" said Judge Roderick.

Astrid Olsen stared at Sheriff Sizemore for a moment as what he said over her objection sunk in. Then she said, "Withdrawn, Your Honor," and sat.

"What did you find, Sheriff?"

"As I said, nothing related to the case."

"What was in this new unit?"

"A few tools, carpet remnants, and some new wood flooring."

"What kind of wood flooring was it?"

"It was called zebrawood. I've never heard of it, personally."

"And you said a moment ago that it's not related to this case?"

Sheriff Sizemore shook his head. "No. The wood flooring

that was burned in this case was different. That was Patagonian Rosewood, so I assume this was for another job."

"And Sheriff, at Ms. Lake's request, you also checked your police reports for the week before and after the Mission Road Fires, right?"

"I did."

"Did you find any relating to the U-Store facility?"

"There was one report from the manager, Scooter Derry, of a break-in on April 8th, but we didn't have an opportunity to investigate it before the fire."

"A storage unit break-in is pretty low priority, I assume?"

"Yes. We have had to prioritize calls since the funding cuts."

"I'm sure. Thanks, Sheriff. That's all, Your Honor."

I checked the back of the courtroom. Nothing.

Good.

I sat down and looked at Cyn. She turned her notepad toward me.

I texted her.

I nodded.

Astrid Olsen stood. "Sheriff Sizemore, you're not surprised that Mr. Chase had another storage unit since the Mission Road U-Store unit burned down, are you?"

"No, I'm not."

"And to be clear, the wood flooring that burned in the Mission Road fire was Patagonian Rosewood, right?"

"That's right. That's what was listed in the police report and the insurance claim form."

"So in your opinion, nothing in this second storage unit was relevant to this case?"

"That's correct."

"So, Mr. Shepherd wasted your time?"

Sheriff Sizemore shrugged. "I can't fault him for looking. It's a murder case."

"It certainly is. No further questions, Your Honor."

I stood as Sheriff Sizemore stepped down. As he walked past me, I leaned in.

"You may want to stick around."

He stopped, stared.

"Not for long." I gestured to the front row.

He pursed his lips, turned his hat in his hands, and took a seat.

"Any more witnesses, Mr. Shepherd?" said Judge Roderick.

I gestured to Emily, who was already on her way to the door.

"Yes, Your Honor. May I check the hall?"

"Quickly."

She ducked out.

A moment later, Tommy Chase walked in. With Cade Brickson right behind him.

I turned to the judge. "Your Honor, the defense recalls Tommy Chase."

Astrid Olsen stood. "Your Honor, how much more time are we going to waste here?"

"Is this about something new, Mr. Shepherd?" said Judge Roderick.

"It is, Judge."

"Is there a reason it wasn't brought up the first time he testified?"

"Yes."

"Very well. Mr. Chase, please retake the stand."

With his work clothes and yellow cap, Tommy Chase didn't look any more ready to appear in court than Patrick Dabbs had. Given that he kept looking over his shoulder at Cade, I wasn't surprised. Once the judge spoke though, he took a seat, removed his hat, and gave me a scowl.

"You're still under oath, Mr. Chase," said Judge Roderick.

Tommy Chase nodded.

I stepped forward but stayed in the center of the courtroom so the jury and Astrid Olsen had a clear view of the witness chair.

"Mr. Chase, we heard from Patrick Dabbs this morning. He said you were at the BeachHead with him the night of the Mission Road Fires. Were you?"

Tommy Chase shook his head. "I'm not sure. We've been there at the same time now and then."

"Any reason to doubt Mr. Dabbs?"

"Well, I mean, I don't want to talk sh—I don't want to talk smack, but Dabber does have a tendency to get his drink on pretty regular."

"So he might not be the most reliable source?"

"I wouldn't want to say that, but yeah."

"If we wanted to know if you were really there that night, we should check something more reliable, like maybe your credit card records, right?"

He cocked his head. "I guess. I wouldn't know."

"Mr. Dabbs also said that you did not go to Pappy's with him that night. Is that true?"

Tommy Chase looked a question at Judge Roderick, who gestured to go ahead.

"I guess I wasn't a lot of places that night," Tommy Chase said. "Pappy's could be one of them."

I nodded. "You rent a storage unit over on Pineview Road, don't you?"

Tommy Chase's face went blank. "Had to put my stuff somewhere after the U-Store went up."

"What would we find if we searched it?"

Astrid Olsen stood. "Objection, Your Honor! Sheriff Sizemore has already testified that he found wood flooring that was not related to this case!"

Tommy Chase's eyes widened.

"I think we should still hear the witness's answer, Judge," I said.

"Overruled," said Judge Roderick. "And you know better than to make a speaking objection, Ms. Olsen."

I didn't care. This was better than I'd planned.

"What's in the unit, Mr. Chase?"

Tommy Chase looked from me to Astrid Olsen to the jury.

Then he folded his arms.

I let the silence stretch out.

"You have to answer the question, Mr. Chase," said Judge Roderick without looking up.

"Not if he's invoking the Fifth Amendment, Judge," I said.

Judge Roderick's head snapped up. "Is that what you're doing?"

"I'm not answering anything," said Tommy Chase.

"Based on your Fifth Amendment right against self-incrimination?"

"Whatever it is. I don't have to answer anything."

"Zebrawood is expensive, isn't it, Mr. Chase?"

Tommy Chase was silent.

Judge Roderick stepped in. "Mr. Chase, you have to say that you refuse to answer based on the Fifth Amendment if that's what you're doing."

I asked it again. "Zebrawood is expensive, isn't it, Mr. Chase?"

He lifted his chin. "I refuse to answer."

"It's almost impossible to get, isn't it?"

"I refuse to answer."

"It's worth an awful lot of money, isn't it?"

"I refuse to answer."

"That zebrawood was what was stored at your Mission Road U-Store unit, wasn't it?"

"I refuse to answer."

"There's no varnish on that zebrawood flooring, is there?"

"I refuse to answer."

"You use varnish all the time in your job, though, don't you?"

Tommy Chase had settled back in his chair, calm now, giving his response by rote. "I refuse to answer."

"A fire is a good way to hide a theft, isn't it, Mr. Chase? Better than a false police report, right?"

Tommy Chase just sat there, arms folded. "I refuse to answer."

I walked closer. "You know, as Ms. Olsen likes to point out, I'm not from here so I don't know folks the way you all do. What is John Warhelm going to do when he finds out you stole his wood?"

Tommy Chase's calm collapsed. His face went white and he sat straight up, gripping the sides of his chair, eyes darting as if he expected John Warhelm to walk in right then.

Astrid Olsen stood. "Objection, Your Honor. Mr. Shepherd can't just keep asking questions about whatever he wants."

I shook my head. "The Fifth Amendment grants Mr. Chase the right to refuse to answer, Judge. It doesn't limit my right to ask questions." I looked at Astrid Olsen. "Especially if this case continues as it is."

Judge Roderick took those brown glasses frames between his thumb and forefinger and straightened them twice. Then he said, "Members of the jury, I think this is a good time for lunch. We'll continue to this when you come back."

We all stood as the jury left. When they did, Judge Roderick said, "Counsel, in chambers. Sheriff Sizemore?"

Sheriff Sizemore nodded. "I'll see that he doesn't leave, Judge."

"You can't arrest me," said Tommy Chase. "I haven't done anything."

Sheriff Sizemore smiled. "I'm detaining you pending an investigation."

"Now, counsel," Judge Roderick said.

57

As soon as we sat down in front of him, Judge Roderick sighed. "What are we going to do with this?"

"You have to limit Mr. Shepherd's questioning, Your Honor," said Astrid Olsen. "We can't have him up there all afternoon just asking whatever he wants—"

"—I'm talking about the murder charge, Ms. Olsen."

She blinked. "What do you mean?"

"I mean that it seems to me that there is a high likelihood that you have the wrong guy."

"I don't see it that way, Judge."

Judge Roderick shook his head. "At the very least, it seems that further investigation may be in order."

"But jeopardy has attached!"

"Yes, it has. But I'm not the one who investigates the case, Ms. Olsen. Or chooses when it's ready for trial."

I stayed silent as Astrid Olsen said, "All Mr. Shepherd has right now is a theory, Judge. And don't even get me started on the causation end of this—even if Tommy Chase did go in there and douse the place with varnish, Mr. Shepherd can't prove that the two fires didn't unite into one and cause the deaths."

"You have to prove that, Ms. Olsen," I said.

"What?"

"You have the burden of proving that the fire my client allegedly set made it all the way to the end."

"We've done that."

"You've done that assuming wood for fuel was in Tommy Chase's unit. It wasn't. And you're forgetting something else that the jury will find troubling."

"What?"

"If the original fire was still spreading, why did Tommy Chase have to start another one?"

That stopped her. When she didn't say anything, I handed her a piece of paper.

"What's this?"

"Scooter Derry's phone number."

"The manager from the U-Store? Why do I need that?"

"So you can call him."

"Why?"

"To find out which tenant reported a break-in to their unit the night before the fire."

She stared at it.

I pulled out my phone. "Better yet, let's call him now."

"Who was it?"

I shrugged. "You know it's going to be Tommy Chase."

"But—"

"He's on both of our witness lists, Astrid. I'm calling Scooter on Monday."

I'd entered a couple of numbers when there was a knock on the door.

"Yes?" said Judge Roderick.

Sheriff Sizemore poked his head in. "Judge, I just received a call I thought you should be aware of."

"Yes?"

"It was John Warhelm calling to report a theft. Turns out he had paid for a zebrawood floor that was supposedly burned in the fire. He heard"—he cleared this throat—"somehow, that the wood was still around."

"But that's not what was listed in all the forms!" said Astrid Olsen.

I nodded. "I think you'll find that zebrawood is difficult to import, Astrid." I said. "I'm not surprised the paperwork lists something else."

Sheriff Sizemore waved a hand. "Anyway, Warhelm's complaint and that fact that Chase about shit himself when he heard Warhelm was calling me is enough for me to arrest Chase for theft."

He looked at Astrid. "I also think it's enough to reopen the murder investigation."

"But the case," said Astrid. "The press."

Sheriff Sizemore nodded. "We're both going to take some heat, Atti. Comes with the territory. Anyway, thought you should know."

"Hold on, Sheriff," said Judge Roderick. "Ms. Olsen, are we going to continue with Mr. Chase's testimony?"

She didn't say anything.

"Or is the murder charge being dropped?"

She thought some more, then said, "I have to talk to Mrs. Tripp and Mrs. Carmody."

"That's fine. We'll lengthen lunch. Sean, hold on to Mr. Chase until then."

As we filed out, Astrid Olsen made a beeline for Mrs. Tripp and walked her outside. Dagmar, Brock, and Cyn joined Emily and me as we emerged.

"What happened?" said Dagmar.

"A lot," I said.

AT THE APPOINTED TIME, we were all back in the courtroom. Astrid Olsen didn't look my way while Kim Tripp glared at me from the back row, which was exactly what had been going on the whole trial, so no, I couldn't tell which way this was going to go.

Sheriff Sizemore was sitting right next to Tommy Chase in the seats on our side of the rail, waiting.

Judge Roderick entered then indicated we could all sit down before he said, "Ms. Olsen, before we bring the jury back in, please advise the Court. Are we going to continue with the examination of Mr. Chase?"

Astrid Olsen stood. "No, Your Honor."

"Very well. Do we have anything else to address?"

"Your Honor, the State will continue the arson case against Brock Niesen to this jury."

"I see."

Astrid Olsen stared straight ahead as she said, "However, in light of recently discovered evidence, we hereby dismiss the murder charges against him with prejudice."

A murmur went up from the gallery as Judge Roderick nodded and said, "Pierce, bring in the jury."

Pierce did and, once they were seated, Judge Roderick said, "Members of the jury, the prosecution has elected to dismiss the murder charges against the defendant."

There was a little surprise on their faces, but not much. There were a lot of hard looks for Tommy Chase, though, as Judge Roderick continued.

"This happens from time to time and has no impact on the remaining charges. I'm going to dismiss you for the remainder of the day while we determine the form the rest of this trial is going to take. For those of you arranging time off work or child-care, I suggest you keep next Monday and Tuesday free. Does that sound about right, Counselors?"

"Yes, Your Honor," we said.

And with some instructions about not coming to any preconceived notions until the conclusion of the evidence, he dismissed the jurors for the weekend.

The second they were out of the courtroom, Sheriff Sizemore cuffed Tommy Chase.

"Do you need him anymore, Judge?" Sheriff Sizemore said.

"No. I expect by the time you're done processing him, court will be closed for the weekend. There will be no arraignment until Monday."

Sheriff Sizemore nodded and led Tommy Chase toward the door.

When they reached the back row, Kim Tripp stepped out from the pew.

"You slept in our house! You were his friend!"

"Mrs. Tripp!" said Sheriff Sizemore, but he really didn't get in her way.

Tommy Chase didn't say anything, but he looked stricken and bowed his head as Sheriff Sizemore led him out.

Kim Tripp stared at him, then turned to me. She didn't say anything, she didn't nod, she didn't acknowledge her misdirected anger in any way but, to be fair, it's awfully hard to change the direction of that much momentum that quickly. She just turned and left, closer behind Tommy Chase than I'm sure he liked.

"What does that mean?" Brock whispered. "Is it over?"

"No," I said. "But the worst of it is."

"The murder case?" said Dagmar.

"The murder case is done."

She pressed her lips into her hand for a moment, then pointed. "May I?"

I nodded.

She grabbed Brock and hugged him. I smiled as he hugged her back. True, arson still held a potentially years-long sentence, but sometimes you have to celebrate the little things.

Judge Roderick motioned us back to his office. "Counsel, let's figure this out."

58

We spent the next hour arguing about what was left of the case. I said the case should be dismissed. Astrid Olsen argued the destruction of the movie screen, wood pile, and part of the Bird unit still constituted third degree arson, which sounds reasonable until you realize that it's punishable with ten years in prison and a twenty thousand dollar fine. Judge Roderick tried to twist our arms into settling for a plea deal of fifth degree arson, which was a misdemeanor, and I'll admit, I might have been tempted to take it, but Astrid Olsen made it easy and dug in her heels. Eventually, Judge Roderick threw up his hands and told us to deliver the revised jury instructions to him by noon Sunday and to be prepared for closing arguments Monday morning.

Dagmar Niesen was still sitting in the front row when we came out of the judge's chambers, head bowed, shoulders stooped, her phone cupped in both hands. As Cyn and Emily gathered our things, I went down and sat next to her. She looked up, her startlingly blue eyes red from crying.

"We're not out of the woods," I said. "But we can see the clearing."

"The murder charge is still gone?" she said.

"Yes."

"That's good. But they're going after arson?"

"Yes."

"How much?"

"How much what?"

"How much prison time?"

"The judge tried to push a plea deal that would be a year or less. The prosecutor's going for ten."

Dagmar's face twisted in surprise. "Years?"

I nodded.

"For shooting his own dad's movie screen?"

"And the wood pile and the first storage unit."

She choked on a laugh, shook her head, then let go of her phone and put her head in her hands.

Dagmar's shoulders shook, and she began to cry.

I hesitated, then put a hand on her shoulder.

She shook a little longer, then straightened, laughed, and wiped her eyes. I handed her a tissue because yes, a trial lawyer often needs to have them on-hand and nearby.

After Dagmar thanked me and wiped her eyes again, I said, "We have a shot here. I think the jury's going to be a lot less mad after today and I plan to make the exact same argument you just did, that this was just a dispute between a dad and his son."

"That's my point," she said, with one last wipe. "I appreciate what you did today, how you figured out what happened and got them all to admit it. But my son still might go to jail."

"Maybe. But he might not."

"And if he doesn't, if by some miracle Brock doesn't go to jail, he's going to have to go to Indiana anyway."

"What? Why?"

"None of the distillers will take my apples. I just heard from the last one while you were in with the judge. Everyone's filled their orders for this season."

I processed, shifted gears, then said, "But Mrs. Tripp should back off now, shouldn't she?"

"I'm sure she's already gunning for Tommy Chase, but it's too late. Midwest Fruit won't take us back and it's too late to find someone new. I have a bunch of offers to call again next season, but by then it will be too late. I'm going to lose the Orchard by the end of the year." She shook her head. "I've already had a call from Devin Wright. That means the vultures aren't far behind."

She stared at me. "So Brock will still have to move in with his father. Hell, I might have to move in with his father until I find something. We're going to go through all this, win, and Brock's going to have to go to Indiana anyway."

She bowed her head again as she said, "It's cruel."

I couldn't disagree.

∽

It was a weird vibe in the office that night. We'd won the murder case but our client, our fifteen-year-old client, still faced a decade in prison and a fine he couldn't pay. There was relief but none of the celebration that comes with a win.

We did still gather around the office conference table to eat and rehash what everyone had done. Cade and Olivia joined us and brought the food since Cade had found a place that grilled half chickens over an open wood fire because of course he had. As he distributed birds and sides, Cyn described how the night before, she'd gone from the BeachHead to Pappy's and then the Loon before finding Pat Dabbs and, for the price of two Jack and Cokes, learned all that had happened the night of the Mission Road Fires, including Tommy Chase's presence at the BeachHead and failure to show up at Pappy's that night. It had taken a stop for a Bloody Mary that morning, but otherwise, it had not been hard to convince the Dabber to do his civic duty and appear.

That made Cade chuckle. He had caught Tommy Chase as he left his house that morning and told him that he was wanted back at court. When I asked how he convinced him to go, Cade shrugged and said, "I told him that I could beat the lawyer's ass."

"So you lied?"

"No."

"How's your knee?"

Cade suggested that I go enjoy an intimate relationship without a partner.

Olivia, after claiming that she could beat us both blindfolded, explained how she'd found the second storage unit by searching online for someone selling exotic zebrawood directly. She had tried all the usual sites, and some that were unusual, before she found one that she suspected was our man and became convinced of it when she saw the amount he was selling.

"How did you figure out where he was hiding it?" Emily asked.

Olivia pulled a strip of chicken breast off with her fingers. "Our criminal genius offered buyers a pick-up location if they wanted to save on shipping. Nothing to it after that." She popped it in her mouth.

Emily had been surprised at how easily Sheriff Sizemore had agreed to check the second storage unit. He'd been a little reluctant at first, but the minute she'd mentioned that John Warhelm was the homeowner who might have been ripped off, he was up and running.

"You know, from my end of the table, I could hear Sheriff Sizemore and Chase talking while we were waiting for the judge," said Emily. "I think Chase is more scared of Warhelm than of the murder charge."

"Why do you say that?" I asked.

"Chase asked Sheriff Sizemore if he had talked to Mr. Warhelm. When the Sheriff said he had, Chase asked how he seemed. Sheriff Sizemore said, 'He wasn't happy,' and it looked like they were going to have to clean Tommy's pants out right there."

"Sounds like it'll be a race between Mrs. Tripp and Warhelm to see who gets to Chase first," said Cade.

"Oh, Tripp's already re-aimed her social media gun," said Olivia.

"Jail might be the safest place for him," said Cade.

"Speaking of which, we still don't have any idea who burnt the Orchard, do we?" said Emily.

"The Sheriff doesn't have any leads," said Cyn. "He thinks Tripp may have whipped folks up, but she has an alibi for that night."

I thought about what Dagmar had told me, about who might profit from her being pushed closer to ruin. It seemed like a long list.

"One thing at a time, I guess," I said.

We spent some more time eating, more time talking, and more time appreciating what everyone had done to beat the murder charge. Finally, we couldn't put it off any longer and got back to work. As Cade and Olivia gathered the remains of dinner and left, I followed them out the door.

Olivia caught my vibe right away. "What is it?"

"Just thinking that I appreciate you two."

"Bet your ass," said Cade.

"Overdue," said Olivia.

But both knew me enough to wait for more.

I nodded. "How did you two like going on the road?"

"Anytime, anywhere," said Cade.

"If it's near something climbable or hikeable, I'm in," said Olivia.

"Why?" they both said.

I smiled. "Nothing. Just tired and relieved, I think. Thanks. And thanks for today."

They didn't look like they believed me, but they also accepted it. I got a shoulder bump from Cade, a hug from Olivia, and they left.

~

We worked through the weekend. There was more to do than you'd think. Emily had to completely redo the jury instructions, I had to rework the closing, and Cyn had to sift out all of the exhibits that were no longer relevant so that they didn't go back to the jury. By Sunday night, our relief from Friday night was long gone. Brock had purposefully destroyed a structure and caused damage in an amount that could put him away for a decade. And now, there was no question that he did it.

We were all up late.

59

We could have gone to bed sooner. The jury convicted Brock Niesen of a misdemeanor called a Prohibited Intentional Act, which was the crime of willfully burning or destroying low value property and, more importantly, was not arson. In talking to the jury afterward, we had the impression that, if Brock had only damaged the drive-in, they would have let him off completely, but since Benny Bird's woodpile and the outside of the U-Store building had been burned, they felt like they had to do something.

And man, were they pissed at Tommy Chase. A couple of them asked if there was any chance they could get seated on that jury too. When I told them no, they were incredibly disappointed.

In an unconventional move, Judge Roderick held an immediate sentencing hearing. First, he noted that Brock Niesen had already been incarcerated for five months. Then he declared that, given the defendant's age, the intrafamily nature of the dispute, and the minimal property damage, five months was sufficient imprisonment and ordered his release subject to probation, completion of courses on hunter safety, firearm safety, and fire safety, and regular anger management counseling.

As Judge Roderick rapped the gavel, Dagmar Niesen grabbed her son. Brock looked at me over her shoulder, confused.

"Is that it?" he said.

"You're free," I said. "There's more you have to do, but you're going home tonight."

With that, Brock Niesen returned his mom's hug and buried his head in her shoulder.

I motioned to Cyn not to let them leave, she gave me a nod that said, "I'm not stupid," and I walked up to where Judge Roderick was still seated at the bench with Mason Pierce looming behind him.

Both were talking to Astrid Olsen. I hung back until Judge Roderick waved me up.

Astrid turned, looked me in the eye, and offered her hand. "Congratulations," she said.

"You too."

She gave a wry smile. "We're not going to be popping champagne over a misdemeanor conviction."

"You have the right guy though."

She nodded. "We do."

"That's what we were just talking about," said Judge Roderick. "How this case relates to the Tommy Chase prosecution."

"It seems like his deception can be used to explain this case away," I said.

"That's what I thought," said Mason Pierce.

"I have no official opinion, of course," said Judge Roderick. "But yes."

"I'll give you everything we found on him," I said to Astrid.

"I appreciate that," she said. "In the meantime, I have more than enough to charge him with the theft and hold him while I put the murder case together."

"That's about as much detail as I should hear," said Judge Roderick. He stood and reached down over the bench. "You saved that boy, and us, from a mistake, Mr. Shepherd. Come back to Northlake anytime."

I shook his hand. "Thanks, Judge."

"You two can submit the final orders to my staff attorney here. We'll wrap this up before he leaves us to go to the dark side."

Astrid Olsen's head snapped up as I said, "Where to?"

Mason Pierce ducked his head. "Kramer Burns."

"Wow," I said. Kramer Burns was one of the biggest firms in Michigan. "Congratulations. What are you going to do?"

"Trial work. On the civil side."

Judge Roderick slapped Pierce's shoulder, said, "Traitor," and left.

"You didn't tell me," said Astrid Olsen.

"I was going to after I told the judge."

"So when do you leave for Detroit?"

Mason Pierce scowled. "Detroit? Oh, no, Kramer Burns is opening a Northlake office."

Astrid's face lightened. "Your dad will be glad to hear that."

"You know I would never..." he trailed off, looked at me, then said, "So if you agree on the final orders, I'll get them entered. Can you do it by the end of the week?"

I nodded. "I'll have it to you by the end of the day tomorrow if you can, Astrid."

"Along with the Chase materials?" she said.

"Definitely. I'd like to wrap this up."

"Same."

They seemed to have more to talk about so I was about to leave them to it, but I had to ask one more question. "One last outsider question—was it my imagination or was Chase more worried about getting caught stealing from Warhelm than he was being caught for murder?"

"I don't know what he was thinking," said Astrid but didn't say anymore.

I looked at Mason Pierce.

His broken-nosed face didn't so much as twitch. "You weren't imagining it."

And that was all either of them would say about it.

～

CYN REPORTED to her firm when we got back to the office. They were ecstatic. It was late enough in the day that none of us felt like leaving town that night so when she said dinner was on them, Emily and I were happy to take her up on it. We ended up at the Northlake Grill, which specialized in steaks and whitefish, and after we'd been given our drinks and ordered our dinners, Cyn said, "The firm is going to give you a bonus."

I waved her off. "That's not necessary, Cyn."

"Sure, it is."

"Honestly, no."

Cyn calmly took a sip of her drink, then said, "You should think about your employees, Nathan. Some of them have weddings to pay for."

I stared at her. "Do you always win?"

"I'm always reasonable."

Emily cackled as I conceded the bonus.

We rehashed the case, texted a "look what you're missing" picture of the meal to the Bricksons, who'd already headed home, and had a few drinks on Friedlander & Skald. When we'd moved from the case to a more generally decompressive conversation, I said to Cyn, "So where are you off to next?"

"Charlotte."

"You could do worse than fall in North Carolina," I said.

"What's the case about?" said Emily.

Then we spent a good part of dinner learning about a collapsed overpass and just whose fault it might be.

At one point, when Emily left to use the restroom, Cyn said, "The Firm also wanted to know if you've reached a decision on their offer."

"I've been a little preoccupied."

"They know."

"The offer includes everybody?"

"We can accommodate Daniel's practice. But we want you, and Emily, to do what I do."

"Like we all did this week?"

"Exactly."

"Where?"

"Mostly the Midwest. But sometimes, everywhere."

I nodded.

"I'm sending you the financials," Cyn said.

I thought. "Why don't you give me a week before you go to the trouble."

"I'm sending you the financials," Cyn said again as Emily returned.

∽

EARLY THE NEXT MORNING, Cyn left to catch a flight to Charlotte, and Emily, after repeated assurances that I could indeed close up shop and file things by myself, set out for Columbus for the long-neglected wedding festivities, much to the relief of her mother.

I agreed on the orders to close the case with Astrid, packed our files and equipment, and locked the rental office, putting a bow on our presence in downtown Northlake. I was about to leave when I realized that wasn't quite true, so I put our things in my Jeep, locked it, and walked the two blocks down the street to Maggie's.

It was busy with the morning coffee rush, so I waited my turn, watching Maggie sling caffeine and smiles in equal measure. When it was my turn, she smiled and said, "Single or group?"

"Single. I'm the last one."

"Large, black coming up." As she turned to the carafe, she said, "Congratulations."

"Thanks."

"No one can believe it."

"I had a lot of help."

She threw a nod at her cook staff working behind the glass deli counter. "Team game."

"That's the truth."

As she sleeved and capped my cup, I said, "Forgive an ignorant downstater—"

She smiled. "Good Lord, what do you want now?"

"But I've come to appreciate what it took for you to tell me what you did."

"What was that?"

"How to find a certain powerful person."

"It was nothing," she said, but she kept her eyes on the register.

"Two things—First, we wouldn't have won without it. Second, I think that person is happy he was found."

That got her attention. "Yeah?"

"Yeah."

The line behind me kept filling. "I'll tell anyone coming to Northlake where the best pastrami is," I said.

"Don't hesitate to sample it again yourself."

"I won't."

She held out her hand and I shook it.

"Good lunch, Maggie."

"Good luck, Nate."

∽

ON THE WAY out of town, I stopped one last time at the Golden Apple Orchard and parked my Jeep near where the burnt barn used to be. The debris was gone, bulldozed and removed by the looks of it, so that a smooth pad of packed dirt remained. A familiar gangly form walked out of another building to meet me.

"Hi, Brock."

"Mr. Shepherd."

"Nate's fine now."

He smiled. "Thanks, Nate."

"There you go."

"No, I mean for the other thing, the case."

I waved. "You bet. Just no more SafeBoom."

He ducked his head. "No. No way."

We talked then about his obligations—about completing the courses, about reporting to his supervising officer, and generally about staying out of trouble. I think it was sinking in but, if you've ever had a serious talk with a teenager, then you know you can't really tell. He at least acted like it, which I appreciated.

"And you'll need to report to your supervising officer before you go to Indiana until he says otherwise."

"That won't be for a long time."

"No?"

Brock grinned. "Mom said we don't have to go. She found a buyer for the apples!"

"She did? That's great news!"

"It is. She's back with him now. I'll text her. I know she wanted to see you before you left."

A minute later, Dagmar Niesen walked out of the warehouse with a man. He was a tall man in his sixties with a hawkish nose and a mop of steel gray hair. As the two of them approached, he looked at me, stopped, and said, "Hello, Nate."

It was André Lacombe.

Josie Lacombe's dad.

Marie-Faye Lacombe's brother.

In case you've forgotten, I used to date his daughter Josie until his sister Marie-Fay had me run off the road as a warning, to both of us, that I should keep my nose out of her family's business. As far as I knew, André Lacombe was just an enthusiastic distiller of the Lacombe family's traditional whiskey and was not involved in the questionable, and occasionally murderous, business of his sister. But that didn't mean I was happy to see him. Or that I was happy about what his presence meant.

All that flashed through my head, but what I said was, "Nice to see you, André. You're far from home."

He smiled. "You too. I was just telling Dagmar here that the Lacombe Distillery is looking to expand into hard cider. I found another old recipe from my great grandfather. I talked to our people in Lacombe Agriculture, and they told me they'd found a premier orchard up north here that had the inventory and so here we are. It's fate."

"Sure sounds that way."

André Lacombe turned back to Dagmar. "So, like I was saying, we'll take the whole lot. I'll go back and figure out what I need for the Distillery, but my sister has authorized me to tell you that whatever I don't take, Lacombe Agriculture will take the rest."

Dagmar looked cautious. "What price were you thinking?"

André turned and looked back at the Orchard. "Well, I was

thinking that I'd want your best apples for my cider, but now that I've seen them, I have to have your Goldens." He smiled. "I can already see the bottle for 'Lacombe Gold.' Sounds like a premium Hard Cider, doesn't it? It'll sell itself. So I think it'll be somewhere in the neighborhood of market plus ten percent, and I know Lacombe Ag likes to lock up its suppliers, so I'd guess they're going to be somewhere in the area of market plus five percent range."

Dagmar stared. "For all of it?"

André nodded. "All you have, yeah."

Dagmar put her fingers to her mouth and bowed her head.

"Does that sound good, Dagmar?"

She nodded once, then raised her head and smiled. "That sounds great, André. I'll look for your offer."

"You'll have it tomorrow." He grinned. "Start sorting those golds for me!"

"I will."

"I have a long drive back, so I best get on it. But it was worth it." He offered his hand. "Can't wait to get those apples."

Dagmar shook it. "I can't wait to send them to you."

He waved to me. "Nice to see you, Nate. I'll be sure to tell Josie I ran into you."

I nodded. "Say hi to her for me."

As he left, Brock said, "Mom, does that mean…?"

"Yes." She was grinning now. "We're not going to Indiana."

Brock whooped. "And you can tell Devin Wright to piss off because we're not selling!"

"Brock!" She grinned. "But yes."

"Dagmar."

She turned to me.

I thought about warning her to be careful of the Lacombes, that she should not, under any circumstances, trust Marie-Faye Lacombe, that she should be wary of becoming part of that sprawling web of businesses and lies, that she should be careful of the woman who had almost killed me, a woman who had only let me live because of her affection for my father.

And then I realized that I was just thinking about what the Lacombes were to me, that I was shocked André was there and spooked that his presence meant Marie-Faye Lacombe was still keeping tabs on me, even all the way up here, letting me know just how far her power reached.

All of which had nothing to do with Dagmar.

Dagmar was a modest apple grower in northern Michigan looking to keep her family afloat and from what I knew, André, and his daughter Josie, were honest and trustworthy and just part of the wrong family. This contract was a lifeline for the Niesen family. It didn't matter what it was for me.

Dagmar's eyebrows rose in question.

I smiled. "Congratulations."

PART VII - QUENCH

60

My first stop was my brother Mark's house to pick up Roxie, and if you missed her during this trial, just imagine how I felt. I'd only been gone for a month but even in that time, her brindle coat seemed a little whiter around the muzzle and her saunter a little slower, but she seemed just as happy to see me as I was to see her. Though my nephews protested and begged for one more night, I took her home, watched her sniff around, and don't think I'm projecting too much when I say she seemed happy to be in her own bed. She seemed a little stiff on our first walk, but I attributed that to a month being run ragged by three young boys, and when she laid her head on my lap as we watched TV, I told her that I thought it was good to be home too.

The next two days were filled with catch-up as I waded through the emails, messages, bills, and chores that accumulate when you put everything aside for a trial. Danny had the office running fine, but there were things particular to me and my cases that had to be done. I didn't tell Danny about Cyn's offer for us, not yet, because I wasn't sure what I was going to do.

One of the emails I sorted through was from Mason Pierce, attaching the judge's final, signed order on the jury verdict disposing of the case. He also attached, without comment, two articles from *The Northlake Ledger*. The first described the arrest of twenty-eight-year-old Austin Breen for the firebombing of the Golden Apple Orchard after a video of the act was discovered on an app which was supposed to have deleted it. His attorney was quoted as saying that his young client had been swept away by the social media campaign, that he truly believed at the time that the Orchard was supporting a child-killer, and that this one act "is not who he is." The second article was just a single paragraph, stating that Thomas Chase had been arraigned on charges of theft and murder, but had not appeared personally in Court because he was in the jail infirmary receiving treatment for a fractured femur and ribs he sustained after slipping on the stairs.

Finally, at the end of the second day, I went out to see my parents. My mom harangued me about losing weight and I assured her I was eating. My dad wondered if I'd seen the Lions beat the Vikings last Sunday, and I had to tell him I'd missed it. I asked how he felt now that dialysis was done, and he said never better. I thought he was telling the truth—he had a few more lines around the eyes and his cheeks were sharper, but he still seemed like the hale white-haired menace he'd always been even if my mom's gaze did seem to follow him a little longer whenever he left the room.

The next day, I took my medicine and went to the Brickhouse to workout. Olivia literally stopped the music, blew a whistle, and asked everyone there to welcome new member Nate Softserve. I wouldn't have minded except people kept coming up asking if I needed a spot or a tutorial on the piece of equipment I was using. After the fourth one, I saw that Olivia was giving a free Gatorade to each person who did it.

And the day after that, I drove south to Columbus, Ohio for Emily's wedding.

~

Emily had a big family and so did her now husband Josh and despite the fact that there were an inordinate number of Buckeye antennae pennants, class rings, and suit pins, they seemed like very nice people. When her father offered his toast, I saw where she got her wit and when her mother smilingly reined in her sister, I saw where she got her steel, and when she and Josh and their friends and their siblings took to the dance floor, I saw where she got her joy.

I was sitting at the "work friends" table with Danny and his wife Jenny, a couple of other young lawyers from Carrefour, and to my surprise, Cyn.

"I wasn't sure if you'd make it back from Charlotte," I said.

She nodded. "We have a few weeks before trial yet. And, with the way our practice is, the Firm pays for us to come back, or go, anywhere, every weekend. Which you'd know if you read the financial package I sent you."

With Danny on my right, I leaned closer and said quietly, "I don't think that life is for me, Cyn."

Her green eyes were unreadable as she held mine. "You would always have cases."

"I'm sure."

"And the money is considerably more."

"I figured."

"*Considerably.*"

"I understand."

"I'm not sure that you do."

I shrugged.

We were quiet for a moment before she said, "Personally, I would enjoy working with you."

I nodded. "Maybe there'll be another case down the road. Closer to Carrefour."

"You never know." She broke her gaze and precisely cut a square bite of red velvet wedding cake with her fork. "I'll tell the partners. They'll be disappointed."

"Tell them I appreciate it." I realized another thing. "So I suppose I'll never get to know who paid for Brock's defense?"

Cyn nodded. "Client information is for partners." She took a bite. "There's no big mystery though. Dagmar, and Brock, share a common lineage with a certain large sound engineer and lyricist. It's distant, but it mattered to him."

I smiled. "Hank?"

"I think he heard about the case when he was traveling through Michigan. He wanted Brock taken care of. The same way he had been."

"Can you give him my message from Lizzy? That he's welcome again?"

"The Firm already has. But I don't know that it will change his mind."

Another thing occurred to me. "Why didn't Hank help them keep the Orchard?"

Cyn shrugged. "You know Braggi. He'd probably view losing the Orchard as liberating." She looked directly at me. "I'd bet it never occurred to him that someone could *want* to stay in one place."

"I'm sure that seems crazy. To him."

Cyn smiled at me then, a smile that was genuine and warm. "It's not. We'll keep the door open for you for a while if you change your mind."

"Thanks, but I don't think that's necessary."

She shrugged. "Things change."

"Sure."

The young attorney on Cyn's other side asked her then how she knew Emily.

"We're co-workers," Cyn said, and the two began to talk about how great Emily was.

∽

LATER, as Emily and Josh went from table to table, they made it to ours. I stood as Josh shook my hand and Emily hugged Dan and Jenny.

"Thanks for making it down, Nate," said Josh. "It means a lot to us."

"Thanks for inviting me. Everything's great."

He grinned. "If a caterer can't handle his own wedding, he should get out of the business."

"True enough."

"The signing bonus went a long way too!"

I smiled. "Good."

"And a flight allowance we can use for our honeymoon? Amazing."

Then what he said hit me.

I looked at Emily whose head snapped around as I said, "I'm sure you'll have a great time. Where are you going?"

"Aruba."

I nodded.

Emily came over, took her husband's arm, and said, "We have a few more tables, Boss. Then talk?"

I smiled and I meant it. "I'm not your boss, Emily. And of course."

∽

Cruel Sentence

WE CAUGHT up in a quiet corner of the garden outside the hotel's banquet room. Emily looked flustered as she said, "Boss, I—"

"Don't apologize, Emily. Especially not tonight."

"I thought maybe we'd all be going."

"Just because it's not right for me, doesn't mean it's not right for you."

She nodded. "I just—"

"You want more trials where you're the one handling the work."

She breathed. "Yes."

"And you want to make a lot more money."

"That doesn't hurt. But it's really the trials."

"Then this job sounds perfect for you. And we both know what it's like to work with Cyn."

She looked back at the reception. "I'll come back for two weeks after the honeymoon to wrap things up."

"That's plenty."

"I'm sorry you heard from Josh."

"Don't give it a second thought, Emily. I'm happy for you."

She breathed again. "Thanks, Boss."

I scowled at her.

"Thanks, Nate," she said, and hugged me.

∽

I SAT DOWN NEXT to Danny.

"How'd that go?" he asked.

I looked at him. "You knew?"

"She told me about her offer. My partner didn't."

I nodded. "I was only going to bring it up if I was interested."

"You're not then?"

"No. My life's in Carrefour."

Danny nodded. "Mine too."

We watched Emily pull Josh onto the dance floor.

"We need a new associate," said Danny.

"You knew first, you place the ad."

Danny shook his head. "You didn't give her enough witnesses."

I sighed, sipped my beer, then said, "I suppose that's fair."

NEW SERIES-MASON PIERCE LEGAL THRILLERS

Northlake has its secrets.

So does Mason Pierce.

The Concrete Alibi is the first book in the new Mason Pierce Legal Thriller series. Click here if you'd like to order it or look for it on Amazon under *The Concrete Alibi* by Michael Stagg.

New Series-Mason Pierce Legal Thrillers

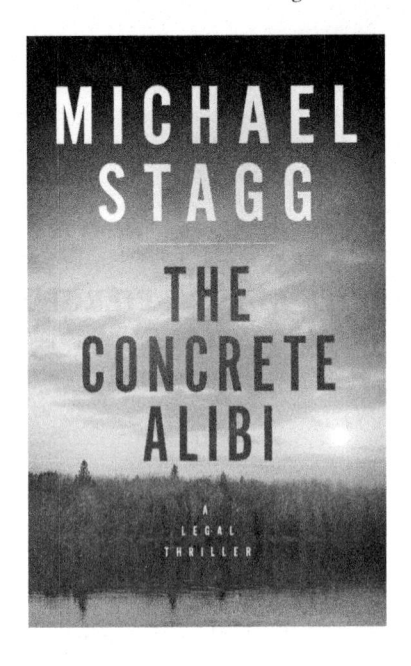

MICHAEL STAGG

THE CONCRETE ALIBI

A LEGAL THRILLER

THE NEXT NATE SHEPHERD NOVEL

There will be more Nate Shepherd books but it will be a little longer than usual until the next one. I'm launching a new series set in Northlake featuring Mason Pierce as he starts at his new firm. Northlake has its secrets, as does Mason, and I'm excited to bring those stories to you. I'm currently planning to write the first two books in the Mason Pierce series, and then come back to Nate.

And I am coming back to Nate. He has too many stories left to tell. He has to find a new associate, Olivia and Cade need to keep him out of trouble, and we all need as much Roxie as possible. And of course, Marie-Faye Lacombe is still lurking out there, held off only by Pop Shepherd's fragile health. Someone is always getting murdered, someone will always need help, and maybe, just maybe, Nate will find someone to share it all with. Or maybe not.

If you'd like to know when the next Nate Shepherd book is coming, sign up for my newsletter here or at https://michaelstagg.com/newsletter/ . That's the first place I'll announce it when the next book is on the way.

The Next Nate Shepherd Novel

Thanks for joining me on Nate's cases. There are more to come.

ABOUT THE AUTHOR

Michael Stagg was a civil trial lawyer for more than twenty-five years. He has tried cases to juries, so he's won and he's lost and he's argued about it in the court of appeals after. Michael was still practicing law when the first Nate Shepherd books were published so he wrote them under a pen name. He writes full-time now and no longer practices but the pen name has stuck.

Michael and his wife live in the Midwest. Their sons are grown so time that used to be spent at football games and band concerts now goes to writing. He enjoys sports of all sorts, reading, and grilling, with the order depending on the day.

You can contact him on Facebook or at mikestaggbooks@gmail.com.

LEGAL THRILLERS BY MICHAEL STAGG

The Nate Shepherd Series

Lethal Defense
True Intent
Blind Conviction
False Oath
Just Plea
Lost Proof
Swift Judgment
Cruel Sentence

The Mason Pierce Series

The Concrete Alibi

Printed in Great Britain
by Amazon